Praise for *The Forsaken*

'Matt Rogers is a bright new talent shaking up the genre. A fresh voice you'll get addicted to – fast!'
Candice Fox

'*The Forsaken* is a thrilling, thoughtful, edge-of-your-seat read that both respects and subverts the genre. I loved it!'
Christian White

'Blood-soaked, relentless, cinematic. A principled killer and a shadowy conspiracy playing out on Brooklyn's streets – *The Forsaken* is simply begging to be made into a blockbuster.'
Hayley Scrivenor

'Fast-paced, sharp and dark. A terrific read.'
Kathy Reichs

'Rogers skillfully plunges readers into a New York where pain and violence reign supreme. Logan Booth is a character who is impossible to look away from and difficult to forget.'
Kyle Mills

'Hold on to your seat. This one never lets up. A relentless, propulsive mix of money, greed, murder, politics, blood and philosophy … A gripping, addictive thriller.'
Michael Brissenden

'*The Forsaken* is gritty, loud, and bears down on you like a freight train.'
Iain Ryan

'With flawed heroes that'll have you shaking your head one minute and cheering the next, Rogers has written a full-throttle action thriller that hooks you from first page to the final, heart-wrenching act.'
Tim Ayliffe

THE DAMNED

MATT ROGERS

SIMON &
SCHUSTER

New York · Amsterdam/Antwerp · London · Toronto · Sydney/Melbourne · New Delhi

THE DAMNED
First published in Australia in 2026 by
Simon & Schuster (Australia) Pty Limited
Level 4, 32 York St, Sydney NSW 2000

10 9 8 7 6 5 4 3 2 1

New York Amsterdam/Antwerp London Toronto Sydney/Melbourne New Delhi
Visit our website at www.simonandschuster.com.au

NATIONAL LIBRARY OF AUSTRALIA

A catalogue record for this book is available from the National Library of Australia

ISBN: 9781761427848
Cover design: Luke Causby/Blue Cork
Typeset by Midland Typesetters, Australia
Printed and bound in Australia by Griffin Press

FSC www.fsc.org MIX Paper | Supporting responsible forestry FSC® C018684

The paper this book is printed on is certified against the Forest Stewardship Council® Standards. Griffin Press holds chain of custody certification SCS-COC-001185. FSC® promotes environmentally responsible, socially beneficial and economically viable management of the world's forests.

A concerted country team effort should be made now to select civilian and military personnel for clandestine training in resistance operations in case they are needed later. This should be done with a view toward development of a civil and military structure for exploitation in the event the Colombian internal security system deteriorates further. This structure should be used to pressure toward reforms known to be needed, perform counter-agent and counter-propaganda functions and as necessary execute paramilitary, sabotage and/or terrorist activities against known communist proponents. It should be backed by the United States.

General William P. Yarborough's
report to the Joint Chiefs of Staff, 1962

PROLOGUE

CAUCA PROVINCE, COLOMBIA
MAY 1964

The children don't understand.

The girl is six, the boy eight. Together with the girl's beloved uncle, Luis, they form three points of a triangle on the grassy plateau, the gentle decline tugging at the tattered *fútbol* they kick back and forth. Luis graciously positioned himself furthest down the slope, electing to fight the gravity that aids the efforts of his niece and her young friend. The girl is old enough to understand it's the least her *tío* would do for her.

Luis would sacrifice the rest of his life's happiness if it meant bolstering hers for only a moment.

So both she and the boy are confused when she kicks the ball down the plateau and Luis makes no effort to lunge for the pass. Sure, she was slightly off the mark, but her *tío* isn't even watching as the *fútbol* sails by. The ball gathers momentum down the slope, lurching and bouncing toward the huge peasant enclave sprawled across the base of the plateau.

Luis stares trance-like at the nearby tree line.

A vein thumps triple-time in his throat.

'*Tío*.' The girl's voice wavers as she calls to him. His gaze snaps to her. His pupils expand. In their short lives, they've never seen an expression quite like the one Luis wears. Neither child can interpret the terror.

All her uncle manages, in a voice like a hoarse whisper, is, '*Corran*.' *Run*.

The boy makes to say, '*¿Qué?*' but he doesn't get the word out before Luis's head explodes.

The bullet enters through the left side of the man's temple, from the direction he was just looking, and rips out the other side of his forehead in a bloom of wet crimson, taking half his face off before he slumps to his knees.

He knew the shot was coming. He must have glimpsed the rifle barrel protruding from the undergrowth, and still he looked away.

Much later, the children will come to understand he wanted his niece to be the last thing he ever saw.

They honour his final wish. The boy snatches the girl's hand and they cascade down the slope in a tangle of rapid footfalls, oblivious to all but their instructions. They don't see the men pouring from the trees. They don't hear the war cries.

They just run.

As they careen into one of the muddy lanes on the outskirts of the enclave, four familiar faces burst from a ramshackle dwelling ahead. Their mothers and fathers are dear friends, so close the kids are like siblings. The boy may as well have lost his own *tío*. He sobs uncontrollably as he leads the girl by the hand, tugging her hard toward the adults crying out in relief. Hands paw desperately at the air until the children close the gap and spill into their parents' arms.

The group embrace lasts the briefest of moments before automatic gunfire engulfs the plateau.

The girl shrieks and covers her ears; the boy's father instinctively wraps his son in a bear hug. But the violent rifle reports and the guttural death cries are still a few lanes over, and the boy's mother swats at the group, screaming, urging them away. Then they're all running. Surrounded by their parents, the children can only see bodies in motion. The humidity encases them, the air a wet blanket as they churn through the mud. The huts and tents fall away and they're on harder ground now, putting more and more distance between themselves and—

Suddenly there are more bodies around them.

The children can't discern what's happening.

A big man they don't know grunts like an animal as he tackles the boy's father to the dirt, ripping him away from the kids. Another man scoops up both mothers at once, and yet another pair wrestle the girl's father away from her. The children stumble to a halt, panting, their little worlds spinning.

They watch what happens next through a veil of incomprehension. One of the huge strangers has a machete, and he holds the boy's father facedown, squashing his victim's head into the dirt as he hacks again and again at the back of the man's skull. Blood erupts like treacle, matting the curly hair. The boy sees his father's brain matter exposed to the overcast sky. The dying man twitches, arms and legs jerking like he's been electrocuted. The same thing happens to the girl's father. It takes two men to hold *him* down. He's bigger, stronger, and he struggles hard. But another blade thunks into the side of his neck, half-decapitating him, and his lips flap soundlessly like a fish out of water.

The mothers scream. The stranger who intercepted them holds both women airborne, hinged at the waist as they drape over his broad shoulders. He turns slowly around to face them away from their slain husbands. In doing so, he winds up staring at the children, who stare back.

A jagged mauve scar carves its way down one of the stranger's cheeks. He's heavyset with a bull's neck, but looks Colombian. His dark eyes bore into them as he notes the shock on their young faces. Their mothers kick and thrash in his arms to no avail. The stranger juts his chin away from the enclave.

The children don't realise he's shooing them away.

'*Corran*,' the stranger growls.

They listened before. They listen now.

Acting on autopilot, the boy takes the girl's hand again, and they turn and flee. Their mothers continue to wail behind them, until two more gunshots ring across the plateau.

By the time they disappear into the hills, the children are orphans.

PART I

CLEAR

Be true to the thought of the moment and avoid distraction. Other than continuing to exert yourself, enter into nothing else, but go to the extent of living single thought by single thought.

Yamamoto Tsunetomo, *Hagakure: The Book of the Samurai*

1

Jacinta Murphy wakes soundlessly in the master suite as a pewter dawn blankets the Executive Residence.

She sleeps on her back, her eyes floating open from a position her husband affectionately describes as corpse-like. Lying beneath the covers, she stares unblinking at the convex northern wall. Upon stirring, she permits herself a single minute of stillness—a habit formed naturally, unintentionally, in order to locate some measure of composure before the assault of the day.

The presidency comes with an overbearing weight she used to assume she would adjust to over time, but tomorrow marks three hundred days since she was sworn in and the pressure constricting her chest only seems to be worsening.

No big deal.

She never wished for a comfortable life.

No matter how many obligations she burns through, thousands more await. You can win an election, but you can't win being the president. Even a whole term of utterly perfect decisions would be critiqued from every angle. In the quiet, she steels herself for the inevitable derision, the scorn of half the country. When her internal timer buzzes, she lifts the dark silk sheets and extricates herself from the four-poster bed.

At fifty-seven, they consider her a young commander in chief. In any other vocation, she'd be approaching retirement. What remains of her knee cartilage requires the lubrication of movement, and she pads stiffly to the adjoining dressing room. Before she slips out, she glances back at the bed.

A decade her senior, Beau Murphy sleeps undisturbed. His firm chest rises and falls, white hair peppered across tanned pectorals. He was already making heads turn when she met him in her mid-thirties, but she finds herself begrudgingly agreeing with the gossip outlets when they claim he's ageing like Clooney. Of course she's aware of her own beauty, but maintaining her appearance is a full-time job heaped upon her presidential obligations. Beau barely considers how he looks.

She's learned to live with her envy surrounding the ease with which he sweeps through life. It's no matter, really. Their love is an authentic thing, the foundations of their partnership sincere, and a little jealousy would never compromise that. In any case, she sees nothing wrong with negative emotion. Long ago, she found a bottomless fuel source within the feeling of inadequacy. Her insecurities propelled her forward. Beau, on the other hand, never reached for more than he needed. He took exactly what he wanted from life and nothing more.

It's why she wound up Madam President, and he the First Gentleman.

Anyhow, Beau's fine with the dynamic. It's not like he lacks accomplishments. He retired at forty-nine after amassing a fortune through the PR firm he founded. With a law degree from Harvard, Jacinta was already independently wealthy as a cutthroat corporate litigator, but she always harboured political aspirations, and from the moment Beau exited his own firm, he turned his attention to supporting his wife's ambitions.

She counts herself lucky. Not everyone finds their person.

She enters the dressing room and sheds her thin nightgown, then gives herself the once-over in the full-length mirror. Acceptable. People speak of beauty and brains like they're opposites, but it takes a sharp mind to properly utilise good looks. She understands the complexity of the presentation she offered the masses, the perfect blend of intelligence, attractiveness, and humility which put her in the White House. Swaying the swing voters requires compassion and strength in equal measure. It takes a powerhouse to defy convention.

As the first female President of the United States, nothing less than the full package would have sufficed.

Poised before the mirror, she looks deep in her own eyes to recite a collection of lines curated from the works of James Allen. Although not religious, she's certainly spiritual. This is her morning prayer, an anchor for the day's inevitable storm.

'Do not long to do great and laudable things,' she mutters. 'These will do themselves if you do your present task nobly. See that your every fleeting moment is strong, pure, and purposeful. You do not live your life in the mass, you live it in the fragments, and from these the mass emerges.'

She takes a step closer to the mirror, until her face hovers inches from her reflection in the glass. Several months ago, she tacked an addendum onto the spiel. She wishes it weren't necessary, but she's found it crucial to assuage a deeper fear.

'You do not fear Logan Booth,' she whispers.

2

Logan Booth once read enlightenment is nothing but clearing the obstacles from your vision, so you may see reality unobstructed.

He believes it.

The wiry delivery driver offers to lend a hand, but he refuses. The boxed tatami mats must weigh sixty pounds each; Logan heaves four at once out the back of the box truck. The exertion in itself means very little. He was always able to put in sickening effort at the drop of a hat, even after whiskey and nicotine for breakfast. What separates him from the man of four months prior is his stillness of mind.

Even at the peak of his operational career, his thinking wasn't as clear as it is today.

Quadriceps flare beneath faded gym shorts as he balances two hundred and forty pounds of authentic Japanese straw on one shoulder. Tribeca shines under morning sun, its industrial façades aglow. Logan walks the long boxes through a sunbeam cutting between two neighbouring warehouses, a natural spotlight trained on his open front door. Half the floor in the entranceway lies torn up as he toes over the threshold and lowers the payload before starting back for the second trip.

He's in the process of single-handedly renovating this rundown condo, which he managed to snatch up at a steal of a price from a developer going under. Even after acquiring the unfinished loft-style space for $2.8 million, he could have easily outsourced the makeover without putting much of a dent in his personal fortune. But Logan has a complicated relationship with the money he earned in his thirties. It's been difficult to shed the idea the funds are tainted.

For a decade, he accumulated millions as a contract killer, taking assignments from what he believed to be a band of vigilantes hellbent on addressing injustice. Only at the end of his career did he learn the truth: all along he was an unwitting asset of the CIA's Special Activities Center, tasked with furthering US interests at home and abroad.

Given his rugged individualism and detest of politicians, the revelation left him broken. Today marks a full year since his handler carted him to a black site and the Director of the CIA revealed his true function. When Logan staggered out into the civilian world, he spiralled into despair, grasping for every coping mechanism in reach. Then a chance encounter with a young woman named Alice Mason altered the course of his life, and for the last four months he's shed self-pity like a snakeskin.

He now sees that labelling his earnings as 'blood money' was only ever a story he was telling himself—an unnecessary guilt, he likes to think. He tells himself that, in the end, it wasn't his fault he was manipulated. The truth is, even with an undergrad in journalism and a BS/MS in computer science—credentials an old friend said made him a truth-seeking missile—his vetting process for the gigs paled in comparison to the power of the military intelligence community. Their desire to deceive, coupled with a limitless black budget, meant he was helpless to stop them pulling the wool over his eyes.

It doesn't make his burden any lighter. His memories are what they are, but he figures he's punished himself enough since his career drew to a close. Only recently did he allow himself to dip into his earnings, but he refuses to use them to shy away from strain or toil. So he won't sit back and let interior designers and construction workers handle this renovation. He will undertake every step of the process himself.

Not like he hasn't got the time.

After dumping the second load of tatami in the entranceway, he back-pedals into the laneway to slip a hundred-dollar bill into the driver's palm. As expected, the guy protests and tries to hand it back, but Logan just claps the baffled driver on the shoulder, turns on his heel, and disappears inside. Then he re-dons protective gear—gloves, eyewear, face mask—and resumes the floor demolition process in the front hallway with chisel and hammer, a project which will soon encompass all the cheap tiling across the ground floor.

Sweat beads along broad forearm muscle as he hammers and pries.

The day he finalised the condo purchase, he stood alone beneath the kitchen's vaulted ceiling, stared out the huge windows at the gently flowing Hudson, and envisioned an extensive remodel. He wanted to utilise Japanese Zen design principles to create something elegant and understated. A sanctuary.

So he committed to the choice and got down to business.

He's a far cry from the man who gazed glassy eyed at a sea of oxycodone pills, contemplating the end of the road. For the first eight months of his retirement, he destroyed himself to flee from responsibility. For the last four, he's been trying to get back to what he used to be.

Speaking of . . .

He checks the Garmin on his wrist: 10:32 a.m. Sometimes he can be too effective at emptying his mind. He's been on his knees in the front hallway since he received the tatami mats at nine, consumed in a trance-like focus without noticing the time slipping away. Now he's late. He rears up from the dust cloud and jogs upstairs to change into his trademark attire: flannel shirt, cargo pants. Athletic wear is thrown in a duffel bag and the strap goes over one shoulder. He hurries back downstairs, weaves through the gutted entranceway, and slips out.

The 2 train leaves from the station on Chambers Street at 10:47. He makes it with a minute to spare, riding the subway two stops to Wakefield—241st Street. Then it's back to street level and into the heart of Midtown. He finds the sign reading JUNKYARD above a narrow set of stairs between two shopfronts. Despite himself, he swallows apprehension. Before the CIA, half his waking life was devoted to grappling, but he hasn't stepped foot in a civilian jiu-jitsu gym in years. From what he's heard, Junkyard's as exclusive as it gets, and he hasn't so much as called ahead to establish if he's welcome.

But it doesn't matter.

He made a promise to himself that he'd show up to Junkyard's morning practice on the one-year anniversary of his retirement; whether or not they let him participate is outside his sphere of control.

He can only roll the dice.

He heads upstairs as the digital watch face on his wrist ticks over to eleven.

—

The guy at reception looks as no-nonsense as it gets.

Late twenties, bald, a little chemical enhancement reddening his skin and hardening his musculature to concrete. He taps away at the phone charging behind the desk, deliberately ignoring the newcomer, until he's forced to finally relent. 'Help you?'

Logan juts his chin out at the mats. More than a dozen jiu-jitsu practitioners and professional mixed martial artists mill below a faded gym banner, JUNKYARD up top, the gym's slogan below: BLOOD, SWEAT, NO TEARS. Ten men, four women, clad in rash guards and grappling shorts. Their bodies are like rawhide, and no wonder: they spend nearly every waking moment dedicated to weaponising themselves.

Logan says, 'Thought I'd see if I could get some work in.'

'Not this place, bud. No walk-ins.'

Logan's aware. Junkyard's infamous on the global jiu-jitsu stage as a private compound for an elite cadre of New York's most ruthless and talented practitioners. The tight-knit crew branched off from the esteemed Renzo Gracie Academy down the street a little over a year ago, favouring a brasher approach. There's no bowing or humility here, only relentless work and vicious social-media trash talk between the Junkyard clique and their competition. But they're the best in the country at what they do, and Logan figured it was worth a shot trying to talk his way into training here.

If he fails, no harm done. He can handle a bruised ego. He sees how many opportunities he missed over the last year by simply being unwilling to swallow his pride.

'I'll pay any fee,' he says.

A glint of anger in the guy's snakelike eyes. 'No fees. Invite only.'

'Right.'

'So take a hike.'

'I'm a black belt.'

The man rolls his eyes, like, *That means nothing here*. But perhaps only to satiate his curiosity, he asks, 'Under who?'

Logan hesitates. Eleven years ago, he was a brown belt at the Marcelo Garcia Academy here in Manhattan, where he trained for the duration of his time at NYU. After he was unwittingly swept into CIA employment weeks before his thirtieth birthday, his handler, Thoreau, proceeded to bring in renowned instructors for one-on-one tutelage, each of them sworn to secrecy. So Logan can't name names, even though he received his black belt from one of the most respected practitioners on the planet.

Of course, he then honed his skillset hundreds of times in the field, which taught him more than the training rooms ever could.

No choice but to be honest. 'I can't tell you. But I'm legit.'

A long pause. 'Oh, you're *legit*?' The bald guy gives him the once-over, visibly amused. 'Big man, huh? Know who I am?'

'Should I?'

Silence.

'Aaron Maker,' the guy finally says. 'Eight–zero amateur MMA, six–zero pro. I'm one regional win from the UFC. But I was a black belt under Renzo before I even transitioned to MMA.'

Logan stays quiet. If only those who rattle off their accomplishments understood how ridiculous they sound.

'Still want a round?' Aaron asks.

'I'm here, aren't I?'

The air hangs quiet, Aaron's disbelief palpable. He looks back and raises his voice—'Guys'—then jerks a thumb at Logan. 'Says he can't tell me who he got his black belt under. Y'know, or he'd have to kill me.'

A few chuckles, some louder laughs. A woman shouts, 'McDojo!' referring to martial arts schools that focus exclusively on collecting gym fees rather than teaching anything worthwhile. Reading the room, Logan can tell they're no strangers to delusional walk-ins. They're lumping him in with the rest of them.

Maybe he's wrong. Maybe he's bitten off more than he can chew.

Only one way to find out.

He cocks his head at Aaron, who shrugs and beckons him to the mats. Logan ducks behind a privacy screen and changes into a long-sleeved rash guard and training shorts. He kicks his shoes off and heads back out barefoot, then slaps his palms to his thighs and takes a small bow before stepping on the mats, prompting jeers of derision.

Aaron rolls his shoulders in their sockets. 'One quick round, then you move yourself along and let us train, yeah?'

Logan nods. He appreciates that Aaron isn't deterred by his physique. Most get edgy when they see that Logan looks carved from stone. Aaron notices, but seems to shrug it off.

'You want to warm-up?' Aaron asks.

Logan shakes his head.

So Aaron charges like it's a running of the bulls.

Being juiced to the gills on steroids, he must outweigh Logan by twenty pounds, but Logan is faster. He sprawls his legs back with lightning speed when Aaron shoots a blast double-leg takedown. Aaron clearly assumed he'd be able to pick Logan up and dump him on his head, so Logan winds up with the positional advantage, leaning all his weight down on the man's upper back as Aaron flails desperately to get his hands locked around his opponent's thighs. The millisecond Logan gains the upper hand, he ratchets the intensity up. He uses a heap of strength and a splash of technique to drive Aaron facedown into the mat, and their four hundred collective pounds detonate off the vinyl like a bomb blast. The *slap* of skin on mat echoes off the walls.

Instead of trying to take the back and secure a choke, Logan elects to exhaust his foe by defending the explosive burst he knows is coming. Sure enough, enraged by having his takedown stuffed, Aaron taps into fast-twitch fibres. He rears up like a man possessed, grunting as he strains. Tries to just brute-force Logan off of him in the way the Junkyard squad specialise: animalistic intensity.

Unfortunately for Aaron, Logan spent a decade crushing the resistance out of men fighting for their lives. That's a tightrope most will never walk, not even pro fighters.

Logan predicts the explosion of effort and uses Aaron's desperation to his own advantage. He leans away as Aaron heaves upward and loses his balance, stumbling a half-step to keep himself upright. The moment Aaron's feet are set too wide, Logan hits a double-leg takedown of his own.

He spears Aaron to the mat, and the back of the man's skull lashes the vinyl. You can't strike in jiu-jitsu, but momentum is often more devastating than a punch. Given the Junkyard training ethos, Aaron must be no stranger to getting stunned in the middle of scrambles, but his reactions are nevertheless impeded for the second it takes Logan to slice one leg over his opponent's midsection and straddle his abdomen, pinning him to the mat. Full mount.

Aaron bucks, wasting energy; Logan rides it out like a rodeo pro. He traps Aaron's neck along with one raised arm in an arm-triangle choke and leaps to one side, with Aaron still bucking like a mule from his back.

Logan squeezes like a boa constrictor on meth. Aaron waits longer than he should to tap.

That damn ego.

When Aaron finally relents, slapping Logan's shoulder twice in submission, Logan releases the hold. Too late: Aaron lost consciousness as he tapped out. No big deal. Happens all the time in grappling, and getting choked to sleep doesn't damage the brain. Out of respect, Logan moves to lift Aaron's feet in the air, thereby hastening the return of blood flow to the brain. But when he reaches for the man's ankles, someone steps in and shoves him double-handed in the chest.

Logan tumbles back to a seated position.

Another man looms over Aaron's limp form. 'You fucking held that.'

'I let go,' Logan says. 'Soon as he tapped.'

Veins pulse across the guy's forehead as he growls, 'You don't get to come in here and tell us what you did and didn't do.'

Logan wears no expression. He knows there's no point defending himself; the man will see what he wants to see.

Aaron sits slowly upright, bleary-eyed, his gaze vacant. The lights are coming back on.

Logan stays quiet, which only seems to further irritate the guy towering over them.

Sure enough, the newcomer takes it up a notch. 'You know what?' he spits. 'Got a little something for you. I stay strapped. You still here when I come back, I'm putting one through your head.'

Then he's storming past the rest of the pack and disappearing out an exit door along the back wall.

Logan doesn't move a muscle.

At some point during his teammate's tirade, Aaron's blank stare solidified into awareness. His pupils swivel over to lock on Logan, the two of them now seated beside each other.

'Does he really have a gun,' Logan asks flatly, 'or is he gonna mope back in here in five minutes?'

Aaron glances at the exit door. 'It won't take five minutes.'

They sit in strangely comfortable silence until, no more than sixty seconds later, the man reappears empty-handed. A muted grimace spreads across his face when he notes Logan's presence.

'Congrats, Wade,' Aaron calls across the room. 'Earned yourself mat-cleaning duty.' One of the women punches Wade in the back in mock derision as he returns to the pack, and Aaron glances at Logan. 'You ever think about going pro?'

'No.'

'There's seven-figure paydays if you make the UFC, go for a belt . . .'

'I'm forty-one.'

Aaron looks him up and down. 'I'll be damned. What were you doing at thirty? You could've been an all-time great.'

Logan doesn't answer.

'You live round here?' Aaron asks.

'Uh-huh.'

'Train here whenever you please, then. Think you could show some of us a thing or two.'

Just like that, Logan has a place to keep his skillset sharpened.

He looks over. 'How's right now work?'

Aaron nods. Even finds a smirk. 'Works just fine.'

Nothing like being bested in unarmed combat to strip away all pretence.

Aaron pushes to his feet. 'Guess warm-up's over.'

Logan rises alongside him, satisfied.

It was his first self-imposed test in months, and he passed with flying colours.

3

Logan staggers off the mats nearly two hours later, panting like a dog.

The ferocity with which he trained has left even the Junkyard crew perplexed. Sooner or later, even professional athletes have to stop to catch their breath, but Logan doesn't work that way. The instant they backed off the pressure, he went at them hard, no matter what he had left in the tank. It's hard for them to comprehend that some guy off the street set a higher pace. They clap Logan on the back and offer praise as he heads for the showers, but he catches the wary looks in their eyes. They wonder what he's made of.

They wonder if he's human.

But he's just flesh and blood, and the exhaustion hits hard. After showering off the salt, rinsing skin rubbed raw from mat burn, and throwing his street clothes back on, he can barely stand. He slings the duffel over one shoulder and stumbles out, checking the time as he descends to street level: 12:50. With a muted groan, he sets off. He's a stickler for punctuality—how you do anything is how you do everything. It's only half a mile north to his next rendezvous, a packed café near the New York Times Building, though the walk seems to take forever. But he makes it.

One on the dot.

It feels like years since he last met Jorge Romero at Empyrean, but Logan still wants to scan the tables for his best friend. For as long as he visits their old meeting spot, Logan will instinctively search for the reporter's features: rosy cheeks, a mop of curly hair, a wide mouth always ready to contort into a smile at the slightest encouragement. The memories still hurt. They always will.

But despite the horrific nature of the journalist's murder, despite the fact that, in his panic, Jorge mistakenly thought it was Logan who ordered him dead, despite the endless list of mistakes, none of which can be rectified . . . at least some semblance of good came from the ordeal.

Logan takes one of the only free seats in the café, in the corner of a broad wooden communal table. Seconds later, someone drags a stool over beside him. The young woman sheds her apron and drops down next to Logan. She applied for the gig at Empyrean after Logan noticed a flyer on the window, the first time he went back after Jorge's death.

He can't resist a smile. Alice Mason is unrecognisable from the woman he met four months ago.

She returns the smile, which renders him speechless. Her grin widens in recognition of his shock. 'Yeah, I know.'

He blinks. 'When?'

'Last week.'

'How much?'

'A lot,' she says softly. 'Like, *a lot.*'

'Did you have the money?'

'I took a little credit card debt.'

'A little?'

She shrugs, then offers a knowing smirk, like, *Okay, a lot.*

Twin rows of pearly whites rest behind her lips. Whichever dentist she visited for the procedure knew what they were doing. At first glance, you can't even tell they're veneers. They don't shine in her mouth as though radioactive, like you see in those who buy a new smile solely to appease their social media following.

Logan knows she has no interest in vanity.

Four months clean now, Alice has risen like a phoenix from the ashes of a crippling crack addition, but there are qualities she will never reclaim. A while back, during one of their weekly catch-ups at Empyrean, she showed him a photo of herself in college, to prove that even though she's come a long way, she won't ever get back to what she once was. Staring at the photograph of teenage Alice beaming in a dorm room, Logan realised that if she hadn't gone straight from her hometown of Lexington to study mathematical economics at MIT, she could have modelled. Some people are so beautiful as to be magnetic.

Having only recently turned twenty-four, her youth meant much was salvageable once she got sober. Her skin cleared, her cold sores healed, her hair found its old shine, and healthy body-weight began returning to her emaciated frame. But her mouth had been a mess of yellowed teeth riddled with cavities and abscesses.

She must have decided that if credit card debt was the price she had to pay to eradicate a visible reminder of the errors of her past, so be it.

'Let me pay it off,' he offers now. 'Pay *me* back, avoid the interest. They'll hammer you, especially if you miss a payment.'

'Logan.' Her tone's blunt. 'I don't care about the interest. I *want* the interest.'

He could pretend not to understand, but he does. If the roles were reversed, he'd have a similar aversion to accepting help.

This is her journey, no one else's. She gets to decide how much responsibility to bear on her own shoulders. He wouldn't dare take that away from her, so he leaves it at the initial offer.

She notices they're almost shoulder-to-shoulder. 'Let's not get too cosy.'

There's sarcasm in her tone, but he straightens up a little anyway. 'No?'

'Fourth time we've met on my break. My coworkers'll be thinking I've got a sugar daddy.'

'They'd think that? I'm nearly twice your age.'

'Oh, Logan.' A genuine laugh erupts from her. 'You sweet summer child . . .'

'What?'

She stares for a beat. 'Sometimes I forget how different you are to the rest of them.' She notes his silence. 'You're six-three with baby blues and you're built like fucking Hercules. You could date several impressionable young women at once, if you were so inclined.'

'Why on earth would I want to—'

She touches a finger to her lips, half-mockingly. 'It's not *me* you need to convince. But now you're not drinking, you're very nice to look at. Your skin's cleared up. It's . . . distracting. And I don't even swing that way.'

He glances over her shoulder, at the two aproned women in their early twenties busying themselves behind the counter with coffee grinders and milk jugs who tear their gazes away as soon as he looks in their direction. One mutters something to the other; they exchange smirks. He averts his eyes. 'What have you been telling them, Alice? Fuck's sake . . .'

She smiles—his discomfort is her entertainment. 'Oh, nothing at all, sweetie,' she croons. 'And even still, Francesca asked when you'd be dropping back in.'

'Francesca could be my daughter.'

'You don't even know which one she is.'

'Exactly.'

She gets serious. '*Are* you dating? Y'know, someone your age . . .'

Logan raises a hand, tilts it side to side. 'Guess I'm open to the idea. But . . . I don't know.' He glances left and right, assessing earshot range. 'Wasn't long ago I almost took my own life.'

Her demeanour shifts. 'You and me both.'

'What about you? Met anyone?'

'I'm not looking yet. I'm not ready. Last time . . .' She trails off. She can't finish.

She's opened up to him a little about Ruby Fisher, the ex-girlfriend she ventured down the rabbit hole alongside. The couple chased their vices from the leafy suburbs of Massachusetts to the crack dens of New York, where Ruby's adventure came to a stark end in a puddle of her own puke. Alice described her most visceral memory from the time: reds and blues flashing off cold, pale skin. She spent half a year alone on the streets before she met Logan. It's a miracle she survived as long as she did.

Same goes for him.

Today, they're on the same page. Given the depths of the abyss they crawled from, four months isn't close to enough. But they're on their respective paths, and they've yet to waver.

They haven't expressed to each other the importance of these weekly catch-ups, but there's little need to state the obvious. They both know how fortunate they are to have found each other.

To divert from memories of Ruby, they turn to general chitchat until the clock strikes one-thirty and Alice peels herself off the stool, her break concluded.

'Back at it.' She dons her apron a touch reluctantly. At five-foot-nothing, she's barely taller than his seated frame.

He looks up at her at a shallow angle. 'You like it here?'

She thinks a moment, then her voice comes quiet. 'Look, I'm sure it's a shit job. I could brainstorm a dozen ways I'm getting exploited. But I'm just . . . this is heaven. Staying the course. It's been so long.'

He nods.

She lays a soft palm on his shoulder. 'See you next time.' She sweeps away, manoeuvring between tables with a practised calm.

He heads to the counter and orders a takeaway double espresso from one of the two young baristas, who's noticeably awkward as she serves him. Must be Francesca. He offers a warm smile and says, 'Thank you so much,' as he takes his coffee and heads out. It's only to embarrass Alice; he has precisely zero interest in such an age gap. He figured most men would, but as he reintegrates with civilisation, he's learning common sense isn't so common.

4

One hundred and eleven days. This is how long it took Alice to stop craving the pipe every waking moment.

At first, she didn't understand what it meant *not* to experience a crippling wave of desire to start the day. The first morning the sensation was absent, she assumed there was something physically wrong with her. She sat up in bed and clawed at her chest, strangely out of breath, unsure what was happening. Then it clicked.

The unrelenting urge to inhale lungfuls of beautiful smoke . . . Gone.

The weeks since have been confusing. She's coming up on two months at Empyrean, but she got accustomed to spending her shifts grappling with the need to find the nearest dealer and light up in an alleyway. When the cravings receded, it was somewhat surreal having room to breathe.

Like, *This is what life can be?*

She still feels pangs of craving, of course – she figures she always will – but it's nothing like what it used to be.

She can't be certain which part of her sobriety journey did the trick – probably a combination of several things. When she went cold turkey four months ago, Logan let her crash in his spare room and covered the costs of anything she thought could help as she slowly put herself back together.

She saw a therapist as many times as she could afford, attended a few Narcotics Anonymous meetings, experimented with meditation. At the same time, she gathered up the missing pieces of her old life, renewing documents and updating records in something of a frenzy – Social Security, bank account, license, passport. She left all the broken friendships behind, making peace with a fresh start, a clean slate.

When she deemed her foundations sufficiently solid, she went job hunting, affording her the means to find her own accommodation just as Logan finished negotiating for that unfinished condo in Tribeca.

And here she is.

Nowadays, no matter how chaotic it gets at work, it's effortless to let it go. The world's bullshit seems to glide right off her. She looks deep in the eyes of the banker giving her an earful because his large, extra-hot, three-quarters-full soy cappuccino wasn't as scalding as he might have liked, and she thinks, *You've never known real problems.* Still, she can't find it within herself to be offended by the naïvety of privileged strangers. In a strange way, their ignorance is a blessing. When you've rolled in the gutter, it's hard to relate to those who've always had their shit together.

It's only that Alice sometimes wishes her memories were different.

In order not to dwell on her past, she compensates by staying busy, putting her whole being into what lies before her. To mitigate the risk of going the other way with it, she makes sure this painstaking attention to detail never borders on obsessive, and she allows herself to fully experience any emotion that bubbles to the surface in day-to-day life. She doesn't bottle anything up, and she aims for moderation in all things. The result, to her mounting disbelief, is fairly stable mental health.

It's hard to fathom how fast she righted the ship. She still makes sure to see her therapist whenever she senses turmoil brewing within, but none of those moments of wavering have led to a relapse. She figured even if she escaped her addiction she would be an emotional mess, tossed about by the winds of life into varying states of hysteria. Instead, she found productive habits that delay gratification, and now she's just good at whatever she prioritises, which, for the moment, is a minimum-wage job.

Her shift ended forty-five minutes ago, and the last customer of the day stepped out of Empyrean fifteen minutes before that, but she hangs back to prep for tomorrow. She's almost finished descaling the La Marzocco espresso machine, moving with clean, practised motions, when a man clears his throat behind her. She looks over one shoulder. 'Hey, Pierre.'

At thirty-one, her manager is younger than a handful of his staff – no small feat. He wears his dreadlocks in a bulky ponytail. The trace of a Cameroonian accent is still detectable as he says, 'You know I don't force you to stay back.'

She blinks. 'Of course I know that.'

'Just getting it out there. So it's on record, y'know.' When she doesn't respond, he goes on. 'Sometimes feels like you're doing it for a reason. Paranoid hunch, I know. But you keep going like this, there might come a point where you start complaining about unpaid overtime or something. I don't know . . .'

The silence is painful. She suppresses a sigh as she finishes running the last brew cycle, then turns away from the machine, wiping her hands on her apron. 'I'm not scheming, Pierre. I just like putting things right.' She glances up at his face long enough to note the glint in his eyes.

'Hey,' he says quietly, 'what are you doing after this? I was gonna grab a bite—'

'I'm busy.'

'Right.'

She has no interest in disclosing her sexuality to her boss—she doubts she'd be interested even if she were straight—so she stands patiently in the quiet. Her unflappability is a recent development.

In college, she used to eat herself alive with anxiety trying to cater to the various eccentricities of her friends. She shape-shifted personalities to make everyone comfortable in her presence, desperate to belong. She assumes she unconsciously inherited this fear of abandonment from her mother. Yet for the most part her efforts paid off, and she thrived socially at MIT. Cynically, she figures that's only because she was pleasant to look at. She doubts her neediness would have been swept under the rug if her smile didn't make the frat boys weak at the knees.

Since she got clean, she's come to realise that uncomfortable silences in conversations are par for the course. She's learning to sit within those silences without disturbing herself. She doesn't need to mould her character based on whoever's in front of her. It was precisely that kind of neurosis which first led her down the road to addiction: the need to constantly consider every opinion, and then find a way to shut her mind up, numb herself.

Pierre can't seem to handle the quiet the way she can. 'You know, I really appreciate that mentality, Alice. People your age'—he shakes his head—'they don't understand how important it is. Putting things right. They'd see it as a burden, staying behind the way you do. They'd only use it as an excuse to claim they were underpaid . . .'

'I am underpaid.'

She sees him trying to form a response, maybe even a quip to return fire with, but it seems to stump him. He clearly doesn't know what to say.

She doesn't give him the chance to figure it out. 'See you tomorrow, yeah?'

He hesitates. Nods.

Alice hangs her apron, skirts around him, and moves through the empty café toward the exit. She senses his eyes boring into her from behind, staring at her the way she's seen people stare at Logan. There's a magnetism to those with definiteness of purpose—she knows what she's doing and why she's doing it, and she's dedicated and attentive enough not to have to suck up to anyone along the way.

She rides the F train eight stops from 42nd Street—Bryant Park to East Broadway and hustles up to her apartment, opposite Seward Park on the Lower East Side. She shares the tiny place with two women: Rose, a first-year student at NYU, and Zuri, a paralegal in her late-twenties. It should have been illegal for the landlord to list the apartment as three-bedroom, but the rent is cheap—by New York standards, at least. A windowless bedroom the size of a closet is still a step up from her previous accommodations.

She unlocks the front door, spills inside, and finds Rose chopping onions in the kitchenette.

The young woman flashes Alice a bitter look as she turns. 'You left your mug out for me to wash again.'

Alice hesitates. 'I—'

'The world doesn't revolve around you, Alice,' Rose snaps. 'How about a little awareness in future?'

Alice never claimed to be perfect. Call it bad timing, call it rash impulse, call it weeks of mounting frustration with the nineteen-year-old, but before she can stop herself, the words escape her lips. 'How about you shut your mouth, Rose?'

She may as well have launched a nuke.

No matter her laundry list of grievances with the entitled teenager she shares an apartment with, she knows she shouldn't have said it.

'*Excuse* me?!' Rose splutters.

She's deliberately heightening her outrage, artificially cranking her horror up to eleven, which reminds Alice of her own mother. The deeper frustrations of a traumatic childhood flare within her.

'Come on,' Alice says, dumping her tote bag on a dining chair. 'I mean, seriously . . .'

'What?' Rose snaps, slamming the knife down on the cutting board. 'Something to say?'

'Your shit is everywhere.'

Rose's eyes practically bug from her head, so total is her shock.

Alice gestures around the apartment: 'Those clothes on the rack—they're all yours, they've been dry three days. Your portfolio work's all over the sofa so the three of us have never been able to watch TV together, like Zuri and I keep suggesting we should. We have to move your tripod and ring light out of the passthrough every time we want to get in the kitchen—'

'What,' Rose snaps, 'are you gonna call me vain? Because I film cooking videos?'

'Did I say that?'

'You wanted to. You think I'm an airhead.'

Alice takes a breath. 'I'm not implying anything about your character. I'm just highlighting everything you overlook, Rose. Because, really, it's no big deal. You're a fine roommate. You're still a teenager and you're independent, out of home, studying hard.

I respect you. But if I leave a mug next to the kitchen sink because I'm in a rush to make my shift on time and not get fired—a mug I was going to take care of the moment I got home—I'd appreciate you not lecturing me on awareness. Because it would be so easy to do the same to you, and I refrain.' She finishes with a mighty exhale. 'I'm sorry I lashed out.'

There. The best she can do, given the frustration trying to claw its way out.

Then Rose scoffs. 'Fuck off, Alice.'

Alice doesn't react.

Rose doesn't appreciate the quiet. She was looking for a retaliatory outburst of emotion. So she keeps going. 'I'm out of home, studying hard? I can *smell* the sarcasm. Just say how you feel. Say I'm funded by the Bank of Mommy and Daddy, studying a liberal arts degree, filming TikToks for my vapid followers . . . I know all the things you and Zuri want to say to me, so just say them.'

Alice clenches her new teeth together. Her neck pulls taut with tension.

But Rose can't stop. 'You two think you're so special for working. Like that's not what I'll be doing a couple years from now. At least Zuri's a paralegal, actually going somewhere. You're a *server.* And you have the gall to act like this.'

'Rose,' Alice says quietly, 'stop.'

'Or what? All you'll do is stand there and tell me to shut my mouth, when all I asked for was a simple courtesy. Clean up your dishes, Alice. It's so simple. Then again . . .'

Alice's blood runs cold. 'Then again what?'

No answer.

'Go on. Say it.'

Rose throws her hands in the air. 'You said you respect me, right? Total bullshit, but you said it. So I respect you too. Takes a lot to stop being a junkie, but you did it. So don't you worry about anything else. Cleaning up after yourself, that's too much to ask. I get it. You just stay away from the crack and keep patting yourself on the back.'

Alice stomps forward, just one step in Rose's direction, slamming the sole of her shoe against the hardwood floor.

Rose flinches like she's been shot. She's several inches taller than Alice and almost fifty pounds heavier, but Alice sees now that the teenager hasn't a clue how to operate when the scenes of her life don't follow the envisioned script.

'Get out!' Rose screams, like there's an axe murderer in the apartment. 'I'm calling the police!'

Alice snatches her bag off the chair. 'You do that. Maybe when they laugh in your face, you'll see how the real world works.'

She throws the door open and storms out.

5

Logan reclines in a state of semi-consciousness.

He rests on a minimalist armless sofa with a dark plywood base. It's built low to the ground, positioned parallel to the streams of sunlight that flood in through the broad windows facing the Hudson. It was the first piece of furniture he selected for the loft; the rest of the furnishings scattered across the ground floor are cheap, temporary measures. His exhaustion is pleasant, a world away from the restless tiredness that used to follow his binge drinking.

But nothing had come close to how exhausted he'd been four months ago, when he wound up with a badly broken orbital bone, three missing teeth, a torn left calf muscle, and violent bruising covering more than half his body. Alice fared little better, collecting a fractured rib and a cracked septum for her troubles.

The grievous injuries were the result of an all-out war with Daniel Datvyan, a real-estate billionaire who used troves of blackmail to enact a hostile takeover of the government's black-operations resources. Datvyan flew too close to the sun and wound up with a hole in his head, but not before convincing the President of the United States to lend him CIA wet-work soldiers for his own nefarious plans.

Logan tries not to dwell on what happened—frankly, it terrifies him how close Datvyan came to pulling it all off. And, sure, Logan could make a case for going to war with the current administration for their complicity, but he's always believed in choosing your battles wisely.

Jacinta Murphy was caught between a rock and a hard place, and after Datvyan's demise, she and Logan agreed on a begrudging truce, using the mayor of New York as a mediator.

Anyway, once the dust had settled, the world-class specialists at the NewYork–Presbyterian Hospital patched Logan and Alice up and sent them on their way without so much as asking for their health insurance providers—likely the result of a persuasive phone call from the mayor, who owes Logan a sizeable debt.

Upon discharge, Alice committed to abstaining from all substances besides coffee, and Logan figured he should follow suit, if only to bolster her morale. He tossed all his booze and nicotine gum when he got home from the hospital, along with a few emergency packs of cigarettes. They spent the next few weeks letting their bodies heal, clawing their way slowly out from the shadows of their old lives.

It was hard to tell if he even went through withdrawals, so distracting was the pain of his injuries. In hindsight, the timing may have been a blessing in disguise. Easy to ignore the craving for liquor when there's a tennis ball of swelling under your eye that stabs your nerve endings every time you turn your head.

But humans are remarkably resilient, and Logan's eye eventually re-emerged from the inflammation. Alice abandoned her sling and her nose lost its rancid purple hue, enabling her to begin rebuilding the life she'd lost.

Resting against the plush cushioning, Logan stares at the space in front of the sofa where an artisanal coffee table will soon be placed, perhaps a Japanese *chabudai*. He recalls a different sofa in front of a different table, upon which rested fifteen oxycodone pills and a bottle of Jack Daniel's Tennessee Fire. He couldn't be prouder of how far he's come since then.

Outside, across the Hudson, the sun dips behind the towers of Jersey City. The buzz of his phone echoes in the loft. It's Alice.

'Miss me already?' he asks.

A tense silence.

'Alice?'

Her voice is small. 'Can we meet somewhere?'

He listens closely to her tone, reads between the lines. 'Sure. Where?'

'Um . . .'

'Bite to eat?'

'Can we do, like, an activity? Need my mind off things.'

'An *activity*?'

'I don't know how this shit works. What do people even do?' She swallows. 'Rock climbing . . .?'

'Rock climbing?'

'Just humour me. I need this.' She coughs, muffled by the crook of her elbow. 'Isn't that all the rage now? Bouldering?'

'Sure.'

'You were training today, weren't you? And renovating? If you're too tired . . .'

His muscles feel like cement. He's unsure if he can even peel himself off the sofa. But Alice needs distracting, from something possibly sinister. For that, he'd move heaven and earth.

'I'm good as new,' he says.

—

The climbing gym lies burrowed down a lane branching off the Bowery's main artery, its signage inconspicuous.

From the street, you can't tell Sisyphus Bouldering is one of the trendiest climbing gyms in all of New York. Logan found the place online, roughly equidistant from Tribeca and the Lower East Side, the opposite sides of Manhattan where he and Alice live.

They meet out front, and only discover the establishment doubles as an after-work drinking hole once they head inside. A solid barrier divides the warehouse cleanly in half, with inclined bouldering walls on their left and a bar overlooking a sea of circular tables on their right. Loud signs disclaim the obvious: you boulder, then you booze, exclusively in that order. Staff in emerald polo shirts survey the visitors, ensuring no one hurls themselves up a rock wall under the influence.

Alice takes one look at the shelves of glittering spirit bottles and throws Logan a sideways glance. 'We can go somewhere else.'

He ushers her toward the reception desk. 'Relax, would you? I can be in the same room as beer.'

As they pay for a session, rent their climbing shoes and find a free wall, Logan studies the crowd. Hordes of men and women in their twenties and thirties, lean and wiry, haul themselves with reckless abandon up set routes. Faces scrunch in determination, chalk dust falling from calloused palms as they lunge for brightly coloured holds. Here, nothing separates the software engineers from the manual labourers, the investment bankers from the hospitality workers. Each generation laments the laziness of the next, but you only need to step outside and take a look around to see the truth: people aren't so bad.

They climb for half an hour. The pull of gravity punishes Logan's heavy build, not to mention the overbearing fatigue he tries his best to ignore, but he's not here to excel personally. Alice weighs 115, max, and although she's never bouldered before, her teenage dedication to ballet has left her with frightening dexterity. He watches her spring up intermediate routes without difficulty, her compression leggings and thin tank top highlighting the muscle reforming across her frame. More important is the concentration on her face; she's wholly absorbed by the task before her.

Whatever happened today, in this moment she's empty of worry, and that warms Logan's heart.

Eventually she notes his exhaustion and, herself satisfied, gestures him toward the exit. He shakes his head and juts his chin at the sea of barstools.

She places a hand on her hip. 'You sure?'

He rolls his eyes as he beelines past her, rounding the barricade that divides the spaces. He pulls out a stool, waits for her to take the one opposite, then leaves her at the table. He heads for the bar and returns a minute later with two beers.

When he places the bottles on the rough wood, her hazelnut eyes bore into him. 'What the fuck are you doing?'

He drops to the stool opposite, raising an eyebrow. 'Non-alcoholic.'

Alice relaxes. 'Oh. Right.'

They share a smile and take sips in unison. He savours the moment for a beat before asking, 'What happened today?'

Her grin dissipates. She puts her beer down, lowers her face in her hands, and groans. She recites the quarrel between her and her roommate, almost verbatim, so as not to gloss over detail that may be crucial. When she's finished the story, she bows her head. 'I'm a piece of shit, right?'

'Because you had an argument?'

'One I could have avoided by keeping my cool. A teenager set me off. It's pathetic.'

'What specifically set you off?'

'I don't—'

'A phrase, a word, maybe just a look. Something made you snap.'

She moistens a fingertip against the bottle's condensation. He waits patiently. Finally, she says, 'Rose said the world doesn't revolve around me.'

'And what about that made you—?'

'That was Mom's go-to. That line.'

'Ah.'

Alice meets his eyes. 'You remember that train ride? Not long after we met. You'd just killed those guys, in your old building . . .'

'You mean the first time I opened up about my childhood to anyone in years? I'm not *that* old, Alice. I've still got my faculties. That's just about the last thing I'll ever forget.'

'Your dad. He still around?'

Logan rotates his bottle in a calloused palm. His mouth seals in a hard line. 'Somewhere.'

'How long since you two spoke?'

He calculates. 'It'd be eighteen years now.'

'Shit.'

'What?'

She shakes her head. 'No, it's just—I'd have been, what, six? I haven't contacted Mom in two years. Which is nothing, really. Not compared to—'

'Stop comparing.'

She eyes him knowingly. 'Right.'

'You thinking about reaching out?'

'No. *God*, no.' She looks like she's seen a ghost.

A flat-screen television fixed to a support beam behind her catches his eye. Tuned to the evening news, the picture displays a familiar face in a familiar location, and before he can help himself, he's entranced.

She notices his attention shift. 'What . . .?' A glance over one shoulder. 'Oh.'

On-screen, a towering African-American man in a slim-fitting dress shirt tucked into woollen slacks shakes hands out the front of a pristine building with ceremonial ribbon stretched across its entrance. Mayor Terrion Young is effortlessly personable; emerald eyes blaze as he flashes his trademark smile. The crowd he works his way through buzzes with adulation. A banner beneath the footage reports the grand opening of three new addiction treatment centres in Hunts Point, one of the most dangerous neighbourhoods in the Bronx.

Alice can't take her eyes off the screen. 'He really is repenting.'

Logan's transfixed, too. 'Seems so.'

Only they know what for.

Despite his best efforts to discredit Young's focus on aiding the forgotten swathes of New York, Logan can't find it within himself to be cynical. Hard to admit, but he's impressed. Perhaps even inspired.

He finally tears himself away from the news segment, and his gaze falls to the back of Alice's head. Then he has an idea.

'I think I'll wander a little farther out. Into the unknown. I might pay my father a visit.'

'To test who you are now?' she asks. 'To see if it affects you? Whether it wobbles your new foundations?'

There's real fear in his gut as he says, 'Right.'

She summons her courage and says, 'Then I think I'll see Mom.'

—

'They've met twice today.'

Jacinta registers the words, but she can't decipher them. At times like these, the oak she rests her elbows on doesn't feel like it belongs to the Resolute desk. She certainly doesn't feel like the President.

But she is, so she ignores the weight on her shoulders and swallows her stress. 'What did you say?'

Jack Riordan, her Chief of Staff, remains unfazed as he looms over the desk. He stabs one of the printouts resting on its surface with his thumb. 'Ma'am, I was referring to the Russia–Iran intelligence briefing within today's PDB—'

She whips a palm skyward, shutting him up mid-sentence.

'Not you,' she says, then curls her hand into a fist and extends her index finger, pointing past Riordan to the man lurking behind. 'Him.'

The spooks never look like they belong in the Oval Office, no matter how hard they try. This one didn't bother trying. He's CIA, but when your business shapes the fate of nations, you don't have to worry about donning a blazer.

The visitor wears a dark pullover, rugged jeans, and weathered boots, and was still let straight in. There's no need to impress—that's real power.

The spook's jaw is rigid as he gazes vacantly across the room. 'They've met twice today,' he repeats.

The air tightens.

Riordan notes the look on Jacinta's face and keeps his mouth shut.

Jacinta draws inward.

None of this would be happening if she hadn't caved to blackmail four months ago. Daniel Datvyan held evidence of corruption within her administration over her head and she deemed the ammunition serious enough to bring her down. Key members of her party had made the mistakes, not her, but as leader, she was responsible for their errors in judgement. Being President is about making the choices no one else is willing to.

So she rolled over for Datvyan. She let him use CIA resources to try and get himself out of whatever predicament he'd wound up in, which she later discovered was a war with one of the most lethal wet-work operatives in Langley's storied history.

Logan Booth left nearly two dozen bodies in his wake, some of them Tier One soldiers from the CIA's Special Activities Center, and then dispensed with Datvyan himself.

He promised the mayor of New York that he wouldn't seek revenge against Jacinta, but she just doesn't believe him. So she's having him followed, along with his new best friend – a young woman Datvyan tried to have killed.

If something's coming, she wants to be ready for it.

You do not fear Logan Booth. She looks up to meet the spook's eyes. 'Why twice?'

The man sports the detached gaze of a predator. 'Hard to say. Both their phones are fortified to the nines, so we can't eavesdrop the way we'd like. He's up to speed on all the latest encryption measures. He didn't exactly rest on his laurels after the computer science Master's in '09.'

'Of course not,' she says quietly. 'You trained him well.'

The spook pauses. He seems mildly irritated. 'So, two meet ups. The usual café this morning, and a climbing gym tonight, whatever that means. Might be a date. Maybe she's straight now. Maybe they'll fuck.'

'Maybe.' Jacinta calculates. 'Keep an eye on it?'

'Sure.'

'And if you so much as catch *wind* he's coming—'

She cuts herself off when the spook's eyes narrow. He quietly points a finger at the back of Riordan's head. The Chief of Staff faces Jacinta, oblivious to the gesture behind him. The Company man then raises the same finger, bringing it softly to his lips.

Jacinta nods her understanding. Riordan looks over his shoulder, but the spook's already folded his arms across his chest.

'Just stay on it,' Jacinta says.

'You got it.' The spook tilts his chin down. 'Ma'am.'

Then he's gone.

Riordan studies the silence for a few seconds, deep in thought. 'This about that shit that went down in New York?'

She lifts the document concerning Russia–Iran relations off the Resolute desk and hands it to him. 'You were saying . . .?'

They exchange a knowing look before he presses on.

Business as usual.

6

Logan has never been one to dawdle.

The very next afternoon, he pulls a nondescript rental car into an expanse of bitumen. A burning white sun torches the lot. It was ninety minutes from the Avis in Manhattan to the Oakview Gardens Retirement Village in Whitneyville on the outskirts of New Haven, yet somehow the journey was over in a flash.

When you're reluctant to reach your destination, time only accelerates, and Logan spent every second behind the wheel dreading this. The Zen ideal of having no preferences is a faraway concept now. He wants what comes next like a hole in the head.

Nevertheless, he takes one of the hundreds of empty parking spots in front of the long, low building of the retirement home. He hasn't the faintest idea why seventy-two-year-old Roy Booth requires assisted living. It took Logan five minutes to locate his father, but he pried no further than an address. Maybe because he isn't sure how he wants to find the old man.

He kills the engine and sits in the stillness as the air-conditioning dies. The heat immediately encases the hatchback, seeping through the thin gaps in the chassis. He senses the precursor to sweat beads flushing through his face, close to the skin, then he swallows his apprehension and levers out of the vehicle. The lot and its surrounding buildings rest under a blanket of indifference, a distinct lack of urgency permeating everything.

In the cool lobby of the retirement home, a receptionist who doesn't look far off residency herself peers up at him. 'How may I help you?'

'Here to see Roy Booth.'

The old woman nods and taps at a keyboard, verifying Roy's name on the resident list. A wall clock ticks loudly behind her.

Logan feels compelled to add, 'I'm his son.'

He isn't sure why he suddenly felt the urge to justify his presence, but the woman just nods again. Her gaze remains fixed on the screen. She clicks the corded mouse a few times, squints a little, then says, 'Room one fourteen. Just down there, on the left.'

'Thank you.'

She pushes a visitor log toward him. He signs it, then stands there, as if expecting there to be more. She stares at him, confused. Her expression says, *This isn't a prison.*

He sets off along the featureless corridor. Bare white plaster walls, slate carpet. A cloying, artificial smell masks the stench of the elderly. He runs his fingertips gently along the metal handrail as he strides, the lack of stimuli stirring long-buried memories. Blurry and unfocused, the past rotates through his mind as he takes the first left and reads numbers on white doors: *101, 102* . . .

He remembers when he was seven, he and his father transfixed by the cable debut of the previous year's *Die Hard.* Swigging from a pint of Jim Beam, Roy turns to his son, eyes wide with intensity, jerking a thumb at the blocky television: 'You see? That McClane there ain't no pussy. Ain't no fuckin' bitch. You ain't gonna be one either . . .'

Logan's confused, unable to grasp the nature of the gulf he senses between the stoicism displayed on-screen and the loud and frightened man across from him. All he recalls thinking is: *You don't understand, Dad.* Unsure how to communicate this to his father, he keeps quiet, nodding in vague agreement.

The next year, at a Little League game, Logan takes an unsuccessful swing at a pitch that looks like a strike, but it's called the other way, and Roy jumps to his feet in the bleachers and screams at an umpire. 'Are you serious?! You must be breaking my fuckin' balls!'

Surrounding parents cringe. Logan eyes spit flying from red lips as his father continues his tirade, until another dad rises, lays a hand on Roy's shoulder, and says, 'Hey, Roy, pipe down, why don'tcha?'

His father manages a small, frantic laugh and sinks back to the stand like someone let the air out of him.

Eighteen years ago, Logan went home for the final time. It was the last of a series of annual trips he made between college semesters that he usually wound up regretting.

Months later, his mother passed from pancreatic cancer, and he realised he felt no obligation to continue speaking with his father. He only ever went back home for her sake.

Mary Booth was a quiet, reserved woman who understandably resented her husband, but with each new outburst from Roy, she only withdrew further. In hindsight, Logan sees how her placidity stifled his relationship with her. *You're here by choice,* he would find himself thinking, often angrily.

Still, he loved her with all his heart. So, at age twenty-three, Logan left her funeral and never contacted Roy again.

It feels like a bad dream as he lays a palm on the handle to a door reading *114* and raps the other fist on the thin wood.

'Yeah?' a gravelly voice grunts from the other side.

One syllable, but the familiar tone almost makes him flinch.

Discipline is nothing to you, Logan thinks, steadying himself. *This here is how you grow.*

He pushes the handle down and steps into the room, regards the old man in the chair by the window. 'Hey, Dad.'

—

The neighbourhood hums with tranquility. Lexington is all trimmed lawns, white picket fences, towering oaks, and generous lots. The American Dream is clearly still alive in some places.

Alice tries to take a deep breath before stepping up on the porch, but an inhale won't quell the terror in her chest, so she goes right ahead and finds herself staring blankly at the screen door of her childhood home.

She briefly considered calling ahead, then dismissed the idea. Surprises were always her mother's Achilles' heel. Carolyn thrives with time to scheme, to formulate an emotional minefield in advance. The false narrative she feeds herself to remain functional requires careful preparation. You need a retort in your back pocket for every possible accusation.

Alice lifts a fist, makes to rap on the fibres of the screen door. Beyond the wire, the front door lies open, and she hears a rustle of movement within the house. Carolyn wasn't far from a recluse by the time Alice left for New York, and it will only be worse now. With her mother's condition, you don't gain awareness, you don't correct course.

A condition, Alice reminds herself. *It's a condition. It's not her fault.*

But her fist won't move. It hangs in the air in front of the screen, and a wave of hot panic rolls up through her, and suddenly she's turning and taking off at a quiet jog away from the house of nameless horrors, the source of all her youthful pain and confusion. Before she knows it, she's run all the way to the end of the street, past where she parked the rental car. She needs distance, or she'll explode. She comes to a breathless standstill at the T-junction, doubled over, hands on her knees. She waits until the veil of panic clears to straighten up.

Dead ahead, a low, dark sedan is halfway through a U-turn, speeding away from her. The engine whines, almost like it slid off the mark the moment she came careening into sight. Her brow furrows, but that's all she manages before the sedan purrs away, its windows darkened to maximum tint. The sun beats down on its gleaming chassis as it recedes from view. She loiters a moment. Confusion tugs at her.

The car's a speck at the end of the street by the time she fishes her phone from her pocket. She's likely just paranoid, but Logan made it clear he would prefer to be alerted to a dozen false alarms than have her overlook danger once and pay the price. Probably nothing, but either way . . .

She swipes to unlock her phone. Then a shrill voice rings out. One word, ripping through the leafy neighbourhood: 'Alice!'

Her blood runs cold.

'Alice! Is that you?!'

She looks back down her childhood street and spots the wide, stooped profile of her mother on the sidewalk in front of the house.

Suddenly Alice is helpless, her decisions unconscious. She forgets the phone in her hand. Forgets the dark sedan. Forgets anything she had planned. As though reeled in, she trudges back past her car, all the way up to her mother, who still dwarfs Alice, hunched as she is.

Short black hair, wet lips, nostrils that seem permanently flared. A thin film rests over the reddened whites of Carolyn's eyes. Not tears—they're watering from the daylight. She mustn't get out much. Her skin is translucent, varicose veins exposed across swollen ankles. Her mouth hangs slightly open, but it seems to be her default expression. Alice doesn't detect any real surprise, certainly no joy.

'Hey, Mom,' she says.

—

It takes Roy a second, then his wrinkled lips tremble. 'Logan?'

The door swings gently shut behind Logan. 'Thought I'd swing by.'

His father fights to steady his quivering mouth and fails. Next thing Logan knows, there are tears in the old man's eyes.

Logan didn't expect it; maybe he should have. He tries to picture the last sight Roy caught of his son before today—a scrawny twenty-three-year-old, yet to correct his awful posture, absconding from his mother's wake with his head down. Now Logan's two hundred and twenty pounds of muscle, standing to his full height with a searing gaze.

He understands why it took Roy a moment to put a name to the face.

As his father sits crying, Logan feels his preconceived judgements fall away. He crosses the space, lifting a chair out from the circular dining table on his way over. He places the chair opposite his father and sits.

Roy chuckles without humour as he wipes the tears he clearly wishes weren't flowing. He was always a handsome man who, through choice of character, made himself ugly. Physical features he passed to his son still exist: the hard blue eyes, the strong jaw, the permanent golden-brown tan. Decades of self-pity have taken the rest. His face hangs like a leathery bag, and his pupils flicker with anxiety. He looks like he's been scared for as long as he can remember.

Roy makes to say something but doesn't seem capable.

Logan folds his hands in his lap. 'Why are you here?' he asks his father.

'Huh?'

'Why aren't you out in the village? Why are you here in the home? Are you sick?'

Roy raises his palms. 'Oh, well . . .' He swallows. 'I'm fine. Not sick. But they say . . .' He trails off.

'What do they say, Dad?'

Roy squirms under the pressure. 'They prefer me in here. S'all I know. They say I don't do good alone. All this modern crap. They got all these terms for it. Y'know, whiny bullshit . . .'

'Right.'

Roy can't take his eyes off Logan's noticeable bulk: shoulders like bowling balls, neck thick as a bull's. 'You, uh . . . you hit the weights?'

'I did.'

Another tense chuckle. Muted laughter that seems pained. 'I must've taught you a thing or two after all, huh?'

'Oh, I never used anything you taught me.'

A dull flare in Roy's eyes. He juts his chin at Logan's chest, old patterns resurfacing. 'Well, you don't get like that being a pussy, do you? I sure taught you not to be a pussy.'

'You taught me to pretend.'

Roy shifts nervously. The scent of stale cigarette smoke emanates off him. 'If that's how you saw it . . . ain't nothin' I can do about that . . .' He keeps trailing off. He lacks the resolve to make a firm point.

You taught me to posture, Logan thinks. *To be hollow. It's a miracle I sought another way to live.* It's too much to heap on his father out of the blue, though, so he says, 'How long you been here?'

'Oh. Let's see . . .' Roy rubs his jaw, faking thoughtfulness. He never did anything genuinely. 'Two years. Comin' up on three.'

'You like it?'

'It's fine. I got no place else to be.' He shakes his head. 'Damn. You really . . . what do you do, boy?'

'I'm retired.'

'Oh. But you're—you're—what, forty . . .?'

'Forty-one.'

'What *did* you do?'

'Defence.'

'Defence? Like . . .?'

'Like I signed things. I can't really talk about it.'

'Oh.' A little relief this time, like he nervously anticipated the revelation of some drab bureaucratic career, perhaps an early medical retirement from symptoms Roy would describe as 'pussy-boy shit'. The old man coughs into a wrinkled fist. 'So you made your hay and bounced?'

'Something like that.'

'Well, ain't that somethin'.' Roy's gaze darts around. He always had trouble with eye contact. 'They beat you into this shape in the military?'

Logan shakes his head. 'My own doing. Long before my defence work.'

'Well, you did good, son. Your generation, they sure don't look like you. Everyone went so fuckin' soft—'

'Dad.'

'Yeah?'

'I've heard about enough of that for one lifetime, don't you think?'

Roy's frown deepens. 'You don't . . . you don't think we're all going soft? I mean . . .' He gestures vaguely to the television in the corner of the room.

Logan rests his elbows on his thighs. 'Eighteen years and we're right back to what the talking heads tell you to think?'

Roy stares. 'You cut me off. Don't go talking about "eighteen years" like I did that to you.'

'I didn't cut you off. I just didn't reach out. Neither did you. I was at NYU for four more years after Mom died. You knew where to find me.' He sighs. 'Look, we did it to each other. Mutual participation, I guess.'

'I never thought I'd see you again.'

'Me neither.'

'Why . . .?' Roy drums his fingers on one thigh. 'Why now?'

'A little while back, I met someone who reminded me of you, and . . .' Logan shakes his head, picturing a slight, sweat-soaked man named Daniel Datvyan. 'I realised I was maybe too harsh on you. Some things you couldn't help.'

'Couldn't help . . .?'

'I judged you. But you didn't have access to other ideas. You couldn't just look up different ways to be. You learned what you learned and . . . anyway, I'm here now.'

Roy looks at him plainly. 'Why?'

Logan shrugs. 'It's just what's right.'

Real emotion bleeds back into Roy's eyes, the macho act falling by the wayside. 'This here . . . you think it's right?'

'Yes, Dad. I do.'

Then Roy does something Logan never could have predicted.

The old man extends a hand.

Logan takes his father's wizened palm in his own.

'What are you doing here?' Carolyn snaps.

Emotion only comes once she discerns how to use it to her benefit. It's why Alice despises crocodile tears.

'It's been a long time,' Alice says. 'I wanted to see you. See how you were doing.'

'How I'm *doing*?' Her mother only ever used words to manipulate, so she unconsciously assumes everyone else is doing the same. 'I'm doing fine—thank you, Alice. You didn't think to call? Let me know you were coming?'

'No,' Alice says. She has the urge to offer apologies, explanations, but she holds herself back. It takes everything. 'I just thought I'd see if you were home.'

'I see.' Her mother scoffs. 'Well, if it suits you, I guess . . .'

'I can come back. If it's not a good time.'

'Not a good time?' A shrill laugh, and Alice flinches as an iceberg of childhood memory cracks the surface. 'No, I get it. Because I've got nothing going on, right? You can just appear when you please—of course. Show up on the doorstep like nothing ever happened. I don't know what I expected.'

Alice clears her throat. 'Should we go inside?'

'I'm fine right here. You'd like to go inside, would you?'

'I just think—'

'All you do, isn't it, darling? *Think*. On and on about everything, all the time. What led you to that nasty little friend of yours,' Carolyn sneers. God forbid she ever found out what the young women were to each other. 'I must admit, I thought she'd be right by your side if you ever came back. Murmuring all those opinions in your ear, like when you left.'

Tense quiet.

'So? Where's Miss Know-It-All?'

'Back in New York,' Alice mumbles.

Technically true. Ruby's cremated remains must be somewhere in the state. Either scattered or buried in an unmarked grave, the set period to claim her ashes likely expired. Alice never thought to, consumed solely by the pursuit of her lifeblood. That guilt will never leave her.

'Mmm.' Carolyn's eyes narrow. 'Your teeth . . .'

'Oh,' Alice says quietly. 'I needed new ones. Had an accident, knocked some of them out. I'm okay.'

The first lie. She came into this determined to be truthful, no matter what. She feels it all unravelling.

'Oh, *you're* okay?' Carolyn's pitch tilts upward. Alice knows what's coming. 'I'm glad *you're* okay. Never one to worry about others, were you?'

'Mom—'

'You've got some nerve, you know that? *"I just thought I'd show up. Me and all my baggage, I just thought I'd show up."*' Carolyn mocks fake tears, one of her specialties. 'Maybe no one wanted you to show up, you *selfish* child. Disappear for two years, turn back up, run off the porch like a little baby, and then *"How are you doing, Mom?"* You want to know how I'm doing, Alice?' Suddenly she's screaming, her voice echoing down the leafy street. 'I'm just wonderful! Your father left me, you left me. Shows where thoughtfulness and consideration get you in this world. All I've ever dealt with are the entitled and the spoiled! You and Jonathan, you take me for granted and you run off with your little friends who whisper conspiracies in your ears about me and—!'

'*Mom!*' Alice yells. 'Let's go inside! Please!'

Wet lips froth as Carolyn jabs a finger at the house and hisses, 'You don't ever get to go back in there. That's *my* house. You used it for what you needed, used *me*. I sacrificed everything to raise you to the best of my ability and you spat it all back in my face. I can't *believe* you showed up here after . . .'

She keeps going, but Alice tunes out when she notices neighbours on porches, a few people peeking through bay windows. She can see her mother's boozing has worsened from the deeper, uglier redness in Carolyn's face and the familiar stench of shiraz on her breath. Her mother used to down half a bottle in the morning before the school run, car rides where she would rave incessantly about the terrible dangers of underage drinking.

Alice turns and takes a step toward the house, hoping her mother will follow. It's fine if Carolyn screams the whole way to the porch, Alice just needs to get her inside so they can talk—

The *crack* feels like it splits her head.

She wonders where her mother produced the baseball bat from, so severe is the impact. As Alice staggers off the garden path, she realises Carolyn just put her massive bodyweight behind the blow, landing the heel of her hand behind the ear. A hot concussion makes Alice stumble. She nearly goes down on her hands and knees in a bush, but rights herself at the last second and comes to a trembling halt on the lawn, nauseous.

Carolyn's still shouting: 'I told you you don't get to go in there—!'

Alice swallows hard, sways a little. Somehow, she manages to ask herself what she was expecting from this reunion and realises the answer is: nothing at all.

The lack of reaction seems to short-circuit Carolyn. She murmurs, 'Alice,' in the smallest voice imaginable.

Alice finds it within herself to understand. To know it isn't her mother's fault, not really.

'I forgive you,' Alice says as the concussion makes her world swim. Already, she feels the flesh behind her ear swelling. 'Goodbye, Mom.'

'Alice, no. My girl. Oh, my baby girl . . .'

Alice hears the pleas as she turns and walks away, but they stopped meaning anything to her years ago. She floats back to the rental car as though above her body, and by the time she reaches the driver's door she can no longer hear her mother screaming for her.

She gets behind the wheel, fires the engine, and drives away.

As she passes Carolyn, she watches the woman fall to her knees. The gesture isn't real. Her mother collapsed crestfallen only so she can paint the memory in a different light in future, so she can pretend Alice is the monster who abandoned a loving parent.

It's none of Alice's concern how her mom twists what just happened.

She remembers a Buddhist concept she came across in the early days of her sobriety: no second arrow. Life hits us with the first arrow—some painful experience—but the second arrow we fire into ourselves, spiralling into self-blame. *This terrible thing happened to me because I deserve—*

No. A terrible thing happened, and that's that. Alice tried to build bridges and got cracked in the head for it. In the past she would have sought to numb herself from this feeling. Now she sits with the sensation.

She can see things she would have previously overlooked. Only four months ago, she'd have fled back to the crack dens and abandoned responsibility, cursing the upbringing she was handed, creating her own destruction. Now, as she turns out of her childhood street for the last time, she just addresses what must be addressed.

She fishes her phone out of her pocket, speed-dials Logan, and when he answers, she says, 'Someone's following me.'

7

Logan relinquishes the grip on his father's hand just as the phone buzzes at his hip.

Very few people on this planet have his number.

He mouths '*Sorry*' at Roy before fishing the phone out. When he sees who's calling, his grimace deepens.

'Someone's following me.'

His heart leaps. Roy must notice, because the old man leans forward, curious. Logan hunches over the phone in concentration. 'Where are you? Lexington?'

'Y-Yeah.' Alice stammers the syllable out, her voice trembling.

'Seen your mom?'

'Yeah.' He gets the sense that if she were any less curt, her composure would shatter.

'So it's—?' He pinches the bridge of his nose with two fingers. Tries to read her tone, but she's not giving him anything. 'What, she didn't want you to leave? She's chasing you?'

'What? No—*no.* Jesus, I wouldn't call if it was that. I can handle that.'

'Then what?'

'It's a black Ford sedan. A Focus, I think. I saw it parked in the next street. Didn't think anything of it, but it pulled a U-turn as soon as I spotted it. I think whoever's inside panicked. I didn't get a look at them. Didn't memorise the plates either. I should have. And I'm—oh, shit. *Shit*—' A sharp inhale.

'*What?*'

Roy flinches in the La-Z-Boy. Never in his life has he heard his son command that kind of tone.

Her voice comes fast, clipped between frantic breaths. 'It's . . . okay . . . okay, I think we're good . . .'

'Speak, Alice.'

'I just passed Trader Joe's. It was there, the sedan. Parked in the lot. Waiting, I guess. Maybe I'm just paranoid . . .'

'Has it pulled out? Is it tailing you?'

'I'm—no. I don't know. I've turned. I don't *know*.'

'Did you see anything you missed the first time? People, plates?'

'No. I freaked out. *Fuck*. Sorry. I should have—'

'Stop apologising.'

'Sorry.'

'How much gas have you got?'

'What?'

'Gas. In the tank. How much?'

'Half full.'

'That's enough. Just drive in broad loops. Stick to busy roads, thoroughfares. As many witnesses around you as possible. Whatever you do, don't pull in anywhere quiet. I can be there in two hours. I'll call you when I hit Lexington—'

'No.'

Logan hesitates. 'No?'

'I'll head across to Boston,' she says. 'What's that, twenty miles? It's fine, it's I-93. Can't get much busier than that. Then I'll do what you said. Drive in circles until you show up.'

'Why Boston?'

'I'm the one who brought this to Mom's doorstep. So I lead them away from here, okay? If something's going to happen, it should happen elsewhere. It's our problem. Not hers.'

He tries to read between the lines. 'So the reunion went okay?'

'No, Logan,' she says bluntly, and all at once her tremors vanish. She sounds lucid now, and it strikes him that her tension had very little to do with the tail. 'It went as bad as I thought it would. But that doesn't mean she deserves to get swept up in this.'

He doesn't know what to say. He only wishes he had her emotional intelligence.

'Yours go okay?' she asks.

He glances up from the floor, into his father's unblinking eyes. 'I'm in the middle of it.'

'Oh.' A terse pause. 'I'm sorry . . .'

'Don't be. I'll be there as soon as I can.'

'Okay. You think this could be something to do with—?'

'Alice.' It's dead quiet in Roy's small unit, and the old man can undoubtedly hear every word spoken in his son's ear. 'Wait until I'm there, okay? We'll figure it out.'

'Okay.'

'We'll figure it out,' he says again. 'I promise.'

He kills the call. Keeps his head bowed. He can't bear to look at his father.

'You gotta go?' the old man says.

Logan finally looks up. 'It's serious. I've made enemies. My . . . defence work.'

'Was that your wife?'

'No.'

'Girlfriend?'

'She's like a . . . sister.'

Roy looks left and right. That unidentifiable fear, gripping him again, threatening to blow his insecurities like a powder keg. Logan watches him grapple with the impulse to voice his frustrations the only way he knows how: *So you're off, just like that, and you ain't even gettin' any pussy for it?*

Yet somehow, the old man avoids the instincts that have ruined every relationship he's ever had. Maybe seventy years of poor decisions was enough. Roy swallows his pride and says, 'Will you be back, my boy?'

'Soon as this is taken care of. I promise.'

Silence.

'If I promise something,' Logan says, 'it's done. I'm a man of my word.'

Roy nods slowly. He takes a breath. 'I'm proud of you.'

Emotion swells within Logan, but he also needs to clarify something. 'I didn't get like this because of how you raised me.'

'I know,' Roy says quietly. 'I know, son.' He rubs his nose. 'You figured out something I never could, huh?'

Logan's eyes turn wet as he reaches over and clasps his father's gnarled knee. 'Good seeing you, Dad.' He rises, looks around the room, and manages to say, 'I'm sorry I didn't do this sooner.'

'Not your fault.'

Logan gives a small nod, mildly shocked that Roy Booth seems to have gained some self-awareness.

Then he recalls the fear in Alice's voice and hustles straight out.

A severe-looking woman barges into the room, her ponytail drawn tight. 'You're on in five.'

Jacinta tries to respond to the producer without moving her face, murmuring, 'Yes, thank you.'

Two makeup artists fill her vision, swapping places every few seconds, their brushes overlapping. An eyeliner needles the skin behind her lashes. She holds herself still and controls her heart rate. It's not her fault she was late to the studio. She's tackled her mountain of duties with haste and diligence. Sometimes these things just get away from you.

But not even the President can delay the programming schedule of a multinational news channel.

'Okay,' one of the makeup artists mutters, her face twisted in concentration. 'Okay, we're good.' She steps back, and a few seconds later, the other woman follows suit.

The producer who just stormed in says, 'Great,' without an ounce of excitement. She beckons for Jacinta and her cadre of senior advisors to follow her. They sweep out of the small makeup station alongside a phalanx of Secret Service agents, weaving fast down a series of corridors that eventually open out into the studio itself. Across the room, the male and female co-anchors—each like wax figures with perfectly coiffed hair—banter amongst themselves as a digital banner projected behind them announces the imminent arrival of Madam President. From behind the cameras, Jacinta absorbs the banner's text as one of her advisors whispers in her ear, rehashing the talking points the President committed to memory between the furore of the day's events.

Jacinta's red lips spread wide in a kind smile you'd never know was false.

'Showtime,' she purrs, testing a certain inflection.

She doesn't consider herself sociopathic. She feels real emotion when it counts, but it doesn't change the fact that most of this job is performance. She's still warming the necessary facial muscles when she gets the tap on the shoulder. She turns smiling, but the expression dissipates when she spots her small entourage hovering a few paces back.

They retreated to make room for the spook with the dark pullover.

He disguises his coldness with a plain stare. Here, he could be a modestly dressed executive, even a big donor granted special access to the studio. Whatever. Those in the know let him through, and the rest of them will see what they want to see.

She inches closer to him. The tiniest gap separates them. 'I'm on in two minutes.'

'Good for you,' he says quietly. 'Now, you told us the girl was a crack addict. But she's not. She's sharp. She spotted the tail.'

Behind them, the female anchor unleashes an over-the-top laugh at some quip her co-host blessed upon the viewers.

'*What?*' Jacinta whispers.

'Precisely what information were you operating off?' the guy asks. 'We had a suspicion she was clean, but you insisted she wasn't. We trusted you. Because you were so involved in that mess in New York.' He bristles. 'You do understand you're a billboard, yes? A mouthpiece for talking points. Not an intelligence officer.'

'Sixty seconds,' the executive producer warns from a distance.

Jacinta leans right into the spook's ear. 'Correct. But I still appoint your director, and I'm too public for you to stifle me before I put a puppet in charge of the CIA and gut you. So when I say dance, you dance.'

'Doesn't change the fact you led us astray. We thought we had a useless junkie on our hands.'

'That's your own sloppiness.'

The producer starts mouthing: *Ten, nine, eight . . .*

'So?' the spook mutters.

Tension builds for a few seconds, then Jacinta sighs. She makes the tough call, because that's her job. 'Just grab her, then. Find out what she's been up to.'

A spark of life in the man's dead eyes.

Jacinta contorts her face into the warmest smile imaginable, turns, and sweeps onto the set with the grace of a runway model as the anchors erupt in greeting. The cameras zoom in on her figure in the tight-fitting dress, and she paints her face with a false smile.

As the spook slips away, Jacinta nurses a terrible fear.

—

Seventy minutes after coming off I-93 into the heart of Boston, Alice realises her error.

As is usually the case with mistakes, she sees too late.

Logan said stick to the busiest stretches of the city, but it must have gone without saying to also avoid the most dangerous. She did a decent job for the first hour she spent trawling through Beacon Hill, Chinatown, Bay Village, but she deemed it imprudent to double back on the same areas, and her unease took her north-east through the Callahan Tunnel, depositing her in East Boston. From there, she coasted a few streets over into Central, a neighbourhood of narrow streets and industrial warehouses lining the waterfront.

Guiding the rental car along Border Street, parallel to the harbour, she coasts past a skate park and spots a group of teenagers milling under a looming tree, hands in pockets. One kid fingers a switchblade as he mouths off to a rival.

She grew up just outside of Boston, so she knows Central's violent crime rate is three times the national average. If the people tailing her are going to try anything, they'll want to be able to obfuscate the snatch and grab. Make it look like an ordinary carjacking.

Here's the place.

'Relax,' she says to herself, slowly letting out a breath.

After she passes the skate park, the traffic suddenly clears. There's only a steelworks on her left now, beside a looming factory with a rusted sign reading: WELDING.

It's quiet.

'Relax,' she whispers again, but one hand drifts to her phone. She snatches it up, glancing down to scroll her contacts for Logan's number.

When she looks back up, she sees the dark nose of the Ford sedan slice into view from the mouth of a connecting street—making to cut her off.

She stamps the brakes, rubber burning as she darts her hand to the buckle at her hip, unclasping the belt. She's shouldering the driver's door open before she's even come to a stop, and hits the asphalt running. Alice erupts from the rental car like a cannonball, phone clutched tight in hand, sprints behind the gently rolling vehicle, across the right-hand sidewalk, and straight down a narrow laneway between two shopfronts.

Blood roars in her ears.

She can just make out muffled male voices rising behind her.

She mutters, 'Fuck,' over and over again as she hurls herself up a low fence at the back of a deserted rear lot. She scrambles over it, slicing her forearms on the twisted wire, but adrenaline makes her impervious to pain. She figures she can run until her heart explodes in her chest. She fears she might well have to until she tumbles to the pavement in the next street in a heap of limbs, lurches back to her feet, and spots a miracle on the opposite sidewalk.

Under a tasteful logo, a sign in front of a four-storey brownstone reads NEXUS BOUTIQUE HOTEL.

She races toward it. A passing car nearly clips her, leaning hard on its horn, but she barely hears it as she sprints up a flight of steps and barrels into a small reception area. The concierge sits behind an ornate desk, a small man in a suit, his eyes wide in the wake of her explosive arrival.

She screeches to a halt in front of him, gulping for air. 'Hi. Sorry. Just been for a jog. Can I get a room, please?'

He blinks. But money's money, and his eyes drift to the computer screen in front of him. 'Uh . . . we only have—'

'It's fine. Anything.' She pulls her wallet from her pocket and hands over a credit card, nearly maxed by her recent dental procedure.

He stares at the card a moment before he takes it between manicured fingernails. 'Sure.'

He starts listing features, amenities, but she's a world away. Faint commotion floats in through the entranceway behind her, coming from across the street, and she positions herself directly in front of the concierge to block his line of sight. Every muscle on her frame stiffens. She tells herself they won't shoot her in the back in an upmarket establishment, with a witness right in front of her.

Won't they?

After minutes that feel like hours, he hands her back her card—another three hundred sapped from her dwindling credit—and a second slice of plastic emblazoned with the hotel's logo. 'So you just swipe this card under the handle to unlock—'

'Thanks.'

She beelines for the twisting grand staircase.

—

Logan takes the call on I-90 with Boston's skyline looming over him. 'Still circling?'

Alice speaks fast. 'No. They tried to . . . I don't know what they tried to do. They pulled out right in front of me. I just ditched the car and ran. I'm holed up in some bed-and-breakfast . . .'

'Where?'

'Nexus Boutique Hotel, in Central. Second floor, room eight. I'll let you straight in.'

'I'll knock four times. Anything else, don't answer. Not even if I say it's me but I knock different.'

'Okay.'

He kills the call and swipes to the GPS. The hotel is only thirteen minutes away. Each pocket of traffic grates on his nerves as he takes the tunnel under the channel. Shadows claw at the car, then daylight crashes through the windshield again and he's speeding past the airport. He exits fast into East Boston and guns it southwest through quaint suburbia, past tall townhouses in pastel shades, until he hits his destination. He parks hard a few feet from the curb in a rush job, shoulders out of the vehicle, and storms straight up the steps and past a small man behind a desk. 'Just visiting someone.'

He's up the grand staircase before the concierge can get a word out.

The second-floor corridor is blanketed in the silence of wealth. Outrageous insulation—you could hear a pin drop. Logan strides fast over plush carpet until he hits a huge door marked *8*. He raps his knuckles against the heavy wood four times, making sure to separate each knock so there's no room for confusion.

Alice rips the door open.

She's alone. Swollen scratches lace her exposed forearms, but she seems otherwise unhurt. He notes her condition and eases his hand gently off the Glock in the abdomen holster under his flannel. But he stays put, doesn't cross the threshold, not even when she steps aside to let him through.

'You coming in, or . . .?' She sounds guilty, like she fears having torn him away from a reunion two decades in the making for nothing.

He looks past her, into the beautiful room, thinking hard. 'Where'd they try to grab you?'

'What?'

'You said they pulled out in front of you.'

'I mean . . . I don't know for sure they were trying to grab—'

'Where, Alice?'

He hasn't questioned her this forcefully in four long months. She points over her shoulder, in the direction of the harbour. 'Next street over.'

He nods. So they're close. Most definitely staking the place out.

His decision comes naturally, without apprehension.

'Okay,' he says. 'This should work. Hang tight.' He grimaces. 'And I'm sorry.'

'For what?'

He recalls the grimy stairwell in New York where she first saw him kill men with his bare hands. 'What you're about to see.'

8

Logan quietly works his way down to the first floor and hustles for a tall, narrow window at the end of the hall.

The lower pane slides up without the slightest groan.

He checks below for signs of life—all quiet—before he levers himself over the sill. Barely wide enough for a vehicle, the laneway leads to a small parking lot behind the towering brownstone. Logan climbs out and drops from the first floor like a deadweight. He lands hard in a deep squat, slabs of muscle in his thighs absorbing the impact. Straightening, instinct drifts his fingers back to the Glock, but he overrides the automatic response to danger and pulls his phone out instead.

They won't be amateurs. They'll be well concealed, and it's usually imprudent to lead with brute force in urban warfare. That comes later, once he has them where he wants them.

Facing the street, he takes a breath, then transforms his face. His neutral expression gives way to artificial horror: eyes bugging, mouth gaping, stress lines accentuated in his forehead. He forces a series of manual gulps until his throat's spasming. Only then does he break into a jog and press the phone hard to his ear. He bursts out onto the sidewalk at a fast pace, crossing the road with powerful strides.

'I don't know!' he barks into the phone, his voice booming in suburbia. 'I don't know, John! I just found her like that!' He pauses. 'Yes, I'm sure she's fucking dead!'

As though oblivious to all else, he mounts the opposite sidewalk and vanishes down an alley, continuing to shout panicked things into the receiver. As soon as he's out of sight from the street, he wheels into the nook of a side entrance to the neighbouring shop, pressing his back to the closed door as he tucks the phone away.

He counts slowly, steadily, to ten.

He can visualise it perfectly: the confused seconds in which they process what they heard, the exchanged glances. *She's what? That wasn't us.*

When Logan's internal clock strikes ten, he explodes into motion again.

Sprints straight back the way he came.

He times it perfectly, catching a glimpse of a heavyset man in dark clothing racing into the hotel. A muted shout of concern floats out the doorway—the concierge protesting the intrusion. Logan hears nothing else until he crosses the street, takes the steps three at a time in bounding lunges, and enters the reception area.

Empty, save for the concierge standing behind the desk, visibly shocked, like, *How the hell did you get downstairs?*

Still in motion, Logan meets his gaze. 'I'm police.'

You believe anything when you're petrified. The man points a shaking finger at the staircase. 'Some guy just ran up—'

'I'll handle it,' Logan says, already mounting the bottom step.

He races up to the second floor.

—

Even through the brownstone's solid brick exterior, Alice hears the yelling.

It's Logan. He sounds beside himself, though she can't make out what he's shouting about. His panicked voice drifts up off the street, creeps through the gaps around the thick window pane. His cries freeze her. She's never heard him like that, not once. If she can hear him, everyone in the building must be able to, if not the whole street. It's so far out of character as to be incomprehensible. She never pictured him as one for hysterics.

Then the shouting fades as quickly as it materialised, and next thing she knows she hears rapid footsteps thumping in the corridor outside, coming toward her room.

Oh.

She barely has time to brace herself before the door crashes open.

It was locked, and she slid the chain on when Logan left, but the building's old and when the man on the other side runs his shoulder into the wood with all his weight behind it, the chain snaps and the whole thing flies inward in a violent blast of splinters. The door shudders on its hinges as it swings into the wall, revealing a stranger in jeans and a dark sweatshirt filling the doorway.

He white-knuckles a pistol as his wide pupils flick around the space, coming to rest on Alice in milliseconds. That's when his lips flap.

'Wait, you're not . . .' His face falls. 'Shit.'

Logan hits him like a truck from behind.

—

Logan reached the second-floor landing in time to see the man break through the door to Alice's room. When he glimpses her alive and well, he short-circuits for a beat. It gives Logan the opportunity to close the gap. He works his way up to a full sprint down the corridor and thanks to the plush carpet muffling his footfalls, the guy doesn't hear him coming until the last instant.

The stranger manages to half-turn before Logan drops his shoulder, picks up a final burst of speed, and crashes into the man's back.

There's the hollow *thud* of bone on muscle, and the guy flies forward into the room, taken completely off his feet. Logan staggers in after him as the collision rattles his brain. He feels it fizzing off the walls of his skull, sudden discombobulation. He almost concussed himself, but the headache remains at bay, buzzing at his temples.

He can still operate.

So he does.

Alice rears back off the bed, away from the violence, as the stranger attempts to scramble to his feet. But the crash-tackle imparted severe whiplash, and the guy's knees wobble as he tries to get his legs under him. He struggles to turn his head, his neck badly strained. Somehow he kept hold of the gun.

Logan rectifies that issue by kicking the man's forearm like he's trying to punt a football fifty yards.

Bone snaps and the guy howls and drops the SIG Sauer to the carpet. His arm flops, useless. He's still down on his knees, so the angle's right for Logan to shut him up by kicking him again, this time square in his unprotected face. His nose cracks and he splays on his back in a heap, nullified. Logan kicks a third time, sending the pistol skittering into the corner of the room, far out of reach. Then he turns and eases the broken door shut, sealing the three of them in the suite.

Behind the bed, Alice stares at the incapacitated thug. Logan notes the awareness in her eyes, the acknowledgment of precisely what's happening. The last time they shared a life-or-death experience, she was deep in the throes of crack withdrawal. Her level-headedness here is night and day compared to New York, and instead of devolving into terror, she gives Logan a plain look and says, 'He looked scared when he saw me.'

'Scared?'

'He had time to shoot me. He didn't.'

The guy's semiconscious, and he works his way woozily up from his back, basically flopping into a seated position. Blood pours in twin rivulets from twisted nostrils. Logan takes a knee in front of him, grabs two handfuls of the sweatshirt, and slams him back against the side of the bed frame. He lowers himself until his face hovers inches from the guy's shattered nose.

He waits until he sees clarity in the man's eyes before he says, 'One chance to stay breathing. Understand?'

A nod.

'So talk.'

The guy opens his mouth to reply.

Logan shakes him hard, silencing him. '*One* chance. Don't fuck this up.'

The man thinks—as best he can, at least, with a broken forearm and a disfigured face. He swallows hard, searching for lucidity amidst the pain drilling through him. He composes himself, setting his jaw. 'We weren't gonna hurt her.'

His voice is flat, gravelly. Neither his nor Logan's composure gels with the sickening violence in the air. The ability to compartmentalise at the heights of adrenaline is the clearest indicator of a professional, and all Logan can think about is that Alice fits in with them. She stands motionless on the other side of the bed, watching. In that instant, Logan gets his first true sense of her evolution.

He pulls himself back to the task at hand. 'Not good enough, I'm afraid.'

He takes a hand off the sweatshirt, pushes his flannel aside, reveals the Glock 43X in its abdomen holster.

The grimace spreads, but the guy's tone remains the same. He slows the pace of his speech down. 'We. Weren't. Gonna. Hurt. Her.'

Logan parrots the cadence: 'Not. Good. Enough.'

He slips the Glock out, holds it low. Pins the guy to the side of the bed with his free hand.

Bloody lips form a sardonic smile. The guy says, 'Shoot, then.'

Logan hesitates.

Never hesitate.

But he does.

'Go on,' the man hisses. 'That's all you're gonna get from me. Do what you want now. Hit me again, break my other arm, stick that gun to my head. Hell, pull the trigger. Torture me if it'll make you feel better. Still won't get a word outta me. You only got minutes anyway. Cops'll descend on this place soon—rich people stay here. You know that guy at the desk shit his pants and dialled nine-one-one. So you got two choices, really. Shoot me or let me go.'

Logan stares. 'Trained to resist interrogation, huh?'

The guy keeps quiet. True to his word.

The seconds tick, each one painful.

Logan tries to envision taking a prisoner. No question they need to flee this hotel, but his ride's directly in front of the building, parked in full view of reception, and there's no chance he's hauling this guy out on foot through the busy streets of Central. Besides, even if he could somehow get the man in the vehicle before Boston PD came screaming up to the doorstep, it would be moronic to abduct someone using a rental car. He didn't plan for a kidnapping when he set off for New Haven.

So the man's right. Two options: kill or release.

Logan doesn't have enough information to be comfortable with the former. This guy could be the devil incarnate, or the whole thing could be a giant misunderstanding. Given the parameters, there's no way to know for sure.

In the end, it falls on Logan's history. Deceived for a decade straight, the ugly truth is that men lie dead in his storied past who may not have deserved it. Nursing that understanding led him to the brink of suicide, but he can't reverse what happened, can't change what was done to him. He can only do better, no matter how inconvenient it might be.

'Fuck,' he spits to no one in particular. In one fluid movement, he hauls the man to his feet. The guy sways, dizzy from the agony, as Logan pats him down. He relieves the man of a black smartphone from the pocket of his jeans: no branding, no identifiable make or model. A custom job, perhaps even assembled from scratch. So that's serious.

Logan pockets the phone and shoves the guy hard toward the door. The man stumbles. He uses the splintered door frame to keep his feet, and looks back over one shoulder. 'Good call, brother.'

'Either of us glimpse another tail,' Logan says, 'I'm killing you all.'

Silence.

'You don't believe me?'

Blood falls from the man's twisted nose. 'Of course I believe you.'

He nurses his shattered arm as he limps away, then he's gone.

Logan stands in the quiet. He turns to Alice.

'I can't see a happy ending to this,' she says.

9

Soft illumination from a desk lamp spills over the briefing materials.

The documents swim before Jacinta's eyes, their words meaningless.

Such cognitive fog would be enough to send high-powered executives racing for emergency, but she's dealt with this wave of exhaustion every night for as long as she can recall. It's a natural consequence of her ambition. At some point in the evening, her brain just stops working. Nothing to do but take it as it comes. She gave up on the concept of balance somewhere in her mid-twenties, electing to simply get up each morning and work as hard as humanly possible until her synapses stop firing and her thoughts become zombified. She hits that limit now, re-reading the same line over and over again, recognising it as English but unable to decipher any further.

She folds her arms atop the open folders and lowers her head into the crook of her elbow.

She couldn't peel herself upright if she tried.

It's okay. She'll stumble from the Yellow Oval Room into the master suite, crash into bed beside Beau, sleep for an uninterrupted six hours, get up, and do it all over again, sufficiently recharged. She expects nothing less from herself. When you run a country, you must exert yourself fully: you can't leave anything in the tank. Well, some can. A select few have half-assed their time in the White House. Personally, she would never forgive herself if she didn't give her all.

She doesn't hear the man coming up behind her until he places his hands on her shoulders.

She jerks up, the shock like a knife in the stomach, then relaxes when Beau's deep voice murmurs in her ear. 'Come on. Let's get you up.'

Burly fingers knead the knots in her neck. When they met, his hands were the first thing she fixated on. His strong grip is careful, attentive. He's always had the magic touch. She allows the massage, then uses some final splash of motivation to rise to her feet. She turns and hugs him. Leans her head against his chest for one breath, two. The only reprieve she'll allow herself, besides her minute of morning stillness. There's no concern in the way he holds her. Never once has he suggested she soften her lifelong crusade: work less, play more. It's what she loves most about him. He understands her.

When they part, he asks, 'What's it tonight?'

She gestures vaguely back at the desk. 'I don't know what to do about Iran . . .'

'You never know what to do about Iran.'

She doesn't take offence. It's not an attack on her abilities, just an observation that there are some fires you can't ever put out, only manage.

'It'll be that way until you leave office,' he says. 'So it's not Iran.'

How can she explain? He understands the burden she carries, but he'll never *feel* it. He'll never be in her shoes. The thing is, the judgement call she made before going on air that afternoon was such an infinitesimal part of her day, a brief flash amidst her deluge of responsibilities. And yet, to Logan Booth, it might be everything. Aside from reaching out to him personally—which would set such a disastrous precedent that she wouldn't consider it—she isn't sure how to pump the brakes on this messiness, not without devoting significant time to brainstorming a solution.

Time she simply doesn't have.

And she can't reverse her decision. As dicey as it's become, she *must* know what the girl is up to. What they're both up to, going their separate ways to visit long-estranged family. Jacinta can picture Logan sitting across from his father at Oakview, saying, *Dad, I had to see you. One last time. I'm taking a one-way trip. I'm headed to D.C. with a gun.*

It's the only reason Jacinta can think of—paying their final respects, perhaps, before undertaking a suicide mission. If only Langley had a heads-up before Logan barrelled to Connecticut, they could have bugged Roy's room with ease. Then Jacinta would actually know, instead of harbouring unconfirmed suspicions.

I do not fear Logan Booth.

Sounds less convincing each time she thinks it.

The huge north door of the Yellow Oval Room whispers open. She pivots, cheeks reddening, ready to lambast whichever poor staff member decided to barge in unannounced.

Four darkly-dressed men slip into the room, three of them carrying heavy briefcases. Her stomach tightens as she recognises the only man with his hands free.

The spook pulls to a halt inside the space, stares at Beau, and says, 'Mr. Murphy, if you'd give us a moment.'

Beau's calm recedes—a rare occurrence—and he says, 'Now's not a great time for whatever this—'

'Go,' Jacinta demands. 'Now.'

She isn't looking at her husband. She can't take her eyes off the four-man procession. She senses Beau bristle, but he knows his place. He nods—either to her or the spook, she can't make out in her periphery—and shuffles quietly off through the west exit. The door clicks closed behind him.

'How bad?' Jacinta says.

The spook flashes the hint of a smile. 'Quite.'

She glances at the briefcases his cadre wield. 'You're here for a definitive plan of action?'

'No one's leaving this room until we form one,' he says. 'I've had about enough of instructions you concoct on the spot. You're the one who ordered this little surveillance job into existence, so you're going to tell us exactly how you want to play it now that it's gone to shit. Or we'll take it into our own hands, no matter how personally invested you are in this mess, and the people you want harmlessly followed might just wind up in the ground. Because right now, *ma'am*'—the title drips with sarcasm—'that solution's mighty tempting.'

'Then sit,' she says, gesturing to the upholstered sofas in the centre of the room, 'and tell me exactly what happened.'

They do.

The spook must have already brainstormed what would make Jacinta most uncomfortable, because he recites the list of injuries with painstaking detail, each word a punch in the quiet room.

'. . . both the ulna and the radius are shattered, split clean in two by a single blow . . .'

'. . . his nasal bones are destroyed, much of the septum cartilage torn to pieces . . .'

' . . . there's a torn latissimus dorsi muscle, too, halfway down his back. It's like he was hit by a car—'

'But he wasn't,' she interrupts.

'Mr. Booth dropped an Oscar-worthy performance, acting like he found the girl dead, and our sentry was convinced enough to race upstairs to check. Fucking moron. Señor Booth then beat him senseless, stripped him of his firearm and his phone, and sent him on his way.'

Out the tall windows behind her, night lies cold and black over Washington. 'And I'm only finding out now because . . .?'

'We only learned what happened'—the spook checks his watch—'forty-eight minutes ago.'

'You said this went down this afternoon.'

'It did.' A weak grimace, like, *Shit happens.* 'Our man stuck his head in the sand a while, licked his wounds. He was considering whether to come back into the fold or high-tail it for Mexico. We scooped him up before he could decide either way. I don't blame him for considering the latter. For such a straightforward assignment, it's a rather spectacular fuck-up. He feared how we might react when he told us what happened.'

'Should he have?'

'Of course.' You'd have to take creative liberty to describe the spook's dull sneer as a smile. 'I already said he acted moronically. We have little patience for morons.'

She adjusts her position on the sofa. 'Where is he now?'

The spook just shakes his head. 'That's not your concern.'

His three colleagues sit mute on either side of him like a guard of honour. Obelisks in the gloom.

She closes her eyes and digs a pair of fingers into the lids. 'And what did Logan get out of him?'

'Nothing.'

Hope never feels authentic. She always doubts good fortune. 'Bullshit. Injuries like that? He would've *sung* . . .'

'Those injuries were sustained in the initial exchange. It wasn't torture. Logan charged him from behind, kicked him a couple times. That's all. Our man said he improvised on the fly, insisted he wouldn't talk no matter how badly he was beaten or maimed, then gave an ultimatum: kill him or let him walk. He was released.' A thoughtful pause, then a shrug. 'Logan was always too soft for the tough choices. The real work.'

'Which is why you kept him in the dark about the real work, as I've learned.' She inhales. Oxygen solidifies her thoughts. 'You're sure your man wasn't covering for himself? Wasn't bluffing?'

'Oh, yes. We made sure.'

Silence.

'So . . .' Her brow furrows. 'We're in the clear?'

No answer.

She looks back up. Flips a switch. 'Tell me now.'

'He has the phone,' the spook says. 'We obviously followed standard procedure, wiped its contents remotely, but . . . I don't even like the idea of him having his hands on an empty shell of a device. I told you last night I'm impressed by his encryption work. You should know I don't distribute compliments lightly. It's frankly incredible we can't eavesdrop on either his calls or Alice Mason's. That kind of technological prowess . . . I may have undersold his skillset yesterday. It sets us Company boys on edge when we can't listen in on—'

'Get to the fucking point.'

The spook blinks. Then he leans forward. 'I don't like that he has the phone. I don't *believe* he can recover any data, but I'm reluctant to stake my career on a belief. I like certainties, and my gut tells me this isn't certain. So I'm telling you it's a problem. Here and now. There's a version of reality where he traces this back to you. I don't know how slim the possibility is, but it's there. My instincts tell me it's there.'

She places her thumbs against the underside of her jaw and folds her fingers in front of her nose, as though in silent prayer.

'How long,' she says, 'until you can be certain the data's taken a one-way trip through a black hole?'

'Langley's best and brightest are on it, but it's a complicated process to establish a specific estimate—'

She snaps a hand up, silencing him. 'Do you think I ended up here by understanding complicated processes?'

He doesn't answer.

'There are three million PhDs in this nation,' she says. 'There's one President. It's not a matter of smarts. Everyone has brains. Few have temperament. What *I* understand is how to make decisions. So I don't need to know the ins and outs. I need to know how long.'

He swallows. 'Forty-eight hours, give or take.'

She digests it. 'So he needs to be distracted a couple of days.'

'We send any more men his way, he'll end up putting two and two together. He's not stupid. Unless you're thinking we just take him out . . .' He leaves the suggestion hanging there.

But what if you take your shot and miss? she thinks. *I've been told he was your best, and he's only a year out of the game. So you'd be sending runners-up after the gold medallist, and if they come back in body bags, who's next?*

She knows the answer.

Me.

All at once, she knows how to play it. She snaps her fingers. 'That woman.'

'What?'

'Logan's final assignment. Before the Company cut him loose. It was Colombia, right?' She acts like she's fishing, as though she doesn't know every detail. 'He was about to turn forty, you knew his expiration date was near, and then he showed his first flash of disobedience. He stayed in Bogotá after his operation was complete, didn't he? For a woman? Ignored his handler for a fortnight, got all lovey-dovey? The flame of passion, yada yada. Which then gave you the excuse to relinquish him of his duties. Correct?'

'That's right,' the spook says, a touch cautiously. He can't fathom how she remembers so much from a quick briefing four months prior, but he seems to sense what she really wants: a name. 'Camilla Peña.'

'You're still keeping an eye on her?'

He shrugs. 'Standard M.O. We see her acting out, breaking routine . . . well, we don't like civilians knowing things they shouldn't. And if we don't like what we're seeing, it's easy to shut her up. Colombia isn't exactly renowned for pacifism. You can always make it look like . . . something else.'

'I don't want her dead,' she says, too forcefully, betraying her fear. 'I don't want either of them dead. I just want Logan distracted. Plenty of ways to do that.' She mulls for a beat. 'Camilla's still in Bogotá?'

'She is.'

'You have assets there?'

'We have assets everywhere.'

'Assets who could organise a kidnapping?' she asks. 'A false alarm?'

His eyes light up as he understands what she's getting at. 'Of course.'

'Okay.' She sits forward. 'Here's exactly what we're going to do.'

10

Alice stirs.

She's in the guest bedroom, which is unfurnished save for a thin mattress atop a bed frame. Even still, the vaulted space could rest within the pages of a real estate magazine.

Sitting up against the headboard, she watches the overcast sky through floor-to-ceiling windows. Dull light plays across concrete flooring, dances over unadorned walls. The lack of vibrancy lends the room an underwater quality, as though the loft rests below the throbbing surface of the river it overlooks, but the atmosphere works. Appreciating the careful angles, she gets her first true sense of what is meant by 'less is more'.

By superficial metrics, the condo is a rundown shithole, but that's why Logan was able to snatch it up for maybe a million less than what it should have been priced at.

Looking around now, a lump forms in her throat as she realises why he leapt at this opportunity: he glimpsed the beauty beneath the squalor. He saw this place not for what it was, but what it could be.

Four months ago, that's how they saved each another. They showed each other what they couldn't see themselves.

She leans over the edge of the bed and paws at the concrete floor for her phone. Firing the lock screen to life with the tap of a finger, she reads 14:17 and thinks, *Shit.* Granted, she didn't get to sleep until nearly 5 a.m.—that's how long it took the final remnants of the stress chemicals to leech from her system—but being under the covers with the clock reading past twelve reminds her of her addict lifestyle, so she levers herself out of bed and pads downstairs.

On the staircase, she takes stock of herself. No intrusive thoughts, only a dash of lingering anxiety. She's still half-asleep, and perhaps things will worsen as she crawls from the fog of deep slumber, but for now, what happened yesterday feels remarkably . . . fine.

She'll never see her mother again, but so what? She tried her best and got concussed for her troubles. The memory will only guilt her if she somehow convinces herself she deserved the slap, but she knows who she is, and she won't waste another moment of her life dwelling. The nature of their final interaction is Carolyn's burden to bear, not hers.

And a man tried to kidnap her. Okay. It didn't work. She was sharp and fast enough to get away, and now she and Logan are back in Manhattan unharmed. She could curse the world, but instead she thinks about errors she can rectify. When this has settled down, she figures she'll join a boxing gym, maybe even learn to shoot. She wants to be capable.

Most importantly, she knows she can be.

Logan perches on a stool at the kitchen island, watching the Hudson. The thin smartphone he took off her would-be abductor rests in front of him on the marble slab. She gets the sense he's deliberately averting his eyes. The phone screen rests face-up, dead black.

She crosses the space barefoot and pulls out the stool adjacent to his. Where he would have lowered himself down, she must clamber up. But he's bent like a hook, bearing the weight of some invisible dread, so when she mounts the stool and sits straight-backed, their faces are level.

'What are you doing?' she asks him.

He keeps his gaze fixed ahead. 'I gave myself twenty-four hours. To think it over. Before going back to what I used to be.'

She stares at the device. 'You think you have to get back to that place?' She hesitates. When he doesn't answer, she asks, 'There's no other choice?'

'Not that I can see. This phone will lead places. I don't know if I want to retread that path.'

She drags a finger down one of her own cheeks, the skin supple, soft. She recalls how easily people break. 'You really believe that?'

'No. Absolutely not.'

She doesn't respond.

'If this is the remnants of Datvyan's operation,' he says, 'it'll be war. I'm not sure I'm ready for that again. It, uh . . . it takes a piece of you. You saw . . .'

He makes a vague gesture that she knows is referring to the way he dismantled Datvyan's hitmen, marking the first time she saw someone forcibly take a life. How one man's eyes bulged as Logan choked him to death in a Brownsville stairwell, how the other lay there unseeing, his skull caved in.

She recalls the way Logan hurled himself into the fray yesterday without any forethought. That essential instinct to break whatever lies before him, no matter the personal cost. She considers how quickly that came to him, an uncivilised essence most spend their whole lives trying to avoid.

She says, 'You're always ready for war.'

His grunt neither confirms nor denies. 'Just . . . anyone but the Armenians. They're stubborn.'

'It's already been twenty-four hours. Since you got to Central.'

'I know.' He glances her way. 'What's a few more?'

She smiles.

He nods at the view. 'First impressions?'

'I love it.' She sweeps her gaze over the loft: hard lines, refined shadow. An efficiency so brutal as to be beautiful. Alluring imperfection. 'It's you.'

'Not yet it's not. Just you wait.' He looks over his shoulder at the tatami mats propped against one wall of the living room. 'I'll be that weird guy you know from Tribeca, cosplaying as a samurai.'

She curls her fingers around the sleeve of her oversized shirt, rests her chin on her knuckles. Smiles again. 'I mean, if anyone can pull it off . . .'

He smirks. She always admired the confidence of those who believe deeply in certain principles and can still find room to make fun of their own earnestness. It takes self-assurance to resist justifying your worldview to others. Logan's reinforced by his own vision. She's trending in that direction herself, and she gives silent thanks.

Not everyone can catch themselves drifting. Not everyone can correct course.

They go back and forth a little while, regular life talk, deliberately ignoring the elephant in the room. Around 3 p.m. she considers suggesting he bite the bullet and try to crack the device, but as conversation peters out he extracts his own phone and starts tapping away at various applications: a few government websites providing updates in his areas of concern, along with digital news outlets. She gets the sense he has a long-entrenched habit of closely following the state of the world.

The relics of a past life.

He's scrolling through a news feed specialising in foreign conflicts when he reaches a video thumbnail of a dark-haired Hispanic woman. He freezes with a spasm, like someone hit him with a hundred volts.

Alice couldn't ignore the reaction if she tried. 'What?'

His thumb lingers on the screen as he reads a fuzzy headline again and again. She can only make out two words: GUERRILLA VIOLENCE.

His voice comes in a mutter: 'Oh, fuck me.'

'What?' she says, louder. 'Someone you know?'

Her gaze lingers on the woman in the thumbnail. Maybe mid-thirties, with a mane of black hair flowing like silk, framing a sharp face: full lips, high cheekbones, hazel skin. Deep bags of fatigue rest under her eyes. The woman bites her lip hard as she faces someone off-camera. Her eyes are wet. She's deeply distressed.

Logan says nothing, just stares. Alice is reluctant, but she has to ask. 'She . . . she was, what? Taken hostage? Killed?'

His expression is thunderous, uncompromising. 'I need to go to Colombia.'

'You need to . . .?' The words sink in. 'No, Logan, not now . . .'

He shakes his head, rising off the stool. 'You hole up here'—he stabs a finger at the entranceway—'and you shoot anyone who comes through that door who isn't me. You'll be okay. You'll have to be.'

She doesn't respond. She knows his mind's made up.

His hand droops and the phone screen drifts toward her.

The woman's pixellated face hangs there: flustered, scared.

'Before I met you,' he says, 'she was the only real thing I ever came across.' He swallows. Raw emotion. His voice shakes.

'Maybe you'll hate me for this. It just doesn't matter. I have to go. I don't have a choice.'

All quiet.

'I'm going,' he says again. 'It's done.'

PART II

TRUTH

If you wish to see the truth, then hold no opinions for, or against, anything. To set up what you like against what you dislike is the disease of the mind.

Hsin Hsin Ming

11

Arriving at JFK Airport feels like an uneasy reunion with a vague acquaintance.

In his old line of work, Logan barrelled from one assignment to the next, often hitting thirty, forty countries a year, but he hasn't left the homeland since they relinquished him of his duties. This bustling terminal is unfamiliar, too—he rarely flew commercial.

His globetrotting as a triggerman was facilitated by executive jets, usually Gulfstreams. He knew the planes were off-the-books, owned by private companies within shell corporations. He believed the anonymous vigilante outfit he worked for wielded possession of a vast front organisation which, thanks to world-class talents in both forgery and bribery, they could use to shepherd their assassins between countries undetected. If he ever took off his rose-tinted glasses, he might have spotted obvious similarities between the jets which whisked him all over the world and the fleet of rendition aircraft the CIA use to transport prisoners extralegally between black sites. Having researched the shadowy history of his country in college, Logan knew of the rendition flights long before he ever learned he was a Company man, so why did he never put two and two together? Why didn't he ask himself how many vast and invisible networks of private jets can possibly operate in America at once?

Because the answer is, and always has been, one.

He'll never be able to forgive himself for what he overlooked, but he tries not to dwell on those ten years. He's repented enough.

Turns out he doesn't mind the superficial downgrade. He tugs a ball cap low over his face and boards a United flight to El Dorado Airport in Bogotá, which he booked the moment he finished reading the article hours prior. He carries a rucksack only, no suitcase. No matter which way this goes, he doesn't envision an extended stay.

With a screen in front of him and little to do but mindlessly consume, he opts instead to close his eyes and sink a little lower in the economy seat. He yanks the cap all the way down now, darkening the space beyond his closed lids and proceeds to do nothing at all. It's technically meditation, but he's never seen it that way—not once in his life has he intended to meditate. He doesn't consider this spiritual. He just knows patience is a virtue, and practising deliberate boredom is a way to cultivate self-restraint. It was Blaise Pascal who said all of humanity's problems stem from man's inability to sit quietly in a room alone.

Six hours goes by like nothing.

He refrains from pondering what awaits and only opens his eyes when wheels shudder on tarmac beneath him. The old Hispanic woman beside him jolts as he straightens up. She may have suspected he was dead, sitting motionless for so long. He flashes her a smile and she turns away, shaking her head.

Once the seatbelt light vanishes, he only needs to pull his rucksack down from overhead, disembark, and beeline for customs: no loitering at the baggage carousel. With no time difference between New York and Bogotá, he's facing a customs officer before the clock strikes midnight. The guy seems stuck in quicksand as he stares vacantly at Logan's passport, but there's nothing that reads, *I used to be a contract killer*, so he stamps a sixty-day visa within its pages and waves the big American through with a grunt.

The air is thin. Logan's heart rate inches upward, adjusting to eight thousand feet above sea level. He works his phone as he heads past customs, using the free Wi-Fi to purchase an eSIM card for cell service out in Bogotá. He has perfect reception with a Colombian provider by the time he reaches the first taxi office. A sign above the booth reads IMPERIAL S.A.S.

He pulls up in front of a weary-looking man in a crumpled shirt and says, 'Patio Bonito.'

The guy waves a hand. 'You do not want to go Patio Bonito. You look like you have . . .' He rubs thumb and forefinger together. 'Stay somewhere other.'

Logan pulls out a thick wad of Colombian pesos he exchanged at JFK. 'Patio Bonito.'

The guy stares at the hundred-thousand peso notes and shrugs. 'Patio Bonito. Sure.'

He requests a sum which locals would consider egregious. With no motivation to haggle, Logan hands the money over. The man organises for a driver and five minutes later Logan's dumping his rucksack across the rear seats of a spotless white sedan.

They peel away from the airport and he gazes out at low ochre buildings that look to be squatting under a dead sky. Loud graffiti simmers in the dark. Twisted wire fences, empty lots choked with dust. They pass the Hilton Garden Inn, its red floret logo looming over the avenue as if marking a border between two worlds. When they take a right onto Avenida Boyacá, the gentrification begins to recede. His awareness heightens as streetlights grow farther apart.

He knows it's twenty minutes from the airport to Patio Bonito because he took the journey in reverse a year and a half ago, taxiing from her small abode to make his flight back home, leaving only shattered hopes behind. Sure enough, as soon as an internal timer goes off in his head, the driver veers into the maze of narrow lanes that encompass her neighbourhood. The dust is thicker here, coating narrow streets, clinging to eroding brick, dusting brightly painted doors. The occasional streetlight sputters, but entire swathes of the maze are pitch black. The odd silhouette staggers through the gloom.

Logan says, 'Here,' the moment he recognises a particular intersection. The driver cranes his neck as he looks back, wearing a worried expression, like, *You sure?*

Logan nods.

The vehicle never reaches a complete stop. The driver eases to the sidewalk and slows beside a gutter painted green, red, and white. When Logan levers out with the rucksack in one hand, the taxi races off, abandoning its passenger the moment it's considered acceptable to do so.

Night encroaches until his eyes are wide like saucers. He tries to discern the outline of buildings, and, failing, fires his phone's flashlight to life. Ahead, a lanky shape scurries down an alley. A few streets over, an animal moans. He isn't overly concerned. He knows the difference between real threats and those whose circumstances make them appear threatening. Most people are just trying to get by.

He slings the rucksack over one shoulder, using his phone beam as a searchlight as he takes a series of turns he will always remember. He has no confirmation she still lives here, but it's a place to start. Before he flew out, he tried the number she gave him all that time ago, but it was out of service.

He reaches a certain door painted pale blue—a door seared in his brain—and knocks before he can consider exactly what he's doing. A few beats of silence, then quiet commotion on the other side of the wood. Furious whispering in Spanish, and the peephole goes dark. Someone's looking out at him. He doubts they can make out much.

More muttering, something that sounds like an order, then the door inches open and she slips out onto the dusty sidewalk right in front of him, easing the door shut behind her. Inside, someone pads softly away.

Holding his phone light low sheathes them both in ethereal light. She's exactly how he remembers: five-eight or so, a mane of hair like shining silk, bright eyes that probe unashamedly. She trains her gaze on him, the gaze that occasionally infiltrates his dreams, and mutters, 'Let's go somewhere else,' in heavily accented English.

He looks past her, at the sealed door. 'Sorry. Did I wake your mom?'

She answers by shooing him off the mark. Not a chance she knew he was coming, but still her touch harbours a certain mischief as she brushes her fingers down his shoulder, guiding him west. Only one place she could be taking him; they met not far from here, in a dive bar drenched in neon. He obliges her request and sets off down the dusty lane.

He's only just plunged into the stretch of deep shadow before the next intersection when hands snatch him from behind.

12

When Logan spins, it's without aggression. He recognises the touch.

Camilla adjusts her grip in the darkness, grabs the front pockets of his flannel and pulls him in. Her full lips probe for his. She's up on her tiptoes as he takes her by the shoulders and breathes, 'Wait.'

Primal urges beg him to cave, but he didn't survive a career for the ages just to drop his guard in a dark alley. There's a time and a place, but humans are animals of desire, and despite all the supposed self-control, he lets out a low groan.

'Look at you,' she whispers. '*So* well behaved.'

'You think?' He runs his fingers through her hair as he pans the shadows. 'You know, I expected a different kind of greeting.'

'I'm sure you did.' Her warm breath in his ear. 'I should have slapped you. You left me. But here you are. Back.' She's quiet for a beat. 'You're back.'

'Your English . . .'

He senses her smile. 'I've been working hard at it. How is your Spanish?'

'About the same as it was.'

'So, shit.'

'*Sí.*' He pauses. 'You were expecting more?'

She drags her fingertips down his sleeve. 'Maybe.'

'That right there was my whole vocabulary.'

She laughs, and he takes her by the hand and leads her to the watering hole where they first stumbled into each other's lives. Maybe she's more shaken by what happened this morning than she's letting on, but for now it's them and the night and the bodily sensations he resigned himself to never feeling again. He relishes this warm appreciation for something he never thought he would reclaim.

He'd worried that if he found her safe she would still lash out at him, scream at him, order him back to the airport before he could crush her hopes again. Even if walking beside her in the dark is all he's going to get, that's already enough.

The dive bar's open. Of course it is. It's the type of place that never closes. Men sit out front, perched at rickety folding tables under a rusted awning. The elders play dominoes and the younger guys pound Colombia's national drink, aguardiente: 'firewater'. In their mean and defeated postures, you can tell the men understand this will constitute the rest of their lives. Pairs of haunted eyes snap to Logan and Camilla as they emerge from the night into the halo of syrupy green. Neon pulsates above the entrance.

Seeing a tourist in these parts, at this hour—especially with a local woman—the patrons look ready to throw hands, their stares cold enough to send even the most confident newcomers scurrying for the hills. Logan understands it's nothing to do with him. He's their excuse to inject a little excitement into the collective stupor of their existence. A brawl would be inconvenient, though, and small humiliations compound, so he has no choice but to return their gazes with an even icier look.

No one was expecting such fierce resistance. The thin night air constricts. Logan doesn't blink until every single one of them looks away. It takes a full fifteen seconds, which feels an eternity. Camilla doesn't budge, just stands beside him, one hand on her hip. Only when the last of the observers drops their gaze do they head inside.

The interior is long, narrow, with slick tiled floors and subdued cumbia beats thudding from gaudy speakers, the bass cranked up, the treble lowered. A thin and wizened man behind the bar is happy to serve them. His language is money, so he pays no mind to the rarity of a foreigner's presence. Logan wonders when a tourist last wandered in here in the middle of the night.

It might have been him, sixteen months ago.

Camilla orders two shots of aguardiente. As the anise stench floats off the Antioqueno, she meets Logan's eyes. He shakes his head.

Given the depth of the bond they formed over the course of that fortnight, they spoke relatively little. Their connection was based on perception more than anything else and she's still able to read him now.

Realising he's not a drinker anymore, Camilla shrugs and hands the bartender a crumpled note before picking up both shots. 'I need them. Been a bad day.'

There are only four people inside the bar, so they're cloaked in privacy as they select a vinyl booth up the back. He slides in first, facing the entrance, and she follows. She sits close to him and downs one of the shots with a grimace.

'What happened this morning?' he asks her.

She shrugs, swallows the second shot. 'I was taken.' When he doesn't respond, she says, 'But you know that already. Because you are here.'

'I saw the article.'

'Oh. Yes.' Her face scrunches. 'That reporter was there. This timing was . . . unfortunate.' She elbows him gently in the ribs, using the gesture to scoot closer to him, deeper in the booth. '"Unfortunate." How's *my* vocabulary?'

Her composure allows him room for a smile. 'You're fluent now.'

When they first met, he had to employ total focus to decipher her Spanglish. The improvement is remarkable. If he ever devoted himself to learning a second language, it would take him years to make the leaps she has in sixteen months. He was never the suave, multilingual super-spy, hoodwinking his way through an eclectic mix of cultures. He was the berserker. The human freight train.

He served his purpose, perhaps better than anyone, but he was always aware of his own limitations. He never felt he deserved women like Camilla: razor-sharp, fearless. He was always his own worst enemy.

'The article,' he says. 'Was it true?'

She nods.

'So it *was* ELN?' he asks. 'That wasn't a cover-up?'

She folds her arms across her chest, sinks lower down the vinyl. The denim of her jacket snags on the upholstery. She nods again. 'They said they were ELN, yes.'

Which is the National Liberation Army, one of the major armed rebel groups in Colombia, responsible for a decent chunk of the violence that has gripped the country for six decades straight. As with most endless conflicts, there is no objective truth, only claims. The guerrilla groups prop up the rights of the poor, the paramilitary gangs accuse the guerrillas of terrorism, and the government preaches the need for stability. Maybe one side is more right than the other, but everyone's wrong when they each massacre hordes of innocents in droves.

Much of the article was familiar to Logan; he already knows the statistics. Almost half a million Colombians have been killed in sixty years of fighting, with millions more displaced. Maybe the rebel groups were originally formed with altruistic intentions, but most of the devastation wreaked upon rural Colombia nowadays concerns control of critical drug trafficking routes. You can no longer tell the difference between a freedom fighter and a cartel kingpin, a government official and a power-hungry psychopath. Cruelty on all sides has obfuscated the idea of good and evil. It's a brutal mess, top to bottom. Everyone's fighting everyone for reasons they insist are benevolent. Meanwhile, ordinary citizens suffer horrifically.

Which is pretty much all of human history.

Part of the reason Logan became a hitman in the first place is because he understood there would always be a need for extralegal enforcers, one way or the other. As long as he can remember, he's rebuked impractical idealism. Of course he fights for what's right, but in equal measure he deals with reality, not what he hopes reality would be.

'What, they snatched you?' he says. 'Off the street?'

She nods, makes to explain. But the words snag in her throat, and she holds up a finger—*one moment*—and hustles to the bar for another round. She returns with two more shots of aguardiente, slams them both down for liquid courage, and slides back in beside him.

When she settles, she's composed. Her eyes are hard.

'I was on my way to work,' she says. 'They grab me, throw me into a van. Tie me, gag me. I'm with maybe six others. Not easy to see. I think most of them were women. Everyone's sweating. I think someone . . . what's the word? Urine on themselves, you know.' She shrugs, like, *These things happen*. 'They take us to some factory on the edge of the city, bring us into this big empty space. I'm thinking maybe they hang us up, start cutting us. I don't know. I can't stop crying.' She stares forward, emotionless, as though recalling a dream. 'We are there for maybe ten minutes? Surrounded by these men with guns. Then they all start shouting, there's some big confusion, and one of them is swearing and comes toward me with a knife and cuts the'—she snaps her fingers, searching for the word—'bindings. Sets us all free. He points outside and tells us to go and they all start yelling at each other again. We go, but we can't really believe it. This doesn't happen. We've all heard the stories.'

She swallows.

'Then there is this small news crew at the end of the street—unfortunate, like I say. Just two men, and they keep the camera hidden until they've followed me for a while, until they know they will not be spotted talking to me. They ask me some questions about what happened, about guerrillas, things like that. I am in a . . . daze? Yes, a daze. So I just answer their questions, I don't even really see there's a camera, and then I go home. And life goes on. I'm scared, but I can't just stop. I go to work. In the afternoon I see this story and read that it was ELN who took me, that they made a . . . misidentity? Whatever the word. Anyway, they get the wrong people and they release them and their top commander tells the media it was a big mistake. The reporters write things about the rural violence coming to Bogotá, how this is very bad, but, like, what changes? Tomorrow I go to work again . . .'

He watches her. 'And nothing since? No one following you?'

She shakes her head. She seems fixated on him, captivated by his presence. She's waiting for him to reach the obvious conclusion.

'So that's it?' he says. 'It was really just a mix-up?'

Her fingers dance across the back of his hand. 'This is frustrating, I know. You come to help, but there is nothing for you to do. But you, what? See my face in the news, get on a plane? Why? This looks like you care about me, Logan, but . . .' *History says otherwise.*

'I had the time. I'm retired now.' He's downplaying and he knows it.

'Retired?' Full eyebrows rise. 'So young . . .'

'I took risks. They paid me well for it.'

'These . . . shadow people?'

She knows what he is. He told her, right here, the night they met. Laid himself bare, expecting disdain. He said he was a killer, and instead of running for the hills, she asked him why. He explained, and once he was finished laying out the complexities of his worldview, she told him she understood his function. Her life had not been a sheltered one. They stumbled back to her place after the next drink, each nursing their respective demons.

She knows everything besides who his employers really were, but he didn't deliberately withhold that information—he hadn't known either.

'Those shadow people,' he says, 'expected everything I had to give. That's why I had to leave you.'

She reaches up and grips his coarse cheek, turns his face toward her. 'You did not have to leave.'

'Huh?'

'You chose to.'

'Yes,' he admits. 'That's right. Back then, my work was the most important thing in my life.'

'Not anymore?'

'Like I said, I'm retired.'

She hesitates. 'By choice?'

'No. But now . . .' He cocks his head. 'Now I'm glad it happened.'

She places a palm on the table. 'This was your choice. To come back here.'

'Yes. It was.'

'You didn't have to.'

'No.'

She smiles. 'Then I'm glad it happened, too.'

This time, when she pulls him in, he doesn't resist. Her lips meet his ravenously, like she needs to consume him, and the booths are dark enough for discretion. Her palms search beneath the flannel.

He kisses back. Slow at first, re-familiarising himself with her taste, then faster as his blood warms. She exhales softly into his mouth as her touch drifts upward, nails dancing on the skin behind his ear. She must sense his desire, and it seems to buoy her.

His pulse thudding in his ears, he parts from her, but only to murmur, 'Back to yours?'

The four shots cloud her gaze. Alcohol and passion combine to lend a certain conviction.

'No,' she says firmly. 'We can't do that. My boyfriend is there.'

At first, he says nothing.

She senses the shift in the air. Reflexively, she leans closer. 'I want *you*, Logan.'

He doesn't shrink away. He wears no expression. She can't handle the ambiguity, and her face hardens a touch.

'How could I have told you back there?' she says. 'There was no time.'

He doesn't respond.

'You hate me?' she asks.

'No, Camilla. I don't hate you.' He's still ascertaining what he feels.

But there's a space between them now, an invisible wall, and she scoffs. Four shots of aguardiente in quick succession would have *his* head swimming, and he's almost double her bodyweight. He wonders if they should be having this conversation here, now. Probably wise to clear their heads, compose their thoughts . . . But the train's in motion.

'What,' she says suddenly, 'you expected me to just wait for you? To sit around and cry and hope you come back?'

'That's the last thing I ever would have wanted.'

'Okay, so, what? What is the problem? You should have stayed and you didn't. But you are here now. You are back. I'm not in danger. There is no army of rebels you need to rescue me from. Maybe you wanted it to be this way, so you could kill some people—I don't know—but most things are not so . . . dramatic.' She cups her palms. 'You are here, Logan. That's all I care about. You think I could see this coming?' She shakes her head. 'I will work out what to do about Rubén.'

The primal part of Logan's brain whispers all the things his ego craves. *She wants you, not some schmuck. Go on. Claim your prize.* There's only one problem: he dispensed with his ego four months back. His desires fall on deaf ears.

He can see clearly, and he asks himself when he's ever benefitted from following his baser instincts. In this moment, she's the most beautiful woman he's ever seen, and of course she still possesses the acerbic wit and keen intelligence that drew him to her in the first place, but maybe, just maybe, this was never what he thought it was . . .

'That's who you were whispering to,' he says. 'Just before. Behind the door. Your boyfriend. Not your mom.'

She doesn't blink. 'Mamá died last year. Not long after you left. Heart attack.'

He pauses. 'I'm sorry.'

'Okay.' She stares, unflinching. 'Who cares who was behind the door? Did I send him out to deal with you? No. I looked and saw it was you and it took me one second to know what I want. So I tell him it's a client from work who can't find their hotel and I tell him I'll go deal with it and . . .'

And you try to kiss me, he thinks. *Not twenty feet from your doorstep.*

'Is he good to you?' he asks.

She blinks. 'You mean, does he hurt me?' A wry smile. 'Why? So you can kill him? Like you would have killed everyone in ELN? The whole army, right? If I was in trouble, that's what you would have done? Fight a few thousand of them?'

'I don't know what I would have done.'

'So you would risk your life if I was in danger? But when I'm right here, and I want you . . .'

'Is Rubén good to you?' he asks again.

'Yes,' she says. 'We have our issues, but yes. He is good to me.'

'How long have you been together?'

'I met him the month after you left.'

'More than a year, then?'

'Yes.'

'You love him?'

'I—' A furrow along the ridge of her brow. 'I thought I did. Then I saw you. And . . . I guess I realised what is right.'

He folds his hands on the tabletop, one over the other. No chance this goes smoothly. 'Right is ending things with the person you love before throwing yourself on someone else, Camilla.'

The air goes still.

'What?' Her lips draw tight as a pulse of surprise ebbs through her. 'This is . . . wait . . . this is a lecture? From *you*?' Deathly silence. 'Are you fucking serious?'

'I think—'

'You can't imagine me with another man? You are insecure? That's what this is?'

He sees exactly what this is, what it was: a pipe dream.

He got to know a sliver of Camilla Peña in a breathless two-week romance, then projected what he wanted her to be onto the fuzzy outline he left with. The grass is always greener, and he envisioned a promised land in Bogotá so he could stay sane as the rest of his life fell apart around him. But what did they ever really know about each other besides the places to touch and draw shudders of pleasure? He thought this was special, but it's now clear how easily lust can be mistaken for love. There must be more to the boyfriend situation—Logan doubts this was malicious—but it's brutally obvious he and Camilla aren't aligned. And he's had enough aimless one-night stands for a lifetime.

'Who *are* you?' she says quietly. 'You show back up just to . . . punish me?'

'No. No, I don't ever want to hurt you. I just . . .'

'You just what?'

Don't lie. Don't take the easy road. Be honest.

'I don't want this anymore, Camilla.'

She looks shellshocked. '*Anymore?* So you did until . . .?'

'Just then.'

Silence.

'I'm glad you're safe,' he mutters. 'I'm sorry I intruded on your—'

'Fuck you.'

She grabs her purse and rears up out of the booth.

He stares down the barrel of the bar, through the entranceway, to the dusty night beyond.

'Let me walk you home,' he says.

'Fuck you.' She looms over him. 'Stay right there. Don't come near me again. I don't need your *help*. Your *protection*.'

He can hardly process the sight of her sweeping away, and then . . .

Well, she's gone, isn't she?

He cuts a solitary figure in the booth, anonymised by the lowlight. He lets his head droop and his eyes drift closed. No one ever told him doing the right thing was easy, but turmoil churns so intensely within him that he questions whether it's even worth aiming for virtue. If this is the reward . . .

He doesn't know how long he sits there, paralysed by dejection. A long time to be staring glassily at the slick tabletop. But at some point, when the cloud of his personal woes finally recedes a moment, he finds himself fixating on something she said.

There is this small news crew at the end of the street.

So the reporters were, what, following an armed rebel group around Bogotá? Unlikely. Their heads would be on sticks already. Better chance they were tipped off in advance. But by who?

He finally allows a touch of paranoia.

Someone who wanted me here? he thinks. *Someone with intimate knowledge of where I look for my news?*

He lurches to his feet.

'Shit.'

It could have been different.

Camilla considers just picking a direction and walking, letting the night absorb her. She needs open space, fresh air.

There's a dull burn in her oesophagus, and a pounding in her head. The aguardiente sloshes against her stomach walls.

As she stands outside the bar, processing the whirlwind, a small voice asks, *What were you thinking, handling it like that?* Her relationship with Rubén is strained, and she always knew he wasn't the one, but to give Logan that kind of impression right off the bat? Short-sighted, to say the least.

Shows where operating on impulse gets you.

She wants to stride into the darkness and allow herself vital thinking room, but the black void ahead gains an intimidating quality, so she swallows hard and beelines for home.

She's still flustered when she unlocks her front door and slips inside.

She hoped Rubén would be asleep, but he stands at the end of the shadowy hall, hands in pockets. Waiting. He's six-two, thin, pushing forty, but he's got fight in him. He's capable enough.

She feels no fear. He would never lay a hand on a woman. But his voice contains a deep concern when he asks her where she's been.

Her frustrations mix with an overbearing guilt, all compounded by alcohol. In Spanish, she says, 'That wasn't a client from work.'

His eyebrows rise to his fringe of wispy hair. 'No?'

'No, it was this . . . man.' She isn't sure where the words are coming from. 'An American. Someone I used to love.'

She watches his eyes widen in anger.

She knows what'll happen now.

13

The second Logan makes the connection, he pulls out his phone and hauls himself out of the booth.

It's no guarantee, but the mere possibility that he was coaxed here warrants an immediate return home. He's deep in his own head, contemplating how quickly he can get himself on a flight back to New York, so it takes three full paces before he notices the wiry man blocking the exit.

Logan would have dismissed the guy for the knockoff designer clothing if not for the FN Five-seven pistol in his shaking hand. It's a fearsome piece, manufactured in Belgium, but Logan's not surprised. Foreign-made weapons enter South America through several channels, so they're not uncommon in the region.

Four more men mill behind the man with the gun. Logan even recognises two of the gang from the folding tables out front, clearly buddies of the ringleader, yanked from their late-night drinking session to serve as reinforcements. The whole group shifts restlessly from foot to foot. They swell with righteous fury as Logan pulls to a halt.

The man with the gun takes a step forward. Though his fingers tremble, his aim's tight, squared neatly on Logan's chest. Thin hair, dyed jet-black, falls in a strange fringe over one eyebrow. He seems genuinely outraged.

'Drop the phone,' he says, stifling emotion. His accent is thick.

Logan assesses him. Doesn't like what he sees. The guy is a splash more rage away from a trigger pull. Loose cannons can be harder to deal with than trained professionals. Logan empties his tone of all emotion and says, 'I need to leave.'

'Drop it.'

'I need to leave now.'

'*Fucking drop it!*' the guy screams. He shakes the pistol. His finger's in the trigger guard, and Logan isn't ready to die for pride.

He opens his hand, lets the smartphone clatter to the tiles. His only lifeline.

'Now sit back down,' the man hisses.

Logan backtracks and lowers himself slowly into the booth. The gang are practically salivating. One man barks something at the bartender in Spanish, who extricates himself from his duties by slipping out through a door behind the bar. The handful of patrons scatter outside. They know the drill.

The gang stride for Logan, simmering. One man grins wildly. Another claps his buddy on the shoulder and whoops. A third stomps on Logan's phone as he passes, cracking the screen, crushing the internal circuitry.

Neon soaks twitching limbs, lending them a resemblance to dancing skeletons.

They're hard guys—they'd probably give your everyday Bronx gangster a run for their money—but none of them are in the profession of violence. These men clearly have regular jobs and just live in a tougher society. With their law enforcement usually preoccupied by graver matters, they need to be capable of something like this when push comes to shove.

The man with the gun pulls up directly beside Logan and aims the barrel at the flesh above his ear. Two feet away—mediocre spatial awareness. Understandable: he's furious.

His posse surround the gunman in a shallow semicircle, a wall of flesh barring their target from leaving the booth. Five might be an issue in the confines of an urban environment, based sheerly on bodyweight.

Logan faces forward. 'I need to leave.'

The armed man says, 'You know Camilla?'

Logan turns slowly to face him. 'Are you Rubén?'

One eyelid twitches.

'Is this the part where you do the long speech about how important you are? About how badly I've fucked up?'

Eye contact heightens Rubén's rage, and he leans down. The barrel drifts an inch. 'You should not have—'

Logan aims for a point in space several feet behind the man and, from a seated position, pivots into the hardest left hook he's thrown in months, just as Rubén's revving up for the big spiel.

No choice but to give it his all. The punch must be a whip to land before Rubén adjusts his aim. Logan's knuckles crunch into Rubén's stomach with a *thud* that resonates through the bar, and the man snaps forward like a hinge as breath explodes from his lips. The pistol goes flying into the recesses of the booth. Rubén's bent at a right angle as Logan clamps a palm down on the back of his neck and wrenches him all the way down, bouncing his unprotected face off the wooden tabletop—which, of course, makes Rubén rear back up, recoiling away from the terrible pain of a shattered nose, but Logan was banking on that, and he bursts up into the free space as Rubén falls back into two of his buddies.

The pair catch Rubén's deadweight and hold him upright, because it's the natural reaction, but Logan's on his feet now and he taps into twenty years of Muay Thai and scythes a body kick into Rubén's compromised midsection. Consistent combat sports training hones limbs into baseball bats of calloused flesh and calcified bone, and Logan's shin cracks like a gunshot as it smashes Rubén's belly. The fringe of hair bounces like cotton candy and Rubén screams a guttural noise and vomits whatever he had for dinner in an ugly geyser.

The two guys who caught him shrink away, horrified, but one of the others rides the wave of adrenaline and lunges, swinging a fist. Close quarters, six bodies in a condensed space: you can't dodge punches. It doesn't work like that. But Logan just leans away and shrugs his giant shoulders like a turtle retreating into a shell—a defensive action in boxing known as the shoulder roll—and the punch hits his deltoid muscle instead of his jaw.

He feels basically nothing as his sinew distributes the force of the impact.

Logan understands the critical importance of setting an example, so he abandons restraint and just rips into the guy who took the swing. He slams a low kick into the side of the man's calf muscle, just below the knee, which deadens the leg and takes the limb out from under him, and when he skids wildly on the slick floor, Logan ducks low and clenches a tight fist and swings a right hook into his rib cage, producing cracking noises. As the guy crumples, debilitated, Logan bursts up and times a final front kick perfectly, catching the man in the jaw with the toe of his boot. The guy hits the floor like a corpse.

Two men out of the equation, and the two who caught Rubén are frozen, paralytic.

One unaccounted for.

Logan pivots hard and finds the last man halfway through the process of snatching up a barstool. The guy's about to heft the whole thing off the ground when he eyes the aftermath of his friends' destruction and hesitates. Instead of attacking him, Logan steps forward, jabs a finger hard in his face and roars, '*Help your friends up and get out!*'

Most warfare is psychological.

As the guy thinks it over, Rubén lets out a dull moan of agony behind them. Nail in the coffin.

The man releases his grip on the stool legs.

Logan steps back to give the group enough space to help the injured parties back to their feet. Rubén's down on all fours, retching, saliva dangling from the corners of his mouth. The pair who first caught him now scoop him up by the underarms, bearing most of his weight. The other guy's semi-conscious, making macabre grunting noises as he resurfaces. The one who was about to arm himself with the barstool is now desperate to leave. He simply throws his incapacitated pal over one shoulder in a fireman's carry and strides for the door. With Rubén supported between them, the other pair follow. Blood drips from Rubén's twisted nostrils as his feet drag, dripping a trail over the tiles.

Then they're gone, as quickly as Camilla vanished.

Logan stands there with his chest heaving, giving them time to scatter before he strides out after them—he has to get to the airport.

Before he can leave, the door behind the bar creaks open and the bartender reappears. The man registers Logan, notes the absence of Rubén and his friends, and says, 'Huh.'

Logan shrugs.

The bartender surveys his establishment, taking stock of the damage. Logan tried to minimise collateral, but bouncing Rubén's face off the booth table ripped a jagged splinter through its surface. He points to the crack in the wood, says, 'I apologise,' and reaches for his roll of pesos.

The bartender waves him off. 'That nothing. You trouble.'

Logan eyes him. 'I didn't mean to—'

'No, no. You trouble now.'

Logan hesitates. 'I'm *in* trouble?'

A vigorous nod. 'Yes. With—' The bartender jerks a thumb at the doorway.

'That's okay. I don't think he's coming back.'

'No. He . . . family.'

Logan grimaces. 'You're related?'

'No. *He* . . . the family.'

The bar's empty, everyone having fled the chaos, so there's no one left to help bridge the language barrier.

'It's fine,' Logan says. 'I'm leaving anyway. Going home.' He mimes a plane lifting off a runway. 'New York.'

The bartender grimaces, pulls out an old, fingerprint-smudged smartphone, and taps away furiously. With his face twisted in concentration, Logan doesn't have it in him to walk out on the guy. In the interim, he fetches the FN Five-seven from the back of the booth, slotting the pistol firmly into his waistband. After another minute or so, the bartender looks up. 'Eight next. To New York.'

'The next flight out? Eight a.m.?'

'*Sí.*'

Logan palms sweat off his brow. Through the entranceway, the night beckons. 'Guess I'll walk awhile.'

The bartender murmurs something, jerks a thumb toward the door he took shelter behind. 'No walk. Danger. Rest here. Here, I live. Morning, I call you taxi.'

Logan could refuse, but he can't see much point. He can't exactly trust the guy, but it's still safer in here than it is out there—until daylight, that is.

Gripped by exhaustion, Logan simply says, 'Thank you,' though he can't shake the sense he's being treated like someone beset with a terminal disease. A strange pity rests behind the bartender's grunting machismo.

When he closes the front door and slams the bolt lock home, Logan watches the man shake his head softly, staring at the metal rod.

Like he knows that won't stop what's coming.

—

Their roles have been reversed.

Now it's Camilla who lurks at the end of the hallway, though she hasn't the strength to stand. She sits cross-legged and stooped, transfixed by the frayed rug underfoot. She questions everything. After Rubén stormed out, the house's silence slowly stole her anger away. She no longer sees red, but she doesn't allow herself to fully contemplate what she's done.

She jerks up when the front door shudders open.

Rubén lurches inside like a zombie. His face resembles a swollen pumpkin; flecks of blood and puke stain the corners of purple lips. Someone makes to follow him inside, but he dismisses them with a growl. He slams the door shut on whoever helped him home and loiters with his palm on the handle, his back to her. She thinks she hears a soft whimper.

'Rubén,' she says, clambering to her feet. He sobs, and she grimaces. 'Oh, Rubén . . .'

But this is what you wanted, she thinks, *isn't it?*

What you knew would happen.

Guilt prevents her from dwelling on such insidious knowledge, and she takes a step toward the front door. Still faced away, he spits a gob of blood on the welcome mat.

She twitches. 'Rubén, come on . . .'

He hacks up more blood and spit, lets the string dribble between his feet. A tooth tumbles out with the strand of fluids.

'Oh, baby,' she mutters. 'Come on, let's clean you up . . .'

Finally he turns around, the movement sudden enough to scare her; she jolts back a half-step in reaction. He leers at her through the mask of injuries. 'I'm calling someone.'

She swallows. 'Who?'

He doesn't answer. Just slides his phone out.

Her heart thuds in her chest. 'Who, baby?'

He grins like a clown from a horror movie. 'None of your concern, my love.'

She can't shake an unsteady feeling. She told Logan she and Rubén have their issues. They mostly concern his reluctance to open up. He's been a closed book since they met. The tales he shared from Cauca in southwestern Colombia, where he spent his childhood and young adult life, she had to pry from him. But he loves her, and he works himself to the bone as a bricklayer—a good, clean job—and for the most part stays out of trouble, which is saying something in Patio Bonito, so she learned to begrudgingly accept his reticence.

Now she sees his eyes and fears she missed something vital.

'No,' she says. 'I need to know.'

In response, he storms into the spare room and slams the door behind him. She hears the lock click. Next thing she knows, she's slamming the side of her fist against the wood, knocking hard.

'Rubén, what are you doing?!' she shouts. 'Tell me what you're doing!'

'I'm handling this!' His roar practically shakes the house, and she rears back, horrified. *'Shut the fuck up, Camilla! Stay out of it!'*

She has a vague notion of continuing to bang on the door, shake the handle, crash her shoulder against the wood, but it's futile. Nothing works.

As she continues shouting pointless things, she goes elsewhere in her mind, harbouring grim visions of what's to come.

Intentions mean nothing, she sees that now.

All that matters are the consequences.

14

Sonia Serrano doesn't mind dripping sweat at two in the morning.

You've got to get the work in whenever you can.

Most pump the brakes when they enter their sixties, but at sixty-five she's fitter than she was at thirty, and not for no reason. She's witnessed the direct correlation between her physical condition and the strength of her mind. All the little details are so much more important than people realise. You live a life of ordinary moments, small fragments added together to form the full package you present to the world. Few realise this. But that's why they're in the dirt, grovelling for attention, like the new recruit downstairs waiting for her to finish her workout.

'Five more,' her trainer demands, and she curls her washboard stomach to squeeze out the final crunches. Six distinct abdominals rest tight against the tanned flesh of her exposed midriff. She grunts with each rep, perspiration pooling on the yoga mat beneath her sacrum, and when her trainer says, 'Time,' she collapses on her back, limbs starfished. Fully exerted, she pants for breath, but he doesn't dare say, 'Good job.' He made that mistake only once, when she first brought him on four years ago, praising her after a gruelling session that left her in a heap. She peeled herself upright and shot him a dark look and said, 'This is nothing. Never compliment me for something so simple.'

Now he knows his place. He clasps his hands behind his back and waits for her to compose herself. Once the lactic acid has settled, she pushes up to her feet. She fetches a towel draped over a bench on her way to the showers and kisses him gently on the lips as she floats past. She showers, yanks her hair back in a tight bun, and slips on a white one-piece bodysuit, skin-tight. The designer leisurewear leaves absolutely nothing to the imagination—she doesn't work on her body to hide herself away.

She heads downstairs, through a building so large she often forgets parts of it exist. Mansion doesn't cut it; palace might suffice. She pads barefoot down the grand staircase and finds the sitting room they use for inductions arranged precisely the way she likes it. Her husband, Gabriel Serrano, reclines on a velvet chaise longue, one leg straightened atop the other. He sips Macallan Exceptional Single Cask from a crystal tumbler balanced on his chest. He stares at the ceiling far overhead, ignoring the younger man in the filthy nylon shirt on his knees in the centre of the room. Plenty of spare seats surround the dirty man, but the Serranos make new hires wait like this, with their eyes downcast. No matter how tough they are out there in the world, the act of submission makes them pliable by the time she comes sweeping in.

Gabriel doesn't bother sitting up as she enters. He takes another sip of ten-thousand-dollar scotch and settles back with his eyes closed, smiling in anticipation.

She pulls up in front of the kneeling recruit. Her Spanish is clipped, authoritative: 'Miguel, isn't it?'

The young man keeps his head down. Curly hair, face tattoos, full lips. Big, strong hands. An attractive man. And she can smell the violence in his bones. He says, '*Sí, señora.*'

'You can look at me.'

He raises his gaze, locks it firmly on her face when he registers what she's wearing. He's terrified of being caught ogling.

'It's okay,' she says. 'You can look.'

He glances down at her cleavage, then back up.

She says, 'Do you like what you see?'

His mouth opens and closes. 'I don't know what answer you're looking for.'

'Do you think life is a competition, Miguel?'

He kneels in silence. Thinks hard. *'Sí, señora.'*

'Many men of your generation pretend it isn't. Because they are scared to compete. They act as if they are above the savagery of it all. They don't participate. Therefore, they never win. Do you know what that makes them?'

He hesitates, then says, 'Losers?'

'Losers. This plague of victimhood is everywhere, Miguel. I'm sure you know plenty of infected. I'm sure you've seen it first-hand. These young men are already dead, you understand. They have let themselves become slaves, and they have died. Do you see how much worse this kind of death is than a real one? I am speaking of a spiritual death. Do you follow?'

He nods. 'Of course, *señora.*'

'Do you notice how undisciplined these men are, Miguel?'

'Yes.'

'Everything they know is wrong. Everything they say is wrong. Everywhere they look is wrong. The way they shake another man's hand is wrong. Do you ever look at these men, Miguel, and want to snap them out of it? Do you ever want to tell them how fucking simple life could be if they would just get things *done*?'

'*Sí.*'

'Have you ever killed men for being adult babies? Ever taken your frustrations out on the morons of the world?'

A glint in his eyes, and he seems to register she may be laying a trap, but determines he should tell the truth. '*Sí*. Many times.'

For the first time, she smiles, and she can tell it hooks him.

From this point forward, he's hers.

'Now,' she says quietly, 'you have come over from FARC, correct?'

'*Sí*.'

They poached Miguel from the Revolutionary Armed Forces of Colombia, much the same as you would in the corporate world. It only ever comes down to a better offer. He was one of the group's most vicious and effective guerrillas, and the loss of his talents will hit the FARC dissidents hard, but she actually prefers when the rebels are angry. They're all red-blooded hotheads, tumbling into the bed of problems they make themselves. Give it another decade and she'll have them all under her heel.

She uses two fingers to stroke Miguel's cheek. 'We are the professionals. Everyone else—FARC, ELN, the whole country, really—are the undisciplined cowards, scared to truly compete. They act with emotion. We act with objectivity. So you will serve us, you will violently and ruthlessly execute our orders, and we will pay you more money than you know what to do with. You will do something with your life, Miguel. You will *win*. And all it's going to take is the simple act of grinding the losers of this world into the dirt when we give the word. Does this make sense to you?'

His eyes are wide. He looks like he's seen God as he says, '*Sí, señora*.'

'Now go,' she says, shooing him off. 'Wait for our call.'

He rises shakily, drunk on her magnetism, and stumbles under the passthrough on legs still refilling with blood. As his palm touches the ornate handle of the huge front door, she calls after him. 'Miguel?'

He looks back.

'If you obey for six months,' she says, 'without refusing an order, without getting squeamish, next time it will be me on my knees for you.'

His lips flap, he throws a confused glance at Gabriel—who's unreadable—then he sweeps out. She knows he'll do anything now.

Her husband tuts in the silence, still reclined. 'You shouldn't give them false hope.'

She watches the closed door. 'I don't.'

'They never last six months. Our churn rate is insane.'

'As is our progress. They don't last six months because they do what the others won't. They'll sacrifice themselves for *mami*. And if they make it half a year, well . . .' She eyes him. 'What, you don't like it anymore? Should you and I drop our arrangement?'

He holds his hands up, his thick fingers riddled with gold bands. 'Do what you need to do.'

That's right, she thinks. *You're happy. You get your own privileges.*

She's thinking it's about time for bed when the personal phone buzzes at her hip. A rare occurrence; she can count her inner circle on one hand. She extracts the slim device from the bodysuit as Gabriel takes another sip, notes the contact name.

Huh.

She answers. 'Very late to be calling.'

Rubén Álvarez says, 'I know. And I know it's been a long time. I know you're . . . busy.'

'I always have time for you, Baby Ru.'

And it's true. She and Gabriel only spent a year in Popayán with her extended family in the late eighties, but one of her only cherished memories is of her second cousin's zest for life, how furiously that little boy pedalled his rusted pushbike. She was thirty, Rubén was ten. Even then, she sensed greatness in the child, a quenchless strength of spirit. Such a shame he amounted to nothing. Last she heard he was an unambitious bricklayer up in Bogotá.

'Listen.' He clears his throat. His speech sounds strange, like he's talking through a grille. 'Have I told you about my girlfriend? Camilla?'

'How long have you been together?'

'More than a year now.'

'You and I haven't spoken in years.'

He coughs again. Something sounds stuck in his windpipe. Then the sound of faint banging in the background of the call, muffled shouting. A woman.

Sonia sighs. 'That's her, making all that commotion? What do you need, Rubén? For me to send someone around, get her in line?'

'No, no.' He seems perplexed, choked by emotion. 'I just . . . there's a situation. Can you hear me slurring?'

'Are you drunk?'

'No, a man just . . . beat me up. Very badly. Camilla's ex.'

She stifles a sigh. 'Rubén, how many times did I offer you work in your twenties? How many times did you refuse?'

He doesn't answer.

'You could be a trained fighter,' she snaps. 'Capable of putting any man in their place. But you chose not to walk that path. The consequences of your naïvety are on you.'

'No, I know . . .' She hears him gulp. 'Maybe I'm weak, but that path will never be for me.'

Irritation tickles her throat. 'Something else I can do for you?'

In the background, barely perceptible, Sonia thinks she hears the woman shout, *Rubén, no!*

Rubén ignores the plea. 'Not for me, Sonia,' he says. 'This call is a favour. For you.'

She rolls her eyes. 'You have yourself a good night, Baby Ru. Stay safe.'

'He was an American.'

Her whole body jolts, a nervous-system reaction. Ice in the air; volts in her blood.

She takes the phone away from her ear and stabs the speakerphone button with a shaking finger. She faces her husband. 'You hear that, Gabriel? An American beat up my little cousin.'

The man's jaw clicks, his five o'clock shadow pulsing with tension. He finally levers himself into a seated position. He swallows the rest of the Macallan and slams the empty tumbler on the coffee table. His pale eyes are that of a predator's.

Rubén's voice comes through the tinny speaker. 'I thought you might want to do something about that.'

'You thought correctly,' she says. 'It'd be my pleasure to crush him for you.'

A pause. 'The way he beat us . . . there were five of us, Sonia. I don't know what he is, but . . . he's serious. He must be trained. I thought that might pique your interest. I think he might even be—'

'This is an unsecured line.'

Another nervous bout of throat clearing. 'Just don't underestimate him.'

'Certainly not.' She blinks. 'You're still in Bogotá?'

'Yes. Patio Bonito. He attacked us in a bar—I know the owner. The American trusts him, the idiot. The owner called me, said this guy's catching the next flight out, but he's putting his feet up out the back for a few hours before he heads for El Dorado. You've got time.'

'Give me the address.'

He does. She commits it to memory.

Then there's only tension.

Rubén's the first to fill the silence. 'What, uh . . . what happens now?'

'You just lick your wounds, Baby Ru. Leave the rest to us.'

She hangs up. There'll be no sleep tonight.

She's practically trembling as she turns back to her husband. She finds Gabriel riding out a similar stress response. His voice comes low. 'This American beat five men down at once?'

'Sounds like it.'

'That doesn't happen in real life.' Gabriel stares. 'You understand? Someone like that . . . maybe one in a million. Rarer, even. And the warmongers would never waste that sort of talent. So he might actually be trained.'

'Yes, Rubén said he was trained.'

'No. *Trained.* You know what I mean.' He smacks his lips. 'Might be a war.'

The fury is a molten thing inside her. 'Then let's go to fucking war.'

15

Stretched out across a cheap vinyl sofa in a storeroom behind the bar, Logan stays vigilant.

Thanks to the unique demands of his old profession, he knows he can go days without shut-eye. The room is windowless, but he imagines dawn light ebbing into the sky outside. He lies prone with one hand behind his head and the other rested gently on Rubén's gun at his hip. He stares at a round clock ticking on the wall and tells himself he'll head out at five-thirty. Three hours ago, the owner said he was crashing in his own quarters and scurried deeper into the building. Before the man slipped away, Logan borrowed his phone and booked a last-minute seat on the eight o'clock flight to New York. If he flags a cab down without incident, he should be back at El Dorado with two hours to spare. Ample time.

Besides, Alice is fine. While using the owner's phone hours prior, Logan pulled up an encrypted messaging website, used his memorised login details, and fired her a message he knew she'd respond to within minutes, no matter the hour. Even when her phone's on silent, notifications from this particular service chime regardless. She messaged back thirty seconds later: *All good. Nothing happening here. You okay?* He returned with, *I'm back in twelve hours, talk then,* exited the site, cleared the browsing history, and handed the phone back, his nerves satiated.

Now he hears rustling on the other side of the door the owner disappeared through. It's 5:16. He swings his feet off the tattered sofa. The door cracks open. The owner leans his head in. 'You are good here?'

'I'm leaving. Thank you for your hospitality.'

Obvious concern on the man's face. A hand curls around the door, and he pats the air. 'Wait. I make the coffee.'

Logan stares at the guy's hair. It's as bouncy as the last time Logan saw him, no part of it flattened. 'Have you slept?'

'Yes.'

What, standing up? Logan rips the Five-seven from his belt. The owner doesn't have time to move an inch before he's staring down the barrel of the pistol. His face drains of colour; one eye twitches. Logan sees him considering running.

'I'll just shoot you through the door,' he warns. 'Don't be stupid.'

The guy's frozen, his voice tiny. 'What you want?'

'Step in here. All the way inside.'

Dread cloaks the man as he reluctantly toes inside. The door clicks shut behind him. He stands there, hands in pockets. More guilty than scared.

'You don't live here, do you?' Logan juts the pistol at the closed door. 'There's nothing back there.'

'No,' the man confirms. His pupils keep skittering, panicked glances thrown at the door leading out to the bar space.

'How long?' Logan asks.

'Huh?'

'How long do I have?'

The man shrugs.

Logan slips a finger inside the trigger guard.

The owner swallows. 'They say five-twenty.'

Just my luck. Logan eyes the clock. The minute hand ticks from eighteen to nineteen. The owner's knees begin to tremble.

Logan says, 'If I use you as a shield . . .'

The owner shakes his head, tears in his eyes. Dark acceptance. 'They just shoot me. They no care.'

Decision. Fast. Logan snaps two fingers on his free hand, points to the far corner of the storeroom, past free-standing shelves. 'Get over there.'

The man appears confounded. 'But I . . . sell you out . . .'

'Yeah, whatever.' Logan clicks his fingers again. 'Get over there. Now.'

The guy shuffles into the corner, unsure why his safety's being considered. Clearly his world requires self-preservation, and Logan can't hold much of a grudge against someone just trying to survive.

He springs to his feet and positions himself beside the other door, the one leading to the bar. Presses himself hard to the wall, holding the Five-seven low. His trigger finger drifts to the ambidextrous safety; he flicks it off. He slows his heartbeat as best he can and listens to the throbbing silence.

Nothing.

Another glance at the clock: 5:20 now. All quiet.

Then he hears the tiniest noise. The scuff of a shoe, right on the other side of the door. Someone who was previously padding silently toward the storeroom is backing up a step. Preparing to breach.

Reality sharpens. The hyper-awareness of life or death.

Then a great weight smashes the door open, and all hell breaks loose.

The lock snaps and the door swings inward at full speed. Logan braces for impact and slams his shoulder into it. The impact rattles him, but the door shudders and reverses course, almost as fast as it was coming at him. The man in the bulletproof vest trying to force his way into the room wasn't expecting immediate resistance, and when the door he breached comes crashing back into him, it knocks him off-balance.

He staggers a step, keeping a tight grip on the Kalashnikov AK-47 rifle in his gloved hands. In his desperation to keep hold of his weapon, he ignores all else. Logan has room to step in, plant the Five-seven against the side of his skull, and pull the trigger.

Crimson blooms and the guy goes down in a bloody heap.

Logan wastes no time. He hurls the door all the way aside so he can aim out into the space behind the bar. Sure enough, he makes out the blur of bodies lined up, at least five more men wielding automatic weaponry, and he figures he can get a couple of quick shots off before hurling himself back behind cover.

During the milliseconds in which he lines up his trajectory, he spots the stun grenade in the gloved hand of the first man in line. Logan processes the sight just as the guy processes him.

The soldier reacts first, snatching for the AK-47 dangling from a shoulder strap by his side. But impulses lead unerringly to mistakes, and the primal part of the soldier's brain that screams *Threat!* forgets about the grenade he planned to throw into the storeroom. The hand clutching the flashbang smacks into the underside of the rifle's stock, and the grenade springs from his palm.

Logan sees the grenade clatter to the floor and suddenly all else is irrelevant.

Oh, fuck.

Someone up the back of the procession fires a shot, which scythes through the air above Logan's head, but he ignores it, already turning away, dropping the Five-seven, clamping his hands over his ears, squeezing his eyes shut—

The flashbang blows.

Being blinded and deafened is a mere inconvenience on the big screen. In reality, it's apocalyptic. In the confined storeroom, the blast is all-encompassing, and Logan feels his knees give out underneath him, his eyes burning as he loses his proprioception. He has a vague sense of spilling to all fours, nursing the sensation of his head splitting in two, but all that lies within his control is his ability to fight for composure, so that's what he does.

The world is faraway, a white-hot imprint seared on his closed lids. He paws desperately for a wall, screaming at himself to maintain what little awareness he can.

His palm slaps something hard and cold: the metal shelving. He rubs his face hard on one sleeve, groans through the agony. He sways violently on the spot. His surroundings are no clearer. But if he can't see, neither can they, and if he knows where the shelves are he can orient himself—

He pivots hard, aims for where he believes the open doorway to be, and sprints blindly out into the bar itself. He doesn't run directly into the wall, a minor victory, and he can sense he's out of the storeroom, in a bigger space. His gag reflex spasms and he dry heaves, but his debilitation doesn't dissuade him—they're going through the same thing.

He runs blind into another body, knocking the guy back. Probably the man who was first in line, the one who dropped the grenade. Logan retches as he paws at the man's chest, feeling first for a vest, then an arm, then the rifle slung across his body. His head's an inferno as he rips the AK-47 away from the guy. Logan uses the stock as a melee weapon and swings the rifle with savage intensity, aiming for the space he believes the enemy's head to be.

The first strike glances off a collarbone, but Logan uses the clue to adjust his aim and the second ricochets off the man's temple, hard enough to knock him unconscious.

Logan crouches low and blinks hard, again and again. Maybe ten seconds since the stun grenade went off. Tinnitus needles his eardrums, he knows they're all shouting, but he can't hear it. Can't hear his own moans, either. Grunting, he keeps blinking, willing his vision back. No major changes, but at the edge of his perception he now catches outlines amidst the blur of fiery white. Silhouettes, some crouched, some stumbling about on their feet. Unlike him, the flashbang went off directly underneath these men.

Logan gets his bearings first.

The figures crystallise into distinct targets. With his awareness ebbing back, he aims underneath or above the bulky vests and squeezes off tight three-round bursts. The Kalashnikov AK-47 is a rugged, reliable weapon. Logan's familiar with its weight, its stopping power. He doesn't need to see the bodies hit the ground to know he found his targets.

By the time his vision comes most of the way back, everyone's dead.

It's hard to comprehend what he's done when the bar materialises before him. Blood coats shattered spirit bottles; men lie dead atop one another; limbs twitch in death throes. Logan catches a marked whiff of some uglier stench: voided bowels, the metallic stink of blood. He counts six bodies, including the man he shot in the storeroom doorway. He rears to his feet, only now registering the fact he vomited all over his own flannel at some point in the furore. He staggers back to the storeroom doorway and stands in it. He finds the owner still cowering in the far corner.

The man squats facing the wall, his hands over his ears. His skinny back heaves, trembling with fear and pain.

'Hey!' Logan screams. He can barely hear what leaves his own mouth.

The owner turns shakily.

'Make sure you're out of here before the rest of them show up!' Logan yells.

The man offers a sad smile.

Logan cocks his head.

The owner says, 'They need . . . make sure . . . we dead.'

Logan can only read his lips. 'What?'

The far wall explodes.

A steel bumper blasts through crumbled brick and shattered plaster. Then the rest of a Toyota Hilux follows, the truck jacked up on modified suspension.

The reinforced pickup crushes everything in its path as it roars into the storeroom. Logan watches the grille smash the bar owner forward like a rag doll, sending him tumbling under the wheels in a bundle of broken limbs. There's no time to process the grisly demise. Logan's connecting dots.

This was their plan.

Breach from the barroom, toss a flashbang in, stun him just long enough to keep him in place before the truck came through the wall and obliterated everything in the storeroom.

Shelving twists and topples, tossed aside by the huge vehicle. One massive tyre swallows the sofa Logan was lying on minutes earlier. The Hilux grinds to a halt, taking up most of the floorspace. Doors pop and there's just enough room on either side for the passengers to leap down—more sinewy men with Kalashnikovs.

Any other time, any other place, this would be overkill. But their target is Logan Booth.

They didn't expect him to be up on his feet, watching them come through the wall. Because he stands a couple feet outside the storeroom, the only consequence of his proximity to the explosion of debris is a few fragments of plasterboard peppering his flannel. He has a clean line of sight and ample time to take aim as the reinforcements spill from the truck, and he guns all three men down without fanfare. Just cold, efficient execution shots, rounds from his AK-47 snapping heads back, and through the tinted windshield he sees the driver panic and, wide-eyed, snatch for a weapon he never expected he would have to use. Logan shoots him through the glass, spider-webbing the pane as lead punches into the man's chest. Logan doubted it was bulletproof, and he was right. Polycarbonate isn't cheap. Resources are finite amongst even the most prosperous guerrillas.

So four more men are dead in as many seconds. The truck's unmanned now, its engine chugging idly away, bodies draped on the side skirts.

Alone in the building, surrounded by the aftermath of the massacre, Logan takes stock. He figures if he tries to flee out the bar entrance, they'll just gun him down the moment he makes a break for it. He can't imagine sprinting across the dusty patch of land out front without taking a bullet to the head for his recklessness. It would be foolish to assume there aren't more men lying in wait.

No, he must leave another way, and he sees an opportunity right in front of him. The instant he decides, he acts, taking a breath and holding it before charging into the storeroom.

The dust cloud swallows him whole, but he soldiers forward undeterred, hustling along the thin corridor between the wall and the driver's side of the vehicle. He heaves the dead driver out of the bloodstained seat, lurches up into the cab, and slams the door shut, rattling the chassis and showering himself with shards of the driver's window. But that hardly matters—by this point, the whole world is blood and sweat and dust and glass.

The only priority is staying in motion.

With his chest heaving, he tosses the AK-47 on the passenger seat, leans over to close the passenger door, throws the Hilux in reverse, and stamps on the pedal. The suspension shudders as the pickup fights for traction, accelerating back over the mangled sofa and twisted shelving, everything coated in rubble. Finally the massive tyres find purchase and the vehicle roars toward dawn light. As soon as the truck bed is out under the indigo sky, Logan twists the wheel hard, trying to spin the Hilux out of the hole it punched in the side of the building. But the front-right wheel snags on jagged brickwork, and the pickup only rotates ninety degrees before slamming to a halt outside, jammed parallel to the exterior wall.

He wrenches the gear selector down into drive and accelerates again, but extrication proves impossible. The right-hand wheels spin uselessly, trapped amid debris. The passenger doors are pinned tight to the brickwork. The only way to exit the cabin is out the driver's side.

Logan snatches the rifle back up and pops his door, revealing the worst-case scenario.

The bar backs onto a maze of dilapidated laneways, one of which unspools in a straight line away from the building. Logan finds himself staring down this alley, which must have provided the Hilux the necessary space to pick up speed before smashing through the wall.

Another vehicle is barrelling toward the bar.

A Renault sedan with a faded paint job is already doing thirty miles an hour, beelining for a T-bone collision with the driver's side of the pickup. Logan's trapped in place; he can't accelerate or reverse. If he leaps down from the cabin, he won't have time to hurl himself aside before the Renault crushes him like a bug. And he's a sitting duck if he stays where he is. The sedan's hood will thrust up into the cabin upon impact, a vehicular projectile.

He sees only one option before him, and it might kill him. At the very least, injury is guaranteed.

With no time to brainstorm alternatives, he raises the AK-47 and puts the last few bullets in the curved magazine through the Renault's windshield. The driver and passenger already ducked down in advance, anticipating Logan to fire at them, and the bullets do nothing to stop the oncoming vehicle. If anything, the sedan seems to quicken in response. But Logan wasn't looking to kill the occupants, or make the car swerve.

He only needed to weaken the glass.

An undercurrent of fierce energy surges through him. Thoreau, his old handler, always said he was a sucker for mutually assured destruction. He prefers when everyone hurts equally, because he knows he's best at handling pain.

He hardly has time to inhale before the Renault closes the gap, but instead of sitting there and getting squashed, he leaps out of the open driver's door at the last second and lands directly on the spiderwebbed pane.

Logan weighs two hundred and twenty pounds, and the Renault's going thirty miles an hour.

Force equals mass times acceleration.

His bulk shatters the glass like a bomb going off, and he crashes straight through the windshield into the cabin.

No time to discern how much damage he just inflicted upon himself. He lands across the driver and passenger, glass cutting him up as he uses their laps to blunt the impact of his fall.

He splays uncontrollably when he lands, the steering wheel in the small of his back, someone's elbow inadvertently catching him in the jaw. The Renault hits the Hilux half a second later, the G-forces of deceleration staggering, but Logan managed to wedge himself down across both seats, so he doesn't go flying back out the windshield when the sedan obliterates the truck cabin he just leapt from.

No sooner has the vehicle come to a violent halt, half-embedded in the side of the Hilux, than Logan starts whaling on the driver and passenger, swinging limbs in the confined space. He thunders a haymaker into the driver's face; the guy was already semi-conscious, and the fist to the mouth knocks him all the way out. Logan then rolls and kicks hard, stabbing the sole of his boot into the side of the passenger's head, and the second man slumps unseeing against his door. A third guy sits behind the passenger seat, but he thought he was too tough for a seatbelt, and bouncing off the seatback upon impact disoriented him. Logan scrambles to a half-seated position, spots another FN Five-seven pistol in the driver's footwell, and snatches it up. He fires a trio of kill shots—three rounds in three heads—then kicks the passenger door open and spills out of the Renault.

He can't believe he's alive.

He's in bad shape though. The agony is different now, sinister, nauseating, suggesting more than superficial damage. No matter how hard he sucks for air, he can't catch his breath. His balance is fucked. He stumbles all over the place in his quest to find stable footing. A wave of dizziness nearly dumps him down in the dust, but he somehow stays upright. Planting a palm on the Renault's crumpled hood to steady himself, he gazes all around, searching for more hostiles.

He isn't sure what to do if he spots them. He hardly has the strength to keep his feet.

No one materialises. He stands swaying as the laneways hang in stillness. He can faintly hear the screaming in neighbouring streets. Dogs are going ballistic; a baby howls. The weak light of predawn is ghostly. He gasps for lungfuls of the thin air and prays nothing's broken, which is unlikely.

Then an old Mazda hatchback rumbles into the alley he stares down. *Fuck's sake.*

He tries to raise his pistol. His hand shakes.

But the Mazda has only one occupant, and the wide-eyed man who spills from the driver's seat is clearly a civilian. Terror hastens his movement. The guy sees Logan standing against a backdrop of twisted metal, aiming a gun at him, and he practically tumbles from his vehicle and disappears between two residential buildings.

Logan limps toward the hatchback and shouts, '*Hey!*' trying to coax the man back as his vision pulses. Despite his condition, he's determined not to mirror his old employers. Most of his hatred of the CIA stems from their habit of charging into foreign lands, razing them to the ground, and retroactively claiming they did it for the good of the people. Logan never much believed in what powerful nations pretend to stand for. He would never ruin innocent lives to preserve his own.

So he staggers up to the hatchback and peers down the shadowy alley the guy fled into. He spots a silhouette in the darkness and roars '*Hey!*' again. The civilian pulls to a halt and turns to face the vehicle he just abandoned. Judging by the filthy attire Logan glimpsed him wearing, and the way the ancient Mazda's fenders are secured with electrical tape, Logan understands this car might be all he has in the world.

'Come back,' Logan shouts. Blood pools in his mouth. 'Take your car.'

The guy doesn't budge.

He's listening.

A faint wave of sirens rises in the distance, the screams of civilians intensify, and men shout at one another in front of the bar. Their furious exchanges drift over the top of the building. Within minutes, it will be bedlam. Logan killed more than a dozen people here. Given the public nature of the massacre, it will make national headlines.

The Mazda driver understands that, too. He doesn't want to be caught in the wrong place at the wrong time. He'd rather escape with his life than go back for his ride and get hauled in by the National Police as a witness.

Logan sees him preparing to run.

With a grunt of agony, Logan fishes in his bloody flannel for his roll of pesos. He exchanged four thousand USD at JFK, wanting to be prepared for anything. Without fanfare, he tosses two thirds of the money into the mouth of the alley, where it flutters into the dust like scattered flowers.

The driver is motionless in the shadows, perplexed. Logan jerks a thumb at the banknotes, then at the Mazda. *I'm buying your car.* It'll take too long to bridge the language barrier and receive explicit permission, so he just dives through the open driver's door and reverses the hatchback the way it came.

Within seconds he erupts into the wider road in front of the bar. Someone spots him behind the wheel and shouts, but he rips a tight U-turn, throws the car in drive, and tears away from the scene. Half a minute later he slices into the throbbing dawn traffic, a sea of mopeds, motorcycles, and cars overflowing with passengers.

Airport? he thinks, fighting off hallucinations. *I can still make the flight.*

He stops thinking when he spots the roadblock ahead.

Scrawny men in tank tops and cargo shorts openly wield AK-47s as they shepherd traffic. Their movements are erratic as they duck down and peer hard into each car that trundles past, the procession moving at a snail's pace.

Logan wipes blood off his face, hacks up a gob of crimson to clear his throat, and grips the wheel tight.

He envisions similar roadblocks all around El Dorado Airport.

He's got no clue what this is, but it's far bigger than he thought. Four months ago, he waged war through the underbelly of New York, and he just hit the same body count here in a handful of minutes. Not only did he destroy his own body in the interest of survival, leaving him with very little capacity for further resistance, but his conscience won't permit continuing this fight through the bustling streets of Bogotá, with thousands of civilians as potential collateral damage. Nothing good awaits the decision he forces himself to make, but it's his only choice.

He can't go home. He can't go to the airport.

So he must flee the city.

With his heart in his throat, he spins the Mazda into a gap in oncoming traffic and speeds in the opposite direction until he mounts a multi-lane highway heading southwest. His gaze drifts to the passenger seat and he spots an old smartphone that the driver must have dropped in his panic. Its screen glares, a grid of icons displayed. Still unlocked.

Logan snatches the phone up and dials a memorised number.

He has enough experience to know that was just the beginning.

16

Six a.m. The city that never sleeps picks up steam for the morning rush. Thus begins the caffeination of the masses, and Alice arrives for her Sunday shift at Empyrean with time to spare. She called in sick yesterday, bone-tired after what happened on Friday in Boston, but from her brief message exchange with Logan late last night, it seems his business in Colombia has already concluded. She isn't sure if he was being intentionally cryptic—she knows he'll explain everything once he returns—but she can't put her life on hold at the vague possibility of danger. She needs to work.

Bills don't care how frightened you are.

As she unlocks the front door of the café in the lee of the New York Times Building, her phone vibrates in her coat, a steady, insistent ringing. She pulls it out and glimpses an unknown international number. *Probably a scammer.*

She wants to let it go to voicemail, but dark thoughts compel her to answer. 'Hello?'

A second of silence. Then another. She makes to hang up.

As she takes the phone away from her ear, Logan's voice whines from the speaker, distant, broken up. 'Can . . . hear me?'

She jolts. 'You okay?'

No answer.

'Logan, you good?'

'Listen . . . delay . . . might be . . . just go back to work . . . don't worry about . . .'

Frozen on the sidewalk, she squints in concentration. 'I'm *at* work. Where are you?'

Suddenly the connection clears. 'Listen, Alice, I'm in some shit. It's nothing to do with Boston. You just go about your life, stay vigilant. Don't worry about me.'

'What—?'

'Don't worry about me!' he shouts. 'You hear me? No matter what the headlines read. This is . . . look, it's my own fault. Just—'

'What?' Tears come to her eyes. She can't ascertain exactly why, something in his tone. 'Just *what*?'

'Just . . . you know what to do. Right? If I don't make it . . .'

Her stomach falls. 'Logan, what the fuck?'

'This might be bad.' He sounds strained, as though suppressing tremendous pain. 'But . . . you've got it, don't you? You know what to do.' She hears him swallow. 'You know how to live.'

'Just get on a plane.' Her voice quakes. Emotion erupts: '*Get back here!*'

'I can't. Maybe not for a while. Camilla's boyfriend . . . I . . . I've made a serious mistake . . . honestly, I don't know what I've done . . . I'm being hunted . . .'

'Logan—'

'I'm about to be out of range, okay? I don't know when I'll be able to get another phone. But just . . . if this is goodbye . . . you're . . .' He grunts, mustering courage. 'You're the best thing that's ever happened to me, Alice.'

'*Tell me what's going on!*'

A hard click, and the call dies.

Her hand trembles as she stares at the lock screen. Passersby must think she's consumed in a trance; they throw concerned glances as they hustle past. Which is new—pedestrians went out of their way to pretend she didn't exist.

Distress only draws attention if you look put-together. Addicts are assumed to be beyond salvation. She understands—concern for a junkie is an ugly, complicated thing. You don't want to wind up assaulted for your own goodwill.

So she appreciates the newfound interest in her wellbeing, but she doesn't meet anyone's eyes.

Her whole world has shrunk to four words: *if this is goodbye . . .*

She doesn't sense Pierre beside her until he says, 'What's going on?'

She tucks her phone away. 'Nothing,' she says. But she's shaking.

He jerks a thumb over his shoulder. 'Heard you shouting from back there.' He pauses. 'Relationship troubles?'

She finishes unlocking the door. 'No.'

He follows on her heels as she steps into the empty café. A sea of stools rest upside-down on polished tables. Coffee machines lie dormant. His voice echoes in the space as he says, 'Make sure to keep it outside of work, yeah?'

She doesn't respond, just shuffles behind the counter in a daze.

'You hear me?' he says. 'Can't have you shouting down the phone between orders.'

'Mmm.'

'Alice . . .'

She knows what's really motivating this lecture. She wasn't especially polite when she turned him down on Friday.

'Have I ever failed to do my job, Pierre?'

'I'm just saying . . .' But she's already busying herself with the day's duties, and he watches her work for a moment before shuffling away.

Hours later, on her break, she scrolls through the news and reads a headline.

A piece posted ten minutes ago by Al Jazeera is titled: THIRTEEN SLAUGHTERED IN BOGOTÁ MASSACRE.

It's like someone stabbed her in the stomach.

She scans the article itself, absorbing remarks about the unprecedented nature of this hurricane of violence, what with guerrilla warfare ordinarily contained to rural Colombia, far from the big cities and tourist towns. The writer of the piece laments the escalation of the conflict, especially during a time where the government is pushing so hard for peace talks and ceasefires. The current consensus is that a rebel group mowed through more than a dozen rival insurgents in a dingy bar in the dangerous Patio Bonito neighbourhood.

She knows the truth.

It's my own fault, Logan said.

'What are you *doing*?' she mutters.

That's when it hits her. She feared for him four months ago, too, but she was helpless then. It's different now. As a slave to her own desires, the world controlled her. Now she controls herself, and it affords her the space to see clearly.

Logan may be a destroyer, a human battering ram, but he's still human. Fallible. Blind to his own mistakes.

There must be something she can do to help.

She calls the international number back. No dial tone. Out of range, like he said, for who knows how long. She sees a version of reality where she lets it go, lets him wage his vengeful crusade through Colombia until he inevitably meets his demise. But if she can help him see the light, pull him back from his self-destructive tendencies . . .

All at once, she sweeps to her feet and beelines through the busy café toward Pierre. On her way over, she sheds her apron. He gives her a strange look.

'I need some personal time,' she says.

He looks flummoxed. 'You already had yesterday off.'

'I know. I'm sorry. This is urgent.'

'I told you not to bring your personal life into—'

'Pierre,' she interrupts. 'This isn't a debate. I'm saying I need some time.'

'Not a debate?' He scoffs. 'You're replaceable, you understand?'

'I didn't ask you to keep me on. If you need to fire me, fire me. That's in your control. This is in mine.'

'This isn't you, Alice. Don't throw a good job away.'

She shrugs. 'I'll find another.'

Walking away from Empyrean, Alice thinks about what she's about to do: an impossibly dangerous undertaking with zero guaranteed payoff. The risks are staggering, the rewards unlikely.

But if their roles were reversed, Logan wouldn't think twice about risking everything for her. She has no doubts about that because she literally watched him do it four months ago, back when they hardly knew each other.

Bottom line is, if she doesn't try to help, she will question that choice for the rest of her life. If she goes, and she fails, at least she'll fail with the satisfaction of having done her damnedest.

It scares her to the depths of her soul, but she finds she's no longer afraid of fear itself. Not if it comes as a result of doing the right thing, making the hard choice.

Logan might need her. And if she needed him, he'd move heaven and earth.

She books a flight to Bogotá.

—

A full uninterrupted hour with the director of the National Economic Council fries Jacinta's synapses.

By the time he scurries out at 9 a.m., she's having trouble remembering which senior staff meeting comes next. Cognitive fatigue before midmorning is a bad sign. The moment she's alone in the Oval Office, she buzzes her secretary and says, 'I need twenty. Push everything back.'

'Ma'am—'

'You want me rushing through critical decisions and botching half of them? Or you want me sharp? Twenty minutes. There's no function today. No travel time. We're good.'

'You got it.'

'Is Beau in?'

'Yes, ma'am.'

'Tell him coffee's on me.'

Six minutes later, the First Gentleman enters wielding fine china in each hand: a pair of espressos. They could have had the mugs brought in by staff, of course, which would have made it a little easier to visualise this as a genuine coffee catch-up between married professionals, but Beau Murphy understands as well as she does the importance of efficiency. No point sitting around for a minute or two waiting for the caffeine to arrive when he can just take it in himself.

He places the saucers delicately on the Resolute desk and sits across from her. 'This is nice.'

She smiles. Sips the crema off the steaming espresso and relishes the maple notes.

Jacinta watches her husband in pleasant quietude. She appreciates him, and she appreciates her newfound reassurance.

Logan Booth touched down in Bogotá late last night. Job done.

Beau drains his espresso in a gulp and settles back in his seat. He drags manicured nails along his five o'clock shadow. Watches her right back. 'I take it that interruption a couple of nights ago wasn't anything world-ending.'

'What makes you think that?'

'You look stressed. But not *stressed.*'

She understands what he means.

'I sorted it,' she says as her phone pings.

She looks down at the screen and reads, *Thirteen armed rebels killed three blocks over from Camilla Peña's residence around 0530. Media putting it out in 30. National Police kept a tight lid on it, we just caught wind. Advise ASAP.*

She reads the text again. Her ears roar. She hears Beau speaking, but can't make out a thing he's saying.

Almost unconsciously, she mutters, 'Oh my God.'

It takes him yelling, *'What?!'* to cut through her head noise. She jerks upright in her chair. The last time he raised his voice at her was two and a half years ago.

'I . . . I can't tell you,' she says. 'You know that.'

He finds his composure, and she knows it will be years before he shouts at her again. 'I've just never seen you like this.'

It dawns on her that, really, she can do whatever she wants.

Before she knows it, she's venting, telling him everything that happened four months ago, everything that's been happening over the last couple of days. He absorbs each explosive development without reaction. She considers her ability to summarise without extraneous detail to be one of her finest talents, so he has the whole picture within eight minutes.

She finishes her whirlwind recount and leans toward him over the Resolute desk. He's unreadable.

'What do you think?' she asks quietly.

'I'm not a spook. This isn't my wheelhouse.'

'Not on a professional level. Personally. Husband to wife. What do you think?'

He gazes over her shoulder, out at the Rose Garden aglow in morning light. When he looks at her again, he says, 'I think some people in this life are serious.'

'What?'

'I'm reluctant to try putting this into words. I never have before. It's just what I've always believed . . .'

'Well, try,' she says. 'Please.'

When his voice comes, it comes soft. 'I think most people don't want what they say they want. If they did, they would stay true to their word. I believe all else is empty fluff. Broken promises, mental masturbation. We debate and opine and create narratives and make justifications for our behaviour because we are fundamentally insincere.' He hesitates. 'But I think there are rare types who are truly serious about what they want. Who know precisely what's *truly* beneficial. I think you've run into a serious person, Jacinta. I think there are consequences to that. There always are.'

She knows what to ask, but it takes courage. 'Do you consider yourself serious, Beau?'

'Most of the time. Sometimes I slip.'

'Do you consider me serious?'

'Most of the time.'

She cocks her head. 'I've slipped, haven't I?'

'We all do.' He cocks his head in turn. 'Well, almost all of us . . .'

'I didn't think this through,' she admits. 'I rushed. I provoked a serious person.'

Again, he says, 'There are consequences.'

'What do I do?' she asks him, but he won't answer.

He knows she's a better decision maker than he is.

So she alters the question. 'If you were on this side of the desk, what would you do?'

'I'd wait,' Beau says. 'And I'd pray Colombia takes care of him.'

'Oh, you're religious now?'

'When push comes to shove, we're all religious.'

'And if he makes it out the other side?'

'I'd get serious.' Beau's eyes are ice. 'Because that would be the only way to stop what's coming.'

PART III
WAR

Would you like to know how they do not live long? See how keen they are to live long.

Seneca, *On the Shortness of Life*

17

Alone, armed with only his faculties, fleeing toward an uncertain fate. For a portion of his life, it was all Logan knew.

He thought he wasn't going home, but maybe he already is.

He drives one-handed toward a crimson sunrise and pats himself down with his free hand. Even the dregs of stress chemicals can mask serious injury. Through experience, he's found the most effective way to take stock of his condition in the immediate aftermath of a conflict is to slap the shit out of himself. So he gives himself the once-over, striking his thighs, stomach, chest, and arms with an open palm. Each hit produces a hot sting of disturbed nerve endings, but no explosions of agony. He's bruising all over—by sundown, he'll be half purple—but no bones seem to be broken, no muscles torn.

Satisfied he won't be crippled when the adrenaline wears off, he moves to the next priority—being caked in blood and dirty sweat is hardly conducive to keeping a low profile. Each time the morning traffic forces him to slow, bold young men on passing scooters peer unashamedly through the driver's window, curious about the filthy condition of the big foreigner.

Logan knows his options for cleaning himself up will be scarcer once he's all the way out of the city. They're slim enough here. The southwestern edge of Bogotá appears even poorer than

Patio Bonito. Tightly clustered houses form a rolling sea of ochre. Dust chokes everything. Half-completed construction sites, some long abandoned, loom over the highway. A peeling sign identifies this municipality as SOACHA.

He uses the one bar of patchy reception on the smartphone he appropriated to locate a hotel near the highway, and ten minutes later he pulls off into a claustrophobic neighbourhood of dirt roads and faded billboards.

The hotel is situated within a crumbling building beside an open-air market of multicoloured umbrellas and knockoff sportswear. Logan parks, sheds the flannel and leaves it on the passenger seat. The black tee underneath hides most of the bloodstains, but his hands are caked with the stuff, crimson embedded under his fingernails. His left forearm has begun to swell. All the skin is scraped off one elbow. His face is a mess. But the only way to guarantee people remember him is to fall into the trap of self-consciousness, so he shoulders out of the Mazda and strides confidently to the hotel entrance—a narrow passage between two dilapidated shopfronts.

People stare anyway, mostly because he's the size of a house. He senses gazes lingering, like spotlights cutting through the dawn, and he quickens his pace before ducking through the entranceway.

A windowless white corridor, cramped and harshly lit, culminates in a tiny reception area. Beneath the hotel logo, the sign reads 24 HORAS. Sure enough, a middle-aged woman sits behind the small desk, even at six in the morning. Logan lets out a breath of relief.

'Room, please,' he says. 'Just one night.'

'Ah . . .' The woman parts her palms, grasping for the required English. 'Check-in, no. Check-in, twelve.'

Midday. No good. He estimates the room fee, triples it in his head, and slides crumpled pesos across. 'Please.'

She stares at the money. Then she fishes in a drawer and gives him a key. Simple as that. Of course, she seems concerned by his physical condition, but nowhere near enough to turn him away. It's his business what he got up to last night.

He moves down narrow corridors barely wide enough for his frame and unlocks a wooden door so thin it may as well be papier-mâché. No matter. He's not staying long. As soon as he seals himself in the featureless room—nothing more than a white box with a cheap bed—he pulls the Five-seven from his waistband and tosses the pistol on the bed, then kicks his boots off. He sheds his tee and cargo pants, peels off his underwear and socks, and leaves everything in a sweat-soaked heap atop the bedspread, beside the gun. All the clothing is dark, a deliberate choice, so after a quick shower to scrub himself clean of the residue of war, he re-dons what he was wearing. The damp attire clings to his skin, but it doesn't matter how uncomfortable it feels.

Cleansed of visible bloodstains, he tucks the pistol in his belt and drapes the tail of his moist shirt back over the piece. He snatches the driver's smartphone up and uses the hotel's Wi-Fi and his own memorised credit card numbers to purchase another eSIM, its mobile coverage superior to the Mazda owner's network. Equipped now with decent reception, he considers calling Alice again, but what else is there to say? He already told her what she needed to know. It was his fuck-up, beating Rubén down without recognising the possibility that the man may be connected, and now . . .

Now what?

How bad *is* this?

He finds out when he slips back out of the room, six minutes after entering, and doubles back to reception.

The woman jolts when he reappears, slamming a corded phone back into its cradle.

Her eyes dart between the phone and his face, her chest inflating with rising panic. So someone informed her of how dangerous he is. Which means whoever she rang knows precisely what happened a mere half-hour ago in Patio Bonito.

He realises with a prickle at the base of his spine that some kind of alert must have already gone out across Colombian social media channels. Something like, *If you see the big American, let us know.*

He can't see how anywhere in Bogotá is safe now, not even the outskirts. To escape the interconnectedness of a city hooked into technology, he must flee as far from civilisation as he can. That's all he knows.

The woman seems stunned as he nods a pleasant farewell and walks out, but he hardly notices her expression. He's elsewhere in his mind, questioning just how deep into rural Colombia he needs to venture.

And whether that plays into the hands of those hunting him.

He gets on National Route 45 and puts his foot down, heading southwest.

Dawn gives way to a cloudless morning, and for nearly two hundred miles he drives through countryside under a glaring sun. He passes chartreuse hills, hand-tilled fields, and the occasional little town, the pueblos set against the backdrop of distant mountain ranges. Hours pass, largely thoughtlessly—he has little information to work with and sees no need for anxious speculation. He figures every mile he puts between himself and the destruction he wreaked in Bogotá is at least somewhat beneficial. He must create space before searching for the context he lacks.

He stops only once, for much-needed sustenance, chowing down something in the vicinity of two thousand calories of sausage, potatoes and corn from a roadside stall. After heaping salt and butter upon the paper plate, the indigenous woman watches in muted shock as he consumes enough food for three people, right there on the side of the highway. He hasn't eaten since he boarded the plane at JFK, and it feels like he sweated out half his bodyweight. The sodium's much-needed, and there's no telling when he'll next get the chance to eat, so he scoffs as much as his stomach can physically hold, pays for a few huge bottles of water, tosses them in the car, and continues on his way.

When he occasionally gains a cell signal, he refreshes the news headlines.

His hunch was correct: the massacre dropped a bomb on the news cycle. Sure, five hundred thousand have been killed in the Colombian conflict—what's thirteen more?—but like the cartel violence up in Mexico, there are unspoken rules. You absolutely, unquestionably, do not fuck with tourism. Kill each other in droves, displace or butcher entire rural communities if you please, but keep it out of sight, far from the pipeline of cash that foreigners distribute into the major cities and historical landmarks. If people are too scared to visit Colombia, everybody loses. A serious incident in Bogotá is incredibly rare.

So the media are having a field day.

THIRTEEN SLAUGHTERED IN BOGOTÁ MASSACRE, *Al Jazeera* states. Half a dozen peripheral articles from other outlets opine on what the carnage means, whether armed groups are kicking off a turf war in the nation's capital. If that's the case, experts say, there'll be hell to pay. There are rumblings that the Colombian president is preparing a statement.

What's worse, someone has clearly enforced a suppression order on certain details. In all the articles, the bodies are blurred. The organisation whose paramilitary soldiers were slaughtered is supposedly a mystery. They all had mauve patches on their arms; someone must know something. But no one's talking. Whoever's hunting Logan has friends in high places.

In the early afternoon, the Mazda struggles toward the first major city since he left Bogotá.

The hatchback's engine strains, old and overworked, things hissing under the hood. Logan regains reception on the outskirts of the city, and uses the phone's GPS to identify this municipality as Neiva, an agricultural and industrial nerve centre in southern Colombia. High-rise apartment buildings soar over squatter dwellings. Giant palm fronds overhang the main arterial road. The air is thick, lending the city a tropical quality. The temperature's double Bogotá's, already pushing a hundred. The Mazda's air-conditioning whines, fighting a losing battle. Logan sweats freely under the black tee. Fatigue makes his vision pulse. An underlying anxiety makes everything brighter, harsher.

With the tank nearly empty, he has to stop for fuel. Squinting in the glare, he pays the pump worker for a full tank of *corriente*—87 octane—and the guy starts filling the car without a word, unsuspicious, but when Logan glances in the direction of the gas station itself, he sees a bald man behind the counter staring directly at him, barking into a phone.

'Fuck,' he mutters under his breath. He turns back to the worker. The pump displays thirty-five litres distributed, the tank about two-thirds full. It'll have to do. Logan waves the man off. The guy gestures haplessly, trying to highlight the fact Logan paid for fifty litres.

Logan taps his watch, trying to communicate the fact he's in a hurry.

The pump worker shrugs, baffled by such brazen disregard for money, and withdraws the nozzle from the opening. Logan bundles back into the car, fires it up, and veers hard off the baking concrete. He hoped to hole up here, but there must already be a bounty on his head.

Once he's moving, he checks the news again, half-expecting to see a CCTV image of himself, but there's nothing. Which is worse—it means this nationwide crusade for his head is taking place underground, far from official channels.

He guns it out of Neiva, continuing south, returning to rural isolation.

Another couple of hours on Route 45 and the sun starts dropping fast. He passed through smaller municipalities along the way, but by now he's sufficiently paranoid of anything resembling civilisation. At some point, the occasional signs reading 45 change to 24, and suddenly he's on a different route headed west, following the twisting Magdalena River through untouched countryside. Stretches of road with overhanging trees form tunnels of brilliant green. It's like he's left the world behind.

As the sun melts toward the horizon, the choking tunnels of flora recede, giving way again to flat farmland as far as the eye can see.

The GPS tells him he's moving through the Huila department. He figures he'll turn off the one-lane highway soon, see if he can get some more food without drawing attention to himself, perhaps even a bed for the night. He can hardly see straight.

There are limits to how much tension one can handle. It feels like he's been on the road for days.

With perhaps half an hour until sunset, he finds it within himself to admire the scenery. His predicament may be dire, but that's even more reason to savour the quieter moments. There's no guarantee he has many of them left.

He only fixes his gaze on the distant mountain range for a few seconds before he sees it: multiple vehicles in the rearview mirror, erupting onto the straight behind him, previously concealed by the winding road.

Logan counts three cars, then four, five, *six* . . .

His stomach drops. How long have they been tailing him? Since Neiva? He hadn't a clue. Now they're making their move, without a soul around.

As the souped-up vehicles scream closer, gaining easily on the old Mazda, he eyes men leaning out open windows, hefting rifles skyward. He swears he can see them twitching like marionettes on strings. Hopped up on stimulants, no doubt. A couple of them fire into the air. The gunshots crackle. He envisions them whooping, hollering, screaming battle cries.

It's a war party.

Logan pushes his foot all the way down, but the Mazda doesn't respond. The hatchback's given everything today. It redlines at eighty miles an hour.

The encroaching headlights grow larger. Then the first bullet whizzes past the driver's side. There's nowhere to go.

So this is how it ends.

He rips the Five-seven pistol from the small of his back, holds it in his palm. Glancing back and forth between the pistol and the rearview mirror, he watches the six vehicles roar toward him, most of them jacked-up SUVs like the Hilux in Bogotá.

He's one man with a sidearm.

Some battles are unwinnable, no matter your skillset.

With a tightening in his chest, he returns the gun to his waistband and begins to accept his fate.

At eighty miles an hour, everything rushes at you. Before he knows it, a gap between the perimeter fences of two farms materialises ahead, revealing a dirt road trailing up toward the neighbouring mountain range. Maybe five seconds until he blows past it.

Decision. Now.

He stamps the brakes hard and twists the wheel. Faded leather shudders in his hands, tyres scream on bitumen. More than likely the trail reaches a dead end, but if he stays on the straight, his demise is all but guaranteed. So he bounces the old hatchback off-road, its suspension groaning. The engine screams in protest as it tackles the loose dirt, lurching over potholes, speeding toward the lush green slope of a steep hillside.

'Come on,' he hisses, his heart rate through the roof. '*Come on.*'

It's all unfolding too fast to formulate a clear plan, but he subconsciously envisions a slim possibility of losing his pursuers in the mountains, carving out just enough time to abandon the Mazda and burrow down in some hiding place before the war party closes the gap and discovers the empty vehicle. His hard ninety-degree turn already created some space. He sees a bottleneck in the rearview as two of the pickups grind against each other trying to turn onto the dirt road in unison.

He's got a twenty-second lead.

The trail curves, still bordered on both sides by hand-tilled farmland and rusted wire fencing. The mountains loom dead ahead, a sheer wall of rising trees. He spots a cluster of whitewashed houses atop one of the smaller hills, before the more severe peaks. A highland pueblo. If he can make it up there . . .

He completes the turn, and the next stretch of trail opens out before him.

He can't believe his eyes.

Three hundred feet ahead, three off-road jeeps rest nose-to-tail across the widest section of the path. They're all the colour of slate, with men dotting their frames like ornaments. At least eight guys, all of them seated and slouched, legs dangling off hoods and rear bumpers. From this distance the jeeps are like Lego cars, the men stick figures, but Logan can still make out the unmistakable silhouettes of rifles slung over shoulder straps.

It's an armed blockade, preventing passage. *How did they know?*

Then he realises. They didn't.

These jeeps are distinctly different from the trucks chasing him. Their paint jobs are consistent, their modifications expensive. This is not some hodgepodge collection of machinery. And these men seem idle, unalert. They weren't expecting anyone. This is a different armed group. A separate force. And he's in their territory.

Heads snap up as the members of the blockade see Logan's hatchback roaring up the trail toward them. He checks the rearview. No sign of his pursuers yet. Maybe ten seconds until they round the bend.

Thinking at light speed, he glances right. A wall of tree trunks form a swathe of impenetrable forest that ascends into the mountains. No good. On his left, there's the shoddy rear fence of some vast farmland. On the other side of the twisted wire, a natural ditch in the earth runs all the way along the farm's perimeter, parallel to the dirt road.

He cranks the wheel to the left. Only toes the brake.

Rusted wire the colour of bronze fills his vision, then the hatchback smashes straight through the old fence. He intended to drive straight down into the base of the ditch, maybe even barrel all the way past the blockade. But nothing ever goes the way you intend.

The front left wheel is the first to rocket off the edge of the ditch, out into open space, and it drops too hard.

A moment of weightlessness, and Logan only has time to think, *Oh, fuck me.*

The car rolls.

18

He thinks the Mazda rolls twice, but there's no way to know for sure.

His vision blurs and the world goes quiet. There's that indescribable terror of sitting within the eye of the storm, just before the consequences erupt. He can only hope to survive the impact.

The Mazda crashes into the bottom of the ditch on its roof.

He already fought the centrifugal forces to bring his feet as close to the seat as possible and pin his arms to his sides so as not to snap a limb. The landing is an explosion of noise and visceral sensation, nauseating in its ferocity. The chassis screams, the roof twists and buckles, and all the windows blow out, showering him in glass. His bodyweight slams against the seatbelt, but the old nylon holds, keeping him pinned in the seat. If the belt snapped, he'd have landed upside-down on the crown of his head, undoubtedly breaking his neck. The force of the deceleration nearly snaps his collarbone, and a fresh wave of pain rolls over him.

A headache explodes to life. But he's alive. Conscious, too.

Panting with shock, he unbuckles his seatbelt and manoeuvres himself carefully out of the inverted position. He scrambles out the twisted windshield frame onto red-brown dirt, subduing a guttural cough. An observer would think they were hallucinating, seeing him crawl from the wreckage only seconds after the car came down in a heap. But Logan's always seen the world as binary, nothing more than one conscious decision strung to the next.

He has the capacity to move, so he does.

He drags himself away from the mangled vehicle and commando-crawls up the shallow slope. He expects to see Kalashnikov barrels aimed at his bloodied face as he peeks over the lip of the ditch, but he gets lucky.

His complete lack of hesitation paid off. The Mazda was already upside-down in the bottom of the ditch by the time his pursuers rounded the bend. The only visible residue of his kamikaze barrel roll is the car-sized hole in the wire, but the perimeter fence is in such a state of disrepair that the flattened stretch is hardly noticeable. His pursuers blew right past it.

Holy shit, he thinks, watching what unfolds next. *Jackpot.*

His pursuers turned the corner to see nothing but the jeeps ahead. They're war-crazed, ready to kill, and their collective instincts land on only one viable explanation.

This other group must have let Logan straight through their blockade.

The six trucks screech to a halt only yards away from the jeeps. Men from both sides leap down to the dirt, and then everyone's shouting at each other. A couple of guys from the blockade motion vaguely in the direction of the ditch. They saw what happened. Maybe they're trying to say, *The guy you're hunting just drove off the road,* but it must be lost in the furore because suddenly guns are raised, wide-eyed thugs pointing automatic weapons at each other, gunmetal illuminated in the evening glow.

No one's pointing in Logan's direction anymore. There's a certain tipping point of testosterone where reason falls by the wayside. Then all that matters is who's got the bigger stick.

Those manning the blockade are clearly more disciplined, already in better tactical positions. A few of them stand behind the jeeps, using the open-topped doors as gun rests. They'll be able to mow down their enemies from behind cover. If everyone starts shooting each other, Logan's pursuers will lose.

Even they can see it.

So the screaming continues, vile insults hurled back and forth in Spanish, threats, attempts at emasculation, but at a certain point one of Logan's pursuers caves. He shakes his head in disgust, turns, and slaps his buddy in the chest, coaxing him back to their pickup. Thus begins a chain reaction. Soon the whole convoy are back in their trucks, retreating to avoid being massacred.

Logan flattens himself to the slope of the ditch and listens to engines chugging as the six trucks trawl past, one by one, back the way they came. Pressing his forehead to the dirt reduces his vision to zero, amplifying his other senses. He becomes aware of the sickening pain in his body. It's a miracle nothing's broken, but he's taken about as much superficial damage as you can receive. And he's on foot now, in the middle of nowhere, his sole mode of transport reduced to scrap metal. He evaded the war party, but at what cost?

When the noise of engines recedes, he lifts his head again, in time to see the men from the blockade lowering their weapons. One man addresses the group firmly, with authority. He points again toward the ditch.

Logan's choice is simple. He can't set off on foot back the way he came; he'll run straight into his pursuers. So, forward. Whatever that entails. He breathes silent gratitude for seatbelts as he works his way up to a crouched position and sets off jogging along the length of the ditch. His collarbone throbs and whines, but pain lost its gravity a decade ago.

His head is clearer than he expected it to be when he pulls to a halt maybe a hundred feet from the Mazda, a point he imagines to be halfway between the wreckage and the jeeps, but he doesn't dare raise his head to check. He squats low, continues catching his breath as quietly as possible, and waits to hear footsteps.

Sure enough, there they are. The soft clopping of boots on hard-pack dirt. Sounds like all of them, marching down the trail in a tight unit, off to scope out the place they saw the hatchback go flying off the road. He times it carefully, waiting until he's most certain they're milling around the stretch of flattened fence, staring down at the flipped vehicle, their collective attention consumed by the wreck.

Then he clambers up out of the ditch and sprints across the trail, into the forest on the opposite side.

If he's seen, he's seen. But all remains quiet, and seconds later he disappears into the tree line, swallowed by thick vegetation. Once he's out of sight of the trail, he strides fast over the forest floor. A steep slope rises in front of him. If his faculties are still there—at this point, far from a guarantee—the hillside town he glimpsed earlier should be directly above him.

Only one way to find out.

Drenched in sweat, he burns calories like kindling as he stomps up the mountain for half an hour, through heavily wooded terrain.

The physical demands aren't egregious, but stress accelerates energy expenditure, and he's about as tense as you can be. If you saw him in action, moving robotically from one death-defying feat to the next, you'd assume he was composed, but war eats away at even the most hardened of psyches. Internally, Logan's as scared as the first time he was ever sent out in the field. The only difference between now and then is that he's learned to operate no matter what he's feeling.

Through experience, he discovered you can pretty much ignore the senses until the job's done.

What job? he thinks as the sunset warms the back of his neck.

He doesn't know who's hunting him, or whether it's even got anything to do with Rubén. All he knows is that by surviving the bar attack, he made himself their mortal enemy. No matter his efforts to think constructively, the future looks bleak, and he hasn't a clue where to start searching for a way out of this mess. His best hope is finding an airport they're not blocking access to, but given the fact a gas station attendant in Neiva recognised him, he doubts there's a single runway in the country they're not watching.

He arrives at the top of the hill exhausted, depleted to the bone. Like a mirage, a rough stone path appears on the plateau before him, undulating softly toward the village he spotted from the valley below. The pueblo is larger than he expected, eighty or ninety buildings in total. Most of the houses are white with red terracotta roofs, the village outskirts dotted with cheaper buildings that resemble storage sheds. The spire of a small church rises above the lower dwellings.

He turns to check whether anyone followed him up the hill. But the wooded slope below him hovers in stillness, birds chirping in treetops that glow in the sunset. No sound from the town itself.

All clear.

He sits down in the red dirt, just before the beginning of the winding path into town. And there he remains for fifteen minutes, cross-legged, recollecting himself. Only when he feels refreshed enough to keep the dizziness at bay does he rise again and set off along the stone path. Closer to the village, he senses the quiet hum of life: distant voices, the uninhibited laughter of a child. Hope is a dangerous thing, but he allows the tentative thought that everything might just be okay.

The path forms a natural alley as it weaves between a low metal shed and a larger building, perhaps a general store. He turns into the mouth of this laneway and runs directly into a small group of people.

Ahead are two men, a woman, and a pair of small children, separated into two distinct parties.

The men stand side by side, wearing rugged outdoor shirts tucked into dirty jeans. They bristle with a dangerous energy and wear pistols in faded holsters at their belts. They face the woman and the kids, but they don't seem to be trying to intimidate.

The woman must be a local. Black hair pulled back in a tight ponytail and chestnut skin. The dark complexion makes her eyes pop, brilliant greens imbued with a cunning that reminds Logan of a coiled panther. Her thin work shirt hangs over shapeless jeans, but the baggy clothing can't conceal the underlying athleticism. She appears relaxed, but she stands between the children—a boy and a girl—with a hand draped over each of their shoulders. It's hard to tell if the kids are hers. They share her skin tone, but their features are blunter, not as stark. They stare at Logan like they've seen a ghost, but that's expected. He doubts hulking foreigners materialise too often in these parts.

The men watch him, too, wary, unblinking. Logan deems it imprudent to try to push straight through the pack, so he pulls to a halt in front of them all.

One man fires a question: '*¿Quién eres?*'

Logan's grasp of Spanish is rudimentary at best, but it sounds like, *Who are you?* He nods past them, out toward the main street. 'Supplies.'

'*¿Qué?*'

He mimes eating and drinking, then gestures to his dishevelled state. 'Supplies. And medicine. I got lost.'

'*¿Quién eres?*' the other man repeats, because they never got an answer.

Logan shrugs. 'Backpacker. Tourist.'

They share a look, which Logan interprets as, *Brave gringo.* He imagines most travellers are reluctant to interact so casually with armed men in rural Colombia. This pocket of the country is far from the beach resorts. But they seem unbothered by his arrival. Whether they're part of a rebel group, a crime gang, or a larger trafficking organisation, it doesn't mean they need to impose terror upon every stranger who waltzes into their midst.

One of them grunts permissively, and the other extends a hand down the alley. *Go.*

Despite recent history, Logan isn't here to wage war on every guerrilla he comes across. He was never an interventionist. He knows you can't storm into a country, suppress terror, and fix everything in one fell swoop, no matter what his homeland may preach.

So he nods and walks through the middle of them.

Two things happen in quick succession. First, in his peripheral vision, he sees the men turn to one another. One leans in and mutters something in the other's ear, likely a joke at the foreigner's expense. But it means both of them are faced away as Logan passes the woman, and in a quick, decisive motion, she reaches out and pinches his wrist between two fingers and a thumb.

As he notes her touch, she hunches a little closer and whispers, 'Leave this place,' in English.

Stranger still, he swears her accent is Italian.

He stays in motion— anything else would draw attention. He catches a brief look in her eyes on his way past, but her expression communicates nothing. She took enough risk delivering the warning. Her fingertips brush down his wrist as she retracts her hand.

He dwells on what she said as his back turns to the group. Does he try to coax her away from the men? Get more information? Dig a deeper hole for himself?

Before he can decide, one of the men growls something, and Logan spins in time to watch the guy approach the woman. She keeps her face blank as he barks something in Spanish. Logan picks up on one word: '*Inglés.*'

She's sprung. The man didn't know she spoke English.

Undeterred by the gringo's presence, he darts out a hand to snatch her by the throat.

Logan saw it coming. He burst into action half a second before the man reached his hand out, so it only takes one lunging stride to close the distance and enter kicking range. A Muay Thai teep kick is simple enough—you just stab one foot forward and put your whole bodyweight behind it.

Logan executes the strike before he has time to consider what he's doing.

The man's fingers only brush the woman's neck before the sole of Logan's boot cracks him in the guts. The thud is sickening, intestines crushed beneath rippling flesh. A horrible noise splutters from his lips, and he doubles over as he stumbles back away from Logan.

The children scream. The woman keeps deathly silent.

Now both men are several paces away, with pistols at their waists.

Only one choice.

Logan sprints forward, grabs the guy he kicked into temporary paralysis by the collar of his work shirt and shoves the man back into his buddy. Limbs crash together, the noise of bowling balls colliding with pins. Logan's keenly aware of the kids wailing right behind him, far too close to the brawl for comfort. He must create distance however possible. The shed on one side of the laneway is comprised of corrugated tin walls and a rotted wooden door. The door looks barely attached to its hinges. It rests directly behind the second man.

Again, one option.

Logan takes it.

He ducks low and charges, tackles the first man, who's still incapacitated by the kick to the guts. Logan's weight hurls him back off his feet, toppling him into the second man.

Dominoes.

Their collective bodyweight falls into the door; hinges snap.

The whole door falls inward, and all three of them crash through to the ground inside.

19

It's not clean, not pretty.

It never is.

Logan reaches back for the Five-seven in his waistband but it isn't there anymore. It must have come free when their bodies collided. A holster would have done a world of good.

Unarmed, Logan unleashes on the stunned duo. He comes down on top of the first man and uses the momentum to drop a cocked elbow into his throat, crushing thyroid cartilage. He scrambles over the top of the wheezing man and intercepts the second guy making his way back to his feet. The angles are just right to throw an uppercut; Logan aims for the chin and swings for the fences. But he misses. His fist whizzes inches past the jaw, and the guy's fast. He takes advantage of Logan's overcommitment and swings a kick straight up the middle.

Shinbone thunders into Logan's groin.

Terrible, stomach-churning pain. Logan's body begs for mercy and his brain screams at him to go down, cover up, protect himself. He ignores the instinct and responds to the groin shot with a reckless headbutt, thrusting his forehead into the man's unprotected face. He connects, stunning himself, too, but amidst the wooziness he hears the *crack* of the man's nose breaking and knows he inflicted more damage than he received. Which is all the motivation he needs to follow up, swinging a pair of uppercuts with alternating fists into the guy's stomach. The punches crack off the man's midsection and he goes down moaning. Logan spins and kicks the first guy in the side of the head, visualising punting straight through his skull. The toe of Logan's boot tears the man from consciousness when it impacts.

Either pistol is right there for the taking—Logan identifies their sidearms as big Colt M1911s, American-made—but he's reluctant to fire unsuppressed gunshots. He drags his defeated foes out of the open doorway, deeper into the space. Privacy matters with innocents nearby. The guy who's still conscious does what he can to resist, but Logan's musculature is a well-oiled machine.

He pins them both down on the exposed dirt floor and clamps a palm over each of their throats.

He leans all his weight down on them, veins straining in concrete forearms. The man who's awake kicks and struggles, but Logan's strength makes things quick. A fifteen-second squeeze separates him from consciousness, and another twenty seconds of pressure separates them both from life itself. Clean deaths, relatively speaking. Fast, silent. They wouldn't show him the same courtesy. They'd drag it out, relishing their victory.

They'd make him scream.

Few understand war. An observer would label him a psychopath, and maybe they're right; maybe he's naïve. But it was him or them, and there's no world where he could have let them stagger away.

He sways as he rises off the corpses. Dripping sweat again, he leaves the old Colts behind. He doesn't need three pistols. The Five-seven lies in the dirt just outside the shed, and he scoops it up as he steps outside into twilight. The gun goes back in his waistband before he lifts the door crudely into place, propping it carefully against the frame. Good enough. You'd need to stare hard to notice the slim gap between the broken hinges and the frame.

He turns to face the civilians.

He finds the green-eyed woman sporting precisely the same expression he last saw her wearing. Almost a strange nonchalance. A dark understanding passes between them as they meet each other's eyes—he knows she's seen the worst the world has to offer.

Certain horrors are, and always will be, the way of the world.

She acted decisively in the interim. She never let go of the children, and now she holds them tighter, pressing them to the sides of her thighs. They sob quietly, faces scrunched, eyes squeezed shut. But they're not screaming anymore, and his stomach twists as he realises they know how to behave in these situations, too. They know what survival entails.

He stands in front of them. Perspiration drips off his chin. He doesn't break eye contact with the woman. Her gaze is penetrating, like she's trying to see all the way inside him. He feels naked under her judgement, but he allows her to see him. To draw her own conclusions.

Something flashes in her eyes. 'Come with us.'

Definitely an Italian inflection; he wasn't imagining it. He senses harboured secrets. But he also senses her request doesn't come from a place of fear or intimidation. She trusts him.

So he nods. It's all he can manage—he's reeling.

She cranes her neck, checking the coast is clear, then whispers soothingly to the children and guides them down the laneway, deeper into town. He follows at a careful pace.

As he trails after them, he pinches his own forearm, but he feels his nerve endings fire. He's here. This is no fever dream.

She leads them down a twisting main road. Whitewashed houses, terracotta roofs. Her movements are practised, attentive. She bristles with what he interprets as a fierce determination. He hardly considers high-tailing it away, not even after what just happened. The exhaustion is intensifying into something crippling, and he knows his limits. Whoever she is, she doesn't seem to be leading him into a trap. At this point, that's the best he can hope for.

A scattering of villagers observe their little procession. A few older Colombians, bolder and blunter than the younger generations, bark questions from their porches. Most of the queries sound like something to the effect of, *Who the fuck is that?* The woman fires back with curt answers, clearly vague in nature. Her responses are met with scowls, but there's some kind of underlying solidarity here. The exchanges feel like familial bickering, not interrogation.

Logan wonders if he hallucinated her accent.

The children keep throwing confused glances back at him.

She leads them to the western edge of the hillside, where the plateau overlooks lush countryside. Undulating emerald hills roll endlessly away, unspooling into a blurred horizon. You could slap the sunset on a postcard, swirling orange disappearing into deeper blue.

It's hard to believe Logan just killed two men.

Blood, sweat and death, then, minutes later, the best view he's seen in years, brilliant dusk encasing verdant valleys.

The woman ushers the children into a brightly painted house on the outskirts of the village, a far cry from the Spanish architecture of the whitewashed homes. The one-storey dwelling is pale blue, maybe fifty years old, and its occupants seem to have uniformly disregarded upkeep over the years; the structure looks close to collapse.

The woman beckons Logan in after them.

In a gloomy hallway, she points the children toward a descending staircase and says, '*Vayan abajo.*' They follow her instructions with militant obedience, disappearing downstairs in seconds.

Once they're alone, Logan says, 'They're yours?'

She turns and regards him. She doesn't answer. He makes to change topic, but a sudden bout of dizziness forces him to reach out and plant his palm against the wall to hold himself upright. He tries to play it off—he's not sure why—but she sees right through him and says, 'Come. Sit.'

She leads him into a small room. A small window looks out over the sea of hills. Tattered cushions cover a wooden nook large enough for him to stretch out on. He lowers himself down to a seated position and alternates his gaze between the view and the green-eyed woman. Two magnificent sights, but he can hardly appreciate beauty in his current state.

'Who were those two men?' he asks, concreted by fatigue.

She lifts a first-aid kit off a table. 'Clan del Golfo.'

He can translate that much. 'Gulf Clan?'

She nods as she moves to him.

'The gulf's up north,' he says. 'What are they doing all the way down here?'

She crouches, shining a small light in his eyes. 'They are pushing towards the Micay River, deeper inside this department. They would very much like to secure that corridor. Towns like Argelia, El Tambo. Very important for them.'

'Why?'

'It is a trafficking route to the Pacific.'

Logan wishes he was better versed on the peripheral players in the Colombian conflict. 'What's Clan del Golfo? A rebel group?'

'Drug cartel,' she says quietly. 'Biggest in the country.'

'What's that mean?'

Her face says, *Seriously?*

'I know what a cartel is,' he says. 'What's it mean for *me*?'

She exhales. 'It means you are in big trouble.'

He settles deeper into the nook. 'I'm already in trouble.'

'What is your name?'

'Logan.'

She touches her own chest. 'Bella.' She tucks the flashlight away. 'You do not seem concussed. Does anything feel broken?'

'No.'

'Are you sure?'

'I'd know.'

She cocks her head. 'Where have you come from?'

'Bogotá.' When she gives him a strange, probing look, he says, 'Patio Bonito.'

No need to hide what he's done. Better she hates him for what he is than mistake him for something he isn't.

Her eyes widen, as green as the landscape outside.

She grips his wrist. 'Who were they?' She squeezes. 'Who did you kill? The news is not saying, and the photos have blurred the bodies.'

'Why's it matter?'

She makes a sweeping gesture. 'It affects . . . everything.'

He points to his own bicep. 'They had mauve patches on their arms.'

Cold quiet. Then she says, 'Fuck.'

'That's bad?'

'For you, yes.'

'Only for me?'

She shrugs. 'For the conflict, not so bad. Most do not yet know who those men are. They are . . . subtle. They wage a quiet war. They pretend to be dissidents of FARC, just another one of the Mafia cells who refused to lay down their weapons after the peace agreement. Only a few of us know the truth.'

'Which is?'

Her tone is sad as she says, 'They are not rebels. They work for the Serranos.' She sighs. 'And you are American.'

He looks at her, not comprehending.

'If you are American, the Serranos will never stop hunting you.'

She seems to expect the revelation to destroy him. But he's felt hunted for as long as he can remember. 'Why do they hate Americans?' he asks.

She doesn't answer, just gives him a strange look. *You haven't heard?*

He doesn't prod further. He's just grateful she knows things. And she didn't seem reluctant to bring him back here, so it must be safe for now. After the day he's had, he wants nothing more than to turn his mind away from thoughts of fighting, survival, never-ending war.

Answers can wait.

He switches tracks. 'How'd you end up here?'

It takes her a second to process the question. 'Did you just hear me?'

'I heard you. Don't worry. I'll be gone tomorrow. I won't endanger you. Just . . .' He swallows, suddenly emotional. 'Just talk to me. Please. I need someone to talk to.'

She must be debating whether to open up to a madman. He can see in her eyes what she thinks: that he should be fleeing, cowering, but he's here and he wants to know about *her*?

We all need a taste of normal, no matter our plight.

She indulges him. 'This place is not what it looks like.'

'The village?'

'It seems idyllic, yes? The elderly out on their terraces, the nice views. Sometimes a tourist even wanders through, and they never suspect a thing.' She gives him a pointed look. 'A real tourist, I mean.'

'Is that what you were? Once upon a time?'

'No. I am a volunteer.' She inhales, long-buried secrets finally resurfacing. 'I *was* a volunteer. With COOPI.'

He cocks his head.

Quietly, she says, 'Cooperazione Internazionale. An Italian NGO. We were working here in education outreach, but we weren't staying long. Problem was, I bonded with some of the children. So I made a rash decision. I quit. "Voluntary non-renewal." I took surplus food and educational materials and came back here on my own.'

He hesitates. 'Your colleagues didn't care?'

She shrugs. 'The turnover in humanitarian organisations is brutal. New staff come in, old staff disappear. I'm sure I was forgotten as soon as I left.'

'And then . . .?'

She stares into space for a while, as if only now formulating the story.

Once she begins her tale, it's like the floodgates open.

'Everyone in this village, and in all the surrounding towns . . . we are now confined. It started six months ago, when Clan del Golfo first came down from Antioquia up north. I knew they would. Everyone wants to move drugs, guns, precursor chemicals to the Pacific. The money is everything. The cartel wants that trafficking corridor I mentioned, but the rebels have a tight grip on it, on all of Cauca. So the cartel is watching and learning. Studying how the rebels control the population.

'The rebels execute social leaders and activists, so Clan del Golfo now does the same. The rebels confine rural towns so they can move their product undisturbed, and the cartel now does the same. This here . . . this is their trial run. They are testing their ability to confine communities before they take over the Micay River corridor and get the real money flowing.

'After leaving COOPI, I was here for two months on my own before they trapped everyone. I planned a year of aid work in southern Colombia. I guess that makes me eight months in.' A small smile, forlorn. 'I sensed the change before I knew for sure. The villagers, it was like they were resigned to it from day one. Like they always knew something was going to happen, one way or the other. The cartel soldiers started showing up, waving guns around, telling us, "No one leaves this place, not unless we say so." They make drawings on maps, give us the borders of our new world. No one protested. No one said a fucking thing. And even still . . .'

Her eyes grow wet as she remembers.

'They kill so many,' she whispers. '*So* many. To show they are serious. Some of these executions . . . public. In front of their children. You couldn't imagine. That is why . . .' She can't finish.

He waits.

When she collects herself, she says, 'That is why I stayed. I could have gone, believe me. When they first confined these people, I could have told them I was European, a volunteer. They do not fuck with foreign hostages. None of the armed groups do. They would have let me walk. But I see these kids abandoned, their parents slaughtered, and the villagers cannot spare a single peso to care for them, the resources are just not there, the money is gone, the cartel has this whole area in a chokehold, and I realise all of my training is to care for displaced children of forgotten crises, and I just know that I am the only . . .' She's crying now.

He has to suppress tears of his own.

'My father is Italian,' she says, her voice tiny. 'My mother, Dominican. So I'm dark enough. You can see this. I look like a local. My languages are excellent. I have not just English, but Spanish, so I made the decision and—'

'You stayed.'

She nods. 'I do not know what I am doing anymore. But I am needed. That is all that matters.'

Logan glances back at the entranceway, and the staircase descending beneath the house. 'Those kids?'

She takes his wrist again. 'Come.'

She leads him downstairs.

—

Logan isn't prepared for what he finds downstairs.

He touches down on the basement floor, pivots slowly around the corner, and emotion roils up through him as his heart cracks.

There are six of them, ranging from roughly five to eleven years old. Two boys, four girls. Not a shred of excess fat on any of their frames, their thin profiles shrunken in the weak light.

Small beds form parallel rows of three against each basement wall. One of the boys reclines on his mattress, head rested on a yellowed pillow, playing an old GameBoy, and the other sits cross-legged on the dusty concrete floor, in a small circle with the four girls. Their heads bow in concentration as they fixate on a board game: Mouse Trap. Its colourful pieces are faded with age.

Logan stands frozen beside the stairs, providing just enough room for Bella to descend the steps and pull up beside him. She stands close to his hip so they can speak without the children hearing.

'They have nothing,' she whispers. 'Not like I have anything, but . . .' She shakes her head. 'I can care for them.'

He juts his chin at the children, a couple of whom stare at him. 'Any of them speak English?'

'No.' She still keeps her voice down. 'Habit.'

'What, you need to hide them down here?'

She shakes her head. 'The cartel do not care who lives where. They only care if we leave.'

'The other villagers . . .'

She eyes him. 'What?'

'They can't help?'

She sighs. 'These are the children of most of the working-age adults in this village. The cartel targeted their parents deliberately—executed the people most likely to be able to resist. The villagers who remain are mostly older. You saw. And they might seem complacent, but inside they are scared. They have lived hard lives. They have little motivation left. They do not have the capacity to care for young children they do not know. It is a tough thing, you see . . . you must take on all their pain, the trauma of what they have seen.'

The boy on the floor turns the crank on the board, and the little plastic cage falls on the red mouse. The girls remain expressionless, hollow-eyed.

'It takes a certain understanding,' Bella goes on. 'It takes time to learn. I have done training before I came to Colombia. So I know not to take it personally when they lash out. So the villagers, they give me a little money to provide for these children. And I am the one who helps them. Because I am able.'

'You haven't alerted the European Commission or anything like that?'

'I do not trust them.'

He hesitates. 'I don't think the cartel has infiltrated the European Commission . . .'

'No, no.' She waves a hand. 'Not like this. I do not think they are evil. I think they are incompetent.'

'That can be the same thing.'

'They are not useless. They do much good. But . . . they are politicians. At the end of the day, they will, what is the expression? Swing their dicks?' She feigns an authoritative tone: '"Release our volunteer this instant or we will do this, this, and this." It makes them look good on the world stage, makes them look strong. But by the time their little show is over, everyone in this village will be dead. The cartel will execute us all, drive one valley over, throw their hands in the air and say, "That was not us. That was another group." You see?' A moment of quiet. 'Maybe the Commission will handle it better than I think they will, but I do not trust that they will. So I stay.'

They face the children as they converse in hushed tones; now Logan turns to her for the first time since they went downstairs. 'You're very brave.'

'I do not think that way. I do not make it a story.'

'What do you mean?' he asks, although he thinks he knows.

'We always make things so dramatic,' she says. 'We need a story to tell ourselves, you see? Obstacles to overcome. But if I think of all the obstacles in front of me here, I will go insane. So I do not go down that road. I do not treat this as some great burden. I just see there are things that need doing, and I do them.'

He doesn't respond. His old handler's words ring in his ears, uttered in a windswept lot in Long Beach. The last time Logan ever saw Thoreau. 'You lose your identity,' the man said, 'you function perfectly. Trust me.'

The silence forces her to turn to him. 'What?'

'It, uh . . . it's rare to meet someone who shares your worldview.'

He expects her to scoff. He could hardly blame her for despising violent men. Instead, she scours him with her gaze and says, 'Will you tell me how your worldview led you here?'

He glances at the children. 'Yes. Upstairs.'

'It's okay. They hear you, but they do not understand.'

'I know.' He hunches closer to her ear, lowers his voice to a mutter. 'But two of them saw what I just did . . .'

She doesn't flinch. 'They did not see the messy part. And they are old enough to understand why you did it.'

He knows that those raised in dire circumstances often have a different perspective of reality. His career enlightened him to the fact that our experience in the world is malleable, unfixed. Maybe after some deep introspection he'll be able to accept that he may not have scarred two of these kids for life, but here? Now? Impossible. He can't process it.

He shakes his head, the only way to communicate that he feels like a monster. 'I think I've been down here long enough. I'm sorry.' His head bows. Inner frustration spills out. 'I can't do what you do. I'm not strong enough.'

Staring at his feet, he blinks in surprise as she places her hand on his stomach. Her touch is soft as she rests her palm against his abdominal wall.

'You should not sell yourself short,' she whispers. She takes her hand away. 'There is a bathroom upstairs if you want to wash up. There are towels under the sink.'

He nods.

She juts her chin at the children. 'I will be up soon,' she says, implying some kind of evening ritual, time spent settling the kids down.

He takes his cue and heads upstairs, moving carefully so as not to cramp exhausted muscles. He takes a final look back into the basement as he ascends, catching the upturned face of the little girl who was with Bella in town, who saw him tackle two men into a shed, who must have heard the grunting and struggling, the death rattles. The girl stares glassily at him.

She reminds him of a confused puppy, unable to fathom what it did to deserve the wrath of an abusive owner.

He holds it together long enough to make it to the top of the staircase. Then he lurches down the corridor into the small bathroom, locks the door behind him, and slides down the wall to the tiles beneath, puts his head in his hands and cries.

20

Logan lets it all out. He never believed in bottling emotion—he saw where that got his father.

When his reserves of tears are exhausted, he drags the back of his hand over his eyes and clambers to his feet. The shower is old, the piping worn, the water pressure terrible, but he can still shed himself of the day's blood, sweat, and dirt. The weak jet of water unclogs his pores, washing away the full-body layer of grime. He wrings his clothes out under the stream, too, giving them a passable wash, then hangs his tee, cargos, underwear and socks over the shower door. He finds a coarse white towel in the cupboard under the sink. The mottled bruising across his musculature whines in protest as he pats himself dry, but it's bearable. He wraps the towel around his waist, pads to the door, and inches it open.

He freezes.

He expected the same hallway. Instead, he finds a windowless bedroom lit softly by a lamp on a nightstand. For a moment he fears he's losing his mind, succumbing to concussion symptoms Bella must have overlooked, but when he looks back over his shoulder, he realises he just got disoriented. There are two ways into the bathroom; the door he entered through rests on the opposite side. It's an ensuite.

He makes to double back when a silhouette steps into the bedroom, gliding in from the hallway. Bella sees him and says, 'Come in.'

He doesn't move.

'Come in,' she says again, inching the main door closed behind her.

His limbs take on a life of their own, and he complies. She stares at his bare torso the way everyone does, somewhat disbelieving that people actually look like that outside of bodybuilding magazine covers. The lamp casts long shadows, deepening contours, and he can sense all of her beneath the baggy clothing. Against the chestnut skin, her eyes almost sparkle. She rounds the bed slowly.

'The kids?' he asks her.

'Watching a movie.'

'You wanted to know how I ended up here . . .'

'That can wait, Logan.'

After what happened with Camilla, he doubts his own desires, but that doesn't stop him. She's the first to reach for him, and he responds the way he knows she wants. As her fingertips brush the fold in the towel, he pulls her to him, lowers his lips to hers. He drags his fingers slowly down the base of her neck. It turns her ravenous, and from the hot rush that flows up through him, he senses the same hunger in himself.

They both understand what this is: refuge. A different kind of passion to how it was last year with Camilla. Of course there are heightened emotions here, too, outside factors that drew them so quickly to one another, but fear is a very different sensation to inebriation. The former heightens your reality while the latter obfuscates. Sobriety lends him the clarity to see this is right.

So right.

Her stomach's warm as it presses against his, her tongue probing at his neck. His exhale is uncontrollable, drawing a soft laugh from her, and she meets his gaze and presses her forehead to his.

It's been a long time. He forgot how good it can be with the right person.

Before they can sprawl back to the bed, someone knocks on the door.

Bella swallows hard and takes a silent step back away from him. He adjusts his towel without making a sound. She inches the door open a crack, keeping him well out of the line of sight, and he hears low muttering between her and one of the children. He takes a seat on the edge of the mattress as she whispers some kind of promise to the child outside. Then comes the soft pattering of small footsteps moving away.

Bella clicks the door shut and turns back to Logan. Her small smile is a touch forlorn.

'Not the right time,' he says.

She shakes her head. 'I'm afraid not.'

Lowering herself down to sit beside him on the bedspread, she traces a finger down the bruising on his chest. 'Some of the children have nightmares.'

He looks at her. 'You need to be with them?'

'I spend most nights down there. Is that okay?'

'What's one more night sleeping alone?' He adds a smirk to betray his lack of concern.

Her fingertip goes still at the base of his pectorals. 'Still planning to leave in the morning?'

The external world comes flooding back in. Reminded of his situation, he tenses up. 'I have to. There's this roadblock at the bottom of the hill—'

'That marks the border of my world. That's their perimeter. Only supplies come in. No one goes out.'

'The cartel scared off the men hunting me. But if what you said is true, they'll be back. I won't endanger this village.'

She senses the unspoken questions in his statement. Her expression deepens as she grows sombre. 'I do not know as much as you might think. I misled you before, acting like I had answers. I already told you most of what I know. I have heard the name "Serrano". I know they are husband and wife, an older couple. Their forces wear mauve patches. The rumour is, when they were children, the man who butchered their families had a scar the same colour.'

'Jesus.'

'They hate Americans. I do not know why. It is folklore now. Myth. Their fury toward your country is unmatched across all Colombia. Which is saying something. They lie low still, but they will grow and grow until they consume every armed group in the country. Then . . . I don't know their plans. That is as far as the legend extends.'

He stays quiet, thinking.

'What did you do,' she whispers, 'to make them your enemies?'

'I don't know.' She offers a plain look. He doesn't know what to say to convince her, so he doesn't try. 'I just know I need to stop this.'

'How?'

He shakes his head, at a loss. But deep down, he knows. They want a war, he can give them a slow one. Go to ground, sink into the anonymity of rural life, move from town to town like a ghost, employ every guerrilla warfare tactic he ever accumulated in his storied career. Hunt the hunters, pick them off one by one, establish a myth of his own. Sow the seeds of doubt in their regime, so they're always looking over their shoulder, fearing the long-haired brute who has come for so many of them before dissipating back into the jungle.

He's got a fair shot of success if he plays it that way, but an it's inconceivable commitment. He would be in-country for months. What's worse, he would reduce himself to a primal state. He'd become what he always feared he would.

As he envisions this road, she seems to sense his capabilities, the nature of what he's considering. She says, 'There is something I can tell you.'

'Oh?'

'But I do not want to.' Her face is soft in the lowlight.

'Why not?'

She takes a shallow breath. Composing herself, perhaps, before she bares what she feels. 'I would very much like to see you again,' she says. 'I do not often meet someone who . . . you understand things I did not think men were capable of understanding. So I am reluctant to share what I know. Because I like you, and I think you will use this information, and you will die, and then I will not see you again.'

He shrugs. 'I'll die anyway.'

She looks forlorn as she says, 'I know where the Serranos live.'

He sits up a little.

'Just the area,' she explains. 'Tierradentro. It is a national park, west of here, in a valley. Far from civilisation. There are archaeological sites there. Underground tombs, ancient ruins. Anyway, word is they have a compound overlooking the valley.'

'How far west?'

'Not far. Seventy kilometres, maybe.'

Now his blood hums. He convinced himself he was obeying a baser instinct as he barrelled south all day, when he could have fled Bogotá in any direction. Turns out he was beelining toward the enemy all along.

'Do you know where—'

'No,' she interrupts. 'I was only told the general region. I am sorry. It might not help.'

He hesitates. 'Who told you?'

'It does not matter.'

'Tell me.'

A look passes over her, like, *Okay, you asked.* 'When we were first confined, one of the soldiers tried to take me. I knew it would happen. This is the way it has always been in wartime. So I was prepared. Instead of resisting, the way he might have liked, I kissed him. Then I acted frustrated. He asked what was wrong. I convinced him I was diseased. I sold it like I was doing him a favour by letting him know. And he believed me. He was grateful. So grateful that he answered my questions about the conflict. He shared gossip from the rumour mill.

'Clan del Golfo had recently learned of these new players, the Serranos—the cartel was very concerned by rumblings of Serrano spies embedded in rival groups. So that is how I know. I was told by the man who was going to rape me. But he didn't, and no one has touched me since, even though I know they salivate over me. Word must have gone around that I was infectious. For that, I am grateful.' Her lips seal. 'It could always be worse. Always.'

He doesn't respond, which she takes as concern. She manages a small smile, inches her body closer to his. 'This was a lie, you understand. About the disease.'

He strokes her arm. Strong, with thin muscle. 'You just soldier on. Despite it all.'

She blinks. 'Of course.'

'You live by what you believe.'

'Of course,' she says again.

'Sorry.' He snaps himself from his open admiration. 'I'm so accustomed to bullshit.'

'This is the way the world has always been. Everyone bullshits. Pretends they are more than they are.' Her lips brush his cheek, a soft peck, her palm cupping his jaw. 'This is what makes us different, you see? We know our flaws.'

He turns his face to hers and kisses her long and slow. Into her mouth, he murmurs, 'I don't see any.'

'Stop.' She rolls her eyes, but her blush is unmistakable. Then her face hardens. 'In the morning, go east out of town. There is a small dirt flat, a little lower down the eastern hillside. The men you killed before . . . their car is there. Did you find keys on one of their bodies?'

'No.'

'Then go back to the shed in the morning. They will be in a pocket somewhere.'

He pauses. 'Thank you. For everything.'

'Get some sleep. And help yourself to what is in the fridge. There is leftover *sudado de pollo*. Take it with you if you need.' She levers off the bed and takes one last chance to gaze down at him. 'If our paths cross again . . .'

'I hope they do.'

She flashes a smile.

'I never told you my story,' he remembers suddenly.

'I do not need your story, Logan. I can tell who you are.'

She slips out and he settles back against the thin pillow. His head is spinning, and not just from fatigue.

But within moments the exhaustion takes hold, and a deep slumber encroaches before he can process the whirlwind his life has become.

—

Domingo Nuñez lurches down off the porch, snatches the half-finished bottle from where he left it on the bottom step, and staggers out into the dark of the evening.

The aguardiente heats his veins, makes his head sway like the town's church bell, but that doesn't stop him. His disgust is a physical thing. It's not like Yolanda suddenly aged another decade, but lying in bed with her, a moment of clarity wormed its way through the fog of booze and struck him fully. All at once, he could no longer ignore the fact she was seventy-two years old.

Obviously, he knew that last month, when his sexual frustrations reached a fever pitch and he took the old villager as his concubine, but the firewater he swigs before barging into her home has done an exceptional job of suppressing the reality of what he's reduced himself to. The drink is a necessity: he must numb himself to the sight of her lying there underneath him, wrinkled, expressionless, unresponsive. She always stares vacantly over his left shoulder, enduring what he puts her through, aware of what would happen if she were to protest.

Tonight she rolled away from him after he was done, and it was the sight of the sags of skin across her back that precipitated his spiral into self-hatred.

As the night blankets him, he pours more aguardiente down his throat. The town lies silent, its residents squirrelled away behind closed doors. Clan del Golfo has never needed to enforce the curfew. Their word is law, and the sheep obey. So fucking simple.

Humanity was designed to be told what to do. Very few are equipped for independent thought.

Frankly, Domingo has no idea what command is still waiting for. He understands their hesitance to attempt the takeover of Cauca without being certain of victory, but how much more certain can they get? All this shit clearly works. They don't need more trial runs. You confine villagers and they become servants, you execute the loudest activists and the rest scurry away like rats, abandoning their empty beliefs. Controlling a population is the easiest thing in the world.

Domingo's been in this miserable village for six goddamn months, 'testing the compliance' of townspeople who were subservient on day one. And the only beautiful woman in the village is rotten, so he's left with Yolanda.

Pathetic.

So he drinks, swigging from the bottle as he stumbles down the empty main road. He wheels down a laneway to take a piss and reaches out in the dark, placing one hand against a solid wall. By staring at his feet to undo his fly, he sways forward uncontrollably. To prevent falling forward headfirst, he pushes off the stone. Too hard. Drunker than he thought, he careens back, his balance lost, and he staggers a few steps before slamming hard into the tin wall on the opposite side of the laneway—a crash like a cymbal as the shed rattles.

He slumps to a seat, head lolling. *Moron.*

Then a door hits the ground next to him.

He stares at it for a moment, its outline silhouetted by weak moonlight. *Huh.* He works his phone free from the pocket of his khakis and fires up the flashlight. The beam illuminates broken hinges. *Did I do that?*

Unlikely.

He clambers back to his feet and steps into the open doorway. Shines the light inside the shed.

The bodies are fresh.

He stares at his bloodied comrades a moment. Even with their faces twisted in death, he recognises them both. He knows them well.

Vicente. Mario.

Hands shaking, he backs up a step, thinking hard. Then he squats wordlessly and heaves the door back upright, against the frame, the way someone else left it. He kills his flashlight, unlocks the phone, and makes a call.

He prays he's doing the right thing.

—

Sonia hears the hyperventilating.

The sound floats in through the gap between a pair of massive glass doors. She screeches to a halt, listens a moment. She allows herself a sigh of irritation. Fear is so unattractive, so unbecoming, but she made a promise to care for Gabriel, whether the flame of passion is extinguished or not.

Above all, she's a woman of her word.

She's hurting, too, but she always had the steadier nerve. She composes herself with an inhale before wheeling out onto one of the largest balconies in all of Colombia. The deck runs the width of the second floor, nearly two hundred feet in total, with a low pebble-studded wall in place of an ordinary railing. Dotted along the vast expanse are clusters of furniture geared towards either lounging or dining, along with a full-fledged outdoor kitchen. At this hour, the view is obscured by a sheet of darkness, but the sunrise will reveal scenery that defies belief, the valleys of

Tierradentro so green they appear to glow in daylight. Far below this hillside compound lie over a hundred hypogea, subterranean tombs constructed more than a thousand years ago by a pre-Hispanic society.

Sonia always found comfort in the daily reminder that her existence is a mere blink in the cosmos. Entire civilisations have come and gone—what happened to her as a child means nothing in the grand scheme of things.

Gabriel just ignores his trauma until it comes out like this.

She finds him hunched in a wicker chair, staring out at the wall of darkness, sucking wind like an asthmatic. His wide eyes stream tears, his pupils like black saucers. The salt-and-pepper dusting along his jaw wavers as his lower lip wobbles. Every dozen breaths or so, he moans like a dying animal.

She crouches beside the chair. 'Hey.'

'Uhhh,' he moans.

She knows what he's thinking about. She remembers, too: the machete sawing at the back of the head, the brains spilling into the mud. She knows it's not a competition, but it was worse for her. At least Gabriel's *papá* was facedown. Moments later, she watched the life go from her own father's eyes, his lips flapping as he was decapitated.

She reaches up and grips the back of her husband's neck with considerable strength. 'It's not happening again. It *can't* happen again.'

'Thirteen,' he breathes, barely a whisper. 'Thirteen dead. And now the Gulf Clan protecting him . . .'

She tuts. 'No, no. Enough of that. We don't know that yet.'

'What else could it have been? The cartel let him through. They are sheltering him. Because he is our enemy.'

'You think the cartel would *ever* help an American?'

His breathing quickens again, every few breaths interspersed by a guttural sob. She holds him. The only thing to do is wait it out.

They market themselves as a power couple only because every criminal in Colombia would laugh with derision if they knew the truth. No one in this country has the stomach to digest the idea of a sole queen, a modern-day Cleopatra. That comes later, after she's proven herself, once they have no choice but to accept her.

For now, Gabriel Serrano is the rising underworld kingpin, she his doting wife.

Her face is hard as stone as she holds her weeping husband.

One of her work phones shrills in a pocket; she keeps her hand on the nape of Gabriel's neck as she fishes it out with the other.

Domingo Nuñez, the screen reads.

She rifles through the mental list of her spies until she remembers him. She recalls his location: sixty-five kilometres to the east, some colonial hillside town, right near—

Oh.

She releases Gabriel, rises, and walks to the low wall, resting her elbows on its pebbled top. Overlooking the black night, she answers with a purr. 'Yes, darling?'

'You know what happened earlier?' Domingo slurs his words. He's a slave to the drink, but he's still useful.

'Of course,' she says. 'I was going to call in the morning, ask again for your assistance.'

'Yeah, well, two of our men are dead.'

Another rush in her brain; the only thing she lives for. 'Where? That shithole you're confining? Up in the hills?'

'Yes.'

She chews a dry lower lip. 'And you called me. Instead of your command.'

'Fuck the Gulf Clan. They don't know what they're doing. I can't spend another night in this fucking place.' A shaky breath. 'Can I help you, Sonia?'

Calculations unspool across the canvas of her vision, probabilities playing across the dark void. She thinks for ten seconds. Then she makes the decision. 'Yes, darling. Yes, you can. Any idea where the American might be sheltering up there?'

'Not a clue. He could be anywhere in town.'

'Then it all needs to burn. We're accelerating the timeline. Remember that little idea I floated to you last month?'

She hears him swallow his fear. 'I know I bitched out. But . . . things change.' A long pause. 'I'm on board now. I want to help. I'm yours. Are we doing it?'

'Yes. Same plan.' Excitement swells in her.

'When?'

She checks her watch, then turns and looks at her husband. A thick string of saliva dangles from Gabriel's lips, his head bowed.

If they're doing this, they need to put out a video statement through the underground channels, assert total authority.

Sonia sighs. She needs time to clean up the star of the show.

'Dawn. Pass it down the line.'

—

Domingo kills the call with Sonia and gets straight back on the horn.

A man answers sleepily. 'What?'

Domingo says. 'The Serrano men will return at first light.'

'And?'

'We're doing it. Hostile takeover.'

21

The red-eye from JFK deposits Alice in Bogotá predawn.

Disembarking into El Dorado Airport, merging with the throng, she fights disorientation.

The last time she left the country was eight years ago as a sixteen-year-old. It was an ill-fated family vacation to Cancún, most of which her mother spent loudly complaining about the weather or her lower back pain to anyone in earshot. Alice and her father's only reprieve from Carolyn's negativity were the times her mother drank. She always got loud when she boozed, so embarrassing to be around that Alice and her father would unconsciously shrink away. By the time the week drew to a close, it felt like half the population of Cancún despised Alice's mother. In the airport, on their way home, when Carolyn was in the bathroom, Jonathan turned to his daughter and finally said, 'I don't know how much longer I can do this.'

Three weeks later, he handed over divorce papers and bailed.

Alice never really blamed her dad. She even understood why he left his only child behind, knowing it would have been a hell of a custody battle. When her dad first reached out after fleeing to the other side of the country, Alice still answered his call. They spoke regularly through her final years of high school and her time at Harvard, but when she failed to land employment upon graduating and told her dad she was returning to Lexington, he grew distant.

By the time her mother drove her to the edge of madness and she fled with Ruby to New York, she hadn't spoken to Jonathan in months. She loves him, but hasn't felt the need to reach out to him again, not even now she's sober. He was never there for Alice the way he should have been.

She shakes herself free of the past as she shuffles through the airport with her tall hiking pack. Anxiety eats at her as she contemplates the unknowns that lie ahead, but she realises she can handle that. If she maintains this pressure on herself, keeps her foot on the gas, it feels like there's almost nothing she can't handle.

It's terrifying, but so what? She knows terror intimately. A harsh life can be a blessing as much as it is a curse.

Neurotic yet determined, she connects to the free WiFi and purchases an eSIM. Then she approaches the first taxi rank she sees: a sign reads IMPERIAL S.A.S. Her heart's in her throat, but she can keep going. She just puts one foot in front of the other. *Is this what Logan meant,* she thinks, *when he spoke of moving forward in spite of everything?*

She stops in front of a man in a creased shirt and says, 'Patio Bonito.'

He takes a long look at her. She might be imagining it, but he seems stupefied. 'No way,' he says in a thick accent, waving her away.

She reaches for her pocket. 'I have money.'

'No.'

'No?' She hazards a guess at what he might charge her and takes out double that estimate in Colombian pesos.

He stares at the cash, visibly flabbergasted. Then he throws his hands in the air before taking the money. 'Just no kill anyone, okay?' A snort. 'Americans . . .'

So Logan must have used the same service. It wouldn't have taken a rocket scientist to put the clues together; they drop a foreigner who resembles the Incredible Hulk in a dodgy neighbourhood, and the next morning thirteen rebels are dead. The man keeps a wary eye on her as he orders a driver around to collect her, but he seems trepidatious, not conspiratorial.

The driver himself seems oblivious, and next thing she knows, a white sedan is whisking her through Bogotá.

She stares out the window for the first stretch of the drive, absorbing differences both marked and subtle. Hard to believe she's here of her own volition, taking her fate in her own hands rather than being spun from one sensory impulse to the next. It will take some getting used to. After ten minutes of people-watching, her thoughts drift to the notifications she didn't have time to scan at the airport, and she hunches over her phone.

Seventeen missed calls from Carolyn Mason.

Her heart palpitates beneath her chest wall. The calls came one after the other in rapid succession, beginning roughly eight hours ago. All night, as Alice was thirty thousand feet in the sky, Carolyn rang and rang. Before that, the last time she tried to contact her daughter was two weeks after Alice first left for New York.

Fearing the worst, Alice calls back without hesitation. It rings for a long time; Carolyn answers just before voicemail kicks in.

Her mother's voice comes slurred, dripping with fatigue: 'Alice?'

'Mom? Are you okay? What's wrong?'

'Oh.' A sniff of congested mucus, a deep breath. 'Fine. M'fine.'

'Why did you call?' No response. 'Why did you call so many times, Mom?' Still no response. 'How much have you been drinking?'

'*What?*' There it is, such predictable anger. 'Nun'v'ya fucking business. M'alone now, you 'member? If I wanna drink, I'll have a fucking drink. I deserve 'at much.'

'You've been up all night?'

'Mmm.'

'Why?'

'Thinkin' bout . . . why I hit you.'

Alice tugs softly at her own hair, tears brimming behind her eyes. 'Yeah?'

'Mm-hmm. And I needa tell you sumfin . . .'

Despite all prior history, Alice allows a modicum of hope. An apology, perhaps? For the first time ever?

'I forgive you,' Carolyn murmurs. 'For . . . abandon me. Tha's what you needa know. S'not your fault. You make people so angry, Alice, so angry they wanna slap you upside the head, but s'not your fault. You dunno any better. You dunno whatchu put me through . . .'

Alice wants to scream down the phone. This bitch will never, *ever* understand what she is, what she does to people, but, somehow, Alice is able to catch herself and hang up instead.

She drops the phone in her lap and cries uncontrollably, lamenting herself for expecting anything different, hating herself for taking the bait.

No second arrow, she tells herself over and over again, a drum beat in her head. *Life fires the first arrow. Don't fire the second one yourself.*

Teetering on the edge, she manages not to spiral, but there are emotions to bare. She cries the whole rest of the drive, ignoring the driver's concerned glances in the rearview. By the time he pulls over in a narrow street lined with dilapidated buildings, she's got most of it out of her system. She wipes her red eyes with a sleeve and finally meets his eyes in the mirror.

'It okay,' he says. 'Bodies . . . no there now. You no see bad thing.'

She realises he's mistaken her for one of those 'extreme tourists' whose travels revolve around the dangerous and the macabre. He assumes she wanted to see the Patio Bonito crime scene everyone's been talking about, then had some kind of breakdown en route.

'Thank you,' she says as she exits the taxi. She composes herself with a deep breath before beelining for the street where the news sites said the massacre occurred. Her phone's GPS guides her, and she walks fast with her head down, ignoring the lurid stares of men.

She hears the crime scene before she spots it, a hum of concerned murmuring. Locals hover in doorways, arms crossed, muttering disapproving things. A middle-aged woman sits slumped in the dust, her head in her hands. Probably somebody's mother. A scattering of journalists float about, capturing footage of the aftermath for B-roll. Yellow police tape cordons the bar itself, a metal barricade fixed across the building's entrance. Cops in yellow high-vis jackets dot the perimeter, feigning busyness while investigators do the real work within.

Alice loiters on the corner of the intersection, surveying the scene, scanning faces. Eventually a policeman ambles up to her and fires a question in Spanish. She shakes her head. 'Only English. Sorry.'

'You tourist? Not good idea for you be here. You go somewhere else.'

'I'm just looking for—'

'You not hear me?'

She glimpses something in the mouth of a connecting street. Leaning around the cop's wide bulk, she hunts for a better angle, but he catches her by the arm. Fingers pinch her bicep.

'Please,' he insists, not kindly. 'Go. Now.'

She pretends to relent—'Okay, okay'—and he releases his grip. She steps all the way out to the left and spots a woman with a dark mane of hair. The smooth skin, the high cheekbones, she looks the same as she did in the photo attached to the article Logan stumbled upon—beautiful and haunted. The eyes are what seal the deal. They're unmistakable. Alice has never seen anything quite like the intensity of those blues.

It's definitely Camilla.

'There,' Alice says to the policeman. 'I know this woman. She's my friend. Can I go to her?'

He looks over his shoulder, searching for who she might be talking about, then seems to realise he doesn't give a shit. He shrugs and walks away.

Now the hard part.

Camilla must be eight or nine inches taller than Alice, but she seems so small in the street. She looks gaunt, shrunken. Deep black bags ring her eyes. Camilla watches the bar for a while in a trance, her throat rippling with emotion. She's aghast.

Finally, she turns into the sunrise and slinks away from the scene. Alice hitches her hiking pack a little higher up her shoulders and sets off after her.

No stopping this now.

She hustles to close the gap. The next street over, she catches up to Camilla and walks up behind her on the dusty sidewalk. Then she rounds to one side and matches Camilla's pace.

Doing her best to sound authoritative, Alice says, 'I need to find Logan.'

Camilla jolts hard, as though tased. She stares down at the tiny stranger who materialised beside her, but shock keeps her moving. She doesn't slow down. 'Who are you?'

'I need to know where he went.'

A sideways glance reveals Camilla's throat pulsing harder. She's barely holding it together.

'Who are you?!' Camilla demands, firmer this time. Any louder and she'll draw attention.

Alice suppresses a sigh. How does she explain? She ends up vocalising the feeling she's held all along, since that first night. 'He's family.'

Camilla's eyes widen. Suddenly she's openly weeping. '*Dios mío.* I am so sorry . . .'

'Don't apologise,' Alice says, maintaining her pace. 'Just help me find him.'

22

At the crack of dawn, Logan shakes the invisible rust off a body that feels like it solidified overnight.

Sleep allowed the healing process to begin, but he isn't sure that's a good thing.

As he creaks upright, he allows the wave of intrusive thoughts to crash. No matter how many positive mantras you recite, you can't escape the truth. He acknowledges that he is being hunted in a strange land; Colombia may mark his final resting place.

Then he gets up anyway.

Rage against the dying of the light.

The morning air is crisp and the house is still. His stomach growls as he pads through the silent house and into the kitchen. He finds a giant pot of chicken stew, the *sudado de pollo,* on the top shelf of the fridge.

Logan hopes Bella meant what she said about helping himself to food.

He dumps a mountain of cold stew in a faded ceramic bowl, fetches a spoon, and eats until his belly distends, another thousand-plus calories. It's only half the pot, and she told him to take the rest, but he pictures the sea of little faces downstairs and returns the leftovers to the fridge before taking a final look around.

He half-expects Bella to materialise like a vision at the top of the basement stairs, but nothing happens. Maybe it's better this way.

When he slips out into the mountainside chill, he sees tendrils of orange streak the horizon like leaping flames. Somewhere behind the town, the rhythmic *thud* of an axe gouging wood floats through the empty streets. Birds chirp staccato calls; an elaborate warble ripples between the sharp notes.

The village is a picture of tranquility. A drug cartel confines its poverty-stricken residents, yet a hedge-fund billionaire would pay an inordinate sum to simulate this kind of bliss.

Logan moves quickly off the unpaved street, producing his Five-seven only once he's out of sight from the house. Knees bent, he holds the pistol low and jogs in a half-crouch behind a long row of buildings on the outskirts of town, doubling back to the laneway where he first ran into Bella. He frowns as he pulls to a halt in front of the shed where he left the bodies.

Did the tin wall have that dent in it yesterday? He can't remember. At the time, his adrenaline was screaming.

He approaches the door itself. He knows he left it propped in the frame with its broken hinges resting precisely against the connecting brackets, but now it sits slightly off-centre, the wood of the door itself touching the brackets. The wind couldn't do that.

It's been repositioned.

Seeing no need for stealth anymore, he shoulders the door inward, sending it crashing to the dirt floor inside. As he expected, the bodies are right where he left them. No one would have bothered propping the door back up if they'd already carted the corpses out. So it probably wasn't the cartel who discovered the scene, but that hardly makes a difference.

He's blown.

Moving fast, he pats down the dead men, a more comprehensive search than yesterday evening's. Sure enough, a concealed inner pocket of one man's work shirt turns up a keyring sporting a fob emblazoned with the Honda logo.

He takes off running, out of the shed, down the length of the laneway, and out into the arterial main street. A few older locals stare at him as he barrels into view, but discretion no longer means anything. East, Bella said.

Automatic gunfire erupts down in the valley. Sounds like it's coming from the blockade.

His pulse thumping in time with the cracks of discharged bullets, he works his way up to a full-pelt sprint.

Here they are. Right on time.

Juan Blanco barks a warning. As the men around him stir, he takes a final suck on his cigarette and tosses it to the churned earth behind the jeep. Then he swings his legs over the edge of the hood and drops, one boot sole squashing the butt into the dirt. He takes position behind the reinforced vehicle, the window already down, setting his AK-47 on the lip of the door.

The convoy from yesterday has returned.

The pickup trucks rumble up the rural trail, illuminated by the beginnings of a brilliant sunrise. Six vehicles, same as last time, their hoods bouncing as suspensions tackle potholes. Sinister silhouettes behind dusty windshields.

'The fuck do they think they're doing?' Ignacio grumbles beside Juan, dropping into a firing position of his own. 'They couldn't win this last night. They can't win it this morning.'

The leader of their squad, Cesar, is the only man to saunter out in front of the three-jeep barricade. He pulls to a halt in the middle of the road, alone, his arms crossed in front of him. But his broad chest swells with confidence, assuaged by the knowledge that seven of his men aim Kalashnikov rifles past his stationary form, ready to open fire in the blink of an eye.

The convoy slows, the two trucks up front crawling to a halt about the same place they did last time.

Sweat beads across Juan's forehead. Drops slide through his thick eyebrows, pool in his eyes. He wipes the salty sting away with a shirt sleeve. Readjusts his grip on his rifle. The convoy sits there, engines idling.

Cesar screams, '*¡Vete a la mierda!*'

Fuck off.

Juan looks to the east.

Sunrise, Domingo said. *It's time.*

Juan swallows hard and pulls his trigger.

He blows the back of Cesar's head off, then wheels hard to the left and pumps a couple of rounds through the face of the soldier beside him. Ignacio was already half-turned towards him, jaw slack at the sight of their leader executed from behind. Juan's bullets go through his open mouth, shredding the top of his spine. He's dead before he hits the ground.

Juan tries to nail a third ally, but gunfire cracks right behind him, and hot numbness swallows him whole. One of his squad-mates shot him in the back, multiple times, and Juan thinks, *Oh, well.* He did what was asked of him. His grip on the Kalashnikov loosens and he topples forward into the dirt, his lips striking moist earth.

The taste of the bitter sludge is his last bodily sensation.

For you, Sonia. My queen.

—

Domingo crouches low behind a tree trunk and waits for the apocalyptic barrage to fade.

When it finally peters out, he steps out into view with his heart in his throat.

All rides on this.

He registers the scene before him and smiles.

A hundred feet down the road, Juan Blanco is facedown in the dirt, his back bloodied and torn, the life ripped from him. His sacrifice was not in vain. The rest of his squad lies decimated around him. On the other side of the blockade, Serrano shooters whoop battle cries as they survey the sea of the dead from behind open truck doors. A handful of victors run for the jeeps, hauling limp drivers out, clambering up onto bloody upholstery, twisting keys that were already sitting in ignitions, firing the vehicles to life. Then they're reversing the jeeps, turning hard, dismantling the barricade.

And suddenly the road is clear.

The pickups surge through the newly created gap, one by one, toward Domingo. He sees men leaning out windows, Kalashnikov barrels drifting toward him as he stands in the middle of the trail. His heart lurches. *A communication failure? Don't they know . . .?*

Then understanding crystallises in their eyes; they recognise him as Sonia's man. She warned them. As she said she would.

Thank you, Mamí.

Domingo beckons the convoy forward urgently. The townspeople just received the rudest of awakenings—the blitzkrieg must begin.

'Up there!' he screams above the roar of the engines. 'No mercy!'

Everyone will die, including the American. Then Sonia will give him the world.

He cackles uproariously as the pickups rocket past him, gunmetal protruding from open windows.

It's a murder party.

—

Logan picks up speed on the decline.

He pumps his arms like pistons as he fights through the burning in his quadriceps, the hill sloping gently away beneath him. The winding trail, lined with thick copses of vegetation, weaves into a man-made clearing hacked out of a small flat. The makeshift parking lot contains a handful of rust buckets belonging to the townspeople. The only car that looks functional is a Honda hatchback, maybe a decade old, its rear passenger window spiderwebbed with cracks and taped in place. The rest of the vehicles are relics rendered into scrap metal from disuse.

Logan stabs the key fob in his sweaty palm and lights blink on the Honda: unlocked.

Thank God.

When the next burst of gunfire crackles, it sounds closer, and he pivots hard in concern, Five-seven at the ready. Then he identifies why it sounded clearer: this lot has an unobstructed view of the southern face of the hillside, along with the rural road he ascended from last night. Jogging to the edge of the dirt flat, he squints down into the valley below.

His stomach drops.

The bodies draped across the jeeps are specks from this distance, but he can still make them out. He watches the blockade disintegrate, two of the jeeps reversing in line with the third to allow passage. The convoy of Serrano forces accelerates past the jeeps, and a man standing in the middle of the trail waves them on.

Logan watches in horror as the pickups speed past the beckoning traitor. They aren't slowing. They aren't being careful. They know he's somewhere in the village, so they'll raze the whole town to the ground.

Sweating in the sunrise, he turns back to the lot. At the far edge of the small clearing, the trail continues down the eastern side of the hill into dense woodland. Likely a dead end at some point, but he can still tear down the mountain in the old Honda, ditch the car when the trail runs out, vanish into the forest, and lose his pursuers for good. With such a sizeable head start, escape is all but guaranteed. He'll never know what happened to the residents of the town he fled. He can scrub their grim fate from his mind—blissful ignorance.

Yeah, right.

That's not him. Never has been.

He runs to the Honda, hurls the driver's door open, and sinks behind the wheel. The cabin reeks of dried sweat; salt stains paint the upholstery. He drives the key into the ignition and twists. The engine splutters to life.

Continuing down the hill is a retreat from responsibility, the coward's way out, so that's out of the equation, but what will he do once he ascends back into town? Take a last stand?

Nothing's changed since he veered off the highway last night. He's still one man against a small army. He pulled it off in a close-quarters urban environment in Bogotá, all tight corners and smoke and confusion, but out here in the hills? No shot. A tactical impossibility—he can't win.

But does he need to?

Before he can think it all the way through, he's gunning the Honda up the trail. The village materialises once more, porches now dotted with the stooped frames of the elderly, old men shouting to one another, a couple of women up on their tiptoes, trying to ascertain the source of the gunshots. Those who glimpse Logan behind the wheel of the hatchback as he speeds down the main street wear open scowls, furious glares. He doesn't blame them. They were confined before he showed up, but they had adjusted to this routine. The big foreigner threw their placid existences into chaos.

That's when the answer comes to him.

He braces himself as the main street falls away and the town recedes, replaced by the trail curving down the western slope of the hill toward the destroyed blockade. Seconds later, the first pickup truck screams into view, followed closely by its five accomplices. The same single-vehicle column winding its way up the hillside now set for a collision course with the Honda barrelling down the mountain.

Logan hesitates long enough for the driver of the first truck to spot him. Even through the dusty windshield, he sees the man grin. Logan feigns a look of unadulterated terror, his mouth agape, like he never expected to flee straight into the hands of his pursuers.

Sure enough, the head of the convoy senses weakness. He thrashes the pickup to its limits, accelerating up the incline, and swerves at the last second, aiming to sideswipe the hood of the old Honda with his reinforced truck bumper.

The moment he commits to the manoeuvre, Logan wipes the artificial fear off his face and hits the brakes with the composure of a rally car driver.

The driver realises he was baited, but it's too late to stop the pickup swerving hard into empty space and carrying onward, flying off the trail. The vehicle wraps itself around a tree trunk in an explosion of twisted metal.

Logan swears he sees a puff of red mist as he accelerates again. He only hit the brakes for half a second, and aided by the decline, he instantly regains momentum.

He knows he can't bait them five more times in a row. Doesn't matter. There's something else he can do.

The rest of the convoy just saw the occupants of the lead vehicle perish in grotesque and spectacular fashion, and reconsider their approach. So the pickups are slowing down, a couple turning hard, trying to form an improvised blockade. But they do it sloppily, and Logan spots a zigzagging route through the remaining vehicles.

Instead of slowing in the interest of precision, he accelerates, because rifle barrels are already taking aim, lining up, set to open fire, and there's not a hope in hell the Honda's bulletproof.

He goes now, or he never goes at all. It'll be a bumpy fucking ride.

Logan takes a breath and rockets past the first of five pickups, ignoring the glint of gunmetal in his peripheral vision. Gunfire roars and shots thud into the trunk as he stamps the brake and twists the wheel hard, bouncing off the side of the second truck. The chassis shudders, the engine shrieks; the driver's window explodes over him. He gets his foot on the accelerator again and swerves violently around the rear bed of the second pickup, revealing the third and fourth vehicles squashed together, grinding their hoods against one another in an effort to box him in. But they focused too hard on the trail itself, overlooking their peripheries, and a rough patch of forest floor beside the dirt road is wide enough for a hatchback to squeeze through.

Logan doesn't think, just drives, lurching off-road. The front tyres drop off the trail into churned earth and the Honda bounces so hard that the steering wheel almost drives up into

Logan's mouth. It would have knocked all his teeth out, shattered his jaw, maybe killed him, but he hasn't the time to think about what could have been; he's wrestling with all his might to keep the Honda from rolling and then he's past the third and fourth pickup.

Suddenly the fifth is skidding across the trail in front, a last-ditch effort to stop him, but he uses the advantage of the decline again and crushes the accelerator to the floor, bracing as hard as he can.

Bang.

The hood of the Honda basically explodes and the impact rattles Logan's bones in their sockets, but he hit the pickup right where he wanted, in one of its front wheels, and the truck slides just enough for the crippled hatchback to eke past.

Next thing he knows, all five vehicles are behind him and the road lies open ahead, his path unimpeded.

The Honda's on death's door, but he only needs to make it down to the open-topped jeeps, those beautiful, shiny pieces of machinery, and he knows he can get there despite the engine hissing and spluttering, and blood leaking from his mouth and nose, and the mother of all migraines drilling his head like a power tool to the brain stem.

No matter what, he must keep the remaining Serrano forces on his heels, lead them away from this place. By no means can they continue their climb into town.

So as he roars away from the convoy, he sticks his arm out the driver's window frame and thrusts his middle finger skyward.

23

Disbelief dulls Camilla's features.

'How can I help you?' she asks Alice, but her face tells another story.

Alice staves off imposter syndrome. For more than a year of her life, no one asked her a thing. People either ordered her around or told her to fuck off. She was a drain on the world, every street corner made worse by her trembling presence. And now this woman who was snatched off the street by an armed group not two days ago, this woman from the worst part of Bogotá, this woman with real problems outside of her own mind . . . wants to help her?

Alice doesn't try to understand it. She just rolls with it, mostly because she wouldn't know how to process reality if she slowed down.

She remembers her brief call with Logan before his signal cut out. *Camilla's boyfriend . . . I've made a serious mistake . . . honestly, I don't know what I've done . . .*

'Take me to your boyfriend,' she says.

Camilla frowns. 'What?'

'Your boyfriend,' Alice says again. 'Take me to him.'

Camilla swallows hard. 'Rubén?'

No idea, Alice thinks. Logan didn't get that far on the phone. But she doubts there are multiple partners in the mix, so she nods.

'He is not my boyfriend,' Camilla says, forceful.

'Huh?'

'I broke up with him. On the spot. The moment he told me what he did.'

Alice sighs. 'Your ex, then. Take me to him.'

Camilla hesitates.

Alice says, 'Now.'

Camilla relents with a nod.

Alice has never spoken like this in her life. She hasn't an inkling where she's drawing these powers of command from, but they're working.

Camilla leads her through Patio Bonito without protest, her chaperone, glaring at the men who consider approaching the petite foreign woman. Alice faces forward, eyes glued to the small of Camilla's back. She winds up fixated on the hypnotic sway of the woman's hips, the proportions of the hourglass physique beneath the rugged jeans.

Alice sees what the men see, what Logan must have seen. It doesn't sound like their reunion was a fruitful one. Maybe he finally discovered he'd been thinking with his genitals when he met Camilla all that time ago. Oh, well.

It usually takes years for those who have nothing in common with their lover to realise. Better to find out now than even later down the line.

Camilla wheels down a shadowed alley and turns immediately into a hole-in-the-wall bar, several blocks over from the site of the massacre. It's a mere nook—plastic tables, plastic chairs, like an oversized doll house with old liquor posters on the walls. A thin man in fake designer clothing, fortyish, sits alone at a table up the back, head bowed, hands kneading the back of his neck. There's no one else inside. A bundle of keys sit on the table in front of the guy, beside four empty bottles of beer. He must have special privileges to open the place up all for himself. Wispy hair overhangs a face swollen with purple bruising and maroon gashes.

Rubén, no doubt.

As they enter, Alice fears a trap, and she murmurs, 'He told you he was here?'

'No,' Camilla says. 'I just knew.'

'Does he speak English?'

'Enough. I was teaching him.'

Rubén lifts his head as they approach. The golf ball of swelling under one eyelid shifts as he registers Camilla. His broken face hangs in confusion as he processes the sight of her companion.

Alice steels herself. They must not see what she's really feeling. She must project nothing but competence.

Rubén cracks a fifth beer as Alice pulls out the plastic chair opposite and sits. Camilla looms over them both like a mediator.

'Who are you?' Rubén says, his accent strong but decipherable.

Alice sits straight-backed, hands folded in her lap. 'The man who just ruined your life is my family.'

Rubén goes a little pale beneath the swelling. Then he pulls himself together and jerks his thumb at Camilla. 'Does this fucking bitch need to be here?'

'For now.' Alice juts her chin at Camilla's form. 'Everything you told her, you tell me. Right now. Go.'

He hesitates a moment, but only a moment. Then the explanation comes in a torrent of broken English. He doesn't seem to be sure why he's telling her, but he can't stop himself. She hears about Camilla slipping out late at night to meet an old flame, Rubén's resulting hot-headed reaction, the subsequent beatdown and humiliation, followed by the impulsive call to a distant relative—a powerful second cousin.

'All those men who are dead,' Alice says. 'They're your cousin's forces?'

He nods.

'Who is she?'

He seems to harbour a primal terror surrounding anyone even vaguely associated with Logan Booth. It sufficiently loosens his lips. 'Her name is Sonia. She is, like . . . war lord. Down in Cauca. Very bad person.'

'Why would she bother getting involved?'

'She hates Americans.'

'Why?'

'Ask her. She never tell me.' He shakes his head. 'She never like me. Say I'm weak.'

Alice's blood hums. Ten minutes of conversation and she already learned more than she ever expected to. It strikes her that she can do things with this information. *Is this what momentum feels like?*

She turns to Camilla, deadpan. 'You knew Logan's physical capabilities. You told Rubén you'd snuck out to see him after you got home, but not that he was dangerous. You knew your boyfriend would go charging over there and get the shit beaten out of him. You *wanted* that to happen.'

Rubén answers for her. 'She already admit this. She was angry at herself. So she punish me for it. Impulse. I tell you, she is bitch.'

To her credit, Camilla stares blankly down at Alice, refusing to stoop to a battle of he-said, she-said.

Alice doesn't care. She's not their counsellor.

In the midst of the tension, she only sees a way through.

She summons her courage and hunches closer to Rubén. 'Listen to me. Are you close with Sonia?'

His disfigured face trembles. Painful regret in his eyes. He manages a small shake of the head. 'Not very.'

'And how many of her men did you just get killed?'

He doesn't answer.

'Thirteen,' she reminds him. 'Now, do you think your psycho warlord cousin is the forgiving type?'

Dead silence.

'I didn't think so,' she says. 'And you need to understand something.' She snaps her fingers. 'Look at me.'

He raises his gaze from the table's greasy plastic surface. He takes a long swig of the fifth beer.

She looks in his bloodshot eyes and says, 'Logan will kill so many more of her people. Probably already has, out there in the countryside. You have no idea, Rubén.'

She watches his face drain of colour.

'So I need something from you,' she says quietly, injecting command in her tone. 'Because, really, it's your only shot of not winding up dismembered in a barrel.'

He doesn't move a muscle.

She understands the situation now. She rushed here thinking Logan was waging an unnecessary war, when he's only been defending himself. By now, he's in far too deep. This isn't something he can just walk away from. The Serranos won't allow it.

So the Serranos need to go. Simple as that.

'I need you to tell me where Logan can find Sonia.'

Immediately, Rubén says, 'No.' He shakes his head with vigour, like, *Out of the question.*

She just sits there. Keeps staring.

As the seconds tick by, she watches his face start to twitch.

His facade begins to crack.

24

There's time to swerve.

Only a second or two, but still time.

Logan urges the battered Honda forward, relying more on gravity than what little horsepower remains in its spluttering engine. And no wonder; the hatchback just bounced like a pinball between those pickups. But the slope is steep, and it bottoms out at the deserted blockade where he knows he can switch rides.

He rounds a tight bend in the trail as the car rattles and shakes all around him, and the road straightens out to reveal the three jeeps lined up parallel, not three hundred feet ahead. Jackpot.

But there's an obstacle in the way.

The cartel enforcer who beckoned the Serrano convoy through, the traitor, stands in the middle of the trail, staring dumbly at the oncoming vehicular projectile.

Logan pictures men with rifles creeping into a house, descending stairs, finding half a dozen children curled up in terror in a damp basement.

There's time to swerve, but he doesn't. Logan only slams the brakes after the traitor goes under the wheels.

The hatchback shudders to a halt on a stretch of trail he knows will mark its final resting place, the chassis groaning all around him. Fluids splash to the dirt from severed pipes along the underbody as he levers out into cool morning air. Ignoring his body's protests, he runs for the jeeps. As expected, the men who dismantled the blockade took the keys with them, but they only needed to move two of the three vehicles to clear the path.

Beneath a blood-flecked dashboard, the third jeep has its key still embedded in the ignition.

Logan takes advantage of the open top and hardly slows as he approaches the jeep, just vaults over the driver's door. He comes down on a seat slick with blood, leans over to pop the opposite door, and shoves the dead man sitting in the passenger seat out into the dirt. He grabs the ring of keys and twists hard. There's no delay; a powerful engine roars to life.

He'll need every ounce of juice he can get.

Bella said seventy kilometres to Tierradentro, forty-odd miles. He only needs to stay ahead of his pursuers long enough to make it there, to coax them away from this place forever. And then what? *A compound overlooking the valley,* Bella told him. That could be anywhere, across, what, hundreds of square miles?

Doesn't matter. One insurmountable task at a time.

He reverses in a tight ninety-degree arc so the jeep is faced away from the mountains, and he's about to take off for the highway in a geyser of dirt when he checks the side mirror and sees no movement on the trail behind. No pickups bearing down on him.

He pivots hard in his seat, looks back. Adrenaline pumps at his temples.

Come on.

Nothing.

Come on.

If they gave up chasing him, that means they're still climbing toward the village. If so, he must go back. To his own detriment, he still believes in the archaic notion of duty. Nearly a dozen Serrano shooters are still alive, so he will fight and he will probably die. But he brought this to the town's doorstep, and if that's the way it has to go, so be it.

Come on, you motherfuckers.

A cacophony of roaring engines.

Pickup grilles explode into view.

Go.

He throws the jeep in drive and crushes the pedal to the floor.

Logan guns it to the highway, less than a mile away, with the convoy hot on his heels, then veers west as Bella instructed. He picks up as much speed as he can, pushing the jeep up to a hundred miles an hour. Wind roars over the top of the windshield and forms a miniature hurricane within the open-topped cabin.

When the highway starts winding, the turns intensifying, he doesn't slow.

One wrong twitch of the wheel and he's sealed in a metal coffin, but he can't have them on his heels when he comes screaming into the national park. A little breathing room is crucial, to determine his next move.

After fifteen miles of white-knuckled swerving, an old highway sign reads LA PLATA and he spots a large town ahead, a sea of buildings blanketing the countryside. As the jeep blazes toward the outskirts of the municipality, along a relatively straight section of road, he takes the opportunity to fish his phone out.

A single bar of reception.

Finally.

With his gaze flitting between the road and the phone screen, it must look like he's pumped up on stimulants. He punches *Tierradentro* letter by letter into the GPS app. It takes far too long to load, only presenting a route once there's nervous perspiration dripping down his face. It instructs a hard left turn onto a mountain road, Carretera 37, in—

Now.

If he blows past the turn-off, he'll lose the lead he's gained on his pursuers. So he just stomps the brakes, decelerating from a hundred miles an hour in a scream of burning rubber. The wheel almost tears itself out of his grasp as the tyres fight for traction on the old road. He uses every shred of forearm muscle to work it hard to the right, and the jeep skids maniacally into the mouth of the westward turn.

He avoids plummeting into a natural roadside ditch by inches. At this speed, even a shallow drop would have flipped the vehicle and dumped four thousand pounds atop fragile flesh and bone.

Shaking now, having looked death in the eye for a fleeting moment, he regains speed up the increasingly isolated route.

The views are soaring, but he pays the scenery no mind, fighting to keep the jeep on the twisting trail.

The occasional towns he passes are tiny mountain pueblos even smaller than Bella's village. The region's emptiness encroaches on him, along with an inescapable tightness in his chest.

The GPS is all that alerts him of his arrival in the Tierradentro National Park. The scenery is just as staggering as the last forty miles: lush green hills rising and falling like the surface of the ocean in a storm. Thanks to his recklessness, he made it in half the time his phone said it would take—and almost ten minutes ahead of his pursuers, judging by the distance between himself and the ominous dust plume several miles behind.

The only problem: he can't stop.

He expected a larger town to shelter in while he tried to locate the Serranos' compound, perhaps a municipality like La Plata, home to tens of thousands. But the hub of this national park consists only of a scattering of buildings. A handful of villagers stare at the paramilitary jeep as it rumbles into sight with a sweating, blood-soaked foreigner behind the wheel.

Logan makes eye contact with an old woman on a porch step, her ankles swollen and riddled with varicose veins. Her tired eyes say, *Take this elsewhere.*

He nods at her and leaves his foot off the brake. Carries right on through.

Heading westward with no destination, he finds he can't punch in a new GPS route without a cell signal. Tumbledown shacks riddle the unpaved, winding road as he inches further away from anything resembling civilisation. Increasingly desperate, he's of the mind to just drive in random directions in search of a gated compound.

Then, out of nowhere, the trail opens into a larger village, *almost* a town. A wooden signpost reads SAN ANDRÉS. There's a church, a few eateries, even a football field.

Logan slows to survey the small community, but he finds nothing of note. Certainly nowhere that could house warlords.

Hope dwindling, he drifts to the shoulder of the road and pulls the Five-seven from his waistband. He figures that's the extent of his arsenal until he takes a look over his shoulder for the first time since he commandeered the jeep.

The frayed hem of a waterproof backpack in the rear footwell catches his eye. It's unzipped, the two halves of its opening curled away from each other. Curious, he reaches back and expands the opening with two fingers. Sticks of sage green putty, at least a dozen, each carefully wrapped, rest atop a bed of connecting wires and blasting caps, all twisted like brambles. A wireless electronic detonator nestles in the thicket.

Logan's sufficiently experienced to recognise the tubes of hexogen and plasticiser for what they are: plastic explosive. Enough to level a small highland village.

A shudder grips him as he understands what the cartel would have done if they had got the 'confinement's over' order. They would have erased evidence they were ever there by erasing the pueblo itself. Perhaps the Serrano mutiny was the lesser of two evils.

Regardless, the contents of the pack are useless here. The assembly of any kind of practical device—explosive, blasting caps, a connected and functioning detonator—is an art, far more complicated than the simple press of a button.

Behind him, the dust plume that signals his pursuers wafts closer, a single conjoined eddy twirling skyward. No time to set a trap—either he shoots it out with them here or he keeps running. A crisp sun beats down on the back of his neck; his pulse thuds as the idling engine vibrates the jeep.

What does he think he's doing?

Where does he think he's going?

Ten on one on a rural mountain trail. He pulled it off in Bogotá through sheer ferocity, but it took almost all he could give. Maybe, *maybe*, he gets it done again, despite overwhelming odds, but then what? He'll still be on death's door—the Serranos are omnipotent, omnipresent, capable of haemorrhaging the Gulf Cartel from the inside. They'll just keep sending more men.

These facts present themselves to him objectively, without fanfare. Work with what reality is, not what you hope it would be.

Logan calmly pops his door. He steps out of the jeep, into the middle of the trail. Such a gorgeous view, southern Colombia sprawling out before him. He can savour it a moment.

Savour what's left of his life.

One hand clutches the hilt of his Five-seven, the other holds the smartphone. He takes a glance at the dusty screen and finds the GPS urging him back the way he came, given he overshot the programmed destination. He kills the route. To his mild surprise, he finds a single bar of reception remaining, dregs from a cell tower planted somewhere in the region. Maybe it helps being up this high.

He shrugs to himself. Doesn't make a difference.

This is an unwinnable war.

Then he feels a vibration in his palm. Convinced he's dreaming, he forces himself to look down. He's not. It's ringing. An unknown number, the country code Colombian.

He answers without a word.

'It's me,' says Alice.

Logan stifles the groan in his throat and closes his eyes. 'Shit, Alice.'

'What?'

He cracks his lids back open and stares at the approaching dust cloud. 'You haven't caught me at a great time.'

'Where are you?'

He can barely register her words. 'Listen, you need to understand—'

'*Where are you?*'

He's never heard her sound like that—unrelenting urgency. And all for nothing. 'You know where I am. Colombia.'

'*Where* in Colombia?'

Something compels him to force the nihilism aside and answer. 'Cauca Province, but look, I'm not going to make it—'

'*Yes*,' she spits like a one-syllable gunshot.

Confusion makes his head throb. The morning sun seems harsher now. He spots the silhouette of the first pickup truck bouncing up the trail in the distance.

He makes to impart his last words to her, but before he can start waxing philosophical, she says, 'You must be close. Write this down. Two-point-five-eight-eight—'

'Alice.'

'Yes?'

'What are you doing?'

'It's latitude. I'm giving you coordinates. Write them down.'

He can't stifle his sigh. 'Coordinates for what?'

'This is where Sonia and Gabriel Serrano live,' she says. 'You need to finish it. The same way you did with Datvyan. Okay?'

The world spins. All he can manage is, 'Wait, what—'

'*Write this down!*' she yells, cutting him off. 'Two-point-five-eight-eight-four . . .'

He has no pen, but he commits the numbers to memory, searing the numbers into his brain. When she's finished giving the coordinates, he remembers the country code of the incoming call. 'Wait, are you *here*?'

'I'm in Bogotá.'

His heart drops. Suddenly he's shouting. 'Alice, what the *fuck* are you doing?!'

'I thought I could come talk you out of your war, but I didn't realise you weren't the one who chose to wage it. So now I'm trying to help you finish it. Because that's the only way through. I'm not going anywhere without you.'

A thousand questions assault him. He selects one at random. 'How did you know where to go?'

'I found Camilla. She led me to Rubén Álvarez. He knows where his cousin lives, but he's not gonna be much more help. He visited once, almost a decade ago. All he knows is it's a big house in a high-walled compound. Guarded. I'm sorry, I wish I could give you more detail—'

He's reeling so hard he doesn't notice how much ground his pursuers have gained until it's too late.

The first pickup erupts into his vision—and he's standing in the middle of the road.

He cuts Alice off by shouting, 'I'll call back,' and hangs up as he dives into the jeep. He gets one hand on the wheel, throws the vehicle into drive, and takes off into San Andrés.

Rifle rounds crack and a bullet thuds into the rear bumper. Speeding past low dwellings, he recalls the lone bar of reception and realises that if he doesn't act now, any chance of survival will vanish along with the signal.

He re-opens the GPS application with shaking fingers and begins to punch in the coordinates from memory. Villagers are screaming in fright as he speeds past them, but he can't look up, he has to finish this—

An incoming call interrupts him: Alice. He stabs END CALL, frantically swipes back to the GPS app, and initiates the search.

The route starts loading—but it's taking forever. Bad signal.

Logan lifts his eyes back to the road and swerves hard to avoid ploughing straight through a roadside shack encased in vines.

Back on the trail, wheels shuddering, he glances down again and the route's displayed.

Fifteen minutes' drive northeast.

He can hardly believe it, but he starts the route, tosses the phone on the passenger seat, re-applies both hands to the wheel, and roars onto a barely discernible trail out of town—back into mountainside desolation.

The reception vanishes as the trees swallow the jeep, replaced by SOS ONLY, but the directions continue despite the lack of service, because the GPS radio gets its location data from satellites. This technological tidbit is the only thing keeping him alive.

The overhead canopy blocks out the sun, darkening the trail he swerves down.

The jungle has him now.

—

'Logan?' Alice says, but he hung up.

Her front teeth move unconsciously to her lower lip. She starts chewing raggedly, keeping the dead phone against her ear. Camilla is still looming over her, and Rubén is watching warily across the table. She can't meet either of their eyes.

Was that enough? Did I do enough?

Rubén drains the last of the morning's fifth beer and leans forward, swallowing a nervous belch. 'Did that work? Will he . . . will he get her?'

She doesn't know.

Can Logan defy the odds, storm the Serrano compound, kill those at the head of the table—or is he already dead?

Weakness grips her from within, encourages her to break down, succumb to the fear and uncertainty. But she can hold out a little longer.

She isn't sure what she's got left in the tank, but she figures she can find out. That much is within her control.

'Let's go see,' she says, game face back on. 'You're going to drive me.'

A pause. 'Drive . . .?'

She can't help picturing rolling up to the aftermath, wading through bodies, and finding one corpse bigger than the rest.

Long hair splayed everywhere, a huge barrel chest hanging still, breathless. She wonders if the ice in Logan's eyes will vanish in death . . .

Alice forces the terrible visual from her mind. She has to go. It's better to know what happened than live forever in the unknown. Logan taught her to take her pain upfront.

'Yes,' she responds, firm. 'We'll leave now. If you don't take me, I'll call Logan back and tell him to stand down. Then Sonia will be alive. She'll know you betrayed her.'

He drags fingers through his oily hair. 'Is like . . . nine hours. And I drank . . .' A hapless gesture at the empty bottles.

'It's still early. We'll be there before sundown. You can sober up on the way.'

He exhales hard. 'Okay,' he mutters. 'Okay.'

Finally, Alice looks at Camilla, who stares down at both of them. Alice can't decipher the look on the older woman's face, but she thinks she spots a little recognition there.

Camilla's voice is soft as she says, 'I doubted it.'

Alice cocks her head. 'What?'

'That you were his family. You don't look alike. But now I see. You are the same. Underneath. You just . . .' She shakes her head. 'You just make things happen.'

Alice says nothing.

'He's your brother?' Camilla asks her.

'Something like that.' Alice rises out of the plastic chair. Nods to Rubén. 'Let's go. Now.'

Unbelievably, he rises.

His fear of Sonia must outweigh his loyalty.

He leaves the ring of keys on the table and shoots a vile look at Camilla, which says, *You lock up, then.*

As she follows him out, Alice finds it hard to tell whether she's finally taking her life in her own hands, or storming toward her own doom.

Maybe both.

—

The small American girl sweeps out after Rubén, then Camilla's alone in the bar.

She briefly considered protesting, trying to warn the girl that she would only get herself killed, along with Rubén, but she realised she hadn't the energy to defend her argument.

Her self-hatred runs all the way down to the marrow. If she had come home the night before last and kept her mouth shut, none of this would have happened, and that understanding has eaten at her. She hasn't slept a wink in forty-eight hours.

She considers Rubén's mistakes worse than hers, but not by much. For more than a year, he kept his familial link to the infamous Serranos secret from her. It was only yesterday morning that she finally learned, when the automatic gunfire stopped cracking through the neighbourhood and the news broke of thirteen dead and Rubén collapsed in the hallway, sobbing. He explained that he lied to her when they first started dating, that not *all* of his family was dead, that he'd fucked up and made a call to someone he never should have involved and thereby dug his own grave in the process.

She was furious.

But she'd lied to him, too, even if it was by omission. Technically, she'd told him the truth—'It was this . . . man. An American. Someone I used to love.'—but she left out the part about Logan being a human wrecking ball. She let her boyfriend storm out of the house with his chest puffed up, knowing what would happen to him. Some dark part of her *wanted* that. She punished a good man because of her own impulsive mistakes.

If her ex gets slaughtered chaperoning a naïve young woman down to Cauca, so be it. Camilla just needs to lie down.

She stares into space for a few minutes, then saunters out of the drinking hole. No sign of Rubén or the girl. They're already gone.

Camilla doesn't care.

She's so tired.

She locks up and trudges home—too spaced out to notice the men who follow.

25

For the second time, Logan leaves the convoy in the dust. He speeds along the jungle trails with total abandon for his safety.

The men coming after him might think they can match his recklessness. They might imagine themselves as berserkers, marauders, but they aren't. They need to hop themselves up on stims, most likely meth, to generate that kind of salivating war-party fervour.

It also helps that their old pickups pale in comparison to what the jeep's got under the hood.

Logan follows dirt roads winding along mountainsides, past precipitous drops. Every few seconds, he checks the GPS to ensure he doesn't miss any crucial turn-offs.

Just like that, he's less than a mile away.

End game.

A high-walled compound, Alice said. *Guarded.*

No sign of the place yet, but he isn't moronic enough to drive right up to their doorstep like a sitting duck. He slows to a trundle along a steep trail cutting through a dense swathe of highland forest, then turns off-road the moment he gets the chance, slicing through a gap between two huge trunks. He parks in the woods behind one of the trees, kills the engine, and leaps down to the forest floor.

It isn't particularly warm, but the humidity grips him and he can feel fresh sweat pooling. He considers lugging one of the AK-47s with him for the final hike through the woods, but there's nothing he can do with an automatic weapon in this environment that he can't do with the Five-seven. He always favoured careful, precise shot selection over spray-and-pray.

After careful consideration, he zips up the backpack filled with plastic explosive and slings it over his shoulders before he sets off.

He tucks the phone away as he treks. No need for it now—he knows where he's headed. Gripping the pistol double-handed, he moves uphill through lush vegetation, parallel to the trail, letting the undergrowth muffle his footfalls. At any moment, he expects to hear the cacophony of engines as the convoy roars past, but it never comes.

They should have caught up by now; it's almost like they're hanging back. Are they forbidden from approaching their masters' headquarters?

Foreboding creeps up on him then, tickling the base of his spine as he stalks toward the end of a journey that began three hundred miles north in Bogotá. He utilises every scrap of prior training to approach unseen—low and slow. The terrain makes it simple enough.

Logan smears moist dirt on his already filthy face and crawls to the edge of the tree line beneath a dense bush. He takes a peek at where the trail ends, and his heart sinks.

His pursuers kept back not out of fear, but because they knew they wouldn't be needed.

He doesn't know why he expected substandard defences, but the compound's slate-grey perimeter wall sits two storeys high, topped with modern steel parapets. The walls are featureless concrete, physically unscalable, and the front gates are solid steel: bulletproof, blast-proof, *everything*-proof. Four soldiers in his direct field of view patrol slowly along the top of the wall and the guard tower fifteen yards back offers three hundred and sixty degrees of observation over the surrounding area.

It's a fortress. Impenetrable.

He loses track of time then, burrowed down in the dirt, contemplating whether it's even worth pushing up off the earth and persevering. He lowers his forehead to the damp soil and counts a slow three breaths.

In and out, in and out.

In and out.

Go.

He crawls backward, receding into the forest. When he's out of sight of the guard tower, he rises from the undergrowth and strides back the way he came.

So they didn't hand their heads to him on a silver platter. They didn't let him waltz in through the front door, but he never really expected them to.

He recalculates. No more thinking this will be over soon. The idea of a slow war is daunting, but it might be his only remaining option.

First things first: slink back to find a small pocket of reception, get on the horn to Alice, and let her know he'll be here a while. Then order her onto a plane home, no matter her protests.

He's halfway back to the jeep when he hears an engine chugging steadily, out on the mountain trail he's moving parallel to. A single vehicle headed for the compound.

If one of the pickups has branched off from the convoy to report to the Serranos, he'll take the opportunity. He should have been picking them off one by one from the start.

Here's his chance to kick things off.

He moves fast, cutting sideways through thicker vegetation, trampling greenery. Tactical idiocy if you're going by the book, but Logan rarely followed the most prudent combat strategy, and he's still above ground. Thoreau taught him how masters can break the rules in ways that amateurs would never get away with, but Logan doesn't know about all that. He just prefers getting shit done as fast as possible.

He spills out of the woods onto the trail and levels the Five-seven, expecting to see a rusted pickup truck.

Instead, he watches a Mercedes-AMG G-class SUV—three hundred odd grand of German engineering—rumble to a halt in front of him. A layer of dust coats the boxy vehicle. The windshield's darkened to maximum tint, and a hollow pit forms in Logan's stomach as he fears bulletproof glass, but the driver pops his door and steps out is alone and unarmed. Perched on the step, he wears a shapeless black suit, no tie, his shirt open at the neck. A mane of blond-tipped hair flows back away from a tanned and weathered face. He's South American, maybe fifty—hard to tell beneath the Botox and lip filler—and he's furious.

He screams something at Logan in Spanish.

Logan keeps the pistol squared on his chest. 'What?'

The guy flaps his bee-stung lips. He switches to accented English. 'What the fuck do you think you're doing?!'

Logan stares at him. 'I don't know.'

The man raises his palms skyward. 'Do you understand what this means for you?!'

Logan glances over his shoulder, up the trail. They're out of sight of the compound perimeter, and well out of earshot. He turns back. 'Did I interrupt something?'

'*Yes!*' the guy screeches. 'So I suggest you—'

Logan strides for the car. The pistol barrel racing toward the man shuts him up fast.

'Perfect,' Logan says. 'You might be useful.'

He pats the man down first, finding no weapons. Then he jabs the guy in his muscled chest with the Five-seven, ushering him firmly back inside the air-conditioned cabin. Logan slams the driver's door on him, rounds the hood while keeping the pistol trained on the windshield, and clambers up into the passenger seat. He sheds his pack as he mounts the side skirt and dumps it in the footwell. His bulk dirties the pristine leather as he jams the gun against the side of the driver's skull, pinning thick locks of hair to the flesh above his ear.

A woman's whimper floats from the rear seats.

Logan looks over his shoulder, noting the two thin girls in crumpled clothes in the back. They're barely of age. Sunken eyes, hollow cheeks. Rage forms in the pit of his stomach as he turns back to the driver. He wants to shoot the guy right here, but the man still may be of some utility.

'Is the vehicle searched before you're let in?' Logan asks.

He sees the man consider lying, but a touch more pressure through the gun barrel dissuades him of such a foolish notion.

'Of course,' the guy croaks, his whole body tense. 'They search everywhere. Guns train on us whole time. You're not getting fucking smuggled in there. What are you, stupid? Please . . . is hopeless. You know this. And is nothing to do with me.'

Logan considers his next move for about half a second, but there are only two directions to choose from, and they can't go forward.

'Then back the way you came,' he says. 'Right fucking now.'

'Oh, God,' the man mumbles, paling beneath the fake tan. '*Dios mío . . .*'

But he complies.

He carries out a precarious five-point turn on the narrow trail. Paint scrapes off the Mercedes' bumper as he grinds its hood up into the tree line, but he eventually gets the vehicle turned around and sets off at a crawl.

'W-where are we going?' he stammers.

'I'm figuring that out myself,' Logan says.

—

Gabriel's tired. So goddamn tired.

He slumps in a hanging pod at one end of the mammoth balcony, slowly twirling the suspended chair back and forth along a ninety-degree arc. The sunrise over the national park is gorgeous, of course, but natural phenomena lost its appeal a long time ago.

He always asks those who espouse the beauty of nature if they've ever heard of drugs.

From a glass vial strung around his neck, he taps out a little more pure Colombian blow across the back of his hand. He buries his nostrils in the coke and snorts hard. It kicks like a mule. Weapons-grade stuff. But he notes no change in his exhaustion levels, only his anxiety.

He's like a corpse with an electric current running through it.

Gabriel fingers his neck. His pulse thuds more than twice a second, and he's sitting down. Not ideal. His bloodstream's all stress chemicals.

He thought he rode out the last of those panic attacks years ago. They ceased when he nailed down his pharmaceutical regimen, landing on the precise quantities to keep his childhood memories at bay. Uppers until the early afternoon, then, in the evening, a cocktail of depressants and painkillers washed down with Macallan. He's the definition of a high-functioning addict.

That new recruit who was here a couple of nights ago, for example, the one with the curly hair and the face tattoos, he probably thought Gabriel Serrano was a quiet killer. A man of few words and obscene authority. Truth is, Gabriel could hardly see straight as he lay back on the chaise, could barely register the words Sonia used to indoctrinate Miguel. Gabriel only needs enough cognitive power to perform, not to think. His wife runs the show.

He couldn't admit this to himself until very recently. The shift occurred when he realised how much he liked getting fucked up, realised how much *more* he'd enjoy it if he finally accepted he wasn't the one steering the ship. Then it was guilt-free ecstasy.

He's mastered the art of riding the line between worlds—one foot in reality, one in dreamland.

Last night's panic attack shouldn't have happened. He should have been comfortable in barbiturate heaven when he heard the Bogotá hit failed and thirteen of their men lay dead at the hands of an American. It should have been a non-factor.

No matter. Send another thirteen.

But through the tranquilliser fog, Gabriel managed to picture those boys' final moments in that dingy bar.

Suddenly he was eight years old again, alone in the hills. Everyone slaughtered, everyone besides the little girl clutching his hand, the childhood friend he would grow to love.

Sonia was there for him last night just as she was there for him sixty years ago, talking him through the hyperventilation. She's always been there for him. Was their romance ever genuine, or simply a product of their shared trauma? He never liked these questions, so he made sure his wife had a firm grip on the armrests of the throne before forming a drug routine to make Elvis Presley proud. They do love each other, he thinks, just . . . unconventionally. They're doing the best they can with the cards they were dealt.

Gabriel checks his watch: 9:15. Fabio's never late. Gabriel's arteries feel clogged, his blood like syrup, his chest so tight from the coke and the stress. He *needs* the physical release. It's why he summoned Fabio without Sonia's knowledge, no matter how poor the timing. This house is so big she'll never know he's keeping his usual routine. She told him not to, told him to bunker down, but he needs this or he'll fucking explode. Who cares about playing it safe if missing a vital part of your self-medication literally kills you?

Anyway, that's his excuse.

He calls Fabio. Once, twice, three times. Nothing. He's sweating bullets, trying for a fourth, when Sonia emerges onto the balcony.

He stabs end call and tucks the phone away.

'What?' he grumbles, his face wet with perspiration. 'I did what you asked.'

His vision was swaying as he recorded the video message for her in the early hours of the morning. She anonymised him with a black balaclava and voice-deepening technology, identifiable to the rest of the underworld only by his distinctly recognisable eyes. He played his part well.

He's sure the warning is already circulating through the underground channels, spreading like cancer across the dark web, relaying his message to the Gulf Cartel: *Your forces in Cauca are now my forces. The Serrano Mafia is rising. Soon we will own you. You will be our dogs. You will obey.*

'That's good,' Sonia had purred as she stopped the recording. 'That's golden.'

Standing in front of him now on the balcony, she looks shellshocked.

She *never* looks shellshocked.

Gabriel massages his chest, inches above his overworked heart. 'What? The takeover failed?'

'No,' she mutters, her perfect face a sheet of white. 'It went off without a hitch. But the American got away.'

'Surely they chased him.'

'They did.'

'Where?'

'Here.'

He stops massaging. 'Oh.'

There it is again. The panic. The insidious sensation he knows she feels, too; the shortness of breath that makes them both want to lash out, attack, hurt indiscriminately. As far as he's concerned, that's the least humanity deserves.

'Here?' he stammers. 'What do you mean *here*—?'

'He will never find this place,' she interrupts. 'So he's somewhere in the national park, that's all. Sniffing around dead ends. No matter. I've already had him sealed in.'

Gabriel swallows.

Sonia smoothes her hair back with a palm. 'We need to flush him out.'

'How?'

'Another dark web video. Time to take this up a notch,' she says, her eyes dead black holes. 'Can you sell crazy?'

—

As the Mercedes weaves through the forest, Logan keeps his eyes peeled for any sign of the convoy of pickups.

He flinches each time one of the women whimpers from the back.

The risk of running into the men who pursued him here is high, but he's banking on common foot soldiers keeping well away from the Serranos' wealthy visitors. He figures a grunt on ten dollars a day wouldn't dare stop a three-hundred-thousand-dollar SUV traipsing around the area.

He doesn't get the chance to find out if he's right—they make it back to San Andrés unimpeded.

It's now a ghost town, the residents shut up tight after the gunfire that tore through their village.

Logan orders the driver to pull over beside an eatery. The shack has no front door, only an open frame, and Logan peers into the shadows within. He makes out the shape of a woman moving slowly behind the counter, working pans. Life goes on.

Logan forces more pressure through the gun barrel, until he produces a yelp from the driver. 'Got money?'

'Huh?'

'Cash.'

'*Sí, sí . . .*' The man fishes in a jacket pocket and pulls out a thick band of pesos, which Logan snatches and tosses to one of the young girls in the back. He uses his free hand to point to the eatery. 'Go in there. Keep your heads down awhile.'

There's no telling whether they understand the words or just his actions, but they pop the door and run straight off into the shack. Their spindly legs are pale in the blazing morning.

Logan doesn't delude himself into thinking he's saved them. He's no hero, swooping in to rescue the damsels in distress. Life has not been kind to them, and in all likelihood, nothing will change, even if they make it out of these godforsaken mountains.

The harsh truth he learned through experience is that by trying to fix everything, you fix nothing. So he watches the young women disappear inside with a pit in his stomach.

Then the driver bursts into motion, lunging for the door handle. Logan pivots like a whip and slams the pistol so hard into the man's temple that he collapses against the unopened door, shouting in pain against the tinted window.

'Don't you even fucking *think* about it,' Logan says.

'Okay!' the driver shrieks, instantly acquiescent. 'Okay!'

Logan surveys the empty street ahead. No sign of life. 'Did you pass pickup trucks on the way up here? Serrano men?'

'Yes, yes,' the driver splutters. He pants for breath, long locks matted damply to the sides of his head. Swollen lips push taut against his skin. He gestures in the direction of the road Logan used to reach the town. 'They make roadblock. Down there. They let me through. Because who I am.'

The pit within Logan widens to a chasm.

Just as he suspected, his pursuers pulled back when they realised he was headed for the compound, aware his efforts would be futile. Instead, they doubled back and blocked the only way out of these hills. The winding mountain trails must be a closed-loop system, a network only accessible via the single route leading up from the archaeological museum. Cut that road off, you seal everyone in.

Confined once more.

Logan keeps his face neutral. The man beside him is now his only lifeline; it's crucial he remains pliable.

Logan applies more pressure with the pistol and blood runs from a gash above the driver's ear. When the man groans, Logan says, 'Drive up the back of this village.'

'Where?'

'Just drive.'

The man obeys. They climb north toward the desolate trails behind town. Locals who glimpse the boxy Mercedes from inside their dwellings avert their eyes. Logan keeps the driver statuesque with the raised Five-seven as he fishes his phone out—one bar of reception. He doubts it will last any further than half a mile out of town, so he orders the driver to pull over a couple of hundred yards past the outskirts of San Andrés, and the SUV rumbles off the trail, moving between thick trees beneath a bare hillside.

No one in the rearview, no sign of anything resembling civilisation ahead. They're alone, and the one bar remains, reading 4G.

Until he discerns how to proceed, this is their base of operations.

Logan's first out. He rounds the hood and orders the driver out. A fallen tree along one side of the copse forms a natural perch; Logan instructs his hostage to sit. The man slumps against the log without protest.

'What's your name?'

'Fabio.'

Logan looms over him. 'You even *think* about making a break for it, I won't shoot you in the head. I'll put a bullet in your lower back, through the base of your spine. Disintegrate a couple vertebrae. You'll bleed out slow. You won't feel anything below the waist while you do. Picture what that might be like before you decide to run.'

Fabio trembles as Logan sits beside him on the log. For the foreseeable future, he'll do as he's told. Logan hunches over his phone and refreshes the headlines—automatic behaviour.

He navigates to the same website that published the piece featuring Camilla, a channel specialising in frontline reporting and foreign conflicts. As soon as he updates the feed, a new headline displays itself front and centre. He couldn't miss it if he tried.

The blood rushes to his head and his world goes dark as he reads: 'SERRANO MAFIA' RELEASE DARK WEB VIDEO STATEMENT IN WAKE OF BOGOTÁ MASSACRE.

He doesn't need to check the timeline to know the article was organised by the Serranos themselves, no doubt via a labyrinth of shell companies and back-channels. Their version of a press release.

The website wouldn't dare share the actual video itself, only a summary, so Logan opens a new tab and pulls up a lesser-known shock site infamous for hosting all sorts of unsavoury videos YouTube wouldn't touch with a ten-foot pole: beheadings, mass shootings and the like. He doesn't even need to use the search bar. It's right there in the suggested videos, number three on trending: *Serrano Mafia statement re Bogotá.*

The thumbnail shows a pair of wrinkled green eyes set deep in the holes of a heavy woollen balaclava.

Logan swallows and hits play.

The video struggles to load, the resolution terrible, but the audio is clear. An unnaturally low voice erupts from the phone speaker, deepened to an obscene pitch by anonymising technology.

'Hello, American!' the masked man cackles in English. 'Hello, pig! You have been a very naughty boy up in Bogotá, haven't you, pig? Fucking interventionist scum. Don't you have some war to fight, some war no one asked you to wage? Ah, but here you are. Naughty, dirty pig. You are trouble. I'm sure you think you're a hero. Big man. But that is not how it works here, pig. We have no time for the hero shit. So I keep this short. You think you're a hero, filthy pig? You think you're a good man? Let's test this, no?' A rancid cackle. 'Oh, yes, let's test! Here's what we do. One town for every day you do not turn yourself in. You understand?

Tomorrow morning, you not walk up to our gate and hand yourself over, our forces move into a rural village and start shooting. We pick at random, anywhere in Colombia, you see? Oops! All dead. Because you think you are hero. Because you think you can save them all. Silly little pig. So we do this every morning. So many villages no one cares about, you understand? They won't know what's coming. We can do this for a year, you see? Every day!' Uproarious laughter. 'Decide quick! Tick-tock, pig!'

The screen cuts to black.

Logan couldn't move if he tried. He feels encased in an invisible tomb. Fabio could sprint away right now, and Logan wouldn't even have the capacity, let alone the motivation, to stop him. But his hostage doesn't sense the opportunity before him. He's digesting the speech, too.

Sweat-soaked hair sticks to botoxed cheeks as Fabio slowly shakes his head.

The copse is quiet as a cemetery as the man mutters, 'I told you. You fucking with the wrong people. You not listen.'

26

Alice watches the countryside rush by.

Her mind is a storm. The unease makes her want to claw her own skin off.

But someone rather special to her once said that bravery isn't what you are, but what you're willing to try and become, so she chalks it up to growing pains and endeavours to hold the line.

She rides shotgun in an archaic Kia Optima beside Rubén Álvarez. For now, fear makes him malleable. He keeps both hands on the wheel, watches the road, and says nothing.

The first hours of the journey pass in silence.

Tension knots her neck, stiffens her back. An iron clamp squeezes her heart, making a vein bounce in her neck.

Rubén never so much as adjusts his position in the driver's seat, moving as much as a propped-up corpse. His first physical reaction of the whole trip comes on a barren stretch of National Route 45, when a Toyota pickup tears by in the opposite direction with men seated in the truck bed wielding automatic rifles.

Rubén flinches.

Alice notes his anxiety. 'What do you do? For work?'

He faces forward as the Toyota blows past. The swelling over his right eye pulses. 'I am bricklayer.'

Asphalt rumbles under worn tyres.

'You never thought about working for your cousin?' she asks. 'She never offered you a job?'

'Of course she offer me job.'

Alice doesn't respond.

For the first time since they got in the car, he glances over at her. 'I am not made for that work. You think I am soft, yes?'

'No,' she says, reluctant to sympathise but unable to help herself. 'I think you're smart.'

He frowns, facing forward. 'But I get your brother in so much trouble. How I be smart?'

'Everyone fucked up here. All of us.'

His frown deepens. 'What you fuck up? You just get here . . .'

'I didn't stop him from coming. I knew something wasn't right, but I didn't speak up. Didn't push back.' She stares out the window at fields of racing green. 'I'm still learning.'

'What you learning?'

'How to assert myself.'

Sometimes I forget I'm clean now, she thinks. *Capable.*

He shakes his head. Probably didn't register a word she said. 'You going to get yourself killed here. You understand this, yes? Still time to go back. Fly home.'

'That's not who I am.' She chews her lower lip. 'Not anymore.'

'So you use to be soft?'

'Used to be a whole lot worse than soft.'

'So maybe . . .' He trails off, self-conscious, and minutes pass as he searches for the required courage. But they've still got hours of driving ahead of them. He knows he can't hold it in for that long. He inhales sharply. 'Maybe I not have to stay same? Maybe I change?'

'Yes, Rubén,' she says. 'You can change.'

She remembers street corners, crack dens, pipe stems. The soul-crushing desperation of it all. Hard to even comprehend how she made it from there to here. Sure, she may be in worse physical danger now, screaming through cartel badlands toward an uncertain fate, but she's sober and clear-headed and self-sufficient. Of course she can't fight, can't shoot, can't yet defend herself if push comes to shove.

But she can move forward. She can be useful.

'Trust me,' she mutters, 'you can change.'

—

Logan's motionless for the better part of an hour as the sun climbs in the sky.

He tries to formulate some kind of plan—but fails.

He senses Fabio watching him, but doesn't respond to the scrutiny. Only when the man starts shifting restlessly on the log does Logan burst into motion, bringing the pistol up and skewering the barrel against the side of his hostage's head. Fabio jolts with an audible throat spasm, fearing imminent execution. Involuntary tears coat his eyes.

'Alright,' Logan says, allowing an unhinged element to his voice. 'It's finally question time, friend.'

Fabio jackhammers.

First, Logan lies. 'I already know the answers to some of these questions. You won't know which. So think twice before bluffing. I hear one lie I already know the answer to, there's a bullet with your brain's name on it. You aren't ready to die, Fabio. You aren't ready for nothingness, I can see it. Far too scary for a man like you, a man so in love with his own flesh . . .'

The facelift twitches. Stretched skin vibrates, fear simmering underneath.

'So,' Logan says. 'Those girls. You're their pimp?'

'Ah . . .' Fabio blinks faster. Searching for another way to put it. Then he seems to remember he likes being alive. 'Well, yes. Pimp. Yes.'

'They're trafficked? They're slaves?'

'Oh. Well . . .' But the cold touch of gunmetal is truth serum. 'Yes, you could say this. If you want. But you need understand—'

Logan tilts the barrel skyward and slams the underside of the pistol forward, a sharp *smack* against the bruised flesh. Skin splits and fountaining blood paints Fabio's earlobe red. He cries out for no one but Logan to hear.

'I tell you what I need to understand,' Logan hisses. 'You answer my questions and *only* my questions. *¿Sí?*'

Fabio's stress reaches a fever pitch, and he begins to cry uncontrollably. '*Sí, sí* . . .' It's clear he doesn't handle pain well, which makes this particular predicament hell on earth.

Logan ratchets up the pressure. 'Don't hesitate. Tell me exactly what you do for the Serranos.'

Fabio side-eyes him, knees trembling, likely on the verge of pissing himself. 'The Serranos? I w-work for Gabriel.'

The husband. That's something, at least. Before this, Logan only had the information Bella provided: a surname, and the fact they're an older couple. 'Does his wife know?'

'Of course Sonia know. Sonia know everything. Sonia is one who . . . what is word? Approve me? Check me?'

'Vet you?'

'*Sí.*'

Logan makes an educated guess. 'Sonia runs things?'

Fabio frowns. 'I not supposed to know this. Gabriel tell me one night when he fucked up. For now, big secret.'

'For now?'

'She beginning takeover this year. It start today, with Clan del Golfo. Once she have enough territory, she can reveal she is the queen. Until then . . . not smart. Woman taking over? If other groups know, they make more effort to crush her. Because it hurt, uh . . . pride. You know? But if she pretend Gabriel is boss, no one pay attention. Not until she have victory, and then it not matter.'

Logan gets the gist. To keep Fabio on his toes, he veers sharply in another direction. 'And she lets her husband copulate with sex slaves? In the compound *she* runs? Come on.'

'They have arrangement.' Fabio's ghost-white now. 'They are not . . . traditional couple.'

'The marriage is for show?'

'No.' The man looks nauseous.

Logan inches closer. 'Tell me what you know, Fabio.'

Fabio hesitates.

Logan taps his finger against the trigger guard and roars, '*Bang!*'

Fabio leaps out of his skin. He stifles guttural sobs and starts talking a mile a minute. 'Gabriel tell me this, one time. Oh, fuck, please do not repeat. I am dead. I am dead.' He sniffs, coughs. Wipes saliva off his puffy lips. 'They love each other, Gabriel tells me. But not . . . romance. Different love. Something very bad happen to them as children . . .'

A little internal relief as Logan realises he finally knows something. 'I was told their families were slaughtered.'

'Yes. After this happen, they only have each other. As kids, they help each other, keep each other safe. When they become adults, this become love. But deeper love than just happy family. Because they are not happy family. Never will be, because of what happen to them. So they not . . . exclusive. Sonia use herself to get men to obey—you just see this with Clan del Golfo—and

Gabriel use me because otherwise he go insane. He have lot more trauma than Sonia. He need . . . release. He have hurt, so he need to make some hurt.' Fabio shrugs.

Logan feels sick. 'It's a one-way ticket for those girls?'

'What this mean?'

'You drop them off. Do you pick them up after?'

Fabio's teeth clench hard. But he hasn't lied yet. He's not about to start.

'Sometimes,' he admits. 'Sometimes not.'

Logan's seen the darkest parts of humanity. This is up there with the worst of it. 'How often do you provide girls?'

'Once a week.'

Jesus Christ. 'How does it work?'

'I tell you. I drive up to gate, they come hold me with gunpoint. Search me, search girls, search every inch of car. Guns on car from guard tower, too. Then they let me through and Gabriel meet girls at front door. I turn around and I leave. I told you is hopeless.'

'You've never been inside?'

'Once. Gabriel let me in one night. He show me around a little. This when he tell me about him and Sonia. But she find us, scream at me, kick me out. She not approve of the pimp in the house. That was year ago. I never been back in again.'

'What did he show you when you were there?'

'Just some rooms.'

'Is there a control centre?'

'What?'

'A room with a bunch of screens. Where the guards watch the cameras. It's either in the house or the guard tower.'

'Oh.' Fabio furrows his brow. 'That is in house. I remember. On second floor. But what is point of knowing this? You not getting in.'

It dawns on Logan that he already knew that. He's circling the drain of the inevitable realisation. Masking his despair, he says, 'You heard their message. Were they bluffing? About massacring villages . . .?'

Fabio scoffs. 'What you think?'

Fuck. It's over.

Logan turns to his phone and redials the number that rang him earlier. Alice answers straight away.

'Hey,' she says, the syllable crackling. 'Did you get it done?'

'The compound's impenetrable, Alice.'

Silence for a few beats, then, 'Oh.'

'It's time for you to go home.'

'What?'

'I'm out of options. So you need to fly back to New York. Now.'

He can't explain why, but she can't be in-country when he hands himself over. She just can't.

She needs to be half a world away before she hears news of his mutilated body found dumped by the roadside, warnings and insults carved into his dead flesh. He knows how things work down here.

'I'm five hours away,' she says.

'*What?!*'

'Rubén's bringing me to you.'

He grips the phone so tight he fears it might shatter. 'Why, Alice?'

'You can trust him. He fears you more than he fears his cousin.'

'No,' Logan hisses. 'Why are *you* coming?'

He doesn't bother trying to convince her to turn around—they're long past that.

'Share your location,' she says. 'GPS.'

'Alice, the area's under confinement.'

'Rubén can get me in and you know it. He's Serrano blood. Now share your location. Or do you want me floundering about aimlessly once I'm in?'

'Why are you coming?' he yells into the empty countryside.

Her voice cracks as she speaks. 'I told you before. I flew to Bogotá because I thought you were the aggressor in all this. I thought I could talk you out of a pointless fight. I didn't realise you were trapped here. And now . . . well, I'm here. There must be something I can do to help. We wouldn't be here without each other, Logan. There must be some way . . .'

He meets Fabio's eyes, and an idea strikes him, but it's so awful he dismisses it immediately. Disgust ripples through him at the very notion. He quietly lambasts himself for even imagining the possibility—but he doesn't tell Alice there's nothing she can do.

As if she can read his mind, she says, 'I don't need protecting, Logan. Not anymore.'

He feels trapped in a vice, its metal jaws cranking tighter, squeezing him to bursting point.

She's right, though. He's not her caretaker. If she's here of her own volition, demanding to be of assistance . . .

He spits a curse.

'What?' she says.

'Nothing. I'll share my location. See you soon.'

He hangs up, slumps lower against the log, and sets to work undertaking the hardest challenge of his life: relinquishing control.

Alice feels like she's tiptoeing on a wire strung between two high-rises. As they turn off the highway onto a winding mountainous route, she hauls courage up through the veil of terror.

Facing Rubén, and remaining deadpan, she says, 'You have a photo of you and Sonia together?'

'Uh . . .' His brow furrows. 'Yes.'

'Your cousin's forces are confining the mountains around her compound. No one goes in or out. But you're family. You can get through. You understand?'

'Yes.'

'Now pull over, please.'

His head cocks at the polite request, then he looks around and his confusion heightens further. 'Here?'

'Yes. Right here. Thank you.'

He pulls off-road onto a bumpy stretch of churned earth as Alice eyes the sky. Encroaching fog. So the evening will bring rain. *Like this wasn't intimidating enough.*

It's only four, but the sun disappeared behind clouds in the early afternoon, and the hills have lost their emerald shine. The scenery hangs in gloom, a postcard image with the brightness cranked down. Not long until full dark.

She refrains from even imagining what that will be like all the way out here.

Rubén slows to a stop. The engine sputters. She works through her chest pains, feigning calm. She even reaches out and lays a palm on the man's skinny thigh, atop his scuffed jeans.

He goes rigid. He's scared, in pain. Probably wants a drink. Definitely wants this all to end.

'Now, Rubén . . .' She gives his thigh a squeeze. 'I'm going to get in the trunk.'

'Oh?'

'That's right. You obviously understand your options. Once I seal myself in, I'll need you to open it from the outside once we're through. If you want, you can drive right up to the blockade and tell them you have a friend of Logan's in the trunk. They can haul me out at gunpoint, and there's nothing I can do about that. Right?'

He squirms, unsure why she's even drawing his attention to the possibility.

She squeezes his leg harder. 'But then what? I'll either be your cousin's hostage, or I'll be dead. Either way, Logan will go on a rampage. A crusade. You understand? You'll have to sit there and watch it happen and think, *I brought this down on her. Again.* What sort of mood do you think Sonia will be in, even if she comes out on top? You don't have the spine to kill yourself, Rubén. You won't be able to escape her wrath.'

He swallows hard.

'Or,' she says, her voice lower, slower, 'you drive up there and you tell them you're family and you need to get through. If they ask you to pop the trunk, you flash the photo of you and Sonia and you tell them it's none of their fucking business. You tell them it's *family* business. You tell them to know their place and keep their mouths shut.'

She understands that if she asks which option he will choose, it betrays weakness on her end. She must display absolute conviction. So she just says, 'You know what to do,' and levers out of the Kia into the mountain air. Birds shriek in treetops as she rounds to the back of the sedan.

She pops the lid with her heart in her throat.

The trunk is a gaping maw.

Don't hesitate, she tells herself as she hesitates. *Don't hesitate.*

She grunts and clambers down and in. Yanks the lid shut before she can second-guess what she's doing. It slams loudly, sealing her in instant darkness.

Before she knows it, she's hyperventilating. Turns out she's reached her limit. She writhes in her tomb, slapping herself, grinding her teeth. Anything she can do to right the ship, steady herself. She feels the car lurch underneath her and then they're off and it's all real now.

For maybe twenty minutes she derides herself for her decisions, fighting not to pass out.

Should've stayed in Bogotá . . .

Should've stayed in New York . . .

Should've walked the other way the first fucking time you laid eyes on Logan Booth.

By the time the Kia slows and she hears a muffled collection of male voices, her breathing is steady. She keeps herself quiet, clinging to the strength she knows she bears.

She can handle anything.

Up front, Rubén says something, and the men surrounding the car respond with confusion. What follows is tense, indecipherable conversation in hurried Spanish.

Then fingers are drumming on the trunk lid, right above her face.

Well, she thought she could handle anything . . .

27

'Please,' Fabio begs.

'Shut up.'

'Sir, please . . .'

'Shut up.'

'Just tell me what you want—'

Logan pistol-whips the pimp in the eye socket, feeling Fabio's eyeball wobble under the closed lid. Fabio moans and bows against the log like he's praying.

Shadows stretch through the secluded copse beneath an overcast sky. Rain clouds hang swollen and pregnant overhead.

Alice should be here by now.

He figures they pulled off the road around nine in the morning, and they're now creeping steadily toward dusk. Twelve hours until the Serranos greenlight the first massacre. The waiting's been hell, but Logan's out of options—except the plan he can hardly stomach the thought of.

The sky finally cracks, unleashing the downpour. It begins with a smattering of fat raindrops, quickly turning torrential. They're soaked through before they can blink.

Logan uses the natural shower to wash the dirt and sweat off his face. He's about to order Fabio back to the Mercedes to take shelter when they both hear a different kind of rumbling. Not thunder—tyres on dirt.

Fabio snaps upright, his left eye already swollen shut, his right eye wide. He looks rough, the rainfall diluting the blood caked to one side of his skull. No doubt he feels worse. Logan kept the pimp in the dark all day, no matter how desperately his hostage begged for information, culminating in the pistol-whip minutes prior.

Now Logan raises the Five-seven and aims it at the patch of trail visible from within the copse. Just in case it's not who he thinks it is.

A rusted Kia Optima trundles into view, rain coagulating the dust blanketing the sedan. Logan identifies the driver from fifty yards away, even through the wall of water. He'd recognise that wispy fringe anywhere.

Rubén Álvarez slows in the middle of the trail, staring around in confusion. He's on top of the GPS location Logan sent through, but he can't see a thing through the storm. Tentatively, he pops his door and steps out into the rain. Logan watches him flinch under the downpour, fat droplets splashing off fresh facial wounds—he really did a number on him back in that dive bar.

Rubén stands there, motionless. Alone.

Despite his despair, Logan still has the wherewithal to snatch Fabio by the collar before he heads for the road. The pimp groans in protest as Logan hurries him through the trees; they burst out by the roadside in a flurry.

At the sight of Logan crashing out of the undergrowth, Rubén nearly leaps out of his skin.

Logan holds a whimpering Fabio in place and aims the pistol square between Rubén's eyes. 'Where is she?'

Rubén smears thin strands of wet hair off his forehead.

'*Where is she?!*' Logan roars.

Drenched head to toe, Rubén rounds to the Kia's trunk and pops the lid.

Alice clambers up and out into the storm.

Logan has to suppress a groan of relief. Despite it all, tactical prudence remains on his mind. He doesn't want Fabio knowing what she means to him. The less his hostage understands, the better. He tries to maintain a poker face as she turns her face to the sky, squinting against the downpour.

He isn't sure why he expected her to look different. Raindrops splash off the dusting of freckles across her cheeks. She's lucid, aware. It's in that moment he gets his first true sense of what she's becoming.

She runs to him.

To ensure his hostage doesn't flee, Logan trips the pimp and shoves him down into the wet dirt. Fabio splays on hands and knees. It affords Logan room to open his arms, all prudence suddenly forgotten, and Alice throws herself into the hug. She wraps her arms around his stomach, squeezes him tight.

'Hey,' he breathes in her ear. He's glad the rain masks his tears.

'Oh, God,' she mutters as she steps back.

'What?'

She shakes her head, as though rattling demons out. 'Coming through the blockade, there was drumming, right above me, on the trunk lid. I thought I was made. But it was just—' She points skyward at the huge raindrops and emits a nervous laugh.

He pays close attention to her every action. She's in shock, but otherwise remarkably composed. It took him years to find such radical acceptance in the face of near-certain death.

Fabio finally hauls himself upright, half-coated in mud. He staggers to a halt beside Rubén.

'Who's he?' Alice asks him.

Standing there in the clutches of the storm, Logan lays out who Fabio is and how exactly the pimp serves Gabriel Serrano. He hopes with all his heart that she won't reach the same conclusions he arrived at, that she'll remain oblivious and say, *Why isn't he already dead? Put a bullet in him.* But he sees the understanding in her eyes. She knows why Fabio's still alive.

She connects the dots. 'You said the control centre's in the house, right? Not the guard tower?'

Logan swallows. 'Right.'

He glances at Fabio.

'Second floor,' the pimp says. 'I can explain where.'

'Then you know how I can help, Logan,' Alice says.

'I'd never ask that of you.'

'You don't need to ask. Either you hand yourself in and die horrifically, or an entire village of innocents dies horrifically, or I do this.'

'And die horrifically.'

'Maybe. Maybe not.'

He doesn't respond.

She says, 'And that's the best odds we've got.'

It's not his place to stop her. He glimpses the single-minded resolve in her eyes and, for the first time, sees what she might become if they make it through this.

It's those who feel fear and act anyway who change the world.

Gabriel never dealt well with his own company.

Sonia disappeared into the war room early in the afternoon and hasn't emerged since.

He would never dare venture in there himself, no matter how crippling his isolation. He's weak, not stupid. If she's undertaking a marathon stint in the war room, it's for a good reason. Coordinating hundreds of her foot soldiers scattered across the country is, to put it mildly, an administrative nightmare. Her generals streamline the process remotely, but the nature of her leadership style requires constant communication with her men on the ground.

Purred promises.

Dangled rewards.

Visions of her flesh writhing against theirs, *powerful* flesh, the queen of the kingdom whispering in their ear: '*You did so good, baby . . .*'

So he won't interrupt. She's hard at work and that isn't his world.

He swallows a couple more Valium to take the edge off the emptiness of the cavernous house. Sometimes he wonders what a simple life would be like: a small apartment, a modest sum in the bank, a firm grip on your desires . . .

Gabriel stretches out on the same chaise he reclined upon two nights prior, fingering the same crystal tumbler he nursed as he bore witness to Sonia indoctrinating that FARC defector, the one with the curly hair and the face tats. That boy was a looker. Sometimes when the new recruits complete their six months of obedience, Sonia has to pinch her nose and close her eyes as she delivers the promised reward, but Gabriel knows she will enjoy the time she spends with Miguel. If it comes to that.

But he knows it will—that boy had a manic glint behind his eyes as he knelt on the rug. He'll go above and beyond for his queen. Gabriel can always spot the ones who will.

He shifts on the velvet lounge, restless. Outside, the storm rages. Usually he can bear the strange dynamic of their marriage. Not tonight. He should be suppressing his pain with trafficked flesh, but that motherfucker Fabio went silent.

Gabriel pops a third Valium and sips more Macallan, until the huge sitting room starts wobbling.

Sometime later, the front door groans open and a man steps into the house. Gabriel wonders if he's dreaming.

Then the man with the face tattoos opens his mouth and speaks, and it all becomes very real.

'Sonia summoned me back,' Miguel says. 'Says she wants me here for extra manpower. To defend the fort. If it comes to it.'

His thick lips seem to pulse as he talks. Maybe it's the drug haze, but Gabriel can't help himself—he pictures that mouth between his wife's legs.

It rattles him enough to throw him off his game. He should act nonchalant, jerk a thumb into the depths of the mansion and growl, *'Go.'*

But he doesn't.

Gabriel slouches, feeling small and old. He says, 'Okay,' but it comes out all wrong—soft.

Miguel flashes a wry smile before he strides past the sitting room and disappears into the depths of the house.

Gabriel's alone again. That smile eats at him. Those white teeth, those sparkling eyes.

A sob rips its way up his throat, the precursor to another panic attack, and just as he's about to gulp air, his phone buzzes and he reads FABIO.

It's as though the heavens open before him. But going radio silent on a Serrano simply isn't acceptable, so he answers wordlessly.

The apology he anticipates does not come. Instead, Fabio says, 'You owe me one.'

Gabriel can't believe his ears. '*I* owe *you*?'

'I got myself all scratched up. Just for you.'

'What are you *talking* about? When I tell you to be here at nine a.m. and it takes you ten hours to even bother calling to explain yourself—'

'Shut up.'

'*What?*'

'Just shut up and listen. I've been busy. Working hard to make *you* happy. I know you don't care for details, so here's the facts. I have a young American girl for you. I spent the day organising her collection. She's eighteen, nineteen, thereabouts. Some backpacker, a dumb bitch not looking hard enough over her shoulder. I don't need her back. No one knows who took her. Just another solo tourist who took a wrong turn and vanished off the face of the earth. She has some fucking fight in her, though. I know you like that. She cut me on the side of the head, fucked my eye up. You'll see when I drop her off. But it was worth the effort. I know you'll pay a premium. I thought it might be cathartic to punish her, given . . . what your organisation's currently dealing with. I know you aren't fond of the interventionist pigs. So. Interested?'

If he hadn't indulged in a third Valium, if Miguel hadn't shown up when he did, maybe Gabriel would have kept possession of some measure of reason and said no. But he thinks of hurting an American bitch and then he thinks nothing else.

Sonia's busy in the war room. She doesn't have to know.

He smiles to himself, his first grin in months. 'Bring her to me.'

—

Fabio's shaking as he hangs up.

Rain drills on the Mercedes' roof, hundreds of simultaneous impacts forming a background roar inside the cabin. The SUV still rests buried in the trees, encased in darkness.

Logan already sent Rubén away. He's no longer needed, and he can be trusted to keep his mouth shut. He's in too deep now.

But Logan's still tense. He keeps the Five-seven trained on Fabio's head from the passenger seat.

'Did it work?' he growls.

'Wait . . . you no speak Spanish?'

Logan shakes his head. 'I only said I did so you wouldn't get any ideas.'

Sensing the missed opportunity, Fabio whispers, '*Mierda*.' Logan's vocabulary extends far enough to translate the curse.

'Did it work?' Logan repeats.

'Yes. He want her. Right now.'

In the back, Alice murmurs, 'Fuck.'

Logan knows what she's going through. A vast gulf rests in the space between getting an idea and actually following through with it. She knew she would be scared, but it's always worse than you expect.

He looks over his shoulder. 'You don't need to do this. You absolutely don't need to do this.'

'Shut up, Logan,' she says, staring at her feet. 'Just let me deal with it.'

He watches her swallow a ball of pure terror and take a few deep, centring breaths before she finally lifts her gaze.

'Let's go.'

She looks determined, but ten minutes from now she might be panicking, spiralling into catatonia, so they have to move while she's composed.

First, Fabio must be compliant without a gun in his face.

'Are you from here?' Logan asks the man. 'From Colombia?'

'*Sí.*'

Logan nods. 'You hesitate for more than a second, you die. Understand?'

Fabio trembles. 'Yes.'

'What's "I forgot your address" in Spanish? Quick.'

'*Se me olvidó su dirección.*'

Logan nods. Lowers the pistol. 'Now open your phone.'

Fabio complies.

'Open your contacts.'

Fabio complies.

Logan snatches the phone. Scrolls. Finds a *Mamá* in the contacts, no *Papá*. Fabio's pushing fifty, so it makes sense he only has one living parent.

He hands the phone back.

'Call your mother and say what you just said to me. If you add anything else, any kind of warning, you die.'

Doubt, despair, horror in Fabio's eyes as he wrestles with what's been asked of him. But at the end of the day, he cares most about himself. So he makes the call, and when an old woman answers tinnily in his ear, he visibly steels himself and says, '*Mamá, se me olvidó su dirección.*'

'*¿Qué?*'

'*Se me olvidó su dirección.*'

Without hesitation, she rattles off an address. Logan catches every word and commits each syllable to memory. He won't forget it.

'*Bye, Mamá,*' Fabio whispers before Logan takes the phone away from his ear and hangs it up.

Fabio's crying. Logan feels a pang of pity before reminding himself how the man makes a living. He tucks the pistol away, along with Fabio's phone. The pimp stiffens as he figures out why his captor no longer needs to hold him at gunpoint.

Logan explains anyway. 'You are going to do everything I say, Fabio, whether I'm there in-person or not. Because if I find out you've been disobedient, I will make my way out of here, and I will kill your mother.'

Horrified silence.

Logan doesn't blink. 'Do you think I'm bluffing?'

Of course he is. But how is Fabio to know that?

'No,' Fabio whispers. 'I do not think you are bluffing.'

'Perfect.' Logan points through the wall of trees to the dark and muddy road beyond. 'Now go.'

PART IV

SIEGE

How much more damage anger and grief do than the things that cause them.

Marcus Aurelius, *Meditations*

28

Alice sits shrunken in the passenger seat, hands in her lap. She makes herself breathe.

Fabio works the wheel with both hands, his mane of hair scrunched in a bun. His eye's a mess and the side of his head is swollen. He sits ramrod straight like someone has a knife tip pressed to his throat. You could use that same knife to cut the air in the cabin.

It's a plush leather box of misery.

The Mercedes rumbles steadily toward a vast wall, steel gates set deep in concrete. A spotlight rolls idly across the grounds from a soaring guard tower within the compound. Silhouettes dot the parapets. Alice kneads her fingers as she surveys the spectacle.

She thought the drug lord television shows were exaggerating. If anything, they're watered down.

Fabio looks set to spontaneously combust at any moment, which just won't cut it when they reach the gate.

'Breathe,' Alice murmurs out the corner of her mouth.

The pimp tries. He exhales forcefully, willing himself calm, and he seems to have it together by the time he rolls up to the gates.

Alice flashes a glance up through the passenger window to the silhouettes atop the wall, hunched now like looming gargoyles, rifles trained down on the Merc's roof.

With a dull rumble Alice feels in her bones, the gates trundle open, groaning along automatic tracks. Harsh light spills through as they part, like some twisted version of the heavens opening, with the watchtower spotlight fixed on the inside of the gate. Men march through the widening gap one after another. Four in total. All wield heavy automatic rifles. Alice knows a single trigger-pull would turn her to paste.

Fabio was right—there's no chance Logan would have been able to sneak in with them.

The four-man procession searches the vehicle methodically. They pop the driver and passenger doors and frisk the occupants. Alice sits rigid and terrified—only half an act—as one of the men, reeking of dried sweat and stale cigarette smoke, pats down her thighs, her stomach, her underarms.

He's rough with her, practically tossing her about in the seat before thrusting a calloused palm into the side of her head, pushing her away. *You're clear*, she guesses.

Two of his pals check the rear seats and the trunk as the fourth man lies down on his back in the mud, sweeping his rifle barrel along the length of the underbody.

Once they've checked the Merc from top to bottom, the guard who searched Alice slams her door and slaps the window twice.

She flinches as the glass rattles in its frame.

Fabio toes the accelerator and they slowly roll toward the compound. The gates only opened halfway, so the gap is barely wider than the Mercedes. With only inches to spare on either side, it's like they're squeezing through the border between worlds.

The gates groan closed as soon as they're inside, sealing them in.

Alice feels like she's floating underwater as she stares up a gentle incline of perfectly manicured shrubbery at what must be at least twenty thousand square feet of house. The mansion's vaguely reminiscent of a Tuscan-style villa, only gargantuan, its soaring walls tinged a shade of sandstone that must complement the green of the surrounding hills in daytime. Right now, the structure looms like an obelisk in the dark, illuminated sparsely by exterior lights.

Unless fifty people live here, Alice can't imagine the space is properly utilised. Entire wings must lie dormant.

But the vastness achieves its intended effect.

She's suitably daunted as Fabio guides the Mercedes past pristine landscaping and turns into a horseshoe driveway the size of a small neighbourhood. You could comfortably play a tennis match on the mansion's portico, the expanse of smooth stone held up by marble columns.

The man who steps out through the grand entrance looks minuscule in comparison, but Alice realises he's a tall man, well over six feet, as he approaches the Merc.

His suit is ocean blue with subtle spiral patterns like DNA helixes embroidered in the wool. The jacket lies open, the top two buttons of his dress shirt undone. Tasteful wire-rim glasses make his long-lashed eyes pop. He still has all his hair, but it's as snow white as his short beard. His pale locks are combed back off his forehead, accentuating his deep tan.

Despite everything, Alice acknowledges it's a killer package. He reminds her of a more effeminate Sam Elliott: rugged cowboy with a splash of chic-refinement.

Sonia must have carefully cultivated her husband's appearance. You'd never pick this man to be a pawn.

Alice figures that's the point, but subservience to his warlord wife doesn't equal harmlessness.

Moving slowly, she clambers down from the cabin, stepping first to the side skirt, then the gravel beneath. Fabio gets out, too, rounding the hood to stand beside her.

The pimp was kind enough to inform her that he drugs the troublemaker girls with barbiturates before entering the compound, so she forces a defocused, glassy look into her eyes so as not to arouse suspicion.

Her vision blurs as the man in the blue suit walks right up to her.

She mumbles, 'Hello,' but doesn't get another word out before he snatches her by the throat.

29

Alice figures it's still a performance, some kind of power play, but she's dissuaded of that notion when she tries to breathe through his crushing grip and finds herself incapable.

He bends at the knees to put his face eye-level with hers, and stares deep into her expanding pupils as he crunches her windpipe tighter, *tighter* . . .

Fabio shifts beside them, clearly uncomfortable. But he doesn't intervene.

The dead eyes behind Gabriel's wire-rim glasses are inhuman, like she's a lab rat and he's a scientist, his head cocked in cold interest.

Heat flushes her face as she gasps for air. The edges of her vision start going dark when he tears his hand away, and she heaves for breath, shaking hard.

He keeps her in place by clutching a fistful of her hair and leers down at her. 'Not just yet, darling,' he mutters. Impeccable English; barely a trace of an accent. 'I haven't even introduced myself. I am Gabriel.'

'Raya,' Alice splutters, saliva dripping from the corners of her mouth.

Gabriel leans closer to her, tugs her hair harder. 'You look so beautiful when you are choking, Raya. So very beautiful.' Finally he looks at Fabio, and chuckles when he sees the swelling. 'You weren't kidding.'

Fabio nods. 'She get me good.'

Alice makes sure not to fix her gaze on any one thing, maintaining the dopey, drugged-up personae.

Gabriel shakes her viciously enough for her to understand he's taken women's lives with his bare hands. Then he frowns.

'What did you load her with?'

'GHB,' Fabio says. 'Maybe I give too much. I apologise.'

'Oh, that's quite alright. You have her phone?'

Fabio hands it over.

Gabriel slots it in an inside jacket pocket. 'Switched off far from here, I take it? Standard procedure?'

A slow nod.

Gabriel smiles down at his prize. 'Why don't you and I go have some fun, Raya?'

Alice doesn't answer.

He slaps her across the face.

Her world goes hot and ugly before the explosion recedes to a headache.

'Yes, yes . . .' she mumbles.

'Good. Well, thank you, Fabio.' Without hesitation, he uses the fistful of her hair to drag her toward the house. 'Thank you very, very much.'

She feels the hatred seeping from his bones.

She never should have expected this to work.

—

The Mercedes rumbles half a mile away from the compound before it pulls up in the middle of the desolate trail—right where Fabio was told to stop.

Through eyes adjusted to the dark, Logan watches the man's silhouette emerge from the cabin. For Fabio, it must be pitch black. Insects chirp, things rustle in the forest. The pimp doesn't see or hear Logan approaching until he's right on top of him.

Fabio jolts, then exhales hard.

'Okay. I do what you say. I drop her off.'

Logan looms in the night. 'Uh-huh.'

Fabio swallows nothing, his mouth bone dry. 'So now . . .'

Logan doesn't respond.

'I want you to know I sorry for—'

The kick catches him in the groin like a metal bat, and he doubles over moaning. While he's falling forward, Logan reaches out and snatches his neck in the crook of his elbow, locking up a standing guillotine choke. He leans all his weight down on the top of Fabio's spine and squeezes with a full day's worth of pent-up rage.

The pimp doesn't flail for long. Logan feels delicate tissue in the throat give way and Fabio releases a guttural wheeze before consciousness slips away.

The pimp's last moments awake were hell on earth. That must be consolation enough.

Logan applies another twenty seconds of crushing pressure to the unconscious body to strip Fabio of life before dumping the corpse in the undergrowth.

He climbs up into the Mercedes, pulls a U-turn, and heads back toward the compound.

Alice tries to come to terms with her imminent death as Gabriel drags her inside by the hair.

He yanks her over the threshold into an entranceway the size of a cathedral. Her dull moans echo off the walls as he uses his free hand to heave the double doors closed, one by one. It takes all her effort to diminish her cries so that they sound the way someone loaded with date-rape drugs would protest.

She wonders whether there's any point keeping up the act.

If she'd known he would be this rough from the jump, she'd never have come. Not because she can't handle the discomfort, but because her already sketchy plan falls apart if he keeps a superglue-grip on her hair the whole time. And if he had to use self-control to stop himself killing her upon first sight, she can't envision him keeping his hate at bay much longer.

He wheels her into a room just off the entranceway and shoves her hard away from him. The relief in the roots of her hair gives way to the shock of impact as she trips on a purple rug and splays on her hands and knees. Then Alice rolls into a seated position, panting.

The space is some kind of lavish sitting area, furnished with velvet chaises and ornate armchairs, dark oak panelling on the walls. Her position on the rug makes her the centrepiece of the room.

She stares up at his looming profile expecting him to advance, but he just stands there, watching her right back. Maybe she has a little longer than she thought.

She keeps forgetting she's supposed to be drenched in GHB; she's looking at him too intensely. Lowering her gaze to avoid his eyes, she spots two dirty imprints in the violet of the rug and looks back up.

There must be questions in her eyes, because he says, 'A man was kneeling there last night. A dirty man. We haven't cleaned up after him yet. We've been preoccupied. So it hardly matters if you and I get this room a little dirtier.'

'Oh,' she mumbles.

Gabriel doesn't blink. 'Soon the man who knelt there will fuck my wife. A reward for services rendered.'

'Oh.'

What else is she supposed to say? She doubts any combination of words will allow her to leave this room alive, especially if he's already venting to her about Sonia.

You only use a prisoner as a sounding board if you're going to kill them.

Gabriel simmers with something that's not quite anger, and only to break the stiff silence, she mumbles, 'Is . . . is she here?'

'My wife?'

She nods.

Gabriel smiles. 'Would you like to speak with her, Raya? Appeal to her compassion?' He tuts, almost scolding. 'You have the wrong idea.'

'No, I just . . . I wanna please you . . . and I don't want her walking in, y'know?' She lifts glassy, hooded eyes to meet his stare.

He smirks. 'My wife is very busy with the work people think I do. She's bunkered down on the other side of the house. Do you know how big this place is, Raya? She won't hear you scream.'

Alice ignores the threat and lets her mouth hang halfway open, sensuous. She looks deep into the blues of his eyes.

There's a very specific performance she's trying to sell. He can have her by force, of course, whenever and however he pleases. Even the fictional Raya would understand that. But Raya might be stupid enough to believe he'll let her go if she satisfies him appropriately.

Alice needs *him* to buy that. If he gets off on the idea of his sex slaves acting of their own free will, pleasing him to try and save themselves, then he'll let her perform for her life right up until he kills her anyway. But if he forces himself on her now, that leaves her without a chance to execute the plan before she dies the worst death imaginable.

Everything rides on the way she looks at him.

He watches her half-closed eyes until, for the first time, he seems to register what she said.

'You *want* to please me?'

'I wanna show you things you've never seen before, baby.'

She can tell he thinks she's a dumb bitch, but he must at least appreciate the novelty, because his arms spread wide. 'Then why don't we have ourselves a little party?'

'Sure.'

He hesitates. Studies her.

She suppresses the urge to squirm.

He shakes his head. 'You're too low. Way too low . . .'

Her heart crashes. *Did I oversell?*

Then his eyes light up. He snaps his fingers and mutters, 'But don't I have just the thing?'

He strides past her to an ornate chest of drawers, atop which rests a cigar humidor. He pops the lid and extracts a small baggie packed with fine white powder.

Alice has no doubt it's the purest stuff imaginable, uncut Colombian blow straight from the source. An addict's wet dream.

He shakes the baggie in her direction. 'For every downer, there's an upper, huh, baby?'

She knows if she partakes, she'll lose her mind. After four months clean, the rush will be unfathomable, and whatever composure she's still clinging to will fall by the wayside. So she'll have to try and fake snorting a line, however she can. Probably impossible, but for once in her rollercoaster life, her addiction years will serve her. She knows exactly how to sell it.

No choice but to give it a shot.

She smiles groggily at him. 'It's a party.'

—

The Mercedes idles in the darkness, headlights off.

Logan kneads the wheel, his teeth grinding. Just ahead, around a bend in the mountain trail, lies the straight stretch leading up to the compound gates. The perimeter guards won't light him up as soon as he edges the vehicle into view—they'll assume Fabio forgot something—but as soon as they spot him behind the wheel, the jig is up.

So he must wait, just out of sight, and listen for Alice's signal.

'Come on,' he hisses, knuckles straining white as the seconds tick by.

It's unbearable.

Chances are she'll die in there, no matter the strength of her performance; the odds are stacked too high against them. Then he'll have no choice but to hand himself over, and Sonia will probably massacre a village anyway, just to punish him emotionally before they tear him to pieces physically.

All he can do is wait.

'Come *on* . . .'

—

'You kidding?' Alice slurs as Gabriel taps a thin, neat line out on the glass.

Seated on the velvet chaise, he hunches over the coffee table; she kneels on the rug on the other side. He still looms over her, and if she tried to make a break for it, he could simply reach across the table and seize a fistful of hair again. Besides, what good would it do if she got away? She could maybe play hide-and-seek for an hour until they flushed her out. Then it would be over.

Now he bristles. 'Am I *kidding*?'

'May I?' she gestures.

His eyes dance over her. 'Whatever gets you off.'

She shakes a full third of a gram out of the baggie, nearly half its remaining contents, and uses the steel credit card he produced from a snakeskin wallet to shape the small mountain of powder into a fat line.

Out of the corner of her eye, she sees him reaching for his wallet again, maybe to provide her with a banknote. For a split second, he's not looking.

She clamps one nostril shut with a dirty finger, lowers her face to the glass, and snorts like her life depends on it. She cups her other hand around her nose, using it as a shield to obstruct Gabriel's view.

It's an Oscar-worthy performance, given she knows *exactly* what it would feel like.

She imagines the feeling of sharp pins in her nasal lining and the burn down the back of her throat as she rears back from the table. Imagines a wave of sensation in her head, her chest, her loins, the ecstatic rise, and she throws her head back and moans, grinding her hands into the rug.

It's easy to pretend her heart is racing and her hands are shaking because her bodily reactions are real—coming so close to the drug that destroyed her life is a terrifying adrenaline rush.

She uses her actual fear to continue selling the performance, smiling manically at him like she's lost all control.

It works. Her reaction seems to bemuse him, and she can hardly believe her luck.

She exaggerated the way she jerked away from the glass, bucking like a mule to draw attention away from the untouched line she swept off the edge with her cupped hand.

It's already dissipated into the thick fibres of the rug beneath the table.

When she nods to his line, he senses the challenge and accepts. Following her example, he dumps more coke atop the pile he already tapped out and ducks down, snorts hard.

Even if you're a full-blown addict, a third of a gram is rocket fuel.

She sees the drug set him on fire.

'Wow,' he mutters, licking his lips, gaze twitching left and right until he tames the rush and his eyes fall on her. 'You are *fun*.'

'Just you wait.'

He pats the velvet beside him. 'Come.'

Game time. She nods toward the passageway and the cavernous entranceway beyond. 'Bathroom just round there?'

'Come,' he says again, firmer now.

She senses her life slipping away.

'I'm gonna wet myself,' she says, still in that purring tone. 'I've needed to go for hours. You want me distracted for what I'm about to do to you, big boy?'

The dopamine has him now, savaging his critical thinking. He'll still consider the right thing, but not for long. She watches him lean forward, peering at the front doors, considering whether it's worth heading out there and fetching a guard to accompany her to the bathroom. She can practically see his thoughts. *What's the worry? She just did enough coke to give herself a heart attack. And even if she runs, so what? She'll be brought straight back.*

He juts his chin. 'Two doors down. Go quick.'

'Won't be long, baby.' She clambers to her feet and lurches out of the room, stumbling like her legs are jelly.

The moment she's out of sight, she enforces composure and strides into the house.

—

Gabriel can't be sure how long he sits there alone, his world alight.

He isn't worried about the girl. She snorted the same amount as him at half his bodyweight. She must be out of her mind right now, barely functional.

He's more concerned about his own condition—forced to breathe manually, each inhale catches in his throat.

Too much, he thinks, over and over again as he massages his chest, his overworked heart zigzagging up and down, left and right. *Way too much.*

Time keeps rushing onward. How long's it been? Five minutes? How long does it take to piss? His temples buzz like there are gnats in his veins.

Insidious thoughts arise. Low, whispered doubts.

Maybe you should check on her.

Maybe you should never have let her out of your sight.

Maybe you're a fucking idiot.

He sits up just as a woman rounds the passageway. His first reaction is relief, until he notes the broader profile, taller frame, and white bodysuit, and realises it isn't the American girl.

His stomach plummets.

Sonia stares at him, her head cocked. She's wide-eyed, reeling—she knows he's high. But that wouldn't have been the reason she left the war room.

'What?' he says, his voice shaking.

She clutches a burner phone and tilts the dead screen toward him, as if that might explain. Then she finds her voice.

'That was one of the boys from below San Andrés, where they've blocked off the road. They just let Rubén back out.'

Gabriel's head spins. 'Back out? Did he visit? I must have missed—'

'No. I haven't heard from him. He didn't come here.'

Gabriel is still confused. 'When did they let him in?'

'Two hours ago.'

He steels his stomach, keeping vomit down. 'Your cousin drove all the way here from Bogotá, hung around San Andrés for two hours, and then left? Without telling you?'

'He's not answering my calls. Something's fucked.'

His world collapsing, Gabriel lifts a trembling finger and points into the house. 'Sonia, there's . . . there's an American girl here . . .'

Her face swells just before she explodes. 'There's *what?!*'

—

The moment Alice is on her own, everything accelerates.

She hustles beneath a giant staircase, down a long corridor, padding as softly as she can, but her footsteps still patter off the high ceiling. Her vision is a tunnel of harsh light and luxury.

About ninety seconds after she leaves Gabriel, she hears a set of voices floating from an open doorway. All male, all low and conversational. She catches a distinct whiff of cigarette smoke and hears the *whisk* of playing cards swept across wood. She creeps toward the doorway, drops to her hands and knees, and inches a look around the corner. Four men surround a circular table, rifles propped beside their chairs.

Some kind of waiting room. No good.

She's small enough to crawl past the doorway on her hands and knees without them catching sight of her. Alice tries not to think too hard about how a single glimpse spells her doom.

Once she's past the open frame, she rises and continues on, deeper into the house. She starts weaving left and right at random, lost now. No going back.

A deserted staircase burrowed somewhere in the centre of the mansion leads up to another long hallway, also empty. She walks until she catches more muttering voices coming from another room. Two men.

Slinking toward the room, she hears someone tapping a keyboard, clicking a mouse.

This has to be it. If it's not . . .

She takes a silent breath, makes a choice, then forces herself into action.

Alice rounds the doorframe, stepping into view with a practiced nonchalance she learned in the dens of New York. How to avoid suspicion: wherever you go, act like you belong.

Besides, it's not like Gabriel Serrano runs the tightest ship. She doubts she's the first prisoner to wander off—but she hopes with all her heart she'll be the last.

The room is cramped and windowless. Two thickset men sit side-by-side in swivel chairs in front of a huge desk, home to a two-by-three grid of wide monitors. Computer towers rest beneath, amid a thicket of tangled wires. The screens are subdivided into four CCTV feeds apiece, streaming in from two dozen cameras all over the compound.

She only gets a split-second glance at the setup before the men wheel to face her.

'Hiii,' she purrs, re-adopting the GHB performance, her lids hooded once more. She makes herself wobble in the doorway. 'Um . . . *¿Inglés?*'

The man she's staring at shakes his head, reaching for the radio on his belt.

Fuck.

The second man raises a hand and tilts it back and forth. She zones in on him.

'I'm Gabriel's guest. He's very scared. Something about a big American man? Who came over the wall?'

'*Over wall?!*' the man shouts.

The first man freezes up, his transceiver forgotten. He shoots a frenzied look over his shoulder at the monitors, wondering how they missed it.

'Mmm,' Alice mumbles. 'I think Gabriel needs you. Apparently he's inside the house—'

She barely gets the words out before the English-speaking guy launches out of the chair and pulls his buddy up by the collar, yelling urgent orders in Spanish. They shoulder Alice aside in their haste to get downstairs.

The charge takes her off her feet, and the back of her head lashes the carpet. She rides out the discombobulation as she watches them sprint down the hall away from her, ripping pistols from holsters.

Panting, shaking, she staggers to her feet and heads into the empty room.

—

Gabriel wants to die.

The way his wife looks at him, her mouth open—he wishes a chasm would open beneath him and swallow the house and everything in it. He doesn't know how to respond, doesn't know if the words exist to explain himself.

'There is an American girl,' she says again, this time quietly, her voice like death, '*in the house?*'

'I—'

Pounding footsteps echo in the entranceway, coming toward them, and Sonia wheels hard. Gabriel lurches off the chaise and runs to his wife's side—as if there's anything he could possibly do, as if he's ever done anything other than create fires for her to put out.

The guards who man the cameras thunder to a breathless halt in front of them, guns drawn. Gabriel can't remember their names. One of them looks right at Gabriel and says, 'Where is he?'

Gabriel's lips flap. 'What—?'

Sonia backhands him in the mouth. There's a *crack* as a tooth snaps loose from the gum.

His hands fly to his face as she hisses, 'You shut the fuck up.' She pivots to the guard. 'And you talk to *me*.'

The guard blinks, his pistol held low. 'The girl upstairs said the American scaled the wall. That he's in the house.'

Sonia's face is a mask of cold calculation. 'You saw him scale the wall?'

'No . . . we thought we missed . . .'

He pales as realisation strikes.

Sonia's throat spasms. When she screams, it comes from the depths of her being.

'And you left her up there?!'

Tears in his eyes, he mumbles, '*Dios mío* . . .'

She snatches the gun out of his hands and takes off sprinting for the grand staircase, leaving three more useless men in her wake.

—

Alice dumps herself in the swivel chair, grabs the mouse, and starts working the computer in a frenzy.

Files and folders and directories flash before her eyes like strobe lights. She's no software engineer and she can't read Spanish, but it's not exactly rocket science. Icons beside the list of installed programs betray their functions, and she's free to work her way through them in rapid sequence, searching fast. The programs aren't password-protected; the computer itself is, but the guards were too panicked to bother sleeping the monitors.

She checks three separate programs, all with icons displaying padlocks or camera lenses.

No good. Not what she's looking for.

Clock's ticking.

A woman's scream rips through the house—pure rage.

Cover's blown.

Alice opens a program with a simple icon: two boxes, green and red.

A long list appears in Spanish with toggle switches beside each item.

She reads one called *Entrada* and clicks the toggle switch to green.

Then she hears footsteps in the corridor outside.

—

It's been too long. It's over.

Logan bows his head to the steering wheel, trying to hold back the tears, questioning why he ever let her go through with it. Of course it was her choice, it wasn't his place to babysit her, but he should have refused to participate. *That* was his decision to make, but he agreed, let her go off with Fabio, and now . . .

He can't bear to picture what's happening in there.

His eyes are wet beneath the closed lids.

Then the signal he's been waiting for drifts over the forest canopy: the dull rumble of the gate groaning open.

Green light.

Like an uncaged tiger released on its prey, he crushes the accelerator to the floor. The Mercedes kicks mud before its tyres find purchase, then bursts forward in a scream of horsepower. He rounds the bend at twenty miles an hour and climbs all the way up to sixty before he hits the compound perimeter. The guards atop the wall see him coming, of course, but it takes them valuable seconds to compute what's happening.

Why's Fabio back? Who opened the gate? Wait . . .

He's pushing seventy miles an hour by the time the SUV roars through the opening.

Bullets come raining down as soon as he's inside the grounds; most catch the trunk. A couple of rounds fired from the guard tower make it through the roof of the cabin, but even the best-laid plans involve some risk.

For Alice Mason, he'll roll the dice until the bitter end.

One round *thwacks* the empty passenger seat, another shreds the centre console. By sheer luck, he isn't hit. He ducks as low as he can as the maelstrom churns all around him, keeping a sliver of view intact.

Then he's through the worst of it, tearing past no-man's-land, levelling neatly trimmed hedges as the Merc's grille eats foliage. The gunfire from the perimeter dissipates into staccato crackles as most of the guards hold their fire, reluctant to shoot in the direction of their employers.

Logan's sure they're apoplectic, screaming at one another as they sprint down flights of stairs, hustling for the house.

Too little, too late.

He hits the circular driveway. Only slows a touch.

The Merc mounts the stone steps of the mansion's portico at fifty miles an hour. His bones lurch under his skin as the vehicle bounces.

He aims at the grand entrance and sends seven thousand pounds of steel and aluminium through the double doors.

30

Endless unbearable waiting, then a brief flash of action. This is the way war always goes. Logan got used to the rush years ago.

Whether it's him or them, it's only ever over in a blink.

The Mercedes decelerates in a dust cloud, spewing debris off its chassis. Three men in the mouth of a connecting room watch in stunned horror as the vehicular projectile smashes into view. The two in front wear simple beige uniforms; the older man behind them dons an ocean-blue suit. One look at the older guy's wide eyes and Logan knows it's him: the man from the dark web video.

Gabriel Serrano.

Only one of his beige-clad guards is armed. The guard raises a Colt M1911, same as the Gulf Clan soldiers' pieces—must have been a bulk shipment portioned out to multiple rebel groups—and fires on the Merc as Gabriel flees for the staircase. Logan threw himself down in advance, a split second separating life and death, and the .45 rounds destroy what's left of the windshield, showering him in glass fragments. But one look at the guards' soft, pasty bodies already betrayed their inexperience: they're security, not real killers. They must be the men Alice coaxed away from the cameras.

Sure enough, Logan counts seven pops before the Colt goes dry.

The idiot panic-fired everything he had.

Logan leaps down from the ruined Merc and snaps his own pistol up in one motion, expecting to line up on a man fumbling to reload. But the guy just stands there with a dumb look on his face, tears in his eyes. His buddy has his hands down by his sides, palms spread. Unarmed.

No sign of Gabriel. The old bastard took advantage of the covering fire to vanish upstairs.

Above the ringing in his ears, Logan shouts, 'You want to defend these motherfuckers?'

The man with wet eyes shakes his head.

'Then go,' Logan says.

They don't need telling twice; they take off sprinting, beelining for the hole in the front of the mansion where the front doors used to be.

As they part like the Red Sea to surge past him, they reveal what's behind—four men with Kalashnikovs careen into view from the mouth of a ground-floor corridor beside the huge staircase.

By their detached, uncomprehending expressions and the way they rush out of cover like impatient morons, it's obvious they've sat around this place for uneventful years on end, never expecting anyone to even attempt an assault on the compound, let alone make it past the perimeter. Maybe they're rural boys who weren't provided the option of refusing this gig, but it doesn't change the fact they're wielding automatic weaponry in an attempt to defend warlords.

Same as ever, it's him or them, so Logan relieves himself of the morality of it all and holds his breath tight as he pumps the Five-seven's trigger for a four-piece, working his aim from face to face before they have time to raise their rifles.

In two seconds, four corpses splatter the floor with holes in their heads.

Logan wheels back hard in the other direction just in time to see the security guys vault over the rubble, charging out onto the portico.

'Wait, wait—' he roars, but doesn't get another syllable out before automatic gunfire crashes outside, cutting the unsuspecting duo down where they stand.

Crimson paints the smooth stone.

So the perimeter troops are closing in on the house. They clearly don't appreciate deserters, but if the mansion's staff are fleeing, the situation's dire.

The perimeter force understand this now; they're about to hustle inside.

Logan senses an opportunity and sprints deeper into the house, headed for the staircase where the four corpses lie sprawled at its base. Chest heaving, he swaps his pistol for one of the AK-47s before taking the stairs four at a time. Muscle fibres fire in his glutes as he uses every ounce of his athleticism. His heart rate reaches its physical maximum, but he reaches the landing in five seconds flat.

He spins, panting, to survey the entranceway below him. The Mercedes sits just inside the hole where the entrance used to be, more than a hundred feet away, but still too close for comfort—given what's buried in a concealed compartment in the trunk.

He waits, crouching low behind the landing's balustrade.

They don't see him squatted up there when they sweep inside, but they play it right, at least. They're the real killers, after all—hard men in bulky bulletproof vests wielding shiny carbine rifles, moving like wraiths into the entranceway in a precise tactical formation.

Logan counts a dozen silhouettes in total. Even from the high ground, he's a dead man if he fires on them and gives away his position. They'll light the landing up like a Christmas tree.

But he wields another advantage.

He formed it earlier today, during those endless hours of waiting. Putting his mind to use in the downtime, and working with the resources available to him, he sweated ounces of fluids as he worked blasting caps into putty and bundled sticks into one interconnected demolition charge.

Now he fishes the detonator from his pocket: a simple wireless device with a plastic safety lid over a trigger mechanism.

Hold, his rational mind commands as he flips the lid up. Impulse urges him to pull now, as the first few soldiers are flowing around the sides of the Mercedes, but the optimal moment is still a few breaths away.

Patience.

Then above the tinnitus whining in his ears, he hears something new floating out onto the landing from deep within the second floor—the unmistakable sounds of a fight to the death, only higher-pitched.

Two women.

Panic assaults him and he spins, staring down the length of the second-floor corridor. He can't see a thing.

He pivots back and spots eyes on him. A couple of soldiers noticed the sudden movement. Carbine barrels rise. They'll shred him to pulp.

The timing's not perfect, but nothing ever is.

He turns and sprints away.

One of the soldiers gets a single shot off—which embeds itself harmlessly in the vaulted ceiling—before Logan pulls the detonator trigger and everything behind him goes apocalyptic.

—

From the moment she hears the footsteps, Alice has five seconds to figure out what to do.

Hide? Flee? All she can do if she stays in the room is crawl under the desk, which is so pointless she dismisses the idea immediately. And if she makes a break for it, whoever's coming will shoot her on sight, which leaves one realistic choice.

She has to time it right, and she has to fight.

Alice doesn't know how to fight. She had the capacity to start jiu-jitsu and kickboxing months ago, with or without Logan's guidance. That's life: could've, should've, would've. She had enough on her plate; she got herself clean.

Before that, she lived on the streets for more than a year—and learned how to survive.

You only have to know how to fight if you need to win.

She just needs to stay alive.

All this roars through Alice's head and before she knows it she's up out of the chair, creeping closer and closer to the doorway. She waits until the footsteps are right on top of her and the tension reaches a fever pitch before she hurls herself out into the abyss.

At least she times it right.

She throws herself forward just as her attacker rounds the corner, hitting the figure centre-mass.

She expects to bounce off some enforcer's broad frame and watch helplessly as he kneels on her chest, puts a gun to her head, and pulls the trigger.

But the body she charges into is smaller, slimmer: a beautiful woman in a figure-hugging bodysuit.

What—?

As Alice drives her shoulder into a taut abdomen, her gut reaction is that she tackled the wrong person. It only strikes her that this must be Sonia Serrano when they crash to the floor in a tangle of limbs and the woman screams, '*Fucking bitch!*' in accented English, clawing at Alice's eyes. She curses unashamedly with the vitriol of someone watching her whole operation crash at her feet.

Alice catches a flash of gunmetal as the pistol Sonia was holding skitters out of reach, knocked from her grasp by the bone-shaking collision.

Alice lunges for it; Sonia snatches her collar and wrenches her back, choking her. Only then does Alice realise the woman's strength. There's real power beneath the bodysuit and Sonia's several inches taller than Alice.

Survive.

Alice rolls to her back and ignores the instinct to swat at her attacker's face. Instead she swings her boot skyward, as hard as she can, punting Sonia in the stomach. Sonia's forced exhale explodes over Alice, but getting winded doesn't dissuade her. She's animalistic.

Sonia cocks a fist and drops it hard, aided by gravity.

Overstimulated by adrenaline, Alice isn't clear-headed enough to see it coming. It catches her clean in the forehead, like a rock dropped on her skull. A molten *crack* and the world goes fuzzy and distant.

Sonia latches her hands around Alice's throat and furiously squeezes for her life, but it was the wrong call.

Alice still has the room to kick from her back, and she swings the toe of her boot again and again into Sonia's stomach. She feels abdominal muscle tear under the fourth kick.

Sonia loosens her grip to compose herself, to shake off the surge of agony in her midsection, and Alice takes the opportunity to break free. She launches to her feet and kicks again, harder. Sonia's still on her hands and knees, and Alice aims for her face—but her head is swimming. Nothing's where she thinks it is and she misses the mark.

Overcommitting to the kick, she throws herself off balance, and next thing she knows she's stumbling and Sonia rears up and grabs her by the collar again. This time she thrusts Alice forward, runs her head-first into the wall. There's a dull, hollow *thud* . . .

. . . and a time jump.

Alice emerges from a flash of darkness standing six feet from her last known position. She realises she suffered a flash knockout, where your brain momentarily shuts down to protect itself before screaming back to reality. Dazed, disoriented, she now lurches around in the low light, searching for her foe.

Sonia's ten feet away, lunging for the gun she dropped.

Alice can't get to her in time. Sonia just has bend down, snatch it up, spin, and fire.

All over.

From behind a veil of disassociation, she watches Sonia get her fingers on the gun.

Then the earthquake hits.

—

Hours earlier, as he wired the sticks of plastic explosive together, Logan hazarded a guess at how powerful the bomb would be.

He *severely* underestimated.

He's well over a hundred feet from the blast, in the mouth of the second-floor corridor, but still the shockwave hurtles up the grand staircase and smashes him from behind. If he was anywhere near the explosion itself, he'd be paste.

The idea of getting licked by bomb flames as you're hurled off your feet is movie bullshit. You'd have every limb separated from your body if you were that close.

In real-life, consequences come invisibly, but no less horrifically. He feels a *thwack* like a punch in the back and spills forward, stumbling, his shoulders wrenched in their sockets, his rotator cuffs twanging like guitar strings.

It takes him a couple of seconds to confirm his lungs aren't shredded, his heart isn't mashed to pulp. Worse than the impact is the knowledge that if he was still standing at the top of the staircase, he'd be clutching at his chest, pouring blood from the mouth, feeling his life slip away.

The whole mansion shudders around him like the earth beneath it is seesawing, and he throws a glance back at a noxious cloud of swirling rubble erupting where the second-floor landing used to be.

This simplifies things. Only one option: deeper into the house.

He stumbles forward, ignoring his condition. A migraine gnaws on his brain as the hallway opens out into a large space populated by commercial fitness equipment: barbells, kettlebells, weight plates, cable towers, cardio machines. A huge private gym with all the trappings.

He can't tell whether his head spins from the concussion or the surreal quality of the room. Either way, his awareness isn't what it should be as he advances through the maze of equipment.

He sweeps the gym with the AK-47, its curved magazine wobbling before his eyes, but he mustn't have cleared every nook.

If he had made the same call in slightly different circumstances, he'd be twitching lifeless on the floor with a hole in the back of his head.

It's a miracle Gabriel Serrano is unarmed, because Logan strides right past him. He only realises his lapse in judgement when ocean-blue flashes in his periphery.

Gabriel leaps out from behind a bulky Stairmaster with a scream before Logan can even pivot.

The noise is visceral, decades of rage brought to bear, and sheer fury lends the man a strength that belies his age. He claws at Logan's face with manicured fingernails, carving two lines of torn skin down one cheek. The tip of another nail brushes Logan's eyelid, dangerously close to mashing the eyeball to soup.

Logan's response is involuntary. He squeezes his eyes tightly shut, rendering himself blind for a vital couple of seconds as Gabriel thrashes at him.

When he overrides basic instinct and forces his eyes back open, the rifle isn't in his hands.

Gabriel used adrenaline-fuelled strength to rip it away, and now he goes for Logan's eyes again, fingers extended.

Playtime's over. Logan's not losing his vision to this psychopath.

He kicks Gabriel's legs out from underneath him, shinbone shredding through weak ligaments and arthritic knees. As Gabriel crumples in a heap, howling, Logan hefts a cast-iron weight plate off a nearby deadlift platform. Thanks to endless years spent savaging himself physically, the plate feels light as a feather, and Logan raises it as high as his wingspan will allow, then brings it down with all his might, like his life depends on splitting the floor in two.

The edge of the plate hits Gabriel full in the face. The noise is grotesque, the sight worse. Red gunk showers the ocean blue of his suit.

Logan turns away the moment he registers Gabriel is dead. Sure, it may mark one half of the objective completed, but nothing can distract him from the women's screams. There's no sense of victory as he pivots back to face the gym, only cold awareness.

Alice is still somewhere in this labyrinth.

He turns to glimpse a raised pistol barrel moving toward him through the maze of equipment.

Logan throws himself down just as a hulking man with a mop of curly hair and faded face tattoos draws a bead on him and fires through a gap in the cable machine that rests between them. The shot goes over Logan's head, but the man roars, '*¡Larga vida a la reina!*'

He knows enough Spanish for that one. *Long live the queen.*

So Sonia Serrano runs a cult.

Great.

The moment Logan realises the shot missed him, he explodes forward on his haunches. The AK-47 lies just out of reach, so he rounds the cable machine like a rabid dog and bursts up into the man's midsection, before his foe even has the chance to correct his aim.

The tackle makes it clear the man is tough, his frame like rawhide. They're roughly the same weight with equal strength; it'll come down to technique and willpower.

As Logan drives the guy down to the gym floor, he questions his own fortitude. He can outlast any sane foe, but a fanatic? This man wants to kill just as badly as Logan wants to live. Should make things interesting.

—

The mansion can't be shaking. It must be the concussion.

Alice sways as the floor spasms beneath her, cursing her fate, but she isn't the only one caught off balance. The hallway trembled as Sonia bent down for the gun, sending her stumbling onto all fours, the weapon still beneath her. A *boom* erupts like a thunderclap, and Alice feels her bones rattle. Sonia reaches for the pistol, but the corridor's still shuddering, and she snatches at empty air.

One chance for Alice to save herself. The only downside: it's going to come with tremendous pain. How can she fight when she can barely see straight?

Don't fight. Just endure.

She just needs to crash forward. She's seen Logan do it. Why can't she?

Alice leaps on Sonia's back, even though it scares the hell out of her and every fibre of her being urges her to lay down and die. Her limbs feel like wet noodles, but she loops an arm around Sonia's throat and rolls to one side, pulling Sonia over with her, away from the gun.

Sonia spins with the motion, winding up directly on top of Alice.

'Fuck you! Whore!' she screams.

Alice keeps her legs locked around Sonia's waist, but Sonia rears up to make space and starts raining down blows, one after another in brutal succession.

Alice catches knuckles to nose, jaw, chest, eye socket. She feels her face swelling, nerve endings screaming, her breath catching in her throat.

Hold the line, she tells herself.

It used to be Logan's voice in her head. Now it's her own.

She manages to throw an upward elbow from her back, half-hearted, but it splits Sonia's cheek.

The woman curses, spits on Alice.

Alice doesn't move. She can't. She's done. Exhausted to the core, a single mass of lactic acid.

Sonia recognises this. With a smile, she clambers off her unresisting prey and stumbles over to where the pistol rests.

Alice uses her last dregs of energy to drag herself back into the security office. She crawls between the swivel chairs, blood leaking from her mouth and nose as she gulps for breath amidst the crimson flow, waiting for the kill shot to come.

Then she hears a man scream something in Spanish.

A beat of silence.

'Be right back, bitch,' says Sonia, and her light footsteps race away.

Logan must weather the storm. Fortunately, it's something of a specialty for him.

The man with the face tats can't get a shot off with Logan glued to his midsection, so he elects to pistol-whip with the butt of the gun. He smashes the stock twice into the crown of Logan's head, skin splitting like miniature volcanic eruptions. But Logan keeps driving him down to the floor, and winds up on top, in full mount.

The guy still firmly clutches the pistol. He tries to work the barrel against Logan's chest, but Logan smashes the weapon out of his hands. It skitters under a neighbouring treadmill. The man howls a war cry and bucks his hips with manic desperation.

It actually works. He hauls Logan off, but Logan flows with the motion and lands on his feet in a deep squat instead of tumbling.

When the man rises, his mop of hair dripping sweat, Logan's ready.

He thunders a body kick into the man's sternum and then lunges forward with a step-in elbow. The cocked tip of bone detonates off the side of the man's head and he goes down like he's been shot.

But he's not out cold. Swimming in semi-consciousness, he's enough of a fanatic to be back on his feet as soon as his brain makes the command.

Logan flashes a glance at the cable machine beside them. When you pull the bar down from above, a pulley system raises the stack of weights within the machine. The stack is set to maximum weight: one hundred and eighty pounds. More than enough for what he's got in mind.

He waits a second for the guy with the face tats to clamber up to all fours. Then he takes the pulldown bar in a double-handed grip, activates a chain of upper back muscles, and wrenches downward, lifting the whole weight stack a few feet off its base. Both hands are occupied but his legs are free, so he slams the sole of his boot into the small of his foe's back, sending the guy toppling headfirst into the gap beneath the suspended stack.

Nothing to do now but let go.

Logan releases the bar and pivots; he doesn't need to see the result. The whole cable machine shudders as the stack slams back to earth, reverberating through the floor beneath. He hears the *squelch* and knows he pancaked another skull.

The job's not done, though.

He's about to double back for the AK-47 when he registers footsteps. He can't be sure how he even hears them with his skull pulsing and his balance swaying, but he does. A light *pitter-patter* coming from deeper in the house, rushing toward the gym. Someone small.

He's got a direct view down the barrel of the next corridor, but he can't be caught out in the open like this, unarmed, just in case it isn't Alice. There isn't time to go for the rifle anymore, so he sneaks quickly to one side of the room's entrance, pressing his back to the wall. The only equipment in reach is a metal rack of kettlebells lined up neatly from lightest to heaviest. He hefts the largest—a cumbersome ninety-pound deadweight—out of the rack by its bulky handle. Veins throb in his forearm as he fights to hold the kettlebell, using what little energy remains.

The footsteps are coming steadily toward him.

'Alice,' he says.

The footsteps quicken.

'Alice,' Logan says, firmer.

In response, the *pitter-patter* becomes an all-out sprint.

It's not her.

Whoever's approaching racks their pistol slide.

Fuck it.

Only when this new foe is right on top of him does he burst into motion. He taps into every morsel of fast-twitch power, pivots hard on the spot, and hurls the massive kettlebell like it's the heaviest discus in history. The kettlebell rockets airborne into the mouth of the corridor just as his attacker sprints into view.

Ninety pounds of cast iron catches Sonia Serrano in the sternum.

She had a handgun raised, a compact SIG Sauer clutched in a double-handed grip, but the pistol goes flying when the kettlebell hits her like an oversized cannonball, taking her clean off her feet. The noise she makes as she crumples to the floor is inhuman. The kettlebell slams down beside her, just as she retches uncontrollably. Blood sprays off her lolling tongue, flecking the cast iron.

She's already been in a fight. Maybe her midsection was already compromised. Either way, Logan knows death rattles when he hears them.

He expects her to succumb right there, spasming into death like a fish out of water, but something flares in her eyes as she tries to drag herself upright. Swirling red stains the white bodysuit; a ghastly strain twists her face. Sinew in her neck ripples from the effort.

She can't even peel herself up to a seated position. She flops back against the side of a treadmill, sweating profusely.

Panting with shock and pain and rage so black it paints her soul, she stares up at him, her breathing ragged. Somehow, she finds the capacity for speech.

'At least . . . it's you,' she spits. 'At least . . . I can see you.'

He keeps his voice level. 'My friend?'

Sonia manages to smile. Blood cakes her teeth. 'Tough little bitch. I promised I'd be back to finish her off. My mistake. She's alive. You win.' She turns her head. 'Where's . . . Miguel?'

Logan nods at the headless body buried in the cable machine, blunt-force guillotined by the weight stack. 'Him, you mean?'

She stares. 'Well, that's one way to go . . .'

Sonia winces from the effort—it's clearly agonising to talk—but no amount of physical discomfort will hold her back. It's like she's waited decades for this conversation.

He knows most willpower stems from pain. It's why those who grow up rich and coddled seldom amount to much. She may be surrounded by unimaginable luxury now, but she comes from worse than nothing, from torment. One look in her eyes and that's obvious enough.

Having reached his limit, Logan slumps down, taking a knee beside her.

There are so many questions he could ask, but he knows he needs to keep it simple.

'What was this about, Sonia?'

She tries to sit up, but she can't. Storm waves of internal bleeding sink her back to earth. But her eyes hold strong—she doesn't take them off him.

'I always wished to speak with the devil,' she whispers. 'May I?'

He hesitates. 'Me?'

That bloodstained smile again. 'You, baby.'

'Do you even know my name?'

'I don't need to,' she says. 'I know your kind. They made me.'

The way she looks at him, like he's the source of all evil in the world, betrays something that's been with her all her life.

'What happened to you?' he asks.

She takes a couple of sharp breaths to compose herself. 'You were an American soldier?'

He hesitates. How could he possibly explain the truth?

'Sure,' he says, to see how she reacts.

Suddenly she no longer needs to gasp for air—her injuries are slowly killing her, but that may as well be background noise. Nothing matters besides her hatred.

Sneering at him, she says, 'You ever hear of LAZO, American?'

Logan blinks.

'Plan LAZO?' she croons, her tone hypnotic. 'It was a CIA program.'

He knows every detail of his employer's shadowy history, of course.

'I've heard of it.'

'And what do you *know* of it?'

He registers the unmitigated hate in her eyes.

'Not enough, I imagine.'

She sneers, her mouth filled with blood. Rivulets leak from the corners of her lips.

'Me, Gabriel . . . we were damned.'

He waits.

'Childhood friends,' she mutters. 'That's what we were. Before life made us . . . this. We grew up in the sixties, in a peasant enclave. Marquetalia. A community on a mountain plateau . . . Beautiful, you should see it. We didn't choose where we were born. But that didn't matter. More than sixty years since we were attacked, but it feels like yesterday. There were a thousand of us. Sixteen thousand of them. It was a . . . slaughter.'

She pauses to suck in air.

'You want to know a fun fact? It was what happened that day that created this country's largest rebel group. FARC, the People's Army, they were the survivors of Marquetalia. Again, that never mattered to us . . . We were children. We only cared about those we loved . . . My *tío* Luis. My *mamá*, my *papá*. Gabriel's *mamá* and *papá*, too.' She wipes crimson gunk off her lower lip. 'Our fathers were beheaded in front of us. Their skulls hacked apart. Our mothers were shot for screaming too loud.'

His breath catches in his throat.

Her fury swells. 'You Americans trained the men who massacred everyone we ever loved.'

Silence.

'Your plan,' she says. 'Your initiative. Because enclaves like ours were dangerous to your business interests.'

The world sways beneath his feet. As he places a palm against the wall to steady himself, dizziness crashes over him, along with a single terrible thought.

I'm the villain.

He wonders whether his stablemates came to the same understanding six decades prior.

Only history knows for sure.

31

CAUCA PROVINCE, COLOMBIA
MAY 1964

The man with the crewcut taps his cigar, a long Cohiba Lancero.

'Money,' he says.

He sits low on a metal folding chair, legs spread wide, boots planted on damp dirt. Smoke curls out the corners of his mouth, twisting skyward through thick jungle air.

A tarpaulin overhead, pulled taut between two trunks, provides shelter from the downpour. The smoke rolls along the underside of the khaki canvas until it escapes out the sides. Around the clearing, fat droplets fizz off canopy fronds.

'Yeah,' his teammate says. 'Sometimes.'

'No. It's only ever money.'

They still consider one another teammates, though no one's acknowledged them as members of a US Special Warfare team in two long years.

The second man puffs on a Cohiba of his own. When they first came to the jungle, he opted for a shaved head over the effort required to maintain a trimmed top.

The bald man drags a palm over the perspiration dotting his scalp. 'Easier ways to make it.'

Across the encampment, they watch their students shuffle out of the clearing in single file: twenty Colombian natives, all under forty, all still technically civilians. It's as close as they'll come to a graduation ceremony. In lieu of certificates, each man wields an AK-47, the rifles generously donated by the Americans. Despite their months of collective relentless effort, there are no smiles or cheers. Certainly no camera bulbs flash—discretion is crucial.

No one likes being labelled an interventionist.

'Easier ways for *us* to make it,' the man with the crewcut concedes, 'but we're the workers.' His cigar tip flares as he draws smoke. 'The boys who give us the work get to divide the pie.'

'That's the way of the world. I don't mind it.'

A pause. 'You don't?'

'Hell, I like not having to worry 'bout who gets what. Most think like that, they honest with themselves.'

His partner stares.

The bald man shoots him a look. 'You think the boys who give us the work ever manage a good night's sleep? They just lay up stressin' over who's got more than their fair share. So let 'em have their trinkets. You pay your own price for that shit.'

The man with the crewcut points an accusatory finger. A dirt-encrusted fingernail trembles. 'That there's why our chunk ain't ever gonna be anything special.'

'What, you ain't happy with this?' The bald man uses his Cohiba as a pointer—first gesturing to his partner's cigar and the seat beneath him, then across the clearing, at the procession of men with nothing but the clothes on their backs and the weapons in their hands.

The man with the crewcut snorts. ''Course I am. Don't get me wrong. "Nothing special" is a whole lot better than jack shit.'

The graduates up front make their way into the jungle's stewing darkness, the shadows elongated by heavy cloud cover.

The bald man's gaze loiters on the group. 'I dunno if it's *only* money. There's something important about this. I dunno what exactly, but . . .' He shrugs. 'Gut feeling. Maybe I'm naïve.'

'Of course it's important.' Wet lips on tobacco leaf, another dense mouthful of smoke. 'But that's not why it's done. It's done because the enclaves threaten their pockets.'

'Whose pockets?'

'Those boys you mentioned.'

'Bullshit. Plenty other places to make a buck. Easier ways, like I said.'

'You think?' The man with the crewcut side-eyes his teammate. 'You know how we ended up here in the first place?'

'I'm sure you'll enlighten me.'

'Roosevelt wanted the canal.'

A pause. 'What, sixty years ago? Panama?'

The man with the crewcut nods. 'I mean, the Panama Canal ain't exist back then. Hell, *Panama* ain't exist. It was all still Colombia. But connecting the Atlantic to the Pacific was an untapped motherfuckin' goldmine. Colombia were makin' it difficult, though, draggin' their feet. They demanded an extra ten mil from the French company for the right to build the damn thing. So ol' Roosevelt took Colombia right out of the equation. He manufactured a coup.'

Silence.

'But why did we ever give a damn about a French canal company, I hear you ask.'

More silence.

'That's a good question.' The man with the crewcut tilts his Cohiba in mock recognition. 'We gave a damn because the boys on Wall Street had already bought up the whole company. I'm talking J.P. Morgan and his partners, friends'a the Rockefellers, even Roosevelt's brother-in-law . . .'

'No chance.'

'That ain't a conspiracy, bud. Just our history. Right there in the archives. Go verify that shit yourself. That syndicate, they then paid damn near a million to lobby for a US takeover of the canal. Next thing you know, the coup goes down, Panama's born, and we get exactly what we want: control. The Wall Street goons double their investment. Everybody's happy.'

No response.

'And would you look at that?' The man with the crewcut grips his teammate's collarbone, forcibly pans his gaze around. 'Here we still are.'

They observe the encampment for a beat. With most of the training apparatus already scrubbed from existence, only they are to know the clearing's true purpose—one of the first American counter-insurgency schools in Latin America.

'It's only ever money,' the man with the crewcut repeats. 'You forget that, you risk gettin' surprised. So don't forget.'

The bald man has nothing to say.

The man with the crewcut squeezes his partner's collarbone tighter. 'But we don't know anything about that, huh? We're just a coupla dumb hicks. Coupla good old boys.'

He notes the flash of understanding in the bald man's eyes. They know how ugly life can get. Maybe the hustlers on Wall Street think their rugged existence leaves something to be desired, but they know it could always be worse.

One of the students up the back of the procession glances over his shoulder, and the Americans stare at the blistering mauve scar carved down one cheek. The man with the scar stares back at his instructors with dead black eyes, then turns and limps into the tree line.

He's off to take some souls in the Marquetalia Republic.

There's a guy out there—Luis Serrano—making too much noise. He needs to go, along with the whole enclave. It's these graduates' first assignment.

The jungle swallows the last of them.

In the sudden stillness, the man with the crewcut glances sideways and raises his cigar in a toast. His teammate seems to understand—you keep your mouth shut and do what you're told. No matter what you think you know.

32

Logan's head is a mess of conflicting emotions. He spends minutes in silence, trying to discern precisely what he feels.

Sonia stares up at him with a certain satisfaction in her bloodshot eyes. She wants him to hurt.

That's when it clicks—she wants everyone to hurt.

He finally meets her eyes. 'I'm sorry.'

Her lips tremble. 'For what your people did to me?'

'Yes. And for what it made you.'

She gulps blood. 'Your fault.'

He lets the accusation hang there for a second, and then says, 'You're right. It's not your fault. It's still your responsibility.'

Outrage swells. 'How the fuck am I responsible for—?'

'If I didn't turn myself in,' he interrupts, 'you'd have slaughtered a village?'

She says nothing, stumped by the hard pivot.

'Had you already picked it out?' he asks. 'The unlucky town in question?'

She hesitates a moment. He sees the flash in her pupils as she decides to tell the truth. 'Just before, yes.'

'What, at random?'

'Yes.'

'Your men are there now?'

'Soon.'

'They need your green light? Before they start massacring?'

A dull, humourless smirk. 'They do. And I guess I won't be around to give the order. So that makes you the hero, American. You saved the day.'

He ignores her vitriol. 'Women and children, too? Like you said?'

Her left eye twitches.

'Answer me, Sonia.'

'Not the children.'

'Wonderful. So the cycle continues.'

He watches the snarl form as she processes his words and her conscience rejects them.

Her tone's venomous as she spits, 'Don't you fucking dare make that comparison. I am my own woman. My soldiers aren't trained by pigs from—'

'And that matters?' Logan says. 'The kid who watches their family hacked to pieces is going to give a *shit* who trained their killers? Sixty years from now, some orphan will be in a house like this, atop a mountain of blood money just like yours, convincing themselves they had no choice because of what you did to *their* family.'

Fire in her eyes. 'You *fucking*—'

'But why try to persuade you?' He shrugs. 'When you look at my face, you don't see me. You see your dead family. I could tell you I never knew I was CIA, that I was manipulated, that I almost killed myself when I learned the truth, but what does it matter? It won't change your mind. Trying to make you see the light would be for my own sake. And I don't need that anymore.'

Her jaw is slack, her swollen tongue lolling.

He leans closer, his voice a whisper. 'I'm fine being the villain of your story.'

And he really means it. He forgives her for hunting him because he understands.

Like a switch flipping, the fury melts from her, jettisoning so fast from her soul he can tell it leaves a chasm behind. She swallows, as though testing what remains within, and the sob that comes up her throat in response is uncontrollable.

Tears well in her eyes as she mutters, '*Mamá* . . .'

With no fight left in her, she has nothing to clutch to, and he watches her slip away. The way she settles back is almost peaceful.

You can't wash away a life of hate in one fell swoop, but at least she tried. That's about all you can ask of anyone. Her last moments alive were different to the moments that came before, and that means something when the world's given you nothing but pain.

He lays a hand on one of her shoulders and then rises, leaving her there curled in a ball, mouth slack, eyes glassy. She can't hurt anyone anymore.

Not even herself.

—

Alice loses track of how long she lies there waiting to die. When the agony recedes to levels that allow movement, she shakily works her way to her feet.

Practically everything below the neck is numb. She moves with a ragged limp, feeling her face swelling. It probably looks like she stuck her head in a beehive.

Hope is a dangerous thing, but she tries to visualise a possible escape route out of hell. Could she somehow stumble her way downstairs, out to the gate, while everyone's preoccupied in the house?

And then what? Stagger through the forest for one mile, maybe two, before collapsing in the undergrowth, returning to the earth from whence she came? If that's as good as it's going to get, why bother trying?

As she's deciding what to do, she catches the sound of someone approaching the security office. So it's over anyway.

The figure rounds the corner—twice the size of Sonia.

Logan's beat to shit, but that's par for the course. Even the most hardened souls would flinch at the sight of the blood all over him, the strain of absolute exertion in his eyes, but she knows it's superficial. She saw him in worse shape four months ago, and he bounced back from that like it was nothing, like physical suffering was only a perspective issue, something you could accept or deny.

She knows the same strength lies within her, because it's not about genetic gifts. Only choices.

She rests her palm on the nearest chair back to hold herself up as she watches him fill the doorway.

'What now?' she says.

He blinks. 'That's it.'

She senses his shock. Whatever he's wrestling with, he does so in a faraway place. She'll find out what he learned once he comes back down to earth.

'Who's left?' she asks.

'Just staff. The house is clear.'

Disbelief grips her. 'So we just . . . leave?'

'As soon as I make known what happened here. It'll take me a few minutes. Meet you downstairs?'

'Sure.'

He gestures for her walk first. She gets the sense there's something he needs to do with the Serrano bodies, something he'd rather she wasn't privy to, but she's too tired to protest.

Alice staggers out of the office and down the corridor, sensing him moving behind her. She came from the other direction, so the private gym takes her by surprise. She wheels from Sonia's body to the man whose head was crushed by the weight stack.

'Jesus.'

Logan places a palm on her shoulder and guides her gaze past the cable machine, to a second headless man by the deadlift platform. 'Something tells me you'll be happy to see that.'

The ocean blue of his suit is unmistakable. She soaks up the sight for a second or two, but doesn't relish it. She's grateful to have been Gabriel's last attempted conquest.

Whatever broken piece of his brain compelled him to hurt as many women as Fabio could bring him has now been smashed out of existence by a cast-iron plate.

She heads to the body, reaches into an inside pocket of the suit jacket, and reclaims her phone.

When she straightens up, Logan asks, 'Did he do anything to you? Before you got away?'

'No. But it was too close.' She shudders. 'He *hates* Americans.'

She turns to find him staring back at Sonia.

'They both did,' he says.

'Why?'

He tells her.

'Fuck,' Alice mutters. Her head swirls. She sees his pain and doubt. 'You okay?'

He sighs. 'I will be.' He stares into space. 'This kind of life isn't supposed to be easy.'

'Confronting reality,' she says, 'instead of sticking your head in the sand.'

He glances over to her. '*You* okay?'

'I got it done. All that matters, really.'

He looks at her for a long time. 'Imagine who you'll be in another four months.'

She shrugs. 'One foot in front of the other.'

It seems like it shouldn't be that simple, but she's come to learn how badly people overcomplicate things. It's not what happens to you that leads you to guarded compounds and limitless hatred, but how you perceive it, all the stories you tell yourself about why you are the way you are, digging yourself deeper into your own little pocket of hell.

It was thoughts and judgments that led Alice to the crack dens, and it was thoughts and judgments that pulled her out, made her capable, brought her here. And it wasn't her mother who sent her down the path of addiction, or Logan who rescued her.

It was always herself.

—

Logan waits until he's alone to finish this. He sends Alice downstairs and tells her to wait for him there.

When every criminal vies for online attention, you need a certain dramatic flair to capture your intended audience. He tears strips of blue material off Gabriel's jacket sleeve to fashion a makeshift balaclava, tying the bloodstained cloth around his own mouth, nose, and forehead, leaving only his eyes exposed. Then he pulls his phone out, flips the view to front camera, hits record, and erupts into the performance.

'*Hey, kids!*' he shrieks into the camera, doubling the manic energy Gabriel used in his last video. 'Get your translator apps out! You're going to need them!'

Logan looks around.

'Oh? What's this? Who do I have here?'

He pans the camera down to Gabriel's body, to his pancaked head.

'One Serrano!'

He moves quickly round the cable machine and aims the camera at Sonia's crumpled corpse.

'Two Serranos! *Bang-bang!* Don't go calling your bosses, 'cause they sure as hell aren't picking up!' He cackles like a court jester, then gets serious.

'Now, you can stand around guarding your little airports, chewing through your little villages, but I'd like you to ask yourself what the point is. Who are you doing it for? A dead man, that's who! So go. Find a new *patrón*—there are plenty more masters to serve. Forget about me, or I'll do you like I did your *untouchable* leaders. If you hang around, I'll get to every single one of you. And even better, I'll *enjoy* myself.'

He licks his lips beneath the crimson-flecked cloth.

'*Bye for now!*'

Logan stops recording, rips the balaclava off his head, and doubles back to the security office. It takes less than five minutes at the computer to gain access to Sonia's accounts.

To call her cybersecurity rudimentary would be a compliment—she never prepared for anyone making it past the physical walls of her fortress.

He airdrops the video onto the computer, uploads it to the same dark web channel where Gabriel's warning was posted, and walks out.

All remaining Serrano forces will be sniffing for new employment by sunrise.

Alice stumbles out onto the second-floor landing and surveys the hellscape.

The entranceway is a wasteland of rubble. It's a minor miracle the ceiling didn't come down.

She descends the splintered staircase carefully, then picks her way step by delicate step over the sea of debris across the ground floor. The sitting room that nearly became her final resting place is exposed, its front wall blown out. The chaises lie overturned, the coffee table destroyed—ripped velvet, shattered glass.

She considers waiting in the middle of the entranceway for Logan, but the vast space feels too exposing, so she heads into the sitting room.

As though predestined, the bag of coke rests among glass shards. It draws her attention for far too long.

Snapping back to reality, she unlocks her phone to distract herself. Of course there's no signal all the way out here, but to her disbelief she finds there's no password required to connect to the Wi-Fi. It checks out: who's getting close enough to piggyback the connection without getting their head blown off? If you're in these mountains, you've got bigger fish to fry.

As notifications rush in, it feels like a fever dream. There are messages from Pierre, and missed WhatsApp calls, one chime after the next as the banner alerts *pop-pop-pop.* An audio message sits there, too—from Carolyn.

Alice hits play and brings the tiny speaker to her ear.

Her mother's voice slurs. 'Listen, my girl . . . you treat me how you want, you toss me 'side, but know this . . . you know this, girl . . . I'll always have enough love for the both of us—'

Alice snaps the phone down before the voicenote finishes, resolving to never listen to another word.

But it's not enough. Sensation overwhelms her, anger and sorrow in equal measure. It hurts more than she considered possible, and the escape's right there . . .

She moves toward the ruins of the coffee table before she can stop herself, plucks the bag from the broken glass, pops the opening. Digs a finger in.

Then stops herself.

Since she met Logan, she's only relapsed once. Four months ago, she lit a crack pipe in the Bronx to defend herself from a rapist. But there's no physical threat here now, only an imagined one. The enemy is her mind. This is her decision alone.

The pain is awful, but she realises she's going to suffer either way. Life is struggle, and that's okay.

One must imagine Sisyphus happy.

She extracts her finger from the bag, dusting residue off its tip. Only when she tosses the bag back into the glass and straightens up does she realise someone's watching her.

Logan hovers in the rubble where the passageway used to be.

She looks at him. She won't lie.

'Almost,' she says.

'There's no almost, Alice. You either do or you don't. And you didn't.'

A new feeling hums in her veins.

'You don't need me, do you?' he says.

That night they met in New York, he dragged her out of hell, helped her hold the line. She doubts she would have been able to escape her addictions without someone watching over her, holding her accountable.

But just then, she didn't know he was there. That choice was hers alone.

'No,' she says. 'I don't.'

And he smiles. They both know she never did.

Logan and Alice exit the ruined mansion side by side, limping together onto the vast portico. The grounds are desolate.

Logan looks at her. 'Shall we?'

As Alice nods and staggers between the huge marble columns, all she can think is, *What's next?*

33

Seated against the basement wall, hunched over her phone, Bella reads breaking news.

The children play Mouse Trap in silence.

The Serranos are dead. In the early hours of the morning, a grisly dark-web video announced their demise, and headlines say the infighting has already begun. Within hours of the upload, their presence in Cauca is disintegrating, with rebels and drug gangs pouncing on their leaderless forces.

In disbelief, she clambers to her feet and walks to the basement stairs. The empty house above is aglow in dawn light. It's so quiet. It's been a full twenty-four hours since the blockade dissolved, but she didn't dare venture down there yesterday. None of the villagers did. They knew it was only a matter of time until the armed men came roaring back.

She's been waiting for the confinement to resume. But there's a power vacuum now, and the fighting is elsewhere. New plans will be formed by whoever seizes the throne, and no one will remember a tiny highland town.

She turns to the children. 'Come on.'

They take their time peeling themselves upright, but eventually they manage, and one by one they approach her with something close to hope in their eyes.

They're smart kids. They can tell something's different. She leads them up into the light.

EPILOGUE

With no deep shadows for his imagination to fill with nameless threats, Logan strides unconcerned down the dusty sidewalks of Patio Bonito.

Residents hustle past on foot or speed by on scooters, all impatient to get where they're going. The streets hum with a distinct energy.

The more time he spends in Bogotá, the more he finds himself drawn to this freneticism. As long as he can remember, he's operated in similar fashion, moving relentlessly from task to task.

There are things that need doing, Bella told him. *I do them.*

He and Alice detoured via the hillside town on his way back to Bogotá. They found it devoid of paramilitary thugs. No blockade, no men with guns roaming the streets, but little else had changed. The elderly were out on the same porches, in the same chairs.

Some people form mental barriers much stronger than physical ones.

As one of the only working-age adults left in the village, Bella was young enough not to have relinquished hope. The only old villager with a smattering of broken English explained to Logan that had she set off that very morning with the children in tow, in search of a place of refuge for the kids. She did everything she could to care for them, but she was never going to be able to raise them to adulthood. Her mission for the last half-year was solely to keep them alive until either the confinement ceased or the unspeakable happened.

When Logan asked where Bella was headed, the villager only shrugged. No one knew.

He hopes with all his heart that he will see her again one day.

Before he flies out, there's one final box to check. It's why he's here in Patio Bonito, back where it all began, flirting with the risk of running into one of the men he beat the shit out of in that dive bar.

He has to see Camilla.

He has to tell her he doesn't blame her for anything that happened. She couldn't have had an inkling of what it would lead to. She made a rash decision, nothing more—he's made a thousand of them. What unfolded was completely random, a cosmic roll of the dice.

When he turns into her street, he finds her front door ajar an inch.

Dread seizes him.

He toes the front door all the way open, revealing an empty hallway. Her coat hangs on a hook, beside what must be Rubén's jacket. He steps inside and pulls his pistol in one fluid motion, then shuts the door gently behind him.

It's dead quiet now.

He advances down the hall, holding the weapon low. The first door on the left is wide open, revealing the master bedroom. He pivots all the way into the doorway and stops.

His heart lurches.

He puts his gun away.

Maybe a minute later, a shrill ringing tears him from his trance. He pulls his new phone free and registers the unknown number. Something compels him to answer, but he does so in silence.

'Is this Logan?' says a woman—the most recognisable voice in the United States of America.

He doesn't answer.

'Logan?' she says again, softer. 'This is Jacinta Murphy.'

He stays quiet.

'You don't believe me?'

'I believe you.'

Hesitation as she processes his voice for the first time. No way of telling how he matches up to her expectations.

She clears her throat.

'This is, of course, breaking every rule in the history of our nation's clandestine activities. But I felt compelled to speak with you. To explain.'

The phone's casing creaks as he tightens his grip on the device. Such delicate technology. He could crush the thing to dust.

'Logan?'

'Go on. Explain.'

'I think it's important that I own my flaws,' she says quietly. 'I consider it necessary to admit my misguided paranoia, and to ask for forgiveness. And you have to hear these admissions first-hand, from me alone, not through a middleman like last time, with Mayor Young.'

She clearly expects a response, so he says, 'Okay.'

'It's my fault you wound up in Colombia.'

'I know.'

'I thought you might have put that together. Would you like to know why?'

'If you think it'll help you.'

There's a pause, then, 'Like I said, I was paranoid. Needlessly so. I was keeping an eye on you and Alice Mason because I was scared.'

He doesn't respond.

'It was hard for me to admit to myself,' she continues. 'But that's why I had tails on you both. I was weak. Too frightened to reach out, like I'm doing now. It's not so hard, you see?'

'Jacinta.'

'Yes?'

'This isn't therapy.'

Another beat of quiet. 'We weren't going to hurt Alice in Boston.'

'Your man already told me that.'

'I'm aware. Look, I thought you were coming for me. The both of you going to visit estranged family members? It seemed like . . . I don't know, your last rites, before some suicide mission. So I wanted to find out what the girl knew. I deemed that easier than trying to snatch you. But it would have been catch-and-release, I swear to you.'

'Should have just called.'

'I know that now.'

'Why the change of heart?'

'No choice now. This all went nuclear. So I had to break every rule in the book to get in touch with you myself. To show you the risk I'm willing to take to mend bridges. To show you how serious I am about fixing this.'

'Too late, I'm afraid.'

She pauses. 'For what?'

'Forgiveness.'

She pushes on like she didn't hear him. 'You took the phone. And the phone might have led to me. And you might have got all sorts of wrong ideas about my intentions. So we had Camilla snatched. To distract you, while we made sure the data was beyond the reach of the best recovery software on earth.' A short breath to steel herself. 'I'm admitting this to you, you see? Being upfront. That should count for something. But it all went to plan. She was taken and released. Same day. Shaken up, I'm sure, but that's it. No real harm done. I don't know what you got yourself into over there, but we had *nothing* to do with that. I swear on my life, Logan.'

'I know you didn't.'

Her relief is audible.

'You're still the reason it happened.'

She goes quiet.

'An unbroken chain,' he says. 'Unintended consequences. All because you couldn't pick up a fucking phone.'

'It's *not* too late,' she hisses. 'You survived. It's a miracle you did, don't get me wrong, and I'm so sorry you wound up in that situation, but it sounds like you managed to put some terrible people in the ground, where they should be. And we're here now. We're talking. I grew the spine. I—'

'Can you video call?'

Hesitation. 'What, so you can screen record this? Incriminate me?'

'I could be voice recording this already.'

'Doesn't matter,' she says. 'I'd just deny it, claim it's AI.'

Sure enough, he realises her voice sounds different to what he's heard on television. The pitch is slightly lower.

'I'm old, Logan,' she says, 'but I'm not a fossil.'

'Leave your camera off. I only need you to see mine.'

'Why?'

'I'd like to show you something.'

'I—'

'Just accept the request.'

He takes the phone away from his ear and thumbs an icon on the call screen. After a few moments of tense indecision, the ringing subsides, replaced by a featureless black box which would usually display incoming video. He sees his own face in the corner of the screen, deeply bruised, his eyes pale blue against the deep purple.

'You look like shit,' she says. 'Have you slept?'

He doesn't say anything, just taps another icon, flipping the view to the back camera. Jacinta's voice erupts like a jumpstarted engine, 'Oh, fuck. *Fuck*. Logan, listen to me. *Listen* . . .'

He doesn't hear her panic over the roaring in his ears.

Camilla's corpse sits propped up in bed beside Rubén's.

Both bodies are decapitated, the heads nowhere to be found, but Logan recognises the torsos, the limbs, the clothing. A simple navy dress for Camilla, gaudy knockoff Gucci for her ex-boyfriend. Dried bloody stumps sit atop their pallid necks. The bedspread used to be a mustard yellow; now the sheets are stained red.

Logan hopes their heads were sawn off after they were already dead, but he's a realist.

The remaining Serrano forces in Bogotá must have been furious. This was their final act of revenge.

Jacinta's still shouting, 'I am so sorry, but you need to understand that was never our—'

'Jacinta?'

She falls quiet. 'Yes?'

'I am going to do everything in my power,' he says softly, 'to destabilise your administration and force you out of office. Once you aren't so heavily guarded, I'll come for you. I hear Secret Service protection for former presidents isn't so stellar.'

In a flash, her apologetic air collapses. 'That really isn't a good idea, Logan,' Jacinta says in a low voice.

He doesn't grace her with a response.

'You should know I'm a serious person,' she says.

He lets the phone fall horizontal, closer to his mouth, and whispers, 'You think I care?'

She's audibly rattled as she says, 'You should also know—'

No. I don't think I should.

He grips the phone with his other hand and breaks it in half. Crushed internal circuitry scatters like powder. He drops the jagged halves at his feet.

'I'm so sorry,' he says to the empty room.

Then he heads out, and his anger simmers, uncontrollable, encasing him. As a soldier, you're supposed to operate without emotion, of course—a tenet as fundamental to military strategy as it is to Zen Buddhism.

Fuck that.

Just as it was with Jorge Romero, he's going to burn through this fuel for as long as it takes to enact vengeance. He can re-establish his philosophy once he gets the job done.

For now, tunnel vision.

Either he guts the White House, or he dies trying.

ABOUT THE AUTHOR

Matt Rogers is the bestselling author of the Logan Booth series. Matt began self-publishing at the age of eighteen, and in the following eight years he single-handedly wrote and marketed more than thirty-five thriller novels, which have collectively sold over one million copies. His stories weave stimulating philosophy with relentless, page-turning action, and he aims to educate and entertain in equal measure. As an ultramarathon runner and mountain trekker, Matt enjoys exploring the capabilities of the body and mind, lending experiential weight to his visceral writing.

You can follow Matt on Facebook and
Instagram @mattrogersauthor.

WHERE IT ALL STARTED . . .

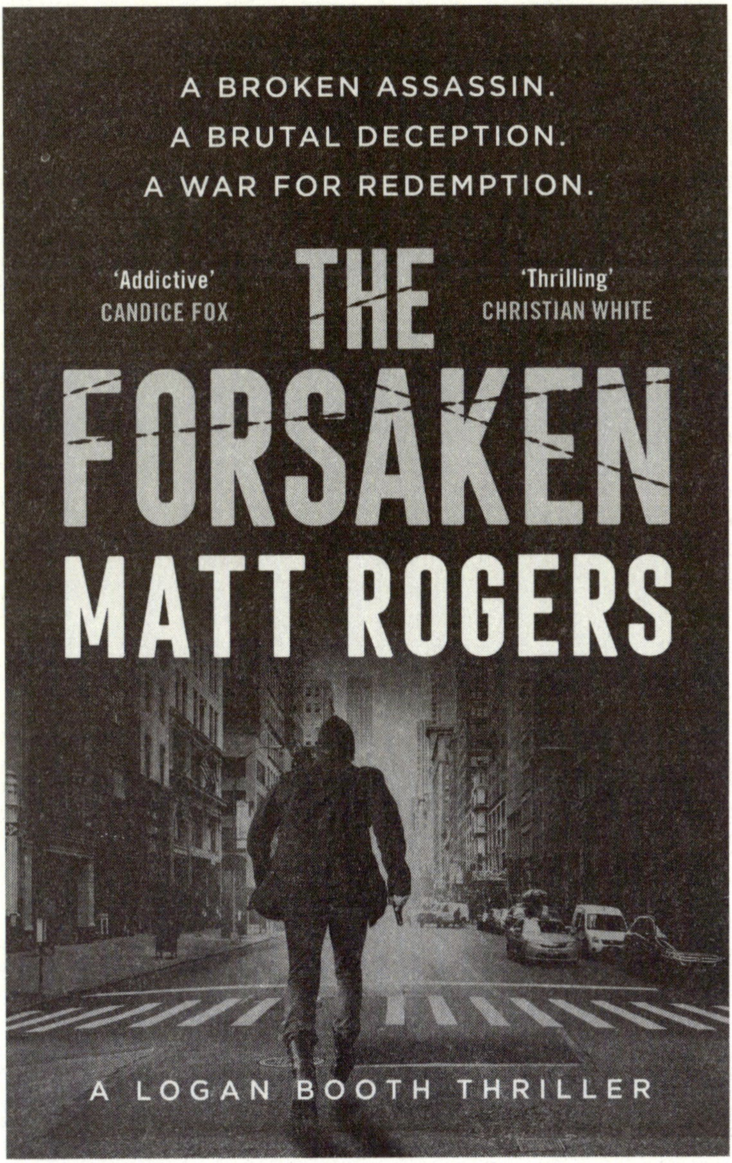

AVAILABLE EVERYWHERE